DELORES FOSSEN

CHRISTMAS AT

Colts Creek

HQN

Recycling programs
for this product may
not exist in your area.

ISBN-13: 978-1-335-45457-7

Christmas at Colts Creek

Copyright © 2021 by Delores Fossen

This edition published by arrangement with Harlequin Books S.A.

For questions and comments about the quality of this book,
please contact us at CustomerService@Harlequin.com.

HQN
22 Adelaide St. West, 40th Floor
Toronto, Ontario M5H 4E3, Canada
www.Harlequin.com

Printed and bound in Barcelona, Spain by CPI Black Print

CHRISTMAS
AT
Colts Creek

CHAPTER ONE

"THIS IS LIKE one of those stupid posts that people put on social media," the woman snarled. "You know the ones I'm talking about. For a million dollars, would you stay in this really amazing house for a year with no internet, no phone and some panty-sniffing poltergeists?"

Frowning at that, Janessa Parkman blinked away the raindrops that'd blown onto her eyelashes and glanced at the grumbler, Margo Tolley, who was standing on her right. Margo had hurled some profanity and that weird comment at the black granite headstone that stretched five feet across and five feet high. A huge etched image of Margo's ex, Abraham Lincoln Parkman IV, was in the center, and it was flanked by a pair of gold-leaf etchings of the ornate Parkman family crest.

"Abe was a miserable coot, and this proves it," Margo added, spitting out the words the way the chilly late October rain was spitting at them. She kicked the side of the headstone.

Janessa really wanted to disagree with that insult, and the kick, especially since Margo had aimed both of them at Janessa's father. Or rather *her father* because he had that particular title in name only. However, it was hard to disagree or be insulted after what she'd just heard from Abe's lawyer. Hard not to feel the bubbling anger over what her father had done, either.

Good grief. Talk about a goat rope the man had set up.

"Do you understand the conditions of Abe's will?" Asher Parkman, the lawyer, asked, directing the question at Janessa.

"Yeah, do you understand that the miserable coot is trying to ruin our lives?" Margo blurted out before she could answer.

Yes, Janessa got that, and unlike the stupid social media posts, there was nothing amusing about this. The miserable coot had just screwed them all six ways to Sunday.

Twenty Minutes Earlier

"Somebody ought to put a Texas-sized warning label on Abe Parkman's tombstone," Margo Tolley grumbled. "A warning label," she repeated. "Because Abe's meanness will surely make everything within thirty feet toxic for years to come. He could beat out Ebenezer Scrooge for meanness. The man was a flamin' bunghole."

Janessa figured the woman had a right to voice an opinion, even if the voicing was happening at Abe Parkman's graveside funeral service. Janessa's father clearly hadn't left behind a legacy of affection and kindness.

Margo, who'd been Abe's second wife, probably had a right to be bitter. So did plenty of others, and Janessa suspected most people in Abe's hometown of Last Ride, Texas, had come to this funeral just so they could make sure he was truly dead.

Or to glean any tidbits about Abe's will.

Rich people usually left lots of money and property when they died. Mean rich people could do mean, unexpected things with that money and property. It was the juiciest kind of gossip fodder for a small town.

Janessa didn't care one wet eyelash what Abe did with

whatever he'd accumulated during his misery-causing life. Her reason for coming had nothing to do with wills or assets. No. She needed the answer to two very big questions.

Why had Abe wanted her here?

And what had he wanted her to help him fix?

Janessa gave that plenty of thought while she listened to the minister, Vernon Kerr, giving the eulogy. He chirped on about Abe's achievements, peppering in things like *pillar of the community, astute businessman* and *a legacy that will live on for generations*. But there were also phrases like *his sometimes rigid approach to life* and *an often firm hand in dealing with others*.

Perhaps those were the polite ways of saying *flamin' bunghole*.

The sound of the minister's voice blended with the drizzle that pinged on the sea of mourners' umbrellas. Gripes and mutters rippled through the group of about a hundred people who'd braved the unpredictable October 30th weather to come to Parkmans' Cemetery.

Or *Snooty Hill* as Janessa had heard some call it.

The Parkmans might be the most prominent and richest family in Last Ride, and their ancestor might have founded the town, but obviously some in her gene pool weren't revered.

Margo continued to gripe and mutter as well, but her comments were harsher than the rest of the onlookers because she'd likely gotten plenty of fallout from Abe's *firm hand*. It was possibly true of anyone whose life Abe had touched. Janessa certainly hadn't been spared from it.

Still, Abe had managed to attract and convince two women to marry him, including Janessa's own mother—who'd been his first wife. Janessa figured the convincing was in large part because he'd been remarkably good-looking along with having mountains of money. But it puzzled her as to why the women would tie themselves, even temporarily, to a man with a mile-wide mean streak.

A jagged vein of lightning streaked out from a fast approaching cloud that was the color of a nasty bruise. It sent some of the mourners gasping, squealing and scurrying toward their vehicles. They parted like the proverbial sea, giving Janessa a clear line of sight of someone else.

Brody Harrell.

Oh, for so many reasons, it was impossible for Janessa not to notice him. For an equal number of reasons, it was impossible not to remember him.

Long and lean, Brody stood out in plenty of ways. No umbrella, for one. The rain was splatting onto his gray Stetson and shoulders. No funeral clothes for him, either. He was wearing boots, jeans and a long-sleeved blue shirt that was already clinging to his body because of the drizzle.

Once, years ago on a hot July night, she'd run her tongue over some of the very places where that shirt was now clinging.

Yes, impossible not to remember that.

Brody was standing back from the grave. Far back. Ironic since according to the snippets Janessa had heard over the years about her father, Brody was the person who'd been closest to Abe, along with also running Abe's sprawling ranch, Colts Creek.

If those updates—aka gossip through social media and the occasional letter from Abe's head housekeeper—were right, then Brody was the son that Abe had always wanted but never had. It was highly likely that he was the only one here who was truly mourning Abe's death.

Though he wasn't especially showing any signs of grief.

It probably wasn't the best time for her to notice that Brody's looks had only gotten a whole boatload better since her days of tongue-kissing his chest. They'd been seventeen, and while he'd been go-ahead-drown-in-me hot even back then, he was a ten-ton avalanche of hotness now with his black hair and dreamy brown eyes.

His body had filled out in all the right places, and his face, *that face*, had a nice edge to it. A mix of reckless rock star and a really naughty fallen angel who knew how to do many, many naughty things.

A loud burst of thunder sent even more people hurrying off. "Sorry for your loss," one of them shouted to Brody. Several more added pats on his back. Two women hugged him, and one of the men tried to give Brody his umbrella, which Brody refused. You didn't have to be a lip-reader to know that one of those women, an attractive busty brunette, whispered, "Call me," in his ear.

Brody didn't acknowledge that obvious and poorly timed booty-call offer. He just stood there, his gaze sliding from Abe's tombstone to Janessa. Unlike her, he definitely didn't appear to be admiring anything about her or remembering that he'd been the one to rid her of her virginity.

Just the opposite.

His expression seemed to be questioning why she was there. That was understandable. It'd been fifteen years since Janessa had been to Last Ride. Fifteen years since her devirgining. That'd happened at the tail end of her one and only visit to Colts Creek when she'd spent that summer trying, and failing, to figure Abe out. She was still trying, still failing.

Brody was likely thinking that since she hadn't recently come to see the man who'd fathered her when he was alive, then there was no good reason to see him now that he was dead.

Heck, Brody might be right.

So what if Abe had sent her that letter? So what if he'd said *please*? That didn't undo the past. She'd spent plenty of time and tears trying to work out what place in her mind and heart to put Abe. As for her mind—she reserved Abe a space in a tiny mental back corner that only surfaced when she saw Father's Day cards in the store. And as for her heart—she'd given him no space whatsoever.

Well, not until that blasted letter anyway.

She silently cursed herself, mentally repeating some of Margo's mutters. She'd thought she had buried her daddy issues years ago. It turned out, though, that some things just didn't stay buried. They just lurked and lingered, waiting for a chance to resurface and bite you in the butt. Which wasn't a comforting thought, considering she was standing next to a grave.

Reverend Kerr nervously eyed the next zagging bolt of lightning, and he gave what had to be the fastest closing prayer in the history of prayers. The moment he said "Amen," he clutched his tattered Bible to his chest and hurried toward his vehicle, all the while calling out condolences to no one in particular.

Most of the others fled with the minister, leaving Janessa with Brody, Margo and Abe's attorney, Asher Parkman, who was also Abe's cousin. It'd been Asher who'd called her four days ago to tell her of Abe's death, and to inform her that Abe had insisted that she and her mother, Sophia, come to today's graveside funeral. Both had refused. Janessa had politely done that. Her mother had declined with an "if and when hell freezes over." That was it, the end of the discussion.

But then the letter from Abe had arrived.

The letter had been postmarked the week before his death, but because she'd been away on business, Janessa hadn't opened it until this very morning. After reading it, she'd dropped everything and made the four-hour drive from her home in Dallas to Last Ride. She'd arrived just as the funeral had been about to start so there hadn't been time to ask anyone about the letter.

"Abe insisted I read his will at the graveside," Asher announced when Brody turned to leave. "He wanted you to be here," the lawyer added, giving glances to Janessa, Brody and Margo. Asher huffed, though, when he reached in his jacket pocket and came up empty. "I just need to get my reading glasses from the car." He kept an eye on the swirling storm clouds as he hurried off.

"Abe wants it read graveside because he probably hoped we'd all get hit by lightning," Margo grumbled. Keeping her purple flowered umbrella positioned over her perfectly groomed head of seriously colored black hair, she walked to the tombstone and kicked it with the pointy toe of her red heels. "You miserable puss ball."

Janessa saw the muscles tighten in Brody's jaw. Felt her own stomach tighten, too. Even if the *miserable puss ball* and *flamin' bunghole* labels applied, those things shouldn't be said at a funeral, and it definitely didn't seem right to kick a man's tombstone.

"I guess you're wondering why I married him," Margo went on, talking to Janessa now. "Since it's obvious I hate every puss-ball inch of him."

This definitely didn't seem like graveside conversation, but yes, Janessa had indeed been wondering that just minutes earlier. Actually, she'd wondered it when she was seventeen and first met Margo, who had already been in the process of divorcing Abe. Instead of asking for an answer, though, Janessa simply shrugged. That lukewarm gesture was apparently enough to keep Margo going.

"I hate Abe because of the way he treated me after our

marriage went south," Margo continued. "After things fizzled, he fizzled, too, and he turned dirty. And I don't mean dirty in a good-in-the-sack kind of way." She paused, and her fit of temper seemed to be waning fast. She sighed. "But before that, Abe did have…appeal when he wanted to have it."

Janessa had never actually been on the receiving end of that appeal. Her earliest memories of Abe were of the custody court battles between her mother, Sophia, and him. Shout-filled confrontations and spearing glares aimed at Sophia, but it had spattered onto her, too. Janessa had seen Abe's angry face plenty of times, and even at that young age, she'd wondered why this man was fighting so hard to get her when he hardly spared her a glance.

Abe had lost his final custody appeal when at age twelve, she was asked by a judge which parent she wanted to live with. It hadn't been a fair question, of course. Live with the mother who'd, well, mothered her or the father who wasn't a father. Of course, Janessa had chosen Sophia, and Abe had walked out. Again, without looking at her. And he hadn't contacted her since.

Not until sending her the letter.

"You didn't know Abe, not really," Margo went on. "I mean, your mother divorced Abe when she was still pregnant with you, and she only lived at the ranch a couple of months before she hightailed it out of here."

True, and Sophia hadn't come back. Ever. Added to that, she hadn't wanted Janessa to come. Ever. Ever. Sophia might have gotten her way on that, too, if Janessa's teenage rebellion hadn't kicked in and she'd made the trip to Last Ride. A trip where Abe still hadn't looked at her and she'd met Brody. It'd been a crazy summer of discovery and mixed emotions.

Margo glanced over her shoulder in the direction of

Asher's car, and she huffed. "Asher's sitting in there making a call while we're all out here risking life and limb."

Janessa looked back to confirm that Asher was indeed in his sleek silver Mercedes, and behind his rain-streaked window, he did have his phone pressed to his ear.

There hadn't been any lightning in the past couple of minutes so that lessened their chances of losing life or limb while waiting for the lawyer. But the rain was still coming down. That's why Janessa maneuvered away from Margo and went to Brody, so she could cover them both with her umbrella. He gave her a look with those amber brown eyes that somehow managed to be both chilly and sizzling at the same time.

"It's not necessary. But thanks," he said, his voice a slow Texas drawl. However, there didn't seem to be any actual gratitude in his tone. Maybe because he believed he couldn't get any wetter than he already was.

"You're welcome," Janessa answered.

And with that brief exchange that barely qualified as a conversation, they seemingly ran out of things to say. Apparently, a past intimacy like tongue-kissing a bare chest didn't keep you connected. Well, except the heat was still there. On her part anyway. She could feel it coming off her own body in thick hot waves.

"Abe had better do right by me," Margo grumbled, taking another kick at the tombstone. "He'd better have put in his will that I can keep my house."

"Her house?" Janessa asked Brody in a whisper.

Oh, my. That set off some more muscle twitching in Brody's jaw, and she didn't know if that's because it was a sore subject or if Brody disliked talking to her.

"Margo got a house on Colts Creek as part of her divorce settlement," he finally said. "She hated Abe, loved the ranch."

Okay, Janessa got that. While she couldn't say she loved Abe's ranch, Colts Creek was indeed beautiful. "If Margo got the house in the divorce, then why is she worried about losing it?"

"Because Abe only gave her the house, not the land beneath it," Brody explained after a long pause.

Janessa pulled back her shoulders. What a crappy arrangement, and yet another example of the angry man she remembered from childhood.

"Why'd you come?" Brody asked, drawing Janessa's attention next to him. Apparently, they hadn't exhausted personal conversation possibilities after all.

It was not the right time to get into the letter so Janessa answered Brody's question with one of her own. "Uh, how was Abe before he died?" She kept her voice low so Margo wouldn't hear.

He stared at her a long time. "Not sick if that's what you want to know. He was just Abe."

Which, of course, could mean a lot of things. "When Asher called to tell me, he said they thought it was a heart attack that'd killed him." She left it at that, hoping he'd either confirm or dispute that.

Brody didn't do either.

Mumbling something she didn't catch, he looked away from her, fixing his attention on the tombstone. "Abe had high blood pressure," Brody finally said several rainy moments later. "High cholesterol, too. He refused to take meds or change his diet so, yeah, the doctors figure it was a heart attack."

She jumped right on that. "*Figure*? They don't know for sure?"

"The autopsy results aren't back yet." Brody paused,

his jaw muscles stirring again. "I wasn't with him when he died. No one was."

The way he said that made Janessa think there was more that he wasn't telling her. Of course, there was more she wasn't telling him, as well. But she also detected something else in his tone. Regret maybe.

"I know you were close to Abe," she threw out there.

He scrubbed his hand over his face. Then he groaned. "Yeah. Abe was an asshole to most people but not to me."

"The son he never had," Janessa said in a mumble. "I remember the way he treated you when I was here that summer."

Abe had invited Brody to eat meals with him where they'd talked about business deals he wanted Brody to be part of. Pretty heady treatment for a seventeen-year-old. Janessa had eaten some meals with Abe, too, but not at his invitation. Abe had done a superior job of freezing her out despite the triple-digit temps that summer.

"He treated you like a son," Janessa added.

"Maybe, but you're Abe's only child," he grumbled, "and he had the DNA test to prove it."

Janessa turned to him so fast that her nose nearly knocked into the umbrella stem. "He did a DNA test on me?"

Brody nodded. "He told me it was something he demanded before he filed his first suit to get custody of you."

Well, heck. Janessa hadn't heard a word about this. "He didn't believe I was actually his daughter?"

"He wanted it confirmed. Abe wanted a lot of confirmations," he added in a snarl. "That included proving to the gossips that he hadn't bedded my mother. He hadn't."

"Why would he want to prove something like that?" she asked.

"Because you and I are both thirty-three, and I'm only

six months older than you. My mother was involved with Abe right before she married my dad and got pregnant. Abe had the DNA test done on me when I was born. I guess because he didn't want your mother to have any ammunition to use against him in the divorce."

Put that way, Janessa could understand Abe's reasoning. At the time Brody was born, Sophia would have been about three months pregnant with her and had already left Abe. Judging from the few tidbits Janessa had managed to glean, Sophia had wanted a quick divorce and gotten one, but the complications started after her birth when Abe pressed for custody.

"Abe told me I was a nuisance." Janessa cringed the moment she heard the words leave her mouth. Words still coated with hurt after all this time. Even if the hurt was justified, the timing was wrong to bash a man at his funeral.

Thankfully, Brody didn't have time to respond to her confession because Asher finally got out of his car. After popping open his huge black umbrella, he started back toward them. Not a brisk pace but rather a slowpoke stroll. The lawyer's expression was like a textbook example of someone bearing bad news.

Swallowing hard, Asher put on his glasses and opened the small white envelope he was carrying. "I'll go ahead and read Abe's opening statement as he instructed, and then we can go over a summary of the will."

Asher stopped, gave each of them a glance, then huffed. "Look, you should know right off that you're not going to like what I'm about tell you. I tried to talk Abe out of doing this, but as you know, he didn't always listen to reason."

Janessa felt her stomach clench into a little churning ball. Margo groaned and kicked the tombstone again. Brody, however, didn't stir from his spot while Asher began.

"'I figure if you're listening to this, then you're wanting to know what and how much I left you,'" Asher read aloud. "'I have some *stipulations*. Now, that's a big-assed word for you, isn't it? A fifty-cent way of saying you'll have to do as I say or you get diddly-squat. My lawyer will tell you all about the terms, but I'll bottom line this for you. My daughter, Janessa Parkman, inherits everything.'"

Janessa froze, then blinked. "Excuse me?" she managed to say.

"Everything," Asher verified.

"Everything?" Margo shrieked.

Janessa shook her head, looking first at Asher, who gave her no clarification whatsoever. He certainly didn't add a laugh and say *wasn't that a fine fifty-cent joke?*

Janessa whirled toward Brody to assure him that she not only hadn't expected this, she darn sure didn't want it. But Brody was already on the move, stepping out from the umbrella and walking away.

"Wait!" Janessa and Asher called out at the same time.

With the rain pelting down on him, Brody didn't stop. Janessa ran after him. No easy feat what with her shoes slipping in the mud. He was already in his truck before she managed to reach him.

"I'm so sorry," she blurted out. "Why would Abe do something like this?"

"Apparently, you weren't a nuisance after all," Brody drawled, right before he slammed the truck door, started the engine and drove off.

There were so many emotions racing through her that Janessa wasn't sure which one she felt the most. She thought about it a second and decided that really-bad-pissed-off fury won that particular award. The ranch should have been Brody's, and nothing should have gone to her.

When Janessa turned back around, she saw a fresh glare from Margo. "I didn't know," Janessa insisted. "And I'll make it right. I can give the ranch and assets to Brody and you."

"Well, actually you can't do that," Asher said, drawing her attention back to him. He got that messenger-of-really-bad-news look on his face again. "I understand Abe sent you a letter."

That cooled some of her anger. "He told you about that?"

Asher shook his head. "No, but Abe arranged for a courier in San Antonio to deliver a copy of that letter to my office in the event of his death. The courier company just found out that his funeral was today so they brought it over. It arrived a couple of minutes ago, and my assistant called to tell me about it. I haven't read it yet," he quickly added, "but on the outside of the envelope there was a sticky note saying you'd already received the exact same letter, that he sent it to you a week ago."

"That's true," Janessa admitted. "It's in the car. I brought it with me." But before she could say more, Asher held her off by lifting his hand.

"Let's get through the will first, then we'll deal with whatever's in the letter," the lawyer insisted. "As Abe said in his instructions, he had stipulations."

"Stipulations?" Margo growled.

Asher nodded, but he left his gaze glued to Janessa. "And when you've heard them, I'm betting that you'll be in just the right mood to kick your father's tombstone."

CHAPTER TWO

BRODY DROVE THROUGH the rain toward the ranch and tried not to think. Especially tried not to think about what had just gone on at Abe's funeral. Now wasn't the time, not when he was on the rain-slick road. Best to get inside his house, change into some dry clothes and then...

Well, then he could start to wrap his mind around the fact that soon, very soon, he might not have a home.

A house, yes, since Brody had bought five acres of land from Abe so he could build his own place. But it was just that, *a house*, if it was no longer a part of what had been his life. And despite his wanting to hold off on the thinking, the thoughts came anyway.

Really shitty thoughts.

He hadn't expected Abe to leave him Colts Creek, but he'd believed down to the soles of his boots that Abe would have given him some kind of assurance he could continue to run the place that he'd helped build.

Hell, he'd worked for Abe ever since he'd been old enough to work. Janessa had spent a single summer at the ranch, and while her absence wasn't all her fault, Brody couldn't believe Abe had chosen blood over everything else.

Chosen blood over him.

His phone dinged with a text. Which he ignored. Brody ignored the next three as well, figuring it was just someone who wanted to know what had gone on at the funeral.

Even though folks had scattered because of the storm, they would have noticed that Asher had lingered. It wasn't much of a leap to guess the lawyer had done that to relay some kind of info to Abe's heirs.

Or rather his heir. Not plural. But rather a solo deal.

It wouldn't take long for news of that to get around, especially since Margo would be pissed. And Brody couldn't blame her one bit. It was possible she no longer had a home, either. If Janessa sold the ranch, which she would most likely do, then the new owner could insist that Abe's ex-wife move her house elsewhere.

Brody drove through the wrought iron gates of Colts Creek Ranch, named for the creek that coiled through it. It had Abe's mark on it everywhere, including the metal fence gate painted Abe's favorite color, black. The main house had plenty of that same color, too, in the trim that created a stark contrast to the white Texas limestone exterior.

Abe's great-great-grandfather had built the original house back at the turn of the twentieth century, but after Abe had inherited it, he'd torn most of it down and rebuilt it to what it was today. Abe had been the one who'd actually started the ranch itself. He'd added to the acreage by buying adjacent land and nearby smaller ranches until Colts Creek had reached its current size.

Sometimes, those other ranchers hadn't wanted to sell, but Brody knew firsthand that Abe always seemed to find a way to get his hands on what he wanted.

Brody drove past the precisely placed displays of hay-bales, pumpkins and dried cornstalks all arranged around and on glossy black wagons with gleaming silver trim. A combination of both Halloween and Thanksgiving decorations, and it was one of Abe's holiday traditions that he liked to show off to anyone who might drive this way. It took a whole lot of man-hours to line the driveways and the front part of the pastures, but Abe had insisted on it. Ditto for the Christmas decorations that were scheduled to go up the day after Thanksgiving.

Of course, this Christmas Abe wouldn't be around to do the insisting.

A reminder that tightened Brody's chest and stomach.

There were no vehicles in the circular drive of the house, but Brody spotted the familiar blue car of the head housekeeper and cook, Velma Sue Bilbo, parked in her usual spot at the back. Since Velma Sue was nearly eighty, she hadn't braved the bad weather to go to the funeral, and soon he'd need to tell her that she might be out of a job. Her and the rest of the household staff. Heck, maybe the entire ranch if the new owner didn't keep them on.

But first, he had to steady himself before he could talk to anyone about that.

Had to deal with the fact that the man he'd thought of as his father had just been buried. That alone would have been a hard sucker punch, especially since Abe had only been sixty-one, but the punch was even harder because of that blasted will.

Brody turned on the narrow gravel road past the first set of barns and drove the quarter of a mile toward his place. It wasn't anywhere close to being grand like the main house. He'd never wanted grand. Nor did it look anything like the fussy Victorian where Margo lived on another section of the ranch. He'd gone with a simple white Craftsman with a wide porch that faced one of the many ponds on Colts Creek. Instead of multiple barns, he'd chosen just one. One big enough to handle the horses he raised and trained.

He pulled into his driveway. And he immediately cursed. Even through the curtain of rain, he could see his mother's car—and his mother, Darcia. Wearing her green nurse scrubs covered by a thick wool sweater, she was sitting on the porch swing. No doubt waiting for him. Brody got out of his truck, and ducking against the rain, he made his way to the porch. She immediately got up from the swing, and he could see the nerves all over her face.

"I'm sorry, but I couldn't go to the cemetery," she said, worry in her eyes. "I just couldn't."

"I understand." And he did.

Unlike Velma Sue, the housekeeper, it wasn't the weather or age that'd kept his mother away. Darcia was only fifty-six and plenty healthy. Her reasons for not going probably had to do with her complicated feelings for Abe. Darcia wouldn't have cursed him or kicked his tombstone, probably not anyway, but it would have cut her to the bone to see her son grieving for a man who had caused more than his share of misery.

Darcia hadn't been exempt from that misery, either.

Brody didn't know all the details, but his mom had let things slip every now and then, so he was aware that Abe had given her the cold shoulder after she'd ended things with him. Brody had never witnessed Abe say or do anything bad to his mother, and he wouldn't have tolerated it if he had. Abe knew that. Brody had made it crystal clear that if it came down to a pissing contest, he'd choose his mother over Abe.

"Why are you all wet?" his mother asked.

"I didn't have an umbrella." He thought of Janessa sharing hers with him. Thought of her being practically shoulder to shoulder with him.

And he thought of her scent.

Not perfume. Something more subtle than that. Soap, maybe. Hell, maybe it was just all her. Either way, Janessa's scent shouldn't have been staying with him like this. Neither should the memories of their one night together way too many years ago.

They'd been teenagers. Horny ones. Added to that the night, the heat and Janessa's anger over Abe, and it had formed a perfect storm. At the time, Brody hadn't realized just how much her anger had played into it. He'd just been focused on the sex with the most beautiful and interesting girl he'd ever met, but considering she'd left both him and the ranch within hours, he was betting her anger had led to regret.

He pushed aside all the old hurt and any lingering thoughts of Janessa so he could deal with his mother. "It's chilly. You should have waited in the house," Brody told her. "Did you lose your key again?"

"No, I just wanted to sit out here for a while." She glanced around, the emotion etched on her face. "I had to make sure you were okay."

He nearly gave her the rote *I'm fine.* That was his go-to response when it came to his mother, but she'd hear soon enough about Abe's will. She needed to hear it from him.

"Come on in," Brody said, unlocking the door. "Let me change, and then we can talk."

Since his mother wasn't a fool, she knew something was wrong, but she didn't press him. She followed him inside, muttering something about fixing a pot of coffee while Brody headed to his bedroom.

His phone dinged again with another text. Margo. In fact, she'd sent several of the other texts. But she'd have to wait. Brody put on dry jeans and a shirt and went toward the kitchen where he could already smell the fresh coffee. However, he hadn't even made it there yet when he heard the sound of an approaching vehicle.

Hell.

He hoped it wasn't Margo coming to gripe about Abe.

Just in case it was, he went ahead into the kitchen and took his mother by the shoulders. Best to drop the bombshell before his visitor did.

"Abe left everything to Janessa," he stated. "*Everything.*"

Brody saw the shock register on her face. Shock that took a couple of long moments to wane and morph into anger. No time to try to soothe that anger, though, because there was a loud knock at the door.

"Let me get rid of whoever that is," Brody told her just as someone called out.

"We need to talk," Margo insisted.

He groaned, and with the intention of still getting rid of his unwanted guest, Brody threw open the door. Unwanted *guests*, he amended, because his porch was filled with the same people he'd just left at the cemetery.

Asher, Margo and Janessa.

Margo obviously took his open door as an invitation to come right in because that's what she did. Then Asher. Janessa, however, stood there on the porch with the rain sheeting off the tiled roof behind her.

Apparently, she hadn't bothered with an umbrella for the trek from her car to his house because her hair was wet, clinging to her face and shoulders.

And she had a wet T-shirt deal going on.

Not that she was actually wearing a T-shirt. She wasn't. But her long-sleeved dark blue dress was wet enough for him to see the outline of, well, pretty much everything about her that he shouldn't be noticing. Hard not to notice that, though, despite the lousy timing.

"I had no idea what was in Abe's will," Janessa insisted. "I hadn't spoken to him in sixteen years, not since I was at the ranch."

Brody believed her, and that didn't have anything to

do with her scent or all those curvy outlines he could see. No, it had to do with that thunderstruck look in her Parkman blue eyes.

"Come in," he said, because unlike the others, Janessa was clearly waiting for an invitation.

She didn't budge for several moments. Instead, she stood there shivering and studying him as if trying to figure out what he was feeling.

Good luck with that.

At the moment, Brody was feeling a lot of things, including confusion because he had no idea in hell why all these people had followed him to his house. He was sure he was about to find out, though. Because judging from the sour expressions from Asher and Margo, this was going to be another kick in the balls, courtesy of Abe.

Behind him, Brody heard his mother politely offering everyone to sit. Offering coffee, too. Leave it to his mom to keep her manners even when a ball-kicking was in progress.

On a resigned sigh, Brody motioned for Janessa to come in, and when she took a few steps, he saw that she was limping. Wincing, too.

"What happened to you?" he asked.

"I kicked Abe's tombstone, and I might have broken my big toe. Serves me right," she added in a grumble.

Yeah, it did. Or rather Brody would have said that before he'd heard what was in Abe's will. It was obvious Janessa had neither expected nor wanted this, and by leaving her everything, Abe had created a very messy situation. One perhaps worthy of some tombstone kicks.

"Sorry about intruding like this," Asher said when Brody and the still-limping Janessa joined the others in the living room. Asher and Margo were already seated, and his mother was in the kitchen, pouring coffee. "But we need to finish talking about Abe."

"And the letter," Margo snarled.

"Yes, that and the will," Asher verified. "I didn't get a chance to finish going over the last parts of the will. What do you know about the letter Abe sent Janessa?"

It took Brody a moment to realize the question had been directed at him. Apparently, this was going to be his day for shocks and surprises. Too bad none of them had been good so far, and Brody wasn't holding out much hope that this one would be any different.

"What letter?" Brody fired back.

"This one," Janessa answered. She took a rain-spattered envelope from her purse and passed it to Brody. "Abe sent it a week ago, but because I've been out of town on business, I didn't open it until this morning."

Brody looked at the envelope first. Not handwritten but rather typed, and it was addressed to Janessa at the Bright Hope House in Dallas. He had some vague recollection of someone mentioning that Janessa ran a place for troubled teens. Why Abe had sent her a letter there, though, he had no idea. Unless Abe hadn't had her home address. That was possible since they likely hadn't stayed in touch. In fact, Abe hadn't once mentioned Janessa in the sixteen years since her last visit.

"FYI, I got the same letter," Asher explained. "A courier delivered it from San Antonio right about the time the funeral started. On the drive over here, I had my assistant read it to me, and I confirmed that the one I received was identical to Janessa's."

Wrestling with his own questions, Brody took out the letter that Janessa had given him and unfolded it. Like the envelope, it was typed, not handwritten. Definitely no pouring out his heart to his only child. Heck, there wasn't even a *dear* or a *hello*.

"'I'm dying,'" Brody read aloud.

That stopped him, and Brody could have sworn his heart stopped for a couple of seconds, too. Yeah, today was definitely the day for shocks and surprises.

There were only a couple more lines of the letter, and after he cleared his throat, Brody read them aloud, too. "'Janessa, I need you to come to the ranch ASAP. There are some things I have to tell you, some things I have to fix. Please come. Please.'"

There was a large *A* scrawled at the bottom.

Well, hell.

Brody read through it again. Then again. To the best of his knowledge, he'd never heard Abe say *please* to anyone, but Janessa had gotten two of them. However, that wasn't what got his attention.

I'm dying.

Yeah, that was an attention grabber all right. Those were the two words that kept repeating through Brody's mind. Along with those repeats, he tried to sort through the past week to see if he could remember Abe giving him any hints or signals that something was wrong. But there was nothing, causing Brody to add another internal round of, *Well, hell.*

His mother came into the living room, set a tray of filled coffee mugs on the table between the two sofas and immediately went to Brody to slip her arm around his waist. It was her protective Mama Bear gesture.

"You might not remember me, but I'm Darcia Harrell," she said, introducing herself to Janessa. "Brody's mother."

Her voice was cool. Yeah, definitely Mama Bear time. Darcia was almost certainly remembering how he'd moped and brooded after Janessa left him all those years ago. Mama Bears had long memories, and it wouldn't do squat for Brody to tell her that was an old-water-old-bridge kind of deal.

"Yes, I remember you. It's nice to see you again," Janessa responded, either ignoring or not picking up on Darcia's coolness. But maybe seeing his mother triggered another memory because Janessa glanced at the mantel.

At the framed family photos centered between two tall slim vases that his mother had made.

There were five pictures, but her attention seemed to zoom in on the shot of Darcia, him and Layla. His sister. A sister Janessa had met and spent time with that summer she'd been at the ranch. Janessa opened her mouth, and Brody could almost see the question she was about to ask.

How's Layla?

Brody didn't realize his expression had changed, but it must have because he saw Janessa table that question and move on to another uncomfortable topic. "I don't know why Abe wanted me here in Last Ride," Janessa said to him. "But I'm guessing it was to tell me about the will."

Probably. There was also a chance that Abe had just wanted to say goodbye to her. Or try to smooth over their rocky past. Of course, Brody had no way of knowing because Abe hadn't seen fit to fill him in.

"Had Abe been sick?" Asher asked Brody.

"Not that I knew of." Then he glanced down at his mother. She worked at the hospital, in pediatrics, but she might have heard something about Abe's claim of *I'm dying*.

Darcia shook her head. "I didn't know."

Even though Brody figured he'd get the same response from Margo, he looked at her. And got the headshake that he'd expected.

Margo wouldn't have kept something like that to herself, even if Abe had sworn her to secrecy. Ditto for Velma Sue. Not that Abe would have told them anyway. Brody considered himself the person who would have most likely heard news like that from Abe, and yet he hadn't heard a word about it.

"I didn't know about any illness, either," Asher supplied. "During my last meeting with him, when he told me he wanted me to draw up some new estate documents for him, including a new will, Abe expressed some concern about how he'd lived his life. That maybe he hadn't always made wise choices."

"A very understated understatement," Margo grumbled. "Did Abe get into specifics about the people he'd screwed over and how he planned for Janessa to fix it?"

"No," Asher said after a long pause. "I did ask him if there was a reason for wanting a new will, but Abe certainly didn't say it was because he thought he was dying. He just said he'd changed his mind about some things."

"Who was his beneficiary in his old will?" Janessa asked.

Asher opened his mouth. Closed it. "I can't say."

"It was Brody," Janessa concluded on a heavy sigh. She groaned and squeezed her eyes shut a moment. "If I hadn't been out of town and had come to Last Ride when the letter arrived, I could have found out what was wrong with him. I might have been able to talk him into not leaving everything to me." She stopped, and some fresh anger lit in her eyes. "Or adding those blasted stipulations."

Brody certainly hadn't forgotten Asher mentioning *stipulations* at the graveside, but he hadn't seen the point of hanging around to hear them. Judging from the scowl on Margo's face, he'd been wrong about that.

This time, Brody didn't bother with the cursing, either mentally or aloud. In fact, he was reasonably sure that nothing else Asher could say would shock him more than he already was.

Asher drew in a long breath. "Abe wanted me to read a summary of his will at the graveside service, but because of the, uh, circumstances, I'll dispense with that and finish reading it here." He pulled some documents from his briefcase. "As I've already told you, Janessa is the only beneficiary."

He handed out copies to Brody, Janessa and Margo. That's when Brody realized some more ball-kicking was about to happen. Ball-kicking that Janessa and Margo were apparently already aware of.

"It's just like I said," Margo griped. "It's one of those stupid online challenges. Would you live in this amazing house for a month with no internet, no phone, some panty-sniffing poltergeists, blah, blah, blah?"

Brody was certain he looked confused. Because he was. "What?"

"It's all spelled out here," Asher went on after a heavy sigh, "but I'll say this started as more of a contract than a will. Estate documents," he emphasized. "Abe wanted me to draw up an offer for Janessa to come to the ranch, not just for a visit but for an extended stay through the holidays. He wanted a chance for them to get to know each other."

"And why would he have possibly thought I'd agree to that?" Janessa asked. Her tone was more like Margo's now, and since she was shivering, Brody took the throw off the back of the sofa. When he handed it to her, she muttered a "Thanks."

"Because he was going to offer to fully fund the Bright

Hope House for the next ten years," Asher answered without hesitation.

Janessa sucked in her breath. "That would have been millions."

Brody could only shake his head. He hadn't heard Abe say a word about any of this. He didn't have to think of Abe's motivation for the funding. Nope. It was the golden carrot to get Janessa here. The "getting her to stay" was the puzzler. Well, not as much of a puzzler, though, as what Margo had said about the panty-sniffing poltergeist.

Then it hit him. Hard.

"Janessa has to live here to keep ownership of the ranch?" Brody asked.

"Like the stupid social media post," Margo said with a finger jab at Asher.

"Like the post," Asher reluctantly admitted. "Janessa does inherit everything if she agrees to live at the ranch for three months, starting now."

The room went silent again, but Brody figured everybody there was doing some hard thinking. He certainly was. Three months could feel like a lifetime for Janessa. This wasn't her home and, added to that, her last three months here hadn't exactly been a cakewalk.

"I've already told Janessa and Margo this particular stipulation, but I'll spell it out for you," Asher said to Brody. "If Janessa leaves for even one night, that'll nullify her ownership of Abe's estate. If she doesn't agree and abide, then the ranch will be sold to the highest bidder at auction, and the proceeds from the sale along with all of Abe's other assets will be donated to various charities."

"Janessa kicked Abe's tombstone when she heard that part," Margo told Brody. "She kicked it again when Asher told her the rest, and then she stormed off like you already had."

"So, I called Janessa and asked her to meet Margo and me here since you were supposed to hear this, too," Asher said before Brody could ask what in the hell was *the rest*. "What I told Janessa before the second kick was that if she stayed the three months and the other stipulation was met, then she would be able to do whatever she wanted with the ranch and the rest of Abe's estate."

Janessa jumped right into the explanation. "Of course, I would have gladly handed over the ranch and all the money to you and given Margo the land under her house," Janessa said in such a way that Brody knew the pisser ball-kicking moment still wasn't over. "Tell him the rest," Janessa insisted.

"There's one other stipulation, an important one," Asher said. "Janessa's mother, Sophia, must also agree. When I tried to contact Sophia to ask her to come to Last Ride so I could discuss some important things with her, she told me she'd be here if and when hell froze over."

Brody was still letting that sink in when Asher continued.

Asher dragged in a long breath. "Janessa has twenty-four hours to convince her mother to live at the ranch for three months. If not, all of you lose everything."

CHAPTER THREE

JANESSA SAT IN the examination room of the ER, waiting for the nurse to return with her X-ray results.

And hopefully some pain meds.

The big toe on her left foot was throbbing nonstop and had now swollen to the point that she'd had to limp shoeless into the Last Ride Memorial Hospital.

Thankfully, she'd been the only patient in the ER and had been seen and x-rayed right away. That quick attention had prevented her from having to sit in a waiting room where she likely would have run into someone who already knew about the mess Abe had created with that blasted condition in his will.

No way would Margo keep something like that to herself.

And it wasn't over yet. Asher had texted her to tell her she needed to come to his office to sign some papers acknowledging that he'd notified her of the conditions of Abe's will. Apparently, she was once again going to be reminded about what her father had done.

Janessa hadn't told Asher that she was in the ER but instead had said she'd get there when she could. Asher hadn't responded, probably figuring that she needed a little time to cool off and contact her mother.

Margo had also tried to call her more than a dozen times. That was understandable since, thanks to Abe's dumbass ploy, she now held the woman's home in her hands.

Or rather Sophia did.

Which was why Janessa had texted and tried to call her mother more than a dozen times since hearing the bombshell from Asher. Sophia hadn't answered even when Janessa had played dirty and mentioned she was in the hospital. She didn't normally use such tactics, but there was nothing normal about this situation.

Ironically, the other person Janessa hadn't heard from was Brody, even though he had the most to lose. Maybe he was still stewing over the way Abe had screwed him. She certainly was and might stew for a long time. Especially if she couldn't pull off a miracle and convince her mother to come back to the one place she'd sworn never to return.

Her phone rang, and Janessa nearly dropped it when she bobbled it to look at the screen. Not Brody or her mother but rather Janessa's own ex, Kyle McKinney. Though *ex* was somewhat of a loose term, and that term was yet something else Janessa had on her plate. Thankfully, Kyle was okay with whatever she chose or didn't choose to call him, and that's why they worked so well together to run Bright Hope House.

"You're in the hospital?" Kyle immediately asked.

Janessa sighed. "My mother told you?"

"Yup. She texted me a couple of minutes ago."

Good. It meant Sophia was at least reading her messages or listening to her voice mails. Of course, she almost always did since she was a family law attorney, a dedicated one, who often took calls from her clients.

"Sophia thinks it's some kind of trick to get her to call you, and she doesn't want to ring you back," Kyle explained. "She figures you'll just want to talk about your father."

"I do want to talk about him," Janessa snapped and then reined in her temper. No use sending anger missiles at Kyle.

"Abe messed over a lot of people in his will, and I need to ask her to do me a huge favor."

Like the *ex*-label for Kyle, *favor* certainly wasn't the right word for something that would throw Sophia's life into chaos. Hers, too. Of course, if she couldn't get her mother to come, then there'd be no reason for her to stay in Last Ride, either. She'd have violated Abe's assery conditions, and the ranch would be sold. Janessa didn't know how much the ranch was worth, but she doubted Brody would be able to come up with the money to buy it in an auction.

"Seriously, are you okay?" Kyle pressed. "Are you actually in the hospital?"

"I am. Well, I'm in the ER anyway. It's just a broken toe." One that was still throbbing.

"How the heck did that happen?"

"Long story." She paused, gathered her breath. "Kyle, there are some things going on, and I might have to stay here in Last Ride for a while."

He grunted, his go-to response, but this one had a you've-got–to-be-kidding-me tone to it. "Because of a broken toe?"

"No, because my father was a flamin' bunghole." Obviously, she wasn't being completely successful holding back her temper. "There really isn't a best-case scenario in this, but if I can talk my mother into doing something, I might be here in Last Ride for the next three months."

This time, Kyle's grunt went up many notches in the you've-got-to-be-kidding-me. "What the heck's going on?" But he didn't wait for an answer. "We need you here. You know the fires we have to put out every day."

Yes, she knew, since fire dousing was a major part of what she did. And there were always plenty of metaphorical fires in a place that housed troubled teens. Some actual fires, too, along with a constant stream of fundraisers since it wasn't cheap to keep a place like Bright Hope running.

"I probably won't end up having to stay here," Janessa said, talking over the string of objections that Kyle started to spew. "I just wanted to prepare you in case I can pull off a miracle."

Kyle quit talking and grunted instead, as if that'd given him some reassurance that she'd soon be back behind her desk. Miracle worker wasn't something on her résumé. Especially when it applied to her mother.

"I'd have to convince my mother to come to Last Ride for three months and live at the ranch through the holidays," Janessa continued. "It's a condition of Abe's will that Sophia and I have to live here."

"Like one of those stupid internet challenges?" Kyle asked.

Janessa sighed and wondered why that analogy had jumped to both his and Margo's minds. "Yes, like that. If my mother doesn't come, people will get screwed over."

A single word of profanity mixed with his grunt response. "Why would your father do this?"

"Because he was a callous SOB who thrived on chaos."

The moment the words left her mouth, she regretted them. Just because Abe was uncaring, it didn't mean she had to be. In fact, she'd built her life around being the opposite of the man who'd fathered her. Kind, helpful, do the right thing, yada yada. Those were her personal mottos—minus the yada yada—and it riled her to the bone that Abe could bring out the worst in her.

Janessa took a breath and gave herself a quick attitude adjustment. "He said he was sick, dying. So maybe he had some kind of brain tumor or some other ailment that messed with his mind."

Kyle stayed quiet a moment. "Okay, so obviously you're doing some juggling there, but I need to remind you of one more ball you have in the air. A huge one. Teagan Cutler."

No, she didn't need to be reminded of that, and this particular ball would result in a baby. One that Janessa had agreed to foster while the adoptive mother was finishing up an overseas tour in the military. Of course, Janessa had made that agreement before Abe's death.

"Teagan's baby isn't due for another two months," Janessa said. "If necessary, I'll come up with an alternative plan before then." And she was afraid she'd need plenty of alternatives if Abe's own plan went through.

She could try to fight the terms of the will, which meant hiring a lawyer. Strange, since this was exactly the kind of fight that Sophia loved to take on. Her mother was a champion of fighting big, rich people who were trying to screw over those who weren't big and rich. Janessa suspected Sophia had become a lawyer because of her bitter custody fights with Abe, so she might be able to lure her mother here by offering her the chance to battle Abe once again. It could work.

But it was just as likely to result in another *if and when hell freezes over* response.

Janessa ended the call, immediately tried again to reach her mother, but she only got Sophia's voice mail. She didn't leave a message, though, because a nurse carrying a boot cast stepped in. According to her name tag, which was outlined with blinking, grinning pumpkins, she was Becky Parkman, probably a cousin, and the pitying smile she gave Janessa was either for the toe or because she'd already heard about Abe's will.

"Well, the toe's definitely broken," the nurse said, already stooping down to fit the boot cast on Janessa's foot.

"It'll be painful for a few days. You can take over-the-counter meds for that or use the script Dr. Michaels wrote for you."

"How long will I have to wear the boot?" Janessa asked.

"You don't have to wear it at all." She tipped her head to Janessa's heels that were on the floor. "But since you can't get back in those for a while, the boot will protect your foot until you can get shoes that won't press against the toe. Even though your feet will get cold, sandals will work best or you can cut out the toe of a sneaker."

Janessa didn't have any sandals or sneakers with her. She'd brought an overnight bag, one that she'd hastily thrown together, but it only had a change of clothes and some makeup. However, her lack of proper foot attire was a problem she'd put on the back burner. At least she'd thought to bring a jacket because the sweater she'd worn to the funeral was soaked.

The nurse pulled the script and a small packet of ibuprofen from her pocket, and then she poured Janessa a glass of water. Janessa downed the two pills and hoped they kicked in long enough for the real meds. She'd get the script filled as soon as she finished up her meeting with Asher.

Janessa thanked the nurse who kindly refrained from asking her anything about Abe, and she made her way out of the exam room and into the waiting area.

Where she immediately spotted Brody.

He was in one of the dozen or so seats and was frowning at his phone. The frown stayed in place when he looked up at her. *Great.* She hoped he wasn't there to deliver another fresh level-of-hell news. Maybe Asher had discovered new stipulations, ones that did indeed include panty-sniffing poltergeists and no internet. Perhaps some flying monkeys to round things out.

Janessa tried not to limp too much as she made her way toward him. Tried not to drool, either. Yes, drool. Even now, Brody's hotness was able to penetrate the pain and her sour mood.

"I saw your car in the parking lot," he volunteered, standing and putting his phone away. "So did some other people who texted me and insisted I check on you." He looked down at the boot cast. "Broken?"

She nodded.

"In pain?" he added.

Janessa nodded at that, too. She usually preferred to keep things like that to herself, but he'd no doubt already seen the answer on her face. She was pretty sure she was grimacing.

"I was about to go to Asher's," she said. Then she could take her grimaces and go…well, she didn't know where. It didn't feel right being at the ranch, but maybe she could find a hotel room.

When she glanced up at Brody, she realized that he still had his attention on the boot, and his jaw muscles were stirring against each other. "Asher's office is in the center of town nearly a half mile from here. Can you drive with that boot on?"

Probably not, but Janessa didn't plan on walking there. She'd drive barefoot if she had to. "I'll take it slow," she muttered. "And thanks for checking on me."

He huffed, and she wished she could interpret that sound as well as she did Kyle's grunts. However, she suspected that Brody didn't want her thanks and that he hadn't actually wanted to check on her. Right now, she had to be the last person in Texas that he wanted to see.

"I'll drive you," he snarled, and she thought it might have been the most unwelcoming offer she'd had. Still, that didn't stop her from limping out with him. She didn't especially want the ride, either, but it would give her a chance to talk to him.

The rain had stopped, and the sun had actually popped out, leaving everything chilly but humid at the same time. He led her to his truck, which was parked right next to her car, and helped her up onto the seat. Which meant he touched her.

Which meant she noticed the touching.

With all the craziness going on in her life, she didn't know why her body had decided it wanted to have another round of sex with this man. She so didn't have time to lust after someone who clearly wanted her off his turf and out of his life.

"By the way, I've tried to get in contact with my mother, but she's not answering her phone," Janessa said as soon as they were out of the parking lot. "I know I keep bringing this up, but have you thought of any reason why Abe would have done this?"

"No. He hasn't mentioned your mother, or you, in years."

That didn't sting. Okay, it did a little. It always would. It wasn't any fun having a father who'd never shown any interest whatsoever in her. Well, no interest until he was on death's door.

"Since he asked you to come and was going to try to lure you here with that funding agreement," Brody continued a moment later, "maybe Abe wanted to make amends with you and your mom."

Fat chance of that happening because she knew of the venom her mother had for Abe. That was probably in part due to their nasty custody battle and divorce. But it might have started before that.

She thought of the DNA test Brody had told her about. Maybe Abe thought Sophia had cheated on him and had given her walking papers. That could explain why Abe was so hostile with the custody challenges. However, it didn't explain what was going on now. Or what had gone on in the week before Abe's death to make him send her the letter.

"Any recommendations for a lawyer I can hire to challenge Abe's will?" she asked. "Someone not in Asher's firm."

"Asher wouldn't have written a will that could be easily challenged," Brody stated. "But there's an attorney on Main Street. Curt Dayton. The Daytons are the other blue blood family in Last Ride."

He hadn't said it with any bitterness, and Brody hadn't spelled out that the top blue blood family was the Parkmans. She didn't know the dynamics here, but if there was any "snooty" rivalry going on, Janessa could maybe use it to convince this Curt Dayton to take on the mighty Abe Parkman.

"Curt's office is there." Brody pointed it out as he turned onto Main Street.

She spotted the shingle outside the yellow Victorian that had obviously once been someone's home. Now, it appeared to be an office building.

Janessa studied the rest of Main Street as Brody drove. It was exactly as she remembered it from her previous visit. Well, except instead of Fourth of July flags and red, white and blue banners on and around the streetlights and storefronts, there were now pumpkins, turkeys and fall leaves. Quaint shops with names like Once Upon a Time, Petal Pushers and For Heaven's Cake. Antique Victorian lampposts dotted the cobblestone sidewalks, and she imagined how the street would look all decorated for Christmas.

Despite Abe never ever rolling out the welcome mat for her, she'd always thought Last Ride was beautiful, and in a way, it had felt a little like home. Probably some kind of genetic memory since the Parkmans had lived here for over one hundred and thirty years.

Janessa looked up when Brody hit the brakes, and she saw the sandy-haired teenage boy with his thumb lifted in a cocky hitchhiker's pose. But it wasn't the pose that quickly caught her attention. Nope. The attention getter was the grim reaper costume, complete with scythe.

Cursing under his breath, Brody pulled into the parking space right in front of the teen, and he lowered Janessa's window.

"Why aren't you in school, and why are you dressed like that?" Brody demanded in a tone that made Janessa very curious about who this was. There wasn't a resemblance between them, but it was possible this was his son.

The boy grinned, causing twin dimples to flash on his pretty face. "Because I'm skipping to do drugs and do some grim reaping."

Brody huffed. "Why aren't you in school, and why are you dressed like that?" he repeated, and this time his tone told Janessa that he knew the boy was joking.

"All right, not drugs. Nachos and a milkshake," the boy amended. "I've got this on because it was wear-a-Halloween-costume-to-school day. As for why I'm here, I was excused early because I got exempt from taking a test. I decided to head over to O'Riley's, grab something to eat and then hang out with friends."

"Does Mom know where you are?" Brody asked.

Mom? Not *your* mom but Mom. So, this was Brody's brother? Janessa hadn't caught even a whiff of gossip about that from Margo's and Velma Sue's letters.

The boy rolled his hazel eyes. "No, but I'll text her while

I'm at O'Riley's." He tipped his head to Janessa. "Is she the one who's going to boot you off the ranch?"

"Janessa, this is Rowan, my brother," Brody snarled before she could even try to come up with an answer to that.

The boy grinned again. "In case you're wondering, I'm adopted so that explains the eighteen-year age difference between us. There's not really a reason why Brody thinks he has the right to boss me around." He said it with some teasing humor, but the humor faded when his eyes met hers. "Are you really planning on giving my brother the boot?"

Janessa definitely didn't want to do that but she wasn't sure she could stop it. She settled for a heavy sigh and a, "To be determined."

"Text Mom," Brody repeated to Rowan. He was scowling when he hit the button to raise Janessa's window and drove off.

"He's fifteen?" she asked after doing the math.

Brody nodded. "And just old enough to get into trouble and still too young to realize just how much Mom worries about that possible trouble."

Janessa did more math. "Your mother adopted Rowan after you graduated from high school?"

"About a year after. She's a pediatric nurse practitioner, and she left Last Ride for a while a few months after I finished high school." He paused. "Things were tough for her, and she had to get away."

She heard the change in his voice. Something that let her know things had been tough for him, too.

"My mother started working as a traveling nurse," Brody went on. "That's how she crossed paths with Rowan when he was just a baby. She got him out of a bad family situation and ended up adopting him. Before that, she'd fostered a teenager about the same age as me. And she's fostered two more since getting Rowan. My mom tends to get involved in her work," he added in a mumble. However, there was affection in his tone, too.

"I understand being overly involved," Janessa admitted. "One of the girls at Bright Hope asked me to foster her baby when she's born until her older sister finishes up a tour of duty."

"That's a lot to take on," Brody remarked.

She shrugged. "I've already done it twice for two other girls while they were sorting out some things in their lives, but that was only for a couple of days. This would be for a couple of months."

"The mother can't take care of the baby on her own?" he asked as he parked in front of the law office.

"She doesn't want to get attached to the baby. It happens," Janessa added. "She's barely eighteen and knows she's not ready to be a parent. Her sister apparently wants children a lot so this is the plan they worked out."

Janessa had worked on it as well by vetting Teagan's sister to make sure she would be an acceptable parent. Everything had checked out.

Brody got out and made it to her side of the truck before she could step down. Good thing, too, because it was obvious the pain meds still had a long way to go before the throbbing stopped.

"Thanks," she said. "I don't want to take up any more of your time. I can get an Uber or some other service from here to take me to Curt Dayton's office and then back to my car." Something she should have thought of when they were at the hospital, especially since it was obvious Brody didn't care for being around her. "Is there anything like an Uber driver in Last Ride?"

"A few." He checked his watch. "This time of day, it'll

be Mary Alice Wilkins who'll have her twin toddlers and a minivan. You going to Colts Creek?"

"To be determined," she repeated.

When Brody gave her a nod, Janessa thanked him and limped inside the law office. A dark-haired woman seated behind a desk immediately greeted her by name, so obviously she'd been expecting her, and she ushered Janessa into Asher's office. It was just as impressive, and rich, as she'd figured it would be.

Asher didn't ask her about her limp, maybe because he'd seen her fit of temper when she'd kicked Abe's headstone and knew the reason for it.

"Thanks for coming in." He motioned for her to take one of the bulky leather chairs next to his desk. "I'm afraid I don't have long because I have a personal commitment, but if you want to call me tomorrow, I'll be able to address any questions you have."

He picked up some papers from his desk, crossed to her and handed her the first page. "As I said on the phone, this is just to acknowledge that I've informed you of Abe's stipulations when it comes to his ranch and other assets. I need you to sign it."

Janessa didn't take the pen that Asher offered, but instead she read through the document. There it was, all in black-and-white, and it didn't have an out that she'd hoped for. She'd thought that maybe the clock on her twenty-four-hour deadline wouldn't start until she'd signed it, but it had started with Abe's graveside service. So, a few hours had already ticked away.

"This is a summary of the assets," Asher said, handing her more papers. Not a single page this time but rather six. "The ranch alone is appraised at over twenty million, but as you can see, Abe had other investments."

He did indeed. As she thumbed through it, she saw the mutual fund accounts, land and even part ownership in several real-estate businesses in San Antonio. Janessa wondered what would happen to those businesses if they were forced to buy out Abe's shares. So many lives could be affected.

She kept scanning, her gaze passing over each account until the gazing came to a screeching halt when she saw Bright Hope House listed. It was the primary beneficiary in the foundation Asher had told her about. The one that Abe had set up if she abided by the impossible conditions he'd demanded in his will. Bright Hope didn't need his money, she assured herself, and she resented that he'd tried to use the funding to try to get her to bend the proverbial knee.

That resentment rolled into a big hot ball in the pit of her stomach. Just as he'd done to her when she was seventeen, Abe set up these asinine rules and now a lot of people were going to get hurt.

A hurt that she probably couldn't fix.

Damn it, but she would try. She'd limp her way to Curt Dayton's office as soon as she was done here. Challenging the will might not put a stop to Abe's meanness, but she could maybe tie the will up in court long enough to come up with another plan.

Janessa stood, snatched the pen from Asher and putting the documents on his desk, she signed her name so hard that it tore a little hole in the paper. She tossed the pen on his desk and headed for the door.

Fighting tears, anger and pain, she went outside to use her app for the driver, but before she could do that, her phone rang in her hand. It felt like a too-late hollow victory when she saw her mother's name on the screen.

"Why didn't you tell me?" Sophia demanded the moment Janessa answered.

Surprised by the question, it took Janessa a moment to respond. "I tried to tell you about Abe's will, but you didn't take my calls."

"No, not about the damn will. The baby. Kyle called me and told me."

Janessa backed up a mental step. "What exactly did Kyle tell you?"

"That you were going to adopt a baby," her mother said without hesitation.

"Uh—" But that was as far as Janessa got before Sophia rolled right over her.

"He said the baby, a little girl, will be born right around Christmas, and that you'll be taking her to Last Ride because you'll need to be there to fight Abe's will."

She did more mental back steps. Either Sophia had seriously misunderstood whatever Kyle had said, or else he'd told a whopper.

Janessa was going with door number two on this one.

Good grief. Kyle had likely been trying to help get Sophia to Last Ride, but this was not the way to do it.

"Did you think that I wouldn't want to be part of my grandchild's life?" Sophia asked.

Janessa sighed. "Mom—" But again, Janessa's part of the conversation was limited to that one word because her mother interrupted.

"Make arrangements for a place for me to stay," Sophia insisted. "I'll be arriving late so don't wait up, but I'll be in Last Ride before midnight."

CHAPTER FOUR

BRODY RODE THORN, his Appaloosa gelding, along the back fence line while he checked for any breaks or needed repairs. It was a job he normally delegated to the newer, younger ranch hands, but he'd put himself on the schedule for it today so he could get away from his office.

And from everybody else.

His office was in the main house. Abe's house. And while it had a separate entrance, Brody figured if he were there, he'd run into someone he would rather avoid. Which at this point was pretty much any and everybody.

Thorn didn't have the best temperament—hence the name—but he was the only company Brody wanted right now. Over the past eighteen hours or so, he'd already heard too much from too many people about Abe's will, and he needed a break. Thorn might be snorting and flicking his tail over this mundane chore, but the crisp late autumn air was pleasant enough and the horse wouldn't be able to go on and on about what might or might not happen to Colts Creek.

Or to Margo, or all the hands and house staff who worked the ranch.

Brody had silenced his phone before he'd gone to bed, and he hadn't turned it back on when he got up and left for work. That would almost certainly piss off some people, including the ranch's assistant manager, Clayton Erle, but

Brody had left a message for Clayton to tell him where he'd be. If it was important enough, Clayton could ride out and speak to him in person. And if the in-person happened, it sure as hell better not be about Abe.

Brody couldn't see the sense of hashing and rehashing something that was in Janessa's hands. If she challenged the will, then he was sure he'd hear about it from her or the lawyer, Curt Dayton. If she was already back in Dallas, then he'd hear about that, too.

He kept riding fence, kept pushing away the thoughts of *what if, why* and all the other bullshit questions that kept popping into his head. Instead, he focused on the quarter horses he spotted in the pasture. Meditation soothed the soul for some, but the horses always did it for Brody.

Abe and he had brought in some prize stock, and it had paid off. The horses were some of the most sought-after in the state. Brody had been part of that. Had loved it. Still did. And if he ended up losing his job here, he'd just start his own damn ranch. It wouldn't be big, and it wouldn't be the same as Colts Creek, but he wouldn't give up raising horses.

He cursed, though, when he spotted another horse, and its rider, coming toward him. Not one of the hands. But rather his mother. She didn't care much for riding so that told him this was important enough for her to tolerate both.

"You aren't answering your phone," she called out to him. She was bundled up in a thick wool coat, and her cheeks were pink from the brisk wind.

Brody sighed. "Because I wanted to give Abe and his will a rest."

She shook her head, and when Brody got closer, he saw the tears shimmering in her eyes. Hell. "What's wrong?"

"This is all my fault," she said, swiping at those tears

with the back of her hand. "I'm the reason Abe did this to you."

Apparently, *rest time* from this subject was over. Brody took hold of the reins of the mare she was riding and got them started back toward his house. The cold wouldn't bother him, but it would his mother.

"No way is this your fault," he insisted.

"But it is," she insisted right back.

Since this was obviously going to turn into a discussion, one that would require him to convince his mom that she wasn't responsible for anything Abe had done, Brody calculated how long it would take to get her back to his house. At least fifteen minutes, and he didn't think he could hold her off that long.

"Okay, I'll bite. Why do you think you had anything to do with Abe leaving the ranch to his daughter?" Brody came out and asked.

"He did it to get back at me, because he was still angry about what happened between us."

Brody had to give that some thought, and he still wasn't sure he was anywhere in the ballpark of what was causing his mother to cry. "You mean when you broke up with Abe nearly thirty-five years ago?" That couldn't be it. Could it?

But Darcia certainly didn't deny it. "Abe was so angry when I ended things with him. So hurt when I told him I was seeing Jimmy."

Jimmy Harrell. Brody's father. But Jimmy had also been Abe's best friend. More like brothers if the gossip Brody had heard was right. Brody had never actually been able to confirm the gossip because Jimmy left Last Ride when Brody was ten. Jimmy had done that after he lost the hardware store he'd inherited from his grandfather, and he didn't visit that often. Abe and Darcia had refused to talk about it.

Until now, that is.

Apparently, his mother thought that long forbidden subject was now on the discussion table. Brody wasn't sure he wanted to hear any other accounts of Abe acting like an ass.

"Abe swore he would get back at me," Darcia went on. "And I think he did that with this will. Because the fastest way to hurt me would be to hurt you."

Oh, he got it now, but Brody had no trouble poking holes in that theory. "I've been working for Abe for seventeen years. If he wanted to hurt me to get back at you, he wouldn't have waited this long."

"But he could have," she argued while more tears fell. "The longer he waited, the deeper the cut would be."

"Well, if that's true, Abe certainly hid his revenge plan well. And you'd think if he wanted to get back at you, he would have taken some jabs at me over the years. He didn't."

Brody mentally went back through his last conversation with Abe. There sure as hell hadn't been any mention of him dying, his will, Janessa or any old bad blood between Darcia and him. It'd been one of those routine discussions about a couple of young hands who'd gotten into a fight at the Three Sheets to the Wind bar and were in jail. Brody had wanted to tell Abe so he wouldn't hear it from someone else, but as usual Abe had told Brody to deal with it as he saw fit.

"About two weeks ago, I was leaving the art studio after I'd finished teaching my pottery class, and Abe was waiting for me by my car," Darcia went on. "He said he wanted to talk. I thought it was something about you, so I agreed. Reluctantly agreed," she amended. "We sat at a table in the little park behind the studio, and he told me the reason he hired you when you were sixteen was because he hoped he could punish me by turning you against me and your father."

Brody reined in and stared at her. His mother wasn't one to lie or exaggerate so he didn't doubt Abe had said that. And did it. But Brody had never picked up on a vibe like that.

"He never tried to turn me against either of you," Brody pointed out.

With a confirming nod, his mother got the mare moving and Brody followed. "Abe said he tested the waters," Darcia explained, "and you made it clear that you wouldn't get involved in what went on between him and me. Or have anything to do with the rift he had with your father."

Even though that'd been years ago, Brody did indeed recall that particular conversation. "Abe did ask me if you'd ever talked about him. I shut down the subject." He paused, cursed. "So, why didn't he fire me then and there if he realized he couldn't turn me against my dad and you?"

"I asked about that, and he said you did good work. Then he added that after a while, he knew he wanted you to run the ranch and that it didn't matter that you were Jimmy's son."

Brody had no trouble believing that was true, as well. Abe had been far more interested in his other businesses than the ranch. He certainly hadn't wanted to get involved with the daily running of it.

"Why didn't you tell me about this conversation before now?" Brody asked.

Darcia sighed. "Because I didn't want to hurt you."

It shouldn't have bothered him after all these years that Abe had had such a twisted reason for hiring him. But it did. It bothered Brody a lot. So did the guilt his mom was clearly feeling.

"Abe's will wasn't your fault," Brody assured her.

"Then why didn't he leave the ranch to you? Or at least arrange it so it wouldn't be sold? Why did he snatch everything away from you?"

That was the million-dollar question, and it took Brody back to something that had been eating away at him. Maybe Abe had truly been the asshole that everyone had believed he was.

They rode the horses through the back opening of the barn and climbed off. Brody was about to start removing the saddles, but he stopped when he spotted the car in front of his house. And the woman.

Janessa.

Wearing a red sweater and black jeans, she was by the huge oak in his front yard, and she was pacing, and limping, while on the phone.

Brody certainly hadn't expected her. Not at his house, not in Last Ride, either. One of the last texts that he'd actually read was from Margo, telling him that Janessa hadn't come to the ranch. So Brody had figured she'd already driven back to Dallas.

"Go ahead and talk to her," his mother said. "I'll deal with the horses."

Brody thanked her, then mumbled, "This shouldn't take long," before he made his way toward Janessa.

Her head whipped up when she spotted him, and even though she still had the phone to her ear, she seemed to freeze. Not freeze in a cold winter kind of way, either. He saw the quick flash of heat in her eyes. Heat that she quickly tried to conceal by looking away.

"I have to go, Kyle," she said to the person on the phone. "I'll call you later to work that out."

Kyle. Maybe a boyfriend? Probably a boyfriend, he mentally amended. After all, Janessa had a life, and that meant there was a high chance there was a significant other.

"That's a good look on you, Brody," she said. "Hard-working cowboy. They make calendars with guys like you on them. You look like a September or October to me. For the August slot, you'd probably have to ditch the shirt, though." She flashed a smile that faded as quickly as it'd come. "Sorry, I got distracted."

Welcome to the club. He always seemed to get distracted around Janessa, and it nearly caused him to blurt out a really stupid question. One that involved her swearing she was going to get a tat on her butt cheek with his name on it. That had been part of the post-sex conversation they'd had after he'd taken her virginity in the bed of his then-ratty truck.

Brody regretted the virginity part. He hadn't known she'd never been with another guy until the deed was done. But he'd never quite managed to regret the actual sex.

He stopped under the tree, but he kept some distance between them. No need to get too close and cause his own flash of heated eyes. Plus, the closeness might bring out stupid questions about butt tats and why she'd left the way she had the night after giving herself to him.

Shaking his head to clear it, he glanced down at her feet. No boot cast. Janessa was wearing black sneakers with sparkly purple hearts on them. A purple almost identical to the color of the bruise on her toe. He could see that bruise just fine because she'd cut out the end of the sneaker to expose it.

"It's too cold to wear flipflops or sandals, and these were the tamest shoe option they had at that store just up from the inn," she explained.

That didn't surprise him. The store, Ink, Etc., was a

tattoo parlor/costume shop and sold plenty of outlandish things.

"It was either these or gold boots with little tiger heads dangling from the laces," Janessa added. "I think I made the right choice. Driving wouldn't be as easy with plastic tiger heads bopping against my legs."

Brody made a sound of agreement, ignoring her attempt to make things light. "You came to say goodbye?" he asked.

He hadn't meant for any bitterness to be in his voice, but it sure as hell was there. Stupid bitterness over something that'd happened the last time Janessa had left Last Ride. She hadn't bothered to say goodbye to him then.

"No. I tried to call and tell you, but...well, when you didn't answer, I figured it best to come and tell you in person." Janessa took a deep breath. "My mother's here. I haven't actually seen her yet, but she got in shortly before midnight."

She held up her hand as if to stop him from speaking, but Brody hadn't even opened his mouth. That was in part because it was the last thing he'd expected Janessa to say, and he was stunned down to the soles of his cowboy boots.

"My mother might not stay so don't get your hopes up," she quickly added. "But just getting her to come here is somewhat of a miracle. It means we have a chance of fulfilling the terms of Abe's will."

Judging from the way Janessa nibbled at her bottom lip, she didn't have a lot of faith in that chance. So Brody tamped down the emotional roller coaster inside him that had been on the verge of skyrocketing.

"How'd you get your mom to come?" he asked.

"A lie," she readily admitted. "Not my lie," she qualified. "But it's a whopper. Anyway, when she learns the truth, she'll probably turn around and go back to Dallas.

Just coming here isn't enough, and I'm not sure I'll be able to get her to stay the entire three months."

Brody gave that some thought, and he didn't like where those thoughts landed. Maybe Janessa had given her mother a sob story about him being destitute and out on the street if the ranch was sold.

"Did the lie involve me?" Brody pressed.

She blinked. "No." She stared at him and repeated it as if trying to figure out why he'd even asked that. Janessa then waved off whatever else she'd been about to say. "Anyway, even if my mom leaves right away, I plan on staying around for a while to challenge the will."

That was slightly less than a shock since Janessa had asked him for the name of a lawyer.

"Look, it'll blast my budget to smithereens if I have to pay for a room at the inn for any extended period of time," Janessa went on. "Do you have a problem if I stay at the ranch?"

She probably hadn't meant to rile him with that question. And Brody wasn't even sure he had a right to be riled, but it hit a nerve. An old, obviously still sensitive nerve that had zilch to do with Abe's will.

"You've always been welcome to stay," he said, hearing the tightness in his voice. "No one asked you to leave sixteen years ago. Besides, the ranch is yours now."

Apparently, that hit a nerve, too, because the new fire in her eyes wasn't from lust. Nope. "No one asked me to leave?" she paraphrased. "You're kidding, right?"

Serious as a heart attack didn't seem an appropriate response, but it was true. Apparently, though, Janessa didn't agree. "I certainly didn't ask you to head out less than twelve hours after you'd talked about inking my name on your ass cheek."

Okay, so he'd gone there after all. And he didn't see what he'd expected to on Janessa's face. No embarrassed apology or regret. Fuming I'm-pissed-off anger. That's what he saw.

"You," she said, pointing a finger at him.

But that was as far as she got. She stopped, limped into a pace. A short one. Janessa only took a few steps before she came right back.

"You," Janessa repeated, "told Abe that we'd had sex, and he said after he had a long talk with you that you'd agreed the right thing to do was for us to get married."

"Married?" That was the only word Brody managed before Janessa just rolled right over him.

"Oh, Abe was going to let me finish college first," she went on, "but after getting my degree, he would be expecting you to propose to me. If you changed your mind, he was going to toss you off the ranch and have charges filed against you since you were eighteen and I was seventeen."

It was as if she were a foreign language. *WTF?* Brody had never ever heard a word of this.

"So, I yelled at Abe to mind his own business," Janessa vented. "I walked out and left the ranch, then and there."

He pointed his finger, too, and like Janessa, it took him a couple of moments to respond. "First of all, I didn't tell Abe that I'd had sex with you. Why the hell would I do something like that?"

"I don't know, but he said you did." She stopped, stared at him. Cursed. If Abe's tombstone had been nearby, she might have kicked it again. "He lied." Her gaze flew back to Brody. "Did he ever demand you marry me or threaten to have you arrested?"

He had to get the muscles unclenched in his jaw before he could speak. "No. And he couldn't have used that threat because Texas has a Romeo and Juliet law. We were close enough to the same age for it to be legal."

She huffed. "And now you know why I never came back." She stopped and squeezed her eyes shut a moment. "I'm sorry. Sorry for a lot of things for both you, me and anyone else Abe tried to manipulate and screw over."

He stayed quiet a moment. Had to. He had to rein in everything he was feeling, but he was failing big time. The grief was colliding with the fresh cuts to the bone.

"Tell your mother the truth about the lie when you see her," Brody advised. "There's already been enough deceit around here."

"True," she agreed, her voice a weary whisper. "But I don't want you to lose this ranch."

Their gazes met again. Held. And for a flash of a moment, he saw the teenage girl who'd come into his life and turned it upside down. The girl who'd stomped on his heart—and she hadn't even known it. In fact, all this time Janessa had believed he'd been the heart stomper.

Yeah, no way had she inked her butt cheek with his name.

"I'll keep you posted," Janessa muttered, limping back toward her car.

Alone, he stood there and watched her drive away. Brody grieved the death of a man he'd loved like a father. But what he grieved more was that the last seventeen years of his life had been one huge-assed lie after another.

CHAPTER FIVE

JANESSA MADE HER way up the porch steps of the palatial house at Colts Creek Ranch. Slow cautious steps. Not because of her aching toe but because she wanted to give herself a few extra moments to settle. Her stomach was churning, and her head was a little light.

She silently cursed both reactions. For Pete's sake, she ran a home for troubled teens and wasn't a wuss. She could handle walking into her father's house. Could handle staying here, too, while she started the process of challenging the will. After all, as Brody had pointed out, it was now hers. Temporarily, of course, but for this moment in time, she owned Abe Parkman's house.

Janessa paused at the door and rang the bell. She waited. Heard nothing. So, she rang it again. The seconds ticked off, turning into minutes, before she huffed and tried the doorknob. It was unlocked so she opened it and stepped inside to the marble floor foyer.

"Hello?" she called out. But again, she got no response.

Maybe the housekeepers hadn't come in, or it was possible that Abe no longer had full-time employees here. Hard to imagine that though with a place this size. Janessa recalled counting the rooms on her previous visit, and there had been twenty-three of them. Twenty-three rooms for a man who'd spent most of his life living alone.

She glanced around and into the large front living room,

noting that both it and the foyer had been redecorated since her last visit. Abe had carried the black-and-white color scheme of the gate and fences into the house. White marble floors here, too, along with sterile pearl-colored walls and ebony wood furniture.

There were no I'm-home-y'all vibes that she'd gotten when Brody had driven her through town. This was like walking into a museum. Abe Parkman's museum where everything looked unapproachable and untouchable.

Unlike the grounds of the ranch, there were no Thanksgiving decorations, and she suspected the exterior ones were all for show. A way of bragging—look here, look what I can afford to do.

Janessa walked into the living room, glancing at Abe's portrait over the white limestone mantel. He looked as unapproachable and untouchable as the house, but it was obvious they shared plenty of DNA. Those were her eyes, a realization that didn't help settle her nerves.

Sighing, she went back into the foyer so she could keep watch out one of the front windows. She wasn't sure why Sophia had insisted on meeting her here. Especially since her mother was staying at the inn in town. Janessa seriously doubted her mom wanted to take this particular stroll down bad memory lane, but maybe it was possible she just wanted to get a look at the place where her "grandchild" would spend the first few weeks of her life.

If that was it, it would give Janessa the lead-in to tell Sophia the truth about the baby. A truth that was going to hurt way more than her throbbing broken toe. Still, Brody was right. There'd already been enough deceit, and if she waited to tell the truth, it would mean only delaying Sophia's exit before the conditions of Abe's will were met. Best to lay all of this on the line and hope for the best.

She heard the clip clops of footsteps and turned to see the housekeeper/cook, Velma Sue Bilbo, coming toward her. The iron-hair woman might have been plenty old enough to retire, but she still looked formidable. She had to be to have dealt with Abe all these years.

Janessa had fond memories of her from the summer she'd spent here. Velma Sue had not only made her feel welcome, she'd written Janessa a few letters over the years. Letters about Abe, of course, and the ranch. Janessa wasn't sure why Velma Sue had taken it upon herself to do that, but she'd read each one and even written back with her own life updates. Just because Abe had been rude to her, Janessa hadn't seen a reason to pass that rudeness on to Velma Sue.

"I rang the doorbell," Janessa said to let Velma Sue know she hadn't just walked right in.

The housekeeper nodded. "I heard it, but I had to take some bread out of the oven, and the kitchen's all the way at the back of the house. I don't move as fast as I used to."

Clearly, since Janessa had been in the house a good ten minutes. "Are you working alone today?" Janessa asked her.

"No, Lottie's cleaning upstairs, but she wears those little earbud things and cranks up the music. It's Stelly's day off. Is there anything I can help you with?"

"No, but thanks. I'm waiting for my mother. She should be here soon."

A ghost of a smile bent the woman's mouth. "Sophia. She was a spitfire."

"Still is. She won't be staying here, but I will. For a little while anyway. I hope that's okay."

Velma Sue shrugged in a suit-yourself gesture that still managed to be welcoming, and with creaky steps that made Janessa wonder just how much housework and cooking she actually managed to get done, she joined her at the window.

"How much of what I'm hearing is true?" Velma Sue asked. "Abe left you everything, but you and Sophia have to stay in Last Ride for three months for you to keep it."

"That's true," Janessa verified.

"Like one of those silly things people post on Facebook," Velma Sue muttered and nearly made Janessa groan and laugh at the same time. "Still, it got both you and Sophia here so it must have worked. Well, it'll work if you both stay."

The question of them staying was indeed the big smelly elephant in the room.

"I don't blame Sophia for leaving like she did," Velma Sue went on. "I hope she's had a good life."

Janessa thought about that a moment. "Good-ish. Depending on your point of view." And she left it at that.

Sophia could champion lost causes with her legal wit, but she had some seriously bad judgment when it came to men. Abe hadn't been her one and only mistake, but it was the only marriage that resulted in a child. Sophia had gone through the "I dos" four times, and Janessa had lost count of the number of engagements and breakups. Her mother made an art form of jumping from one relationship to the other before the proverbial ink had dried on the divorce papers and while the shine was still on the engagement ring.

"Sophia's probably already told you, but Abe didn't treat her right," Velma Sue continued a moment later. "Plus, he married her on the rebound, and that's not a good way to start things off between a husband and wife."

Her mother definitely hadn't told her about that. In fact, Sophia had told her very little about Abe.

"On the rebound?" Janessa repeated, and she hoped the woman didn't realize this was surprising news and just clam up.

She didn't.

Velma Sue nodded. "Abe was all moony-eyed over Brody's mom, Darcia. She was a mite younger than him, five or six years, but I guess she had a little of the moony eye for Abe, too. It didn't last, though. Darcia took up with his best friend, Jimmy Harrell, and that was that."

"His best friend," Janessa muttered. Ouch.

"Best friend and blood brother. Abe kept the scar to prove it. When they were ten or so, the idiots cut themselves a little too deep for their blood brother ritual. Nearly bled to death, and both of them ended up needin' stitches."

It was hard for Janessa to think of Abe being a kid. Or having a best friend for that matter. When she'd spent that summer here, she couldn't remember him once socializing with anyone. Business meetings and parties, yes, but nothing personal.

"So, you think Abe's breakup with Darcia is why he married my mother?" Janessa asked.

"That's the way I saw it. Less than a month after Jimmy and Darcia got hitched, Abe showed up here with Sophia. He'd met her at some fancy cattleman's ball up in Dallas."

Janessa wasn't sure why her mother would have been at a party like that, but she had seen photos of Sophia when she'd been in her early twenties. Plenty of those pictures had involved her being at grand parties. Added to that, Sophia had come from old money and even had family with royal roots. So maybe a fancy cattleman's ball had been part of Janessa's late grandparents' social circles.

"Abe married my mother after only knowing her a month?" Janessa pressed.

"No, it was a little longer than that, but they were already engaged when Abe brought her to Colts Creek Ranch for the first time. It was a month or two later when they had a big wedding right here. *Big*," Velma Sue emphasized. "I think Abe wanted to rub it in Jimmy's and Darcia's faces. Not sure it worked, though," she added.

Since neither marriage had lasted, Janessa wasn't sure how and if any of Abe's feelings for Darcia had played into the divorce. Maybe it'd played into his divorce from Margo, as well. Then again, maybe Abe's personality flaws had been more than enough reason to end the marriages.

"While you're here, you should go through Abe's things," Velma Sue suggested. "Especially the stuff in his storage room next to his office. I think that's where he left some things for you."

That got her attention. "What things? Is it something that'll explain why he did what he did with the will?"

Velma Sue shook her head. "Nothing recent. Just some stuff he got years ago. They stayed in the attic for a long time. Not sure why he didn't give it to you when you were here that summer, but Abe didn't always make sense."

That was true, and it dashed a quick zip of hope that Janessa had gotten over the possibility of there being another letter or some document to tell her why she'd been his only heir. There had to be something, some reason, and while she might be grasping at straws, maybe there had been some condition to Abe's own inheritance. Something along the lines that he could only leave Colts Creek to blood kin.

Velma Sue patted her arm. "You're trying to fix what happened. I hope you can. But sometimes stuff, especially stuff involving Abe, just can't be fixed."

Yes, Janessa knew that, but even if it was unfixable, not righting things would make her feel like a failure. If only she'd been home to read Abe's letter while he'd still been alive, she possibly could have made things right before they'd had a chance to turn so wrong.

"Why'd you work for Abe all these years?" Janessa came out and asked.

That ghost of a smile returned. "I love the house, the ranch. Always did." Velma Sue paused. "Guess I'll have to retire if you can't convince her to stay." She tipped her head to the driveway where Janessa saw Sophia's vintage candy-apple red Mustang come to a stop.

Apparently, it was showtime. One that would almost certainly end the moment Janessa told her mother the truth.

"Good luck," Velma Sue said, giving Janessa's arm a pat. "All of us are gonna need it."

Janessa couldn't agree more. Steeling herself up, she went outside and greeted her mother with a smile and a wave. Sophia stepped out of her car, her gaze sliding over the house and grounds before settling her attention on Janessa.

"Just checking to make sure hell didn't freeze over?" Janessa asked her.

Sophia opened her mouth to answer, probably to say something with more than a smidge of snark, but she frowned as Janessa limped her way toward her. "What happened to you?"

"I kicked Abe's tombstone and broke my toe."

Her mother stared at her a moment and then broke into a loud belly laugh. "Priceless. I might find the cemetery and give it a couple of kicks myself." She pulled Janessa into a hug and kissed the top of her head.

As usual, Sophia smelled like Chanel perfume and freshly laundered cotton. An odd combination, but that scent was Sophia to a tee. The expensive mixed with the environmentally friendly.

Today, she was wearing raw silk pants and a cashmere sweater the color of ripe plums. Probably an outfit bought at some Dallas boutique that specialized in organic fabrics, and she'd paired it with outrageous high-heel lime booties that had likely set her back a thousand bucks.

They stood there for several long moments, just holding onto each other. When she was growing up, Sophia had smothered her with motherly love and plenty of interference and meddling. If Janessa had let her, Sophia would have continued to try to run her life.

"I brought your things," Sophia said when she eased back. She used her key to pop open the trunk of her car. "I didn't stick to the list you gave me, though. I figured you'd want some nicer outfits and such for when you were photographed with the baby. You'll appreciate that when you look back on the keepsakes years from now."

Crap. So, they'd already launched into the baby topic.

"Mom," Janessa said as she lifted the two suitcases from the trunk, "we need to talk."

"Of course, we do. You'll probably want to remind me of just how big the stakes are if I don't adhere to Abe's jackass rules. Rules no doubt meant to take a jab or two at me since that's what jackasses do."

Maybe that had been Abe's reasoning, but after hearing what Velma Sue had just said, it seemed to Janessa that Abe would have preferred those jabs to land on Darcia or Brody's father. Then again, Velma Sue hadn't gotten a chance to get into the nitty-gritty details of what had sent Sophia running from this place.

Sophia took one of the suitcases from Janessa, and they started for the porch. "I won't be going in the house," her mother insisted. "I've already bent my hell-freezing-over rule enough. So, why don't you come back to the inn with me?"

"I can do that, but why didn't you just ask me to meet you there in the first place rather than drive out here?"

"Because I wanted to make the drive. To see the ranch. To see if the place still makes me want to curse Abe. It does," Sophia concluded after another look around. "So, why don't we go to the inn, and then you can tell me all about this Brody Harrell."

Janessa stopped on the top step, looked at her mother. "How do you know about Brody?"

Sophia rolled her brown eyes. "I remember when you ran off to spend the summer here, and you called me all gooey over a boy you'd met."

"You wouldn't talk to me the first month I was here," Janessa quickly reminded her. And then, yes, she might have mentioned a boy when Sophia and she had gotten back to having semi-normal conversations. "I never mentioned his name."

"No, but you doodled it a lot after you got back. Doodled and scratched it out. So, I used my superior deductive skills and figured out that the gooiness hadn't lasted and he'd broken your heart." Sophia paused and stared at her in a way that only a mother could. A prying mother. "Maybe he did more than that."

Since Sophia didn't have ESP, Janessa ignored the fishing expedition. No way would she tell her mother that she'd lost her virginity to Brody, here on the ranch, where Sophia hadn't wanted her to be in the first place.

"Anyway, I did a few computer searches," Sophia went on a few moments later, "and discovered that Abe's ranch manager was—ta-da—Brody Harrell and that he'd been working for Abe while you were here. So, I ran a quick background check on him last night."

Janessa huffed and continued to the front door. "You didn't."

"Don't scowl. There wasn't much to find. No police record. No marriages. No red flags. Just a boatload of financial deals that made Abe richer than he already was." Sophia set the suitcase inside the foyer when Janessa opened the door, but true to her word, she didn't go inside. "Is Brody the reason you're so adamant about staying here for three months?"

"In part," Janessa readily admitted. "But not because I'm still gooey over him." Well, not much anyway. "I don't want him or the other people Abe employed to lose their jobs. I told you about the terms of the will and what's at stake in those voice mails I had to leave for you because you weren't answering your phone."

Of course, Janessa hadn't told her mom everything in those voice mails. There were just some things better spilled in person. Some things best avoided altogether, too, like the attraction to Brody.

Sophia stared at her. "It wouldn't be a smart idea to get involved with him. Even casual holiday nooky could end up causing lots of problems for you."

Janessa thought her mouth might have dropped open. "Casual holiday nooky? I'm here because of Abe's will, not Brody."

"Good, because if you hook up with someone from Last Ride, where would that go, huh?" She didn't wait for Janessa to answer. "Your job, your life and home are in Dallas. His job, life and home are here. It would never work."

"You're giving me love and relationship advice?" Janessa asked after an eye roll.

"Of course. I'm not only your mother, but I've also had a lot of experience with what doesn't work in a relationship. This won't work. That's too big of a bridge to gap, and you'll end up just hurting each other."

Too big of a bridge to gap? Possibly. *Probably*. And it

didn't matter anyway. She wasn't here to hook up with Brody again.

"Brody might not have a job and life in Last Ride if we can't meet the terms of Abe's will," Janessa said, getting this conversation back on track. "And it's not just the ranch. Abe owned businesses all over the state, and they'll be sold if we don't try to do the right thing."

"I'm here, aren't I?" Sophia countered. "But I want a look at Abe's will. If I can challenge it and win, you won't have to be here with my grandchild for even a minute much less weeks. I'm so pissed off that Abe would try to manipulate us this way, and I don't want you and my precious little darling grandbaby to have to live under Abe's roof for a single minute if I can prevent it."

Sophia stopped again, both of them turning in the direction of the road past the barn, and Janessa saw Brody's truck coming toward the house. He no doubt saw them, too, and while he didn't slam on the brakes, she was pretty sure he slowed down. Pretty sure, too, he was muttering some choice profanity. He'd made it clear that he didn't want to see her.

He parked not in front of the house but on the side, and for a moment, Janessa thought he'd just go inside without speaking to them. Something he no doubt wanted to do. However, it wasn't long before he came around to the front porch.

"Brody," Janessa said, her breath automatically rising. Probably her pulse, too. The man looked just as good clean as he did riding back from doing ranch work. "This is my mother, Sophia Wainwright."

Brody tipped the brim of his hat in greeting. "Pleased to meet you." He motioned to the side of the house where

he'd just come from. "I'll be in my office if you need me."
And he turned to walk away.

"We were just talking about you," Sophia called out,
stopping him in his tracks.

When Brody turned back around, Sophia gave Brody
a long look. Not a lustful one that most women gave him,
either. This was a hefty serving of mom stink eye.

"I'm sure there's a lot of talk going on," he said.

And Janessa knew he was doing his own version of
stink eye. The kind where he was silently asking why she
hadn't already remedied that lie with her mother. Kyle's lie
that she hadn't clearly spelled out to Brody, but that didn't
mean Janessa hadn't had a valid reason for not clarifying
it sooner. It was because if the truth had been spilled, Sophia likely wouldn't still be here.

Janessa answered his stink eye with a somewhat cow-
ardly shrug, and she was about to mention that she and
her mom were on the way to the inn. Where much talking would ensue. Fast-talking on Janessa's part where she
would do the non-cowardly thing and fess up about the
nonexistent grandbaby.

However, she didn't get a chance to say anything because
another vehicle turned into the driveway. Another truck,
but this one was scabbed with rust and backfired a couple
of times before the driver pulled to a brake-squealing stop.

Janessa didn't recognize the tall sandy-haired driver
when he got out. At least not at first. But she groaned when
she got a better look at his face.

"Trouble?" Brody immediately asked, and he came back
to the porch. "Who is he?"

"That's Riggs Burkhart, and yes, he could be trouble,"
Janessa admitted. "He's the baby daddy."

"The father of the child you're adopting?" Sophia muttered.

Brody didn't come out and ask, but Janessa could practically see the question in his head. He was no doubt remembering that she'd told him she was *fostering* a baby, not adopting one. And that was the truth. But it was a truth Sophia didn't know yet, and Riggs would surely blab it.

This was so not the way Janessa wanted Sophia to find out.

"Miss Parkman, we have to talk," Riggs insisted, his glare pinned to Janessa.

Wearing jeans and a white tee and a snug black leather jacket that was no doubt meant to show off his muscled body, Riggs strode toward her as if ready to pick a fight. In the handful of times she'd seen him, it'd been his default swagger.

Riggs was young, twenty-two and hotheaded. A bad combination that had led to many run-ins with Teagan. Riggs had resorted to intimidation and stalking, and that had been the final straw for Teagan. She'd broken things off and refused to see him.

"You drove all the way from Dallas," Janessa remarked. "How'd you know I was in Last Ride?"

"I called Bright Hope," Riggs explained in a snarl as he closed the distance between them. "Teagan wasn't working in the office today like she usually does. It was somebody else, another girl, and she said you were away on a trip, that your father had died."

Janessa wasn't sure who would have given Riggs that info, but some of the residents, including Teagan, worked part-time in the office unless they had other jobs. Teagan also worked as a sales clerk in a nearby store because she was trying to earn and save some money. Whomever Riggs had spoken to probably didn't know that Janessa had come to Last Ride, but it wouldn't have been hard for Riggs to do a computer search to find Abe's name and learn where his funeral had been held.

"You shouldn't be here," Janessa said. Like Teagan, she'd made it clear often enough that she didn't want to see or speak to him.

"I had to come," Riggs insisted.

Brody obviously picked up on the young man's riled tone and stiff body language because he moved to Janessa's side. So did Sophia. She was flanked by two people who obviously wanted to protect her, and when this was over, she was going to owe them both an explanation. She'd told Brody that a lie had brought Sophia to the ranch, and now she'd need to spell out for him what that lie was all about.

Riggs stopped right in front of her. "You've got to talk Teagan out of giving up my baby. She has to marry me so we can raise our daughter together."

Janessa's sigh was long and weary, but she straightened her shoulders and looked him straight in the eyes. "We've already gone through this. Teagan doesn't want to marry you, and she doesn't want you to have any part in raising the child. Do I need to remind you why?"

"I'm the baby's father," he argued as if that negated the reasons why Teagan had made her decision.

Janessa commenced with the *reminding him* since he hadn't opted for it. "Along with a lengthy juvenile record, you were also arrested for assault and drunk driving," Janessa reminded Riggs. He might want to gloss it all over, but she certainly wouldn't. "In fact, you're on parole."

Riggs shook his head and jabbed his finger at her. "That doesn't mean I can't have my daughter."

"Actually, yes it does." And Janessa pulled out the big

guns, guns that Riggs was already well aware of. "You signed away your rights to the child."

Riggs cursed, and his face went red, like a toddler about to throw an ugly tantrum. "I did that only so I wouldn't go to jail again for arguing with Teagan," he shouted.

"Lower your voice," Brody warned him and took one menacing step toward Riggs.

Janessa groaned. She couldn't let this turn into a fight. "You didn't just argue with her," Janessa countered, responding to Riggs. "You grabbed her and tried to shove her into your truck. That's assault and attempted kidnapping, and it happened when she was four months pregnant."

"I was trying to make her understand that I didn't want her to give up my baby." Riggs didn't shout this time, but he spoke through clenched teeth while volleying furious glances between Brody and her.

Again, that wasn't anywhere near a valid argument on Riggs's part, and his temper was fueling her own. That's why Janessa reined it in. She didn't want this to escalate.

"He signed away his rights?" Sophia asked.

"Because Teagan blackmailed me," Riggs snarled before Janessa could answer. "She said if I didn't sign papers giving up the baby that she'd have me arrested for that assault and kidnapping shit. That woulda put me back in jail."

"Teagan had a lawyer draw up an agreement that Riggs would surrender any and all parental rights," Janessa explained to her mother.

Sophia turned to Riggs. "You signed the papers for forfeiture of custodial rights?" she pressed, sounding very much like the lawyer she was.

"Because Teagan blackmailed me," Riggs repeated, and this time his voice went up too many notches in volume.

"You're leaving now," Brody demanded, taking another step toward Riggs.

"Not until she tears up those papers and says I can have Teagan and my baby." He flung an accusing finger at Janessa.

Brody got right in Riggs's face. "No, you're leaving now."

Riggs lifted his fist as if ready to throw a punch, but Brody latched on to his arm, holding him in a fierce grip. Brody didn't issue any other warnings. Didn't have to. His entire body was a warning right now.

Even though Brody looked more than capable of kicking his butt, Riggs still didn't budge. He glared at Brody, but he must have seen something in Brody's eyes that told him this wasn't a fight he stood any chance whatsoever of winning.

"This isn't over," Riggs declared, and the moment Brody released his grip, the young man started for his truck. "I'll convince Teagan to take me back," he added from over his shoulder. "You'll see. I'll convince her, and we can raise our baby together."

Riggs got in his truck, and he slammed the door with far more force than required. Gunning the engine, he sped away.

"Well, what an asshat," Sophia mumbled. "What'd you say his name is?"

"Riggs Burkhart," Janessa answered.

Sophia took out her phone, scrolled through her contacts and Janessa saw her text Savannah Maddox, the PI her mother sometimes used for her cases.

"I'm requesting a thorough background check on our Mr. Burkhart," Sophia told Janessa as she composed the text. "I'll also get started on a TRO. A temporary restraining order," she spelled out. "I'll have it include both the ranch and Bright Hope House."

Janessa didn't mind her mother taking such measures, but Sophia might back off when she learned the truth. Then again, Sophia might go into her champion mode and carry through on whatever it took to keep Riggs away from Teagan and Colts Creek.

"When I'm done with him, that asshat won't get anywhere near the baby." Sophia hit Send on the text, brushed a quick kiss on Janessa's cheek and turned to go.

"Mom, we have to talk," Janessa said.

"Later," Sophia insisted. "Call Kyle and tell him what just happened. He'll want to alert Dallas PD in case this baby daddy shows up there."

Janessa sighed as her mother started for her car.

"Who's Kyle?" Brody asked.

Sophia stopped, turned and a twinkle lit her eyes. "Kyle McKinney," she provided. Paused. Smiled. "Janessa's husband."

CHAPTER SIX

HUSBAND.

Of all the things Brody had expected to come out of Sophia's mouth, that wasn't one of them. Nope.

"It's not what you think," Janessa said, whirling around to face him.

Brody was about to tell her that it was none of his business—even if it felt a little as if it was—but her phone rang. Janessa muttered some mild profanity when she glanced at the screen and then added, "I have to take this."

He gave her as indifferent a nod as he could manage and headed around the house toward his office, but he glanced over his shoulder to make sure the hothead idiot hadn't doubled back.

He hadn't.

Riggs's truck was thankfully nowhere in sight. Brody would keep an eye out for it, though. Would alert the hands, too. He didn't know this Riggs Burkhart, but he didn't want him on the ranch. Brody was pretty sure, had he not been there, the man would have tried to bully Janessa. Or worse.

Brody had just reached the porch outside his office when he spotted Margo. Even though she lived on the grounds of the ranch, it was rare to see her anywhere near the main house. Then again, these weren't usual times.

Margo had driven here from her place and parked her car by the side of the barn. She was practically running toward him. No easy accomplishment, considering she was wearing needle-thin silver heels. Margo might have lived on the ranch for going on twenty years, but the woman always dressed as if she were heading to a fancy big-city luncheon.

"Is it true?" Margo asked before she even reached him. "Is Sophia actually in Last Ride?"

"She is," Brody verified. "Not sure how long she'll be staying, though."

He thought of what Janessa had said. About a lie. One that she was supposedly going to tell her mother about and it would send Sophia back to Dallas. Brody was betting Janessa hadn't clarified that yet. Then again, she seemed to be good at keeping details to herself since she hadn't once mentioned she was married.

"But she's here." Margo blew out a long breath and patted her heart as if to steady it. "Did you talk to her?"

"Some."

He figured Margo wanted details but she wasn't wearing a coat, and since the air had a bit of a bite to it, Brody stepped up onto the side porch. He flipped on the switch for the pair of brass column heaters positioned in the seating area. It wouldn't keep her toasty warm, but it would stave off enough of a chill for them to have a short conversation.

Brody didn't want to invite Margo into his office because he really didn't have time for a long talk. He needed to get started on the work schedules for the upcoming week, and conversations with Margo tended to last a whole lot longer than he wanted.

"Some?" Margo repeated in protest. "Surely, you asked Sophia if she was going to do the right thing by staying or royally screw us over by leaving Last Ride before the three months are up?"

"It's Abe's will that'll screw us over," he reminded her.

Margo huffed. "Yes, but the screwing will end if Sophia stays."

"I didn't ask Sophia her plans," Brody settled for saying. He took hold of the doorknob to his office to give Margo a not so subtle hint that he had to go.

"Well, you should ask her," Margo insisted. "In fact, you should ask her other things, too."

Brody gave her a flat look because he was sure he wouldn't care for the rest of what Margo was about to say. "Like what?"

Margo shrugged. "I read about Sophia on the internet. She's a lawyer and has been divorced a whole bunch of times. I didn't see any mention or pictures of a significant other on her social media page. So, maybe you could ask her out or something."

His look got even flatter. "You want me to pimp myself out to keep Sophia in Last Ride?"

"Yes," Margo answered with plenty of conviction. "You could think of it like taking one for the team."

"No. And just to make myself clear. *No*," he repeated.

Margo's eyes watered, and he wasn't immune to the worry he saw there. Colts Creek was as much her home as it was his, but there were lines he wouldn't cross to keep his home. He damn sure wouldn't try to bed Janessa's mother. Or Janessa for that matter. The heat between Janessa and him would stay just that. Heat. And he had no plans whatsoever to act on it.

"I'm not sure where I'll go if I lose my place," Margo went on, blinking back more tears. They were sticking to the thick layer of mascara on her heavily lined eyelashes. "You're the only family I have, and my friends are all here in Last Ride."

"Then stay in Last Ride. You can buy or build another house."

He didn't snap it out. Brody softened his voice and gave her arm a gentle squeeze. Because in a weird kind of way, Margo was his family, too. Heck, so were plenty of others on this ranch. Unlike some of those others, though, Margo could actually afford to move.

She shook her head and stared at him with her watery eyes. "It wouldn't be the same."

No, it wouldn't be. But either way, things would never be the same. Abe's death had stirred their lives around in a big metaphorical stewpot, and he wasn't sure the stewing would stop until they were all cooked.

If by some miracle, Janessa talked her mother into staying and she did end up inheriting the ranch, she might change her mind about offering it to him. And if she did offer it, Brody wasn't sure he would accept.

Correction: he wasn't sure he *could* accept.

Yeah, there was a lot at stake, but he wouldn't feel 100 percent right having Colts Creek just handed to him. If Abe had wanted him to have it, he would have spelled that out in the will.

"You should try to prepare yourself for the worst," Brody murmured to Margo just as he heard the hurried footsteps coming around the corner of the house.

Janessa.

"Sorry about that, but…" Limping toward him, she still had her phone in her hand and stopped when she spotted Margo.

"Is everything okay?" Janessa asked, probably because she'd seen Margo's tears. However, she waved off that question. "Sorry. It's obviously not okay. I'm working on that, though," she added to Margo. "I very much want to make everything as right as it can be."

Margo dried her eyes, managed a smile. "That's good," Margo said with more hope than Brody wanted to hear in her voice. Obviously, Margo wasn't jumping into preparing for the worst.

"I have to go." Margo checked the time. "An early lunch with the Last Ride Society committee." She shifted her attention back to Janessa, and Margo's eyes and tone brightened. "The drawing's tomorrow. I'd love for you to go with me, especially since this is part of your Parkman legacy."

Janessa shook her head and limped up onto the porch to stand beneath the fans. "What drawing?"

"Oh, it's wonderful," Margo gushed, causing Brody to roll his eyes. A wonderful waste of time as far as he was concerned. "The founder of Last Ride, Hezzie Parkman, set up the Society so that future generations of Parkmans would research the tombstones in the local area."

Janessa's forehead bunched up. "You mean like genealogy?"

"More like local history. A legacy," she emphasized. "It also raises money for charity. I obviously wasn't born a Parkman, but it's for Parkman spouses and ex-spouses, too. We usually have the meetings at 6:00 p.m. at the town hall, but we're moving it to the morning because of some repairs that are being done. Please go with me." This time there was a boatload of enthusiasm in Margo's plea.

Janessa shrugged. "Maybe." She paused and met Margo's eyes. "You do know I might not be staying. If my mother leaves, I will, too."

"Yes, I know, but let's not think about that now. You're going to love the Last Ride Society. I'll make sure your name's in the drawing."

With her mood clearly much improved, Margo said goodbye and scurried off on those neck-breaking heels.

"Is it a bad thing that I'm in the drawing?" Janessa asked. "I won't have to do something weird, will I?"

The entire Society was weird as far as he was concerned, but then he wasn't into researching local history. Or researching tombstones. "I think for the most part, it's just a social club."

Obviously not for Margo, though. She tended to treat it more like a once in a lifetime production even though the Society held a drawing every three months.

"I had to deal with something at Bright Hope," Janessa said, drawing his attention back to her. She lifted her phone to remind him of the call she'd gotten moments after Sophia had dropped the *Janessa's husband* bombshell. "I also told them to be on the watch for Riggs just in case he's stupid enough to show up there."

"Since he was stupid enough to show up here, that was a wise move." Brody reached for the doorknob again. A signal to Janessa that he really did need to go in and get started on work.

"It's not what you think," she blurted out. "My marriage, I mean." She shook her head. "I mean, I'm not married. My divorce was final a month ago."

Brody lifted an eyebrow. "A whole month." And no, he didn't pull back on the sarcasm.

"Yes, but it's not what you think, either. Kyle and I split up six years ago, but we didn't get around to filing for a divorce until recently."

"That's a long time to put off doing paperwork," he said and left it at that. And it made him wonder why Janessa hadn't pushed for it to happen sooner. Then he got a flash of Sophia's smile when she'd answered with *Janessa's hus-*

band. "Let me guess. Your mother likes and approves of your ex? She didn't want you to get divorced."

"Oh, yes." Janessa didn't hesitate. "Liked, approved and thinks he's perfect for me. He isn't. We're good friends, and we run Bright Hope House together, but we were never good marriage partners."

Brody hadn't actually met anyone who'd had an amicable divorce, but apparently Janessa had. "So, your mother told me about the ex in case I was thinking about going for a repeat of what we did the summer you stayed here?"

She didn't hesitate with the nod, either. "My mom's no stranger to divorce. She's had four of them. Her own mother had three, and her father had six. Old money, privileged lifestyles, low tolerance for the dips and lows that come with relationships. I think Sophia was just hoping I'd stick it out and break what she calls the family curse. She definitely wants me to try to work things out with Kyle."

Brody nudged aside the ping of jealousy he felt. "And what does Kyle want?"

"Not to work things out with me."

She chuckled and lifted her face to the whirling fans. The chilly breeze kicked up, causing her blond hair to flutter against her neck and shoulders. It got his attention. So did the way her mouth opened slightly when she drew in a long breath.

And that made him stupid.

No way should he be thinking about or noticing such things, and that's why he finally opened the door to his office. Something that Janessa obviously didn't notice because she continued speaking.

"Kyle wants to move on with his life and get more serious about a woman he's been seeing, but he plans to wait a while, until the proverbial ink has dried on our divorce," she said. "I get that. My mother jumps from one relationship to the other, and I believe that's a mistake."

The heat from the open door spilled out onto them. Brody took a step to go in, then he stopped when he thought of something. "Does the lie that got your mom here have anything to do with your ex or the still-wet ink on your divorce?"

Janessa shook her head. "No. It has to do with the baby."

"The one you're adopting now instead of just fostering?" he concluded.

Her forehead bunched up again. "Well, actually I'm not adopting her. That's the lie Kyle told my mother to get her to come here. He knew I was upset about what Abe did, and he was trying to help."

Brody was sure his own forehead did some bunching. "I don't follow you. Did Kyle lie to Riggs, too?"

"No. Riggs's ex-girlfriend, Teagan, is giving up her baby, and she wants her older sister to adopt her. I mentioned that to you when you gave me a ride to Asher's office. The sister is stationed overseas in the military so I agreed to foster the baby for a month or so until she gets back."

Oh, yeah. He recalled Janessa saying that. "Sophia wouldn't have come if you'd told her you were just fostering the child?"

"No way. My mother's in the market for a grandchild. That's another reason she wants me to stick with Kyle. She thinks it'll be too long for a grandbaby if she has to wait for me to find someone else, fall in love, etc." Janessa stopped, met his gaze. "I'll have to tell Sophia the truth."

Brody could tell that wasn't going to be pleasant, but it was best if the truth happened sooner rather than later. Not just for Margo and Sophia but for everyone involved in this mess. It wasn't good to have this hanging over their heads.

"When I tell my mother, I'll try my best to talk her into staying," Janessa added.

He heard the slight waver in her voice. Saw it on her face. That amazing face that had his number.

Hell.

He mentally ticked off all the reasons why he shouldn't do what he was thinking about doing. At best, Janessa was only staying three months, and he didn't want a fling. Didn't want his heart stomped on again, either. Plus, there was the part about the ink barely being dry on her divorce. She'd said it herself that it wasn't good to jump from one relationship right into another.

"You know," she said, her voice like bottled sin, "if I were going to stay through the holidays, I'd kiss you and see where it goes from there."

Like Sophia's husband bombshell, that comment from Janessa hadn't been anywhere on his radar. But, man, did his body latch on to that as a golden-ticket invitation that he should accept.

Brody considered his comeback options. *It'd go nowhere* was a lie. *It'd lead straight to sex* was stating the obvious. *It'd be a mistake*—again stating the obvious.

"All right," she said when he was obviously taking too long to answer, "let's go with an imaginary kiss. I'd like an imaginary hug, too, since it's cold, and I could really use one. I'm betting you could, as well."

A hug would probably also lead them straight to sex. Heck, merely looking at each other might do the trick. But somehow Brody managed to keep his feet planted because he knew one thing that was as real as real got. Janessa wouldn't be staying for the three months.

"Hugging you now," she said, not moving, either. But she did lower her gaze to his chest.

Brody could practically feel her sliding her arms, warm and silky, around him. He had no trouble, *none*, imagining how she'd fit against him. Once that image was burned into his head, his body filled in the rest. The rest being that the hug would quickly escalate with an even tighter grip. A kick of heat.

Then, a kiss.

He knew exactly how she tasted, knew how her mouth would feel on his. Some memories just stayed with you, and kissing Janessa was one of them.

Oh, man.

She could create so much lust with that mouth, and Brody knew if this were for real, he'd be diving in for more. Something long, deep and a final straw that would *lead straight to sex.*

Her lips parted when she drew in a slow breath. Yeah, that would have happened, too, with a real kiss. Maybe not much breathing, though. Air wouldn't be as much of a necessity as was taking every inch of her mouth.

Of course, kissing would lead to touching, and with all the right signals, his hand would slide right down to her breasts. Would slide lower, too, while the kissing raged on. Until there was nothing left to do but to drag each other to the—

Brody cut off that thought before he got a hard-on. Definitely not something he wanted to experience with Janessa while they were on the porch and in broad daylight.

She seemed to do some thought-halting as well, and Janessa shook her head as if trying to clear it. But he saw the arousal on her face. Heard the too-quick rhythm of her breathing.

"Uh, I'll just be going." She fluttered her fingers in no specific direction, and with her breath gusting, she stared at him for several moments. "Going" she repeated, and she turned to limp away.

Brody watched her go. Felt those stupid parts of him start to beg again. And he cursed a blue streak.

Because without so much as laying his mouth or his hands on Janessa, he had just complicated the hell out of things.

CHAPTER SEVEN

WHILE SHE WAITED on hold for Kyle, Janessa walked across
the bedroom to look out the window. She couldn't think of
it as *her* bedroom, but it's where she'd slept that summer
she had spent here. And it was where she'd stay for however long she ended up at Colts Creek.

She was still in the to-be-determined zone as to whether
or not she'd make it the three months or if this would be
her last morning at the ranch. Odds were it would be the
last. But for now, she just held on to a tiny grain of hope
that she could get Sophia's help to fix things.

First, though, she had to deal with telling her mom the
truth about the baby.

That hadn't happened the day before because Sophia had
gone to her room at the inn and immersed herself in getting the temporary restraining order for Riggs and starting
the fight for Abe's will. Janessa had texted her to arrange a
meeting so they could talk, but Sophia had answered back,
Too busy right now. Maybe tomorrow.

Well, it was tomorrow, and that talk was going to have
to happen even if it meant going to the inn and pounding
on her mother's door.

Some movement in one of the corrals caught her eye, and
she saw Brody. He had his forearms on the top of the fence
and his right boot on the bottom railing while he and two
other hands watched a pair of impressive-looking quarter

horses meander around. Brody was impressive, too, in his faded jeans, dark blue shirt and buckskin jacket. The jacket was a reminder of the cold front that'd moved through during the night, and temps had dropped to the forties.

She kept watching Brody and got an instant reminder of the kiss. Well, the almost-kiss anyway. That imaginary kiss, and Brody, had been a huge part of why she'd had such a restless night. She had way too much on her plate right now to have sunk time into that kiss and let it spin her body out of control.

There was more movement, and she spotted Rowan coming out of the barn that was nearest to the house. He obviously spotted her, too, because he grinned, waved and then motioned for her to open the window. Janessa sandwiched the phone between her shoulder and ear so she could do that, and she immediately felt the gush of cold air push through the screen.

"You should bundle up and come out for a ride," the boy called out to her.

She definitely hadn't expected such an invitation, considering she could still give his brother *the boot*. "Maybe later," she said and then added, "Thanks."

"I'm working here part-time, and I'll be around this afternoon. Tomorrow afternoon, too." He paused. "Of course, if you decide you'd rather go riding with Brody, I'll understand." Rowan gave her an exaggerated wink.

Their conversation got Brody's attention because he glanced at them from over his shoulder. No wink from him. He scowled and snarled, "Rowan, check on the mares in the east stable."

Rowan didn't lose his smile or enthusiasm. He gave her a quick wave and headed off at a pace that told her he had a lot more energy than she did at the moment.

"Sorry about the wait," Kyle said when he finally came on the line. "Alisha tried to make a grilled cheese sandwich with her curling iron, and the smoke triggered the alarms. I had an armful of cats at the time because CeeCee has been hiding more strays, and the noise from the alarm caused one of them to scratch up my arm."

None of what he'd said was unusual. Alisha had a penchant for setting off fire alarms with her cooking attempts, and CeeCee was probably on the path to either being a veterinarian or a future cat lady.

"Are the scratches bad?" Janessa asked, closing the window and giving Brody one last glance.

"Bad enough for Mildred to douse me with stuff that burned like hell."

Again, that was usual. Mildred was a retired nurse who volunteered at Bright Hope, and she had all sorts of burning, stinging remedies.

"Anyway, I guess you're calling to check about Riggs," Kyle went on. "No sign of him here."

"Good." Janessa hoped it stayed that way. "How's Teagan?"

"Worried. I had to tell her about Riggs, and she's scared he'll come here. I assured her I wouldn't let the asshole inside, and no, I didn't use the word *asshole*."

Janessa made a mental note to call Teagan. In the five months Teagan had been at Bright Hope, Janessa had gotten fairly close to her. Not exactly a big sister kind of bond, but she might be able to soothe the girl's worries.

"Did you get the budget paperwork I emailed you this morning?" she asked, moving on to something else that was on her to-do list.

"I did. Haven't had a chance to look it over yet, but I'm sure we're as broke as we usually are. How are things going there in cowboy world?" he tacked on to that without so much as a pause.

Oh, where to start. She definitely wouldn't be mentioning the pretend kiss or her real lusting after one particular cowboy, but she could fill Kyle in on the rest.

"Sophia's in Last Ride, and she's staying at the inn, not here at the ranch. FYI, I'm still going to throttle you for lying to her."

"Understood," Kyle said with way too much peppiness that let her know no such throttling would occur. "When will you tell her the truth?"

"Soon." Janessa checked the time. It was already past ten thirty, and even though her mother was probably sleeping in after putting in some long hours the night before on the legal stuff, she should be up by now. "After that, I'll likely be on my way back to Dallas." She paused. "You know, I could have been back there already if you hadn't lied to my mother."

"I know. And trust me, that was a huge sacrifice since I'm the one who has to deal with curling-iron grilled cheeses. But I figured it'd mess you up if you couldn't save that part of the world. That's what you do, Janessa. You save people and things. Me included."

Janessa dismissed that. She hadn't saved him. She'd merely gotten Kyle the help he needed when he was depressed and drinking too much. However, he was right about having this mess her up. She could dump the blame on Abe and his stupid will, but that wouldn't stop her from feeling as if she'd failed. And because of the failure, so many people would lose what they loved.

"How's the broken toe?" Kyle asked. "Will you be okay to drive?"

"It's better." Well, thanks to a steady dose of the over-the-counter meds, it was. As for the driving, Janessa hadn't tested those particular waters today. "If I start hurting, I'll just pull over and wait until the pain stops."

Of course, that meant it could be a very long drive to Dallas. Sophia would probably insist on Janessa going back with her and offer to make arrangements for someone else to bring her car back. But Janessa didn't especially want to listen to Sophia lecturing her for four hours about the lie that had gotten her to come here.

"I have to go," she said when there was a knock at her bedroom door. "I'll let you know when I'm heading back to Dallas."

She ended the call, went to the door and was surprised when she saw Margo. The woman was wearing a corn-colored dress and burnt orange heels and hat. She looked like a walking advertisement for Thanksgiving. A reminder that it was only a few weeks away.

"Are you ready to go?" Margo immediately asked.

Janessa shook her head and started flipping back through all those mental notes to figure out what she was supposed to be ready for.

"The Last Ride Society drawing," Margo supplied before Janessa could come up with the right note.

Oh, that. She hadn't given Margo a confirmed yes that she'd attend, but obviously the woman thought she had.

"We need to hurry or all the snickerdoodles will be gone. Alma's putting them out before the meeting," Margo added, reaching to take Janessa's hand.

Janessa held her ground. "I'm sorry, but I won't be able to go. I need to talk to my mother at the inn."

"Sophia will be at the drawing. You can talk to her there."

That caused Janessa to do a mental double take. "My mother's going? Why?"

"Because I invited her. We had the best chat over coffee last night." Margo chuckled. "Abe was probably turning over in his grave at having his exes roast him."

That required another double take. She couldn't imagine why Sophia would have had a *best chat* with Abe's second wife. Then again, both Margo and Sophia were trust-fund babies so it was possible they'd once traveled in similar social circles. It seemed a little icky to Janessa, though, that they'd bond over ex trash talk.

"I went to see Sophia so I could get a feel for if she was planning to stay," Margo went on. "Don't worry. I was subtle about it. I didn't come out and ask her if she was going to put a stop to Abe trying to screw us all over, but I got the impression that she'd stay because she doesn't want to miss seeing her grandbaby."

Yes, Janessa got that, but she had to shake her head at something else Margo had said a couple of seconds earlier. "My mom accepted your invitation to a Parkman gathering? Why?" she repeated.

Margo shrugged. "Probably because I told her you'd be there. I mentioned there'd be a lot of talk about Abe and that we might be able to get some dirt that could help challenge the will."

At best, that was a long shot, but with Sophia's hatred for Abe, it was possible she just wanted to hear someone else bash him. Still, a small-town historical society didn't seem like something that would lure Sophia away from the inn and her legal wranglings.

"Let's go," Margo prompted. "I'll drive. I told Sophia to hold us some seats, but if it gets crowded, people might give her some sass over saving them."

Janessa glanced down at her black pants and cream-colored sweater. It was one of the outfits that her mother had brought from Dallas. Actually, the only thing Sophia had packed had been dressy clothes and shoes that Janessa couldn't wear. Since she hadn't had a chance yet to find a better pair, the sneakers would have to do. At least she'd already combed her hair and put on some makeup, but she'd done that in case she ran into Brody, not because she'd been expecting to go to a society meeting.

"So, where are Brody and you going on your date?" Margo asked as they headed down the stairs.

Janessa stutter-stepped and nearly tripped. "Our what?"

"Your date," Margo said as if Janessa had simply not heard her. She had. She'd heard, but she didn't understand. "Everybody's buzzing about the steamy way Brody and you were looking at each other on the side porch," the woman explained. "I guess you two will be testing the waters with another romance."

"Uh, no, we won't be, and we won't be going on a date."

Margo laughed and laughed and laughed as if that were a fine joke, and they continued down the stairs and to the front door. Janessa grabbed her red wool coat from the rack in the foyer.

"Brody's the hot ticket here in Last Ride," Margo said. "Don't know how you could resist him."

Janessa wasn't clear on how to go about said resisting, but she had to do it. "Things didn't end well between Brody and me that summer I was here."

"Yes, I heard." Margo led her to her car that was parked in front of the house. "You broke his heart."

Janessa winced. Because it was probably true. They hadn't been in love, but their feelings for each other had been plenty intense.

"Brody got over that, over me," Janessa muttered.

"Don't be so sure of that," Margo insisted as they got in

the car. "I mean, there's a reason he's never been engaged or serious about anyone. Some people just don't mend all the way. I didn't. Abe broke my heart. Darcia broke his. Of course, Darcia had other heartbreaks to deal with. I suppose you've heard all about her daughter?"

"Layla," Janessa murmured. She recalled seeing the family photo of Layla, Brody and Darcia at Brody's house. Like Velma Sue, Janessa had fond memories of Layla, as well. They'd become friendly despite Layla being two years younger.

"That's right. Layla," Margo confirmed while she started the drive toward town. "She was killed in a car wreck a couple of months after you left. It just about crushed Darcia. Brody, too." She paused, sighed. "And I'm sorry I got us off on such a sad subject. Bad timing since this is a happy day. You'll get to meet some of your cousins and be part of Parkman history."

Janessa would have preferred to continue the discussion about Brody and his sister, but since it was obviously causing Margo some distress, she added that to her ever-growing list of mental notes. When she got the chance, she'd do a computer search on Layla.

It didn't take Margo long to make the drive to the town hall. Since it was just up the street from the inn, Janessa immediately glanced around but didn't spot her mother. However, there were people—probably those cousins Margo had mentioned—who were trickling into the brick and red limestone building.

"You find your mother, and I'll get us some snicker-doodles," Margo instructed as they stepped through the open double doors.

Considering how small that trickle of people had been, Janessa expected to see her mom right away. She was wrong. Good grief. The large room was packed, and she nearly choked thanks to the clashing scents of perfume, aftershave, cookies and coffee.

There were two tables at the front of the room, and each one held huge glass bowls. Bowl o' Names was the label on the left one, and Bowl o' Tombstones was on the right. There were slivers of paper inside them, no doubt with the names of her Parkman kin who were eligible for research. And those eligible to be researched.

Hobbling up the rows, Janessa finally saw Sophia. Thankfully, on one of the end seats in the middle of the room. And she'd held the two chairs. Janessa made her way there, creating a path of mumblings and murmurs as she went. Obviously, she was a tasty morsel of gossip right now.

"Janessa," Sophia greeted. She moved in so Janessa wouldn't have to step over her, and they left the aisle seat for Margo.

"Why are you here?" Janessa whispered.

"Because Margo invited me." Sophia smiled that little smile that told Janessa she was up to something. "It doesn't hurt to stir up a little good will for anyone who can help our fight against Abe."

Janessa wasn't sure how much good will either of them were going to find here. "Mom, you and I need to talk."

"So you've said. We can go to Colts Creek after the meeting and talk there."

"Colts Creek? You said you didn't want to go inside the house. Wouldn't you rather go to the inn?"

"There's a pipe leaking in my bathroom, and they said the repair might not be done for at least a couple of hours. I'd rather not have a personal chat with my daughter with a plumber around. We can sit on the porch at the ranch."

While that wouldn't be especially comfortable, Janessa

didn't want to put this off any longer, and there were heaters on the porch. Maybe this meeting wouldn't last too long because it was hard to think about anything else other than just how pissed off Sophia was going to be when she learned the truth.

A thin gray-haired woman in a Christmas red jumpsuit went to the podium and thumped the microphone, causing static to fart through the room. Even though it was plenty loud enough to assure the woman, and possibly people a couple of counties over, that the mike was working, she still said, "Testing, testing," into it. Apparently pleased when her voice poured through the room and silenced the chatter, she smiled.

"How-dee and welcome, welcome, welcome," the woman gushed. She was even more enthusiastic than Margo. And speaking of Margo, with napkins and cookies clutched in both hands, she hurried to take her seat next to Janessa.

"For those who don't know me," the woman at the podium continued while looking straight at Janessa and her mother, "I'm Alma Parkman, president of the Last Ride Society. I'm also performing my stand-up comedy routine at Three Sheets to the Wind every Tuesday night. Join me for some hijinks and shenanigans."

Margo passed down some of the cookies, and since it was there, Janessa took a bite. Then another. Margo certainly had a good argument for not missing out on them.

"Hijinks aside for now," Alma went on, turning her attention to the paper she laid on the podium. "As always, we'll start the meeting with a reading of the rules. Our illustrious town founder, Hezzie Parkman, created the Last Ride Society shortly before her death in 1950, and each and every one of you honor Hezzie by being here this evening.

Honor, tradition, family. Those are the cornerstones that make Last Ride our home."

Janessa was all for honor, tradition and family, but she wondered if Abe had ever stepped foot in one of these meetings. Probably not.

Alma held up one finger to indicate the first rule. "A drawing will take place quarterly in the Last Ride town hall. The winner of the previous quarter will draw the name of his or her successor.

"Second rule," Alma said, lifting another finger. "The winner must research the person whose tombstone he or she draws. A handout will be given to the winner to better spell out what needs to be done, but research should be conducted at least once weekly as to compile a thorough report on the deceased. The report will be added to the Last Ride Society Library.

"Final rule," Alma went on. "On the completion of the research by the winner, five thousand dollars from the Hezzie Parkman trust will be donated to the winner's chosen town charity."

Janessa heard murmurs of those around her, saying how they'd use the money if chosen. Apparently, the rose garden park and the public toilets there needed some attention.

"And now to the drawing." Alma used the gavel to drum out her obvious excitement. "As many of you know, our last winner can't be here because her bunions are acting up so her predecessor will do the honors. Millie, come on up to the Bowl o' Names and get to drawing."

The tall blonde got up from the front row and walked up onto the stage where she got lots of applause. Lots. It turned into a standing ovation, and Janessa was surprised to see some people, Margo included, dabbing tears from their eyes.

"Millie Dayton," Margo supplied. "She won the drawing two quarters ago, and she found true love. It's so sweet how this sometimes works out."

Millie did indeed look happy as she slid her hand into the Bowl o' Names, but Janessa figured that hers was a best-case scenario that wouldn't apply to anyone else. Finding love over cemetery research just didn't seem likely to repeat itself.

"Please tell me you didn't actually go through with putting my name in the drawing," Janessa whispered to Margo. She watched as Millie drew out one of the slivers of paper.

Margo's beaming smile told her that's exactly what she'd done. "Abe's, too," Margo said with a nod. She patted Janessa's hand. "Don't worry. The odds are 375 to one that your name won't be drawn."

"Janessa Parkman," Millie called out.

The room went silent.

Janessa's mind, however, revved up with all sorts of bad words and frustration. She heard herself actually growl when a clapping, cheering Margo pulled her to her feet. "Go up on stage," Margo prompted, taking the rest of the cookie from Janessa.

Janessa didn't want any part of the stage or this drawing. Nor did she want every eye in the room on her. But that's what she got. She wasn't one who liked that attention. Or the fact that she couldn't immediately think of a way out of this. Even a polite *I'm sorry but no* might be taken as an insult to this small-town way of life.

"This could drum up support for our cause," Janessa heard Sophia mutter.

It could possibly do that. If Janessa was going to be in Last Ride long enough. The odds were that she wouldn't be, but she couldn't very well tell her mother that now without a public spilling of the truth about the baby.

"Come on up, Janessa," Alma prompted through the still farting microphone.

Janessa wasn't sure what got her started moving. Maybe it was the nudge in the back from Margo or perhaps her feet just went on autopilot. Either way, Janessa found herself limping toward the stage. The limp caused some murmurs, too, probably because everyone in the room knew how she'd gotten the injury. Margo rushed up behind her, taking hold of her hand to help Janessa up the three short steps to the stage.

Millie gave her a bright smile and a hug when Janessa joined Alma and her on the stage, and both women congratulated her. Obviously, they thought this was a great honor.

Alma directed her to the Bowl o' Tombstones, and Janessa knew she had to allow this to play out. When she ended up having to leave town, then she could ask Alma to find someone else to fulfill Hezzie Parkman's plan.

Janessa reached in the bowl, maneuvering her hand as close to the bottom as she could get. Best to draw someone who had been in there a long, long time. In fact, she hoped it was the oldest tombstone in the entire area.

But it wasn't.

Janessa unfolded the paper, stared at the name and kept staring until Alma came to her side. "Well, shit," Alma murmured. It expressed Janessa's sentiments to a tee.

Because the name on the paper wasn't anywhere near the oldest. It was her father's.

CHAPTER EIGHT

BRODY CURSED UNDER his breath when he saw what was going on in the corral. Rowan was doing some trick riding, again, and while the three hands watching him were clearly amused, Brody sure as hell wasn't.

Ignoring the text that dinged his phone and the whoops and cheers of the hands, Brody made it to the corral just as Rowan crouched and stood in the saddle. His idiot brother was grinning from ear to ear. Or at least he was until his attention landed on Brody. The grin faded some but not nearly enough, and he eased back down into the saddle.

"If you've finished the work on your schedule, I'll find something else for you to do," Brody snarled to the hands. "I'm sure some stalls need mucking, and there are always rocks that need to be dug out from the pastures." Since those were both chores that sucked, it was enough to get them scurrying away.

Rowan didn't scurry. As if he had all the time in the world and no pissed-off brother whatsoever, he dismounted and strolled toward Brody.

"I'm not on shift yet," Rowan said. "Not for another fifteen minutes."

Brody knew that since he'd been the one to make the work schedule. "At what point did you think it'd be a bright idea to break your neck?"

Rowan looked a little offended. "Hey, I'm good at trick riding."

"Hey," Brody repeated with plenty of sarcasm, "even good riders break their necks when doing something stupid." Just in case that didn't drill the point home, Brody pulled out the big guns. "If and when this gets back to Mom, you know she'll be worried."

There. That sank in. Rowan sighed, but what he didn't do was disagree. Because he couldn't.

Darcia had taken worrying about her kids to the extreme, and while it didn't appear Rowan had actually been on the verge of any real neck-breaking, Darcia would imagine a worst-case scenario of losing her son. That's what happened when a parent had already had a worst-case scenario of losing a daughter. It wasn't logical for their mom to transfer her fears and overprotectiveness to Rowan, but logic didn't always apply when grieving for a child.

"I'm really good at trick riding," Rowan emphasized when he repeated it. Again, it wasn't an argument. His tone was more statement of fact. "All the other hands say I'm good enough to do competitions."

Yeah, he was. Brody had seen enough of the boy's antics to know that. "Mom," was all Brody said in response.

This time, Rowan huffed, and he propped his hands on his hips. "Maybe if you explained to her that I'd be safe, that it's actually a sport." He stopped because he probably knew that no amount of explanation would work with their mother, and he leveled his eyes on Brody. "I'm fifteen. She can't baby me forever."

Oh, but Darcia would almost certainly try to do just that. Brody hadn't found a way to get her to back off with him so he wasn't holding out much hope that she'd loosen the reins on Rowan. He loved his mother so it was always hard to find that right balance of soothing her and living his own life.

Brody glanced up when he heard the approaching vehicle. Since he'd been on the lookout for Riggs, he braced in case the moron had made a return visit, but it was Margo. She parked in front of the house, and both Janessa and she got out. One look at Janessa's face, and Brody knew something was wrong. She didn't have an I'll-kick-Abe's-tombstone expression. More like I-broke-another-toe-kicking-Abe's-tombstone.

He'd seen them leave earlier but hadn't known where they were going until Velma Sue had reminded him that it was the first of November and therefore the day of the drawing of the Last Ride Society. Brody was more than a little surprised that Margo had managed to talk Janessa into going with her.

Janessa's gaze zoomed straight to Brody, and she started walking toward him. Margo was right on her heels, and while she didn't seem as upset as Janessa, she wasn't keeping up her usual jaunty pace.

"If you're going to ride, keep your ass in the saddle," Brody added to Rowan as he turned to make his way to a still-limping Janessa. "What happened?" he asked. "Did Riggs show up in town?"

"No, not Riggs." Janessa opened her clenched hand to show him the strip of paper.

Brody immediately put two and two together. "Your name was drawn at the Last Ride Society, and you drew Abe's."

Janessa nodded. "Apparently, fate decided I hadn't been given enough jabs in the eye and gave me one more."

Making a fretting sound, Margo nodded, too. "I shouldn't have insisted that Janessa's name be added."

"No, you shouldn't have," Janessa and Brody said in unison.

There was no venom in Janessa's voice, just the acceptance of that additional eye poke. But Brody held on to a little piece of venom. Janessa shouldn't have been part of that drawing, and Abe's name sure as hellfire shouldn't have been in the Bowl o' Tombstones mix. The man had been dead less than a week. That was way too soon for anyone, especially his daughter, to have to be digging into his life all in the name of historical research.

"You could refuse to do it," Brody pointed out to her, and he motioned for them to move out of the shade and into the sun where it'd be warmer. "Or pawn it off on somebody else. I'm sure there's a Parkman with too much time on his or her hands."

"I could," Janessa agreed. She groaned and muttered some profanity. Profanity that she bit off when Rowan came to stand by Brody.

"Hello, Rowan," she added in greeting, and then she turned back to Brody to continue. "I could try to give this to someone else, but there's probably not anyone who wouldn't think of Abe as the worst kind of chore. I don't like to give someone a chore that I wouldn't be willing to do myself."

Brody thought of the mucking and rock digging. He'd done both of those things too many times to count, but sometimes delegation was the way to go.

"You could go ahead and tell the Society that you probably won't be here long enough to do the research. Which is true," he tacked on to that.

She made a sound of agreement and glanced over her shoulder at the road. "My mother will be here any minute. After we've finally had that talk, I probably will be leaving."

"Janessa told me about the baby when we were driving

back," Margo volunteered, the sadness in both her eyes and voice. She'd been crying again. "If Sophia leaves, our best bet will be to challenge Abe's will. There might be something in the research that can help with that."

That was a longshot. Brody believed that Sophia's leaving was a given.

"I could do most of the research from Dallas," Janessa said. "I would need a picture of his tombstone, that's in the list of rules they gave me, but I could do that before I leave."

"I could help you," Rowan spoke up, causing all three of them to turn and look at him. Rowan shrugged. "I'm good at doing stuff like reports, and I'm only working part-time. I could help," he repeated.

"Thank you," Janessa said, and she even managed a smile. Hard to do, Brody knew, because there wasn't a whole hell of a lot to smile about.

Brody certainly didn't offer any smiles or research help. And he wouldn't. No way did he want to go digging through Abe's past. He had more than enough to handle from the present crap Abe had doled out. Besides, research like that would only throw him together with Janessa. It was best to keep some distance between them.

Apparently, though, Janessa didn't feel the same way because she moved closer, touched his arm and rubbed lightly. "This time, I will say goodbye before I leave."

Hell. Brody had not needed to hear that, because for some asinine reason, it made him want to rub her arm right back. And, yeah, it made him want to kiss her. Then again, breathing seemed to spur the urge to do more kissing.

Their eyes were still locked when Brody heard the sound of a vehicle turning into the driveway. Still locked, too, when Rowan said his shift was about to start and he had to go. Janessa finally looked away when her mother called out to her.

"I'm ready for that talk," Sophia said as she made her way toward them.

Brody turned to leave, but he wasn't fast enough to give them the privacy he'd intended. That's because after one quick breath, Janessa launched right into the confession.

"Mom, since I don't know how to cushion the blow on this, I'll just go ahead and tell you what I have to say. Kyle lied to you to get you to come here."

Sophia's eyes widened. "Kyle wouldn't do that..." But she stopped, huffed and obviously rethought that. "What's the lie?"

Janessa squared her shoulders. "I'm not adopting a baby."

Sophia's stare only lasted a few seconds before Brody saw that sink in. Her mouth tightened, and she huffed. Without so much as a word, the woman turned and headed back to her car.

JANESSA DIDN'T GO after her mother. She just stood there and watched her storm away, but, mercy, the sight of Sophia leaving caused her stomach to twist. She'd failed, and the proof of that failure would soon be driving away.

"I'm so sorry," Margo murmured, and she headed toward her own vehicle.

Janessa watched them while she went over the mental list of what she needed to do. She'd have to meet with her lawyer, get the blasted photo of Abe's tombstone for the Last Ride Society research she could finish in Dallas, and then she could—

Her mental list stopped when her mother did an about-face and came hurrying back toward her.

"Why the hell would Kyle do this?" Sophia demanded when she was still a good twenty feet away from Janessa.

"You want me to stay?" Brody asked Janessa.

It was tempting to have him there for moral support, but Janessa shook her head. No need for anyone else to have to experience the wrath of Sophia. Though she'd need to let Kyle know that the wrath would soon no doubt be heading his way. He'd lose his golden boy, ideal-husband-for-Janessa status for sure.

Brody moved away, heading for the barn, just as Sophia planted herself in front of Janessa. "Well, why?" her mother snarled.

Janessa dragged in a long breath that she was certain she would need. "Because Kyle thought he was helping. And it wasn't a total lie. I am fostering a newborn until her adoptive mother can take her."

Sophia's huff required plenty of breath, too. "Like you did before."

"Like I did before," Janessa verified. "The birth mother's one of the teenagers at Bright Hope, and she's due shortly after Christmas. I figured if by some miracle I was still here, then Kyle could bring the baby to me."

Huffing again, Sophia started pacing. "You know I would have never come if I'd known the truth."

"Yes, and that's why I tried to tell you. You didn't exactly give me a lot of opportunities for discussion."

Sophia didn't acknowledge that was true, but she did stop pacing when the side door of the house opened. Velma Sue came out, and while she wouldn't have won any speed records for making her way toward them, she was carrying two large cups.

"Irish Coffee, heavy on the whiskey," Velma Sue said to Sophia as she handed her the cup. "I remembered it was your favorite. Got your favorite, too," she added to Janessa, and she gave her the second one.

It was hot chocolate with tiny marshmallows, and yes, it was a favorite of hers when she'd been a teenager. At the moment, though, she could have used a shot of the whiskey.

"Thank you," Sophia muttered, taking a big gulp. Since it was there, Janessa drank some of hers, too.

"As far as I know, Abe never stepped foot in the kitchen," Velma Sue explained, speaking to Sophia, "so maybe you can sit in there instead of being out here in the cold. I figure it'd be easier to swallow if you were in a room that Abe hadn't frequented."

"Thank you," her mother repeated, sounding a little calmer now. "But I won't be staying long. I won't be finishing this, either, since I'd rather not get a DUI on my way back to Dallas."

"So, you're leaving, then," Velma Sue said. Not a question, and there wasn't a drop of anger, or surprise, in her expression.

"Yes," Sophia verified.

Velma Sue shifted her attention to Janessa. "And you?"

"After I get a few things done around here, I'll go, too."

"I hope one of those few things you've got to get done will be going through the stuff in the supply room next to Abe's office," the woman added. "The stuff he left for you."

Janessa recalled Velma Sue already mentioning that. "What did he leave for me?" Then she stopped. "Are you positive there was nothing recent, like another letter?"

"No letter that I know of, recent or otherwise. These are wrapped presents. Twelve for Christmas and another twelve for your birthdays. Don't know why he didn't just send them to you, but he said you'd get them when he got custody of you and you moved to Colts Creek for good."

Janessa wasn't sure if that was touching or sick. She re-thought it and decided it was mostly sick. Gifts with strings attached. Live with him and she'd get goodies. Don't live here and she'd get nothing.

"I started to bring them up that summer you were here, but Abe told me to keep quiet about them," Velma Sue went on. "I figured that meant he'd tossed them, but then I found them the day he died."

Janessa had to wonder why Abe had brought them down from the attic. And when. Maybe he'd done it because he knew he was dying.

"Abe stopped at twelve because that's when Janessa told the judge she wanted to live with me," Sophia muttered. Then she drank more and cursed. "The SOB. Did you know he had visitation rights?" she asked Velma Sue but didn't wait for the woman to respond. "He got two weekends a month as part of the initial custody settlement, and Abe never once used those rights."

"All or nothing," Velma Sue commented. "I'll leave out the bad words he used, and he used plenty, but I recall him grumbling that out more than a time or two. He said he wasn't going to visit his only blood kin while she was under your roof."

"That's Abe," Sophia declared, and with a heaping of sarcasm, she lifted her mug in a toast Then she aimed that mug at the ground since she no doubt figured Abe hadn't gone the heavenly route.

On the surface, there hadn't been heavenly acts for Abe, but Janessa figured there had to be more. There was good in all people. Most anyway. And she didn't want to believe Abe was the exception.

"Well, drive safe, and stay in touch," Velma Sue told Sophia as she headed back to the house.

Janessa didn't question the fact that her mother would be leaving. She stood there downing more of her hot chocolate and then cursing when it burned her tongue. Sophia muttered some profanity as well and sank down on the ground, putting her back against the tree.

"It's such a cliché for a woman my age, but I really had my heart set on a grandbaby," Sophia said, closing her eyes a moment.

"I know you did, and I'm sorry." Janessa sat down beside her. It wasn't freezing, but the ground wasn't exactly warm.

Sophia pressed the warm mug to her cheek and sighed. "A big part of that was because I thought a baby would bring Kyle and you back together."

Janessa had to shake her head. "Kyle is seeing someone else. And even if he wasn't, I don't love him."

The sad part was maybe she never had. There were times when Janessa wondered if she'd just gotten caught up in fixing him and she'd mistaken that for love. There'd been some fire, of course, some sexual attraction, but it seemed lukewarm compared to what she'd felt for Brody. Then again, maybe first love wasn't a good benchmark for future fires and such.

"I remember the first time Abe brought me here," her mother murmured. "A lifetime ago."

That got Janessa's mind off her benchmark musings, and she turned toward Sophia. Janessa couldn't ever remember her mother bringing up Abe. She kept that to herself, though, for fear if she said anything, it would cause Sophia to stop.

"Talk about a fish out of water," her mother continued a moment later. "I went from cotillion balls to the smell of horse shit." She sipped more of her coffee. "Old money in Dallas isn't the same as old money in Last Ride."

No, Janessa supposed it wasn't, though, in their own ways, both Abe and her mother liked to display their wealth. Big lavishly decorated houses, nice cars, expensive clothes. It was ironic that their combined genes had produced a daughter who wasn't interested in any of that. For her, it was all about what the money could do, not what it could buy for show.

"You must have been lonely here," Janessa prompted when Sophia's pause continued.

"I was," Sophia admitted. "Lonely. Stupid. And too blind to see the red flags that were right in front of me before I jumped into the lonely and the stupid."

Janessa frowned. "What red flags?"

"That my husband was in love with another woman." Sophia opened her eyes, turned her head and met Janessa's gaze. "With Brody's mother to be specific. And no, that's not the reason I'm so opposed to you being with Brody."

There was a whole lot of information in those couple of sentences. So, Sophia had known that Abe was on the rebound when he'd married her, and it'd likely been the reason for the divorce.

"Then why are you opposed to me being with him?" Janessa asked.

"Oh, let me count the ways. Because you could end up here at Colts Creek and start another fish-out-of-water sob story. And because you wouldn't be getting involved with him for the right reason. He's hurting right now, and you want to help with that since you're Miss Fix-it. But when he comes to terms with the fact that Abe was a dick, the fixing will be done. By then, you'll be sucked into caring about him. You'll come home brokenhearted again and doodle his name."

Janessa wanted to argue with any and all points her

mother had just made—including the Miss Fix-it title that
Sophia had dubbed her with years ago. But she couldn't.
Heck, she couldn't even insist that anything she had with
Brody would be just another holiday fling. So she just kept
her mouth shut and stewed.

The stewing was short-lived, though, because of the car
that came up the driveway toward the house. Thinking that
it might be Riggs, Janessa got to her feet. But it wasn't
Riggs's truck. The dark blue Ford Focus stopped, and when
the passenger's side door opened, Janessa was stunned at
the dark-haired teenager who stepped out.

Teagan.

What the heck was she doing here? Cursing because her
toe had started to throb again, Janessa hurried toward her.

"What happened?" Janessa demanded. "Are you hurt?"

Teagan shook her head and rested her hands on her pregnant belly. "I got scared so I got a friend to drive me here."

"Scared?" Janessa repeated. "Why?"

The girl blinked back tears. "Because I thought Riggs
would come to Bright Hope and try to start some trouble.
I don't want him to hurt me or the baby."

Crap, Janessa didn't want that, and she didn't want Teagan to be afraid of that happening, either. "I spoke to Kyle,
and he said they were making sure the house was locked
up."

Teagan nodded, and when she glanced to the right behind Janessa, she realized that Sophia was walking up to
them. "But I still have to go out to appointments and to
work. Riggs could see me and start something."

Yes. It caused her stomach to clench, but that was the
truth. Even if Teagan were with one of the other residents,
that didn't mean Riggs wouldn't use force to "convince"
Teagan into coming back to him.

"With my mom's help, Kyle filed for a temporary restraining order against Riggs," Janessa assured her. "And I'll see if he can go with you to your appointments."

That didn't ease the fear on Teagan's face, and it sure as heck didn't stop the tears. She clutched onto Janessa, putting her arms around her.

"I don't want to go back to Dallas," Teagan muttered through those sobs. "Please, Janessa. Let me stay here with you."

CHAPTER NINE

Brody stood in the iron archway of Parkmans' Cemetery and looked out at the tombstones that were lined up like dominos. He'd thought that once he arrived he would figure out why the hell he was here.

He hadn't.

There were still a lot of things he hadn't figured out.

A crisp evening wind whipped at him. Both a blessing and a curse. The wind kept the bugs and biting insects away, but it was a reminder that winter was right around the corner. Ditto for the holidays. Normally, that was a quieter time at Colts Creek, but he doubted there'd be much quiet in the next few weeks, especially if the ranch closed down in anticipation of a new owner.

The black granite of Abe's tombstone didn't exactly blend with the night because the moonlight washed over it, spotlighting it as if it were some kind of beacon. Brody could almost see a big-assed cartoon arrow flashing over it and saying, Come Right Over for Another Kick in the Balls.

He didn't go in closer for that kick. It wasn't necessary because he felt it every time he thought of Abe. Not because of Abe's will and the chaos that had caused. But because of Abe himself.

According to the letter that Abe had sent Janessa, he'd known he was dying, and Brody couldn't think of a single reason for Abe to withhold that from him. Abe had trusted him with millions of dollars of payroll and assets, confided in him the ins and outs of too many business deals to count, but he hadn't shared the most important info of his life.

Or rather his death.

That was the cut that would take the longest to heal, and it pissed him off all the way to the bone. Maybe it was some kind of sick karma, but his life had been littered with people who hadn't bothered to tell him goodbye. His father, Janessa, his sister, Layla, and now Abe.

He cursed himself. He was a grown man. What the hell did it matter that the goodbyes hadn't been said? They would have still been goodbyes. Well, except for Layla. If she'd come to him and told him, then he might have been able to do something to stop her from dying.

Brody cursed again when there was a slash of head-lights from a vehicle turning into the parking lot. He'd waited until dark to come because he hadn't wanted any-one around while he did whatever the hell he was doing. Some would call it grieving. Others, a pity party. Brody figured it was more of a search for answers he just wasn't going to get. Ever.

He turned, ready to head back to his truck, when he spotted Janessa. Who else? If he'd had a list of people he hadn't wanted to run into tonight, she would have been at the top. Every nerve in him felt scraped raw, and if any-one would be able to see right through how he was really feeling, it was Janessa.

Using the flashlight on her phone, she hobbled her way to him and panned that flashlight over his face. Brody got a good look at her face, too, thanks to the moonlight. That blond hair was like another beacon, gobbling up the milky rays and making her look like some kind of fairy. Not a waifish one, though. Not with all those curves that were accented in her jeans and thick sweater.

As usual, he felt the pull from the heat. Probably always would. He'd accepted that. Accepted, too, that like his unanswered questions about Abe, he'd just have to learn to live with it.

"Sorry," she said. She had a purse hanging from her shoulder and her coat draped over her arm. "I didn't know you'd be here."

Welcome to the club. Brody tipped his head to her phone. "Let me guess. You came here to get a picture of Abe's tombstone for the Last Ride Society?"

She nodded, lowered her phone and tucked a strand of hair behind her ear. A simple gesture he'd seen her do a dozen or more times, and he wasn't sure why it was punch-in-the-gut sexy.

"I decided to get it done while I still had a chance. I suppose you heard about what happened earlier at the ranch?" she asked.

Oh, yeah. He'd heard all right. No way to keep something like that under wraps, but it was always hard to tell what was pure truth and what was embellished.

"You still like hot chocolate, and Sophia doesn't mind sitting on the ground if she's pissed enough. She also seems to like Irish coffee, and while sipping one of those, a pregnant teenager showed up. Now Sophia knows you're not adopting a baby, and she went back to the inn to pack and leave."

"Nailed it in one," Janessa muttered with a sigh. "There's obviously a bunch of gossips on the ranch."

"Plenty," he confirmed. "I'd already gotten three texts before your mother even drove off." Brody paused. "What about the pregnant teenager? Is she okay?"

Janessa nodded. "Teagan Cutler. Riggs's ex. She's in one of the guest rooms at the ranch."

Brody could see the worry on Janessa's face and figured that worry was tenfold for the teen if it'd caused her to come all the way from Dallas.

"I can text a few of the hands, the non-gossiping ones, and ask them to patrol the grounds," Brody offered.

"Thanks. I'll take you up on that. Velma Sue is staying. Hank Meekins, too, so I thought it'd be safe enough for me to pop out and get this picture. I also turned on the security system before I left."

Hank Meekins was the gardener at the ranch but, yeah, he was a good choice for some extra security. The man was built like an All-Pro linebacker. Turning on the security was the right way to go, too. Abe had spent a ton of money getting a top-notch system despite there never having been a break-in at the ranch.

Brody took out his phone and fired off a couple of texts to hands he knew he could trust. It might be overkill, but he preferred the better-safe-than-sorry mode.

"The person who drove Teagan—a friend of hers—has already gone back to Dallas," Janessa explained. "But Teagan was too upset to go with her. I decided it was best if she stayed the night so I could get her settled down. The stress isn't good for her or the baby."

No, it wasn't. Then again, having an asshole ex who scared his pregnant girlfriend didn't qualify as stress-free, either.

"What about your mother?" he asked. "How is she?"

"To be determined. She said she needed some time to think, but she's doing the thinking here in Last Ride. If she'd checked out of the inn, I'm sure news of it would have already gotten back to me."

No doubt. There were plenty of gossips in town, too, and they'd be on the lookout for Sophia's exit. Especially since that exit would some way or another end up affecting everyone in Last Ride. A new owner of the ranch would mean someone new moving in. Most likely a stranger since no one locally would probably be interested in buying the place.

"Are there any legal problems with Teagan being here?" he asked.

Janessa shrugged. "She's eighteen, barely, so the short answer is no. But her doctor's in Dallas. So is her life. Mine, too." She sighed again. "I'm leaving Kyle with curling-iron grilled cheeses and cat scratches."

Brody was sure he frowned. "Is that some kind of metaphor?"

She laughed, a quick burst of sound that had him smiling, but the lightness was short-lived. Her face turned as serious as, well, a trip to the cemetery. "I wish, but no, it's reality at Bright Hope. We deal with a lot of unwise choices that some of the teens make. Choices sometimes a whole lot worse than grilled cheeses, and with me here, Kyle's taking on the bulk of those dealings."

He heard the frustration but also something else. "You miss being there."

"Definitely," she readily admitted. "I believe in Bright Hope. Believe it makes a difference in those kids' lives."

Brody was certain she did, and if the gossip he'd heard was true, Janessa put plenty of her money and time into the place. A lot of that time included fundraisers to keep the house afloat.

"The home can operate with me working remotely," she added, "but it means Kyle has to deal with the stuff that has to be done face-to-face."

She shivered a little and then adjusted her purse so she could put on her coat. "It's chillier out here than I thought it'd be."

He nearly put his arms around her, but Brody decided that was best left to the coat. Body-to-body contact even for the purpose of keeping her warm would no doubt be just the beginning of even more contact.

"Did you start Bright Hope because of the way Abe treated you?" he came out and asked.

"Oh, I'm sure that's at the core," she readily admitted. "So many of the girls who come to Bright Hope have mommy-and-daddy issues. Of course, their mommies and daddies didn't just ignore or call them a nuisance. It was much worse for some of them. Some endured every kind of abuse and neglect you can think of."

She stopped. Just stopped. And Brody could see her mentally regrouping.

"Anyway," Janessa said several moments later, and then she took a deep breath, "I should go ahead and get that picture of Abe's tombstone. Because it's past the stage of merely being massive, I probably should use a wide angle lens, but the camera on my phone will have to do."

Janessa limped past him and through the archway and toward the graves. Brody had a quick debate with himself as to whether to follow her or do the sensible thing and head home.

He didn't go with sensible.

Even though he knew this was the worst idea in the history of worst ideas, he walked to the grave and stood by her. Janessa snapped a couple of pictures, the flash knifing out like lightning bolts. It reminded him of Abe's funeral. Then it reminded him of Janessa.

It'd been a shock to see her as she'd walked toward the

grave. The people who'd already gathered for the graveside service eased aside, clearing a path for her to the tombstone. All murmurs and chatter had stopped. But then so had his breath for a few seconds.

"It's like one of those penis cars," he heard Janessa say.

That shut down his thoughts about breathing. "Excuse me?"

"You know, one of those overpriced cars that some guys buy to prove they've still got it. Abe seems to be trying to prove something with this over-the-top tombstone. Of course, this is a place where over-the-top reigns."

Yes, it was, and Brody glanced out at the ornate headstones and mausoleums. "It's not called Snooty Hill for nothing."

She made a sound of agreement, took a few more pictures and then stopped again, her attention sliding from Abe's tombstone back to Brody. "You have a right to hate him," she muttered.

"No," Brody quickly disagreed. "The ranch was his to do with as he saw fit. Obviously, he saw fit to handle things the way he did."

She gave him a skeptical look. "So, you didn't come here to curse his grave or kick his tombstone?"

"No," he repeated. Though he still couldn't say exactly why he'd come. Maybe it was going to fall under one of those mysteries-of-the-ages deals.

"You're being more generous about this than I am." Sighing, she stepped back from the grave, and that put her closer to Brody.

He intended to move back. To keep a safe distance between them so it'd lessen the chance of the sparks flying. Sparks flew anyway.

She smiled a little. "If I were going to stay through the holidays, I'd French kiss you and see what happens."

It was almost identical to what she'd said to him on the porch. It'd led to the imaginary kiss that'd felt damn real. This felt real, too, even though he hadn't touched her.

And he wouldn't.

Because the bottom line was she wasn't staying and she had to get back to those curling-iron-grilled-cheese problems. She had to go, and he had to stay so he could try to figure out the new normal in his life.

With all that logic lined in his head, Brody was surprised when he leaned in and kissed her anyway.

His mouth met hers. Not for a light little touch and nip. No. This was a full-pressure kiss, one where he felt the softness of her incredible mouth. Tasted her, too. Also incredible. And it was a taste that raced through him.

He figured Janessa would push him away and ask if he'd lost his mind. He obviously had. So had she because there was no pushing. No asking about mind loss. She made a hungry little sound that was pure sex. Sex right here, right now. Worse, she opened her mouth, deepened the kiss and turned it into the French that she'd been taunting him with.

Hell's bells.

This wasn't right. He shouldn't be kissing her, period, but he especially shouldn't be doing it in the cemetery. A cemetery where someone could drive by and see him having Janessa's mouth for supper. He didn't need gossip. He didn't need heat. But it sure as hell felt as if he needed this kiss.

Janessa finally pulled back and looked up at him. Her breath was gusting, her eyes wild with lust and need. Brody figured he was doing pretty much the same thing because there was plenty of both lust and need firing on all cylinders inside him.

"Well, that's what happens when I French kiss you," she muttered, then laughed. "I might need a cold shower."

He'd need ten of them, and that still wouldn't be enough. Brody resisted the overwhelming urge to go back in for another round. Best to stay put. Then again, he probably couldn't walk with this hard-on anyway.

"Okay," Janessa said after she swallowed hard. "I'm guessing we'll consider that a mistake we shouldn't repeat?"

He didn't hesitate. "Oh, yeah."

She nodded. "Good." But she didn't sound as if that were good at all. She ran her tongue over her bottom lip, causing many of his parts to clench. And beg. "I'm not sure my body is listening to that logic."

Neither was his. In fact, nothing he was feeling for Janessa was logical. It'd taken him a long time to get over her after she'd left without so much as a wave goodbye. And, yes, he understood why she had done that, what with Abe's marriage threat. Still, that long recovery time had been, well, long and common sense told him not to start something that would have pretty much the same ending.

"I should get back to the ranch and check on Teagan," she muttered, finally turning to go.

However, she'd only made it a couple of limping steps before her phone rang. Since it was in her hand, Brody had no trouble seeing the screen in the darkness. And her mother's name on it.

She groaned and hit the answer button. She didn't put it on Speaker, but he still heard Sophia's voice cut through the silence.

"Janessa, I'll stay in Last Ride," was all her mother said before ending the call.

CHAPTER TEN

JANESSA WANTED TO curse when she tried to call her mother again. Because *again*, Sophia didn't answer. Something she'd been doing since her short call from the night before to say she'd stay in Last Ride.

It was somewhat of a miracle, one that her mother apparently didn't want to discuss since she had let all Janessa's calls go to voice mail. The only response that Janessa had gotten from her was a short text saying, We'll talk tomorrow.

Well, it was tomorrow, and Sophia still wasn't talking. That's why Janessa was getting dressed to go to the inn. Then she could see her mother's face and find out what had brought on this miracle decision.

Janessa downed the rest of her third cup of coffee while she dressed and scrolled through her emails. She skimmed most that were related to fundraising events, supply orders and resident applications, but she took the time to read the one from Kyle.

Didn't want to text you in case you were sleeping in, Kyle had emailed. After the night you've no doubt had, you deserve a little rest.

She thought of the sizzler kissing she'd done with Brody at the cemetery. Definitely not on her top ten list of places to make out, but that hadn't cooled any of the sizzling. Unfortunately, that heat hadn't given her a peaceful night. And she'd needed one of those cold showers after all.

All is well here, she continued reading from Kyle's email. No sign of Riggs. Let me know what you decide about Teagan.

That was good about Riggs, and Kyle knew that Teagan was getting settled in at the ranch because Janessa had called him shortly after the girl arrived. Then she'd called him again after getting word from Sophia that she'd be staying in Last Ride. That didn't mean Teagan would be staying as well, though. It was something Janessa would need to work out. After she did the working out with Sophia, that is.

Janessa fired off a quick response to one of the fundraiser emails, saying that she wouldn't be able to attend. She suspected she'd have to bow out of plenty of those, and it wasn't something she could ask Kyle to do. Kyle worked wonders with the residents and keeping the house running, but he was a miserable failure at schmoozing.

She opened the door, ready to head to Teagan's room, and Janessa nearly ran right into Margo.

"I was going to leave them outside your door in case you were sleeping, but since you're awake, you can tell me. What do you think of these?" Margo immediately asked, and she held up a very glittery pair of star-spangled, rhinestone-studded shoes. Not heels like Margo's usual footwear but wedges which were also covered with sparkles.

"Uh, they're shiny." And that was the most complimentary thing Janessa could think to say.

"Aren't they?" Margo thrust them at her. "I figured you'd want to wear something festive for the festival, and these are a size bigger than your usual so they shouldn't press against your broken toe."

"What festival?" Janessa took the shoes but only because Margo actually put them in her hands.

"The one held at the town's fairgrounds. It's the night after next," Margo said as if the answer were obvious.

It wasn't obvious at all. In fact, Janessa had to glance at her phone to realize that it was November 2. So, in two days Margo seemingly expected her to wear the seizure-triggering shoes to some event that Janessa had no intention of attending.

"It's to kick off the holiday season. There'll be carnival rides, rodeo stuff and lots of food," Margo went on. "Oh, and the fireworks, of course. About ten years or so ago, Abe donated a whole bunch of money to the town so they'd name the festival after him. So, it's officially the Abe Parkman Holiday Gala, but nobody actually calls it that despite there being a whopping big-assed sign with Abe's name on it over the arena."

"I wasn't planning on going," Janessa interrupted before the woman could continue.

Margo laughed and laughed and laughed, and even gave a quit-joking flap of her hand. "Of course, you will. Everybody in Last Ride goes. It'll be fun."

It could fall into the fun wheelhouse, but Janessa didn't want to commit to anything until she'd made sure all was well with Sophia. It was possible her mother would play the martyr card and treat this three-month stay as incarceration in a maximum-security prison. Janessa would definitely have to find a way to make that up to her, and that could include spending lots of time with her.

Not at the festival, though.

Janessa seriously doubted that Sophia would want some of that time spent at a local festival in a town she loathed. Especially a *gala* named after a man she loathed even more than Last Ride.

"Thanks," Janessa told Margo, and she put the shoes on the dresser. "I'll get back to you about it."

"Oh, but you have to go," Margo insisted. "You wouldn't want to miss Brody's bull riding."

That caught Janessa's attention. "Bull riding?"

Margo gave an eager nod and fanned herself. "It's a sight to behold, that's for sure. He's been doing it every year since he turned eighteen. It raises money for the local charities."

Janessa was sure it was indeed a sight to behold. Brody in full rodeo mode, looking very Brody-ish and studly on the back of a massive bull. Normally, things like that didn't trigger any heat, but this was Brody. Heat-triggering was a given.

"You should definitely come," Margo pressed. "It'll be a way to celebrate us not losing the ranch."

Janessa started to remind her that she should hold off on the celebrating. Three months, minus a couple of days, was a long time to keep her mother here. But she didn't want to dash that happiness she saw on Margo's face. The woman definitely wasn't in a tombstone-kicking mood this morning.

"I'll get back to you about it," Janessa repeated. She picked up the jacket she'd laid out to go with her outfit. "For now, I need to talk to Teagan." And then she could go to the inn to see her mother.

"Oh, she's not in her room," Margo said when Janessa started up the hall. "She's been up for a while and is in the kitchen with Velma Sue."

The *a while* surprised her. It was a little past eight in the morning, not what some would call early, but like most of the other teenagers at Bright Hope, Teagan tended to sleep in.

With Margo by her side, Janessa made her way down

the stairs and was thankful when she could actually take steps that didn't cause any pain. Well, every third or fourth step still hurt, but the broken toe was improving, and the bruising was now the same color of blue as the shoes Margo had given her.

Janessa passed one of the housekeepers along the way. Chrissy Meekins, Janessa remembered. Chrissy gave her a big smile, something the other household help had been doing. The ranch hands, too, when they spotted her. Apparently, everyone seemed satisfied that they weren't going to lose their jobs.

Margo and she continued down the stairs, and Janessa caught the wonderful sugary scent before she even reached the kitchen.

"Cinnamon rolls," Margo supplied. "I've got to skip them if I want to fit into my festival outfit, but you should definitely give them a try. Tell Velma Sue I'll be by later with those magazines she wanted to borrow."

Margo went out front where she was probably parked, and Janessa headed to the kitchen. Teagan was indeed there and using a spatula to take some of those rolls out of the pan.

"Before I forget," Janessa said right off, "I'm to tell you Margo will bring the magazines later."

With her usual slow calm movements, Velma Sue smiled and took a small plate from the cupboard. "A good news kind of day," the woman said, adding one of the rolls to the plate and passing it to Janessa. "Thought we'd celebrate."

There it was again, that dreaded word. Janessa wished that everyone affected by Abe's will would just wait to see how this all panned out before any celebrations began. Still, that didn't stop Janessa from biting into the results of that good-news-kind-of-day deal.

"Miss Velma Sue said it was okay if I helped in the kitchen," Teagan muttered. She did her usual, too, with the shy downcast eyes and softly spoken words.

"I didn't know you knew how to bake," Janessa remarked, and she emphasized some *mmm* sounds when she chowed down. It wasn't hard to make those sounds because the roll was yummy, but she'd done that with the hopes of putting Teagan at ease.

"I don't, not really, but Miss Velma Sue showed me what had to be done. Can I help her some more, like with lunch or something?"

Janessa knew what the girl was truly asking. *Can I stay?* Janessa didn't want to go with her own usual of *to be determined*, but that was accurate. She settled for, "We'll see. I need to go talk to my mother at the inn, but when I get back, we can discuss what you want—"

"I want to stay here," Teagan said before Janessa could finish.

The girl kept that same nearly whispered tone, but Janessa heard the feelings that came with it. The ranch probably felt safer than being in Dallas and near Riggs. Then again, Riggs had come here before, and he could do it again. Janessa made a mental note to text Brody and ask him if the ranch hands would still be patrolling the property.

"We can talk about that," Janessa assured her, and then she turned to Velma Sue. "When I'm in town, please keep the doors locked and the security system turned on."

"Will do." Velma Sue lifted a large wooden rolling pin. "But I can handle a pissant looking for trouble."

That was possibly true. Anyone who'd worked for Abe all this time had to have some steel in them. Still, it was best not to rely on kitchen utensils for defense.

Taking the rest of the roll so she could put the plate in the dishwasher, Janessa said goodbye to Teagan and Velma and made the trek around the main floor of the house to check the doors again. All thirteen of them were still locked. She'd just made it back to the front of the house when the doorbell rang.

Janessa looked out the side window and frowned when she saw Darcia on the porch. Obviously, the gossips were wrong, because from everything Janessa had heard, Darcia didn't come to the house. Ever.

Licking the sticky sugar off her fingers and hoping there wasn't any on her face, Janessa used the app she'd put on her phone to pause the security system and opened the door. She greeted Darcia with a smile. Which quickly faded. Brody's mother clearly wasn't in a smiling mood.

Darcia was wearing sweatpants and a shirt, both of which appeared to be splattered with clay, and Janessa remembered the woman saying she taught pottery classes. She had pulled back her dark hair in a short stubby ponytail. No makeup, but then she didn't need it. The woman was still beautiful. It was easy to see why Abe had lost his head and heart over her.

"I don't want to come in," Darcia said before Janessa could offer the invitation. She put on her jacket and pulled it tight around her. "And I won't keep you. I just wanted to talk to you about my son."

Janessa did a mental wince and wondered if someone had seen Brody and her in a lip-lock at the cemetery. If so, news like that would definitely make the rounds and get back to Darcia.

"Brody and I had a lapse, that's all," she assured Darcia. "We both agreed it was a mistake." Well, their voices had agreed. Janessa wasn't so sure that any other part of her had listened.

Darcia just stared at her. It soon became apparent that the woman was shocked. Well, crap. Here she'd just gone and blurted out stuff that shouldn't have been blurted. Especially to Brody's mom. Now, Darcia probably thought Brody and she had had sex instead of just a really long, really incredible kiss.

"I'm here about my other son, Rowan." Darcia's voice had gone a little arctic. It matched the frosty look in her eyes, and that wasn't frosty in a cool slang kind of way.

It was mental-note time. Janessa would need to warn Brody about this conversation so that when Darcia confronted him about it, he wouldn't be blindsided.

"What about Rowan?" Janessa asked. She kept her question simple so that she wouldn't blab yet something else that Darcia might not know. Of course, Janessa didn't have anything to dish on Brody's kid brother.

"I don't want Rowan to help you with the research on Abe for the Last Ride Society," Darcia stated. "He's already been doing computer searches and going through old social media pages, and I want that to stop."

Janessa didn't jump to answer. She often had to defuse situations, and while Darcia didn't look especially angry, the emotions were there.

"Rowan asked to help," Janessa finally said, "but I can certainly tell him it's not necessary. Maybe you should do the same?"

Her mouth tightened, and Janessa recognized that gesture, too, since she'd had a lot of dealings with teenagers. They didn't always respond in a positive way to ground rules. Especially when the rule might not make sense to him. So, Darcia had likely already told him and Rowan had balked about it.

"I don't want Rowan to dig into the past, into the kind

of man Abe Parkman was," Darcia continued. "In fact, I'd rather he not work here at Colts Creek, but Brody talked me into it."

Janessa didn't have to guess that Darcia wasn't especially happy about that concession, either. But Janessa could see it from Brody's point of view. Here at the ranch, he'd be able to keep an eye on Rowan. Though Janessa hadn't seen any particular behavior from the boy to indicate he needed such an eye. Still, she'd only run into him twice so maybe there was something about him she didn't know.

"Abe made a habit of using my kids to take little jabs at me," Darcia added. She opened her mouth as if she might say more, but then she seemed to change her mind. "If Rowan comes to you, please remind him I don't want him doing the research."

With that, Darcia turned to leave. Just as Sophia's car turned into the driveway. Janessa figured the two women knew each other. And she was right. When Sophia stepped from her car, there was instant recognition on Sophia's face. Ditto for Darcia's. There didn't seem to be any hot flames of anger but more like the awkwardness because they were both Abe's exes.

"Sophia," Darcia said, though it wasn't much of a greeting. She moved down the steps, obviously heading for her car.

"Darcia," her mother returned, obviously heading for the porch. "Let me guess. You're here to tell my daughter that you don't want her spending time with your son."

Janessa sighed. Was the gossip about Rowan's research making the rounds or did someone else know about Brody and her kissing at the cemetery?

"Just because I agreed they shouldn't be seeing each other," Sophia continued, "that doesn't mean I care much for this visit. It's a déjà vu, isn't it? A lot like your visit sixteen years ago when you came to Dallas to tell me that Janessa shouldn't be with Brody."

What? Janessa had to do a mental double take on that. Darcia must have done one, too, because she stopped in her tracks. So, this wasn't about Rowan but rather Brody.

"You went to Dallas?" Janessa asked, and yes, she aimed that question at Darcia.

Darcia turned back to face Janessa and nodded. "I thought Abe was trying to play matchmaker with Brody and you. Again, as a way of using my kids to take jabs at me. Did you know that Abe lent my daughter the car she was in when she died?" she added before Janessa could respond.

Janessa had to shake her head, and she waited for Darcia to continue. She didn't have to wait long.

"Layla had only had her driver's license a few months," Darcia went on, "and she wanted a car so she could go to and from her part-time job at the florist in town. I told her no, that she was too young, but then she showed up with a car that Abe had lent her. And before you ask why he did that, it was because he wanted to undermine me with my daughter."

It sounded as if that's what Abe had done. But why? Maybe Layla had visited Brody at the ranch, and she'd gotten to know Abe? Still, that wasn't a solid reason for Abe to lend a teenager a car without getting her mother's permission.

"I'm sorry," Janessa murmured because she had no idea what else to say. It was clear that Darcia had connected the dots from long ago and blamed Abe for her daughter's death.

Some of the stiffness went out of Darcia's shoulders, and she nodded before she hurried to her car.

"You didn't mention that Darcia had come to see you in Dallas," Janessa said to her mother.

"No," Sophia readily admitted. "No need. You came home a day or two later, and it was clear you and Brody were no longer together."

Janessa gave her a flat look. "You said you knew Brody's name because I'd doodled it."

"Yes, I did say that." Sophia flashed one of her quick dry smiles. "A white lie. What good would it have done if I told you about Darcia?"

"None," Janessa admitted after she ran it through her head.

"Besides, I agreed with Darcia. I figured Abe was doing some matchmaking and that he was also possibly doing that to take some jabs at her." She paused, gathered her breath and came up onto the porch. "Hell hath no fury like Abraham Parkman when he's scorned."

Maybe. But Janessa hoped that wasn't the reason. Because if so, that meant Abe could have also used Brody to jab at Darcia. Jabs that could have included gaining Brody's trust and love all so he could crush him with this damn will.

Janessa pushed that aside for now and faced her mother. "Are you really staying in Last Ride?"

"I said I would, and I will." But she didn't give Janessa even a second to feel relief about that because she launched into a question. "How's Teagan?"

It took Janessa a moment to switch gears. "She's better. She doesn't want to go back to Dallas."

"Well, of course, she doesn't. Her fixer is here." She patted Janessa's arm and handed her a business card that she took from the pocket of her emerald green coat. "It's for an OB here in Last Ride. I asked around, and everyone says he's the best. Of course, there are only two OBs so *best* might be relative."

"Thank you," she said, taking the card. "This was on my to-do list."

"Now, it's done. So is the temporary restraining order against Riggs. Sheriff Lyle personally handled that for us."

Janessa wondered if that was because Sophia had sweet-talked him or if the sheriff knew the benefits of keeping the woman happy. A happy Sophia would stay in Last Ride.

Sophia glanced at her watch. "Gotta go. I'm having breakfast with Curt Dayton so we can discuss strategies for dropkicking Abe's will."

That seemed a reasonable thing to do, but Janessa caught the twinkle—yes, a twinkle—in Sophia's eyes. "Curt is at least fifteen years younger than you."

Sophia smiled. "Yes, he is. Hey, if I'm stuck here in Podunk for the holidays, I might as well enjoy myself." She waved a perky little wave to go with her perky little smile and went to her car.

"Why did you decide to stay?" Janessa came out and asked. "Was it because of Curt?"

"Nooo," Sophia stretched that out. "It was because I didn't want to see Abe get away with what he tried to pull in his will. I figured I could better fight the terms of that will if I was here. I also wanted to keep an eye on you."

More like an eye on Brody and her, but Janessa wasn't going to look a gift horse in the mouth. Sophia had saved her. Or had at least set up a possible saving.

"And like I said, if I have to be here," her mother added, "then I intend to enjoy myself."

Her mother certainly didn't advise Janessa to do the same in the enjoyment department, but it was something to consider. Three months was a long time when it came to resisting the hottest cowboy in Last Ride. A cowboy she spotted riding toward the barn on an impressive looking Appaloosa.

Definitely the hottest.

Brody didn't look in her direction when he dismounted, and when he immediately started a conversation with a couple of the ranch hands, Janessa went back inside where Velma Sue and Teagan appeared to be waiting for her.

"Is your mom staying?" Teagan immediately asked.

"She said yes." Janessa went ahead and added the asterisk, "But she could change her mind."

"She said yes," Teagan repeated.

Clearly, that news made her happy, and her face lit up. Probably because she knew her chances had increased for staying here. With her fixer. Janessa only hoped that she could indeed fix this by keeping Riggs far, far away from Last Ride.

"You'll need to call for an appointment," Janessa explained, handing her the card for the OB.

"I will. Thank you." Taking out her phone, Teagan stepped aside to make the call.

"If you're wanting to go through those presents now, I can show you where they are," Velma Sue said.

Janessa had already geared up to go back upstairs and tackle some work on her laptop, but she decided it wouldn't hurt to at least get a glimpse of the gifts. First, though, she locked the front door, reset the security and followed Velma Sue through the maze of halls. Following Velma Sue at the woman's slow pace gave Janessa plenty of time to study art and furnishings in his part of the house. Again, it had that museum vibe. A shame since it could have been so much more welcoming with some non-marble, non-gloss and some splashes of color.

Of which Abe's office had none.

When Velma Sue paused in the doorway of that office, and Janessa looked inside, she saw that it was exactly what she'd expected. Black-and-white. Excessively large. And it had an equally excessively large painting of Abe hanging over the black stone fireplace. Unlike the fireplace at Brody's, there were no framed family photos on the mantel, but there was a line of awards. Glossy and shiny, of course.

"The presents are this way," Velma Sue said, leading Janessa past the office and to a large storage room.

The moment Velma Sue opened the door, Janessa spotted the wrapped packages. Now, here was color, a practical rainbow in the wrapping paper that ranged from lavender to bright red. Some had enormous bows, others sparkly coils and stars shooting out like fireworks. Still another had a silk flower arrangement for a topper.

"Wow," Teagan said, coming up behind them. "So many presents."

Janessa made a sound of agreement. So many, and Abe had never mentioned them to her, much less given her any of them. He'd kept them here, close enough to where he worked but out of sight. She wasn't sure what to make of that, but she was quickly learning that Abe had plenty of layers. Not necessarily good ones, but they existed.

"The ones there are for your birthdays, one through twelve." Velma pointed to a stash in the corner. "Those dozen are for Christmas," she added pointing to another corner.

"Why did he stop at twelve?" Teagan asked.

There weren't any puzzling layers about this. "Because that's when Abe knew he was never going to get custody of me."

A rejection, and she wondered how he'd reacted. Janessa

couldn't recall him showing a whole lot of emotion, but it was possible it'd hurt him. Just as possible, though, that he'd flicked it off and shut the door on both the gifts and her.

Teagan went closer to look at the packages. "Are you going to open them?"

Janessa considered the question, nodded. "Maybe a few of them." She pointed to the largest one in the birthday corner. "Why don't you open that one for me?" The equally large tag on it said it was for her first birthday.

Teagan brightened, but then she shook her head. "You should do it. Your father got them for you."

More likely he'd gotten them out of obligation. Or maybe to try to show up Sophia if Janessa had ever gotten around to opening them.

"Go ahead," Janessa assured the girl. "Start with the one that was supposed to be for my first birthday." It was also the biggest one.

With her pregnant waddle, Teagan went to the packages while Velma Sue and Janessa stayed back. "If you don't think it'll stir up too many bad memories, you oughta consider going through Abe's things to see if there's anything you might want."

Janessa thought about that as Teagan carefully loosened the tape on the gift-wrap. Obviously, the girl wasn't a ripper the way Janessa was.

"There might be some old pictures of your mom and him," Velma Sue added.

Now, that was something Janessa might want if for no other reason so she could see that they'd once been happy. "Thanks, I'll do that."

When Teagan finally eased off the wrapping, Janessa saw the dollhouse. No ordinary one, of course. Apparently, Abe hadn't wanted to give his daughter a trendy house of whatever doll had been popular at the time. This appeared to be custom-made and was a replica of Abe's own house. Well, minus some renovations that probably hadn't been done yet when the dollhouse was built.

"Look at all the little furniture," Teagan said, lightly touching her fingers to a tiny Tiffany lamp in one of the upstairs bedrooms.

Janessa hadn't been in that particular room, but she was betting the actual lamp was in there. The living room and library certainly were a match to the real deal. It was the same for the bedroom she used, though the bedding was different. It must have cost Abe a small fortune to have this done.

And, damn it, Janessa felt the little tug in her heart.

Maybe Abe had spent only a few seconds commissioning the job and writing a check for it and maybe it wasn't at all appropriate for a one-year-old, but he'd put some thought into it. Thoughts about her.

Janessa was scowling at the possibility of that when she heard the footsteps, and she whirled around, her body bracing for Riggs. But then her body had a whole different reaction when she saw it was Brody.

She could feel her entire body sigh.

He was in full-cowboy mode today. Those great fitting jeans, boots and long-sleeved blue work shirt that was partially unbuttoned. He smelled like fresh winter wind and saddle leather, apparently a scent combo that caused her to stop scowling. Not Brody, though. He kept his somewhat stern I'm-pissed expression on that dreamy face.

Brody glanced at the dollhouse and the other presents. "Got a minute?" he asked her.

"Sure." Since he headed toward the door, Janessa got a big clue that he wanted this conversation to be just between them and that he wanted it to happen now. "Open any of the gifts you want," she told Teagan. "I'll probably get some work done after I talk with Brody."

As she'd done with Velma Sue, Janessa followed Brody down the hall and to what was obviously his office. It was like stepping into another world. One with at least some color. The love seat and chairs in the small sitting area were merlot leather. The rug, a muted mix of soft blues, greens and various shades of the wine color.

There were no portraits of Brody in here. No impressive mantel with trophies and awards. However, he did have framed photos of some of the champion quarter horses.

She turned to tell him she was impressed that he'd bucked Abe on his decor choice, but she hadn't realized just how close he was to her. She bumped into him.

And felt it in multiple parts of her.

"Yeah," he grumbled as if he knew exactly what she was thinking. What he didn't do was act on those feelings in multiple parts of her.

"I heard our mothers were here earlier," Brody said as he moved away from her to the door behind them.

"Wow, gossip is faster than texting around here." And in this case, Janessa wished they'd held off on that specific gossip until she'd had the chance to talk to Brody about it.

"I had some hands watching the place and told them to text me if anyone came and went," he explained.

She nodded. "Sophia came to confirm that she was indeed staying and that she might be making a play for Curt Dayton. Thought I'd throw that in so when you hear it, you won't be surprised."

Judging from his stony expression, he wouldn't be surprised by anything Sophia did.

"And as for your mother," Janessa went on, "she wants

me to tell Rowan to stop doing research on Abe. Any idea how Rowan will take that news?"

"Badly," Brody snarled, but then he seemed to rein in other snarls. He groaned, scrubbed his hand over his face. "My mother is way too protective of Rowan and me. I can usually find a respectful way to tell her to butt out of my business, but Rowan hasn't developed that skill set yet."

"A lot of teenagers haven't."

"My mother has panic attacks," Brody added before she could say more. "She works herself up when she's worried about one of us, and anything to do with Abe worries her."

Janessa had been around some residents when they'd had panic attacks so she knew how bad and terrifying they could be. "I take it that her job as a nurse isn't a trigger for the stress?"

"No. It always centers on Rowan or me, and this research with Abe paired with her worry over me losing my job could be a perfect storm." Brody paused, and a sleek muscle tightened in his jaw. "On the other hand, I have no intention of telling Rowan to butt out of the research. And I don't want you to tell him that, either. Unless you no longer want or need his help."

She certainly hadn't expected him to say that. "Check both of those boxes on wanting and needing help, but I don't want to cause trouble in your family." Especially since Darcia already looked at her as if she were a fungus that needed treatment.

"I want Rowan to make up his own mind about this," Brody assured her, "and I'll deal with the trouble and fallout from Mom."

Part of Janessa felt this was a small victory. Not for her but for Rowan. But then she thought of Darcia in the full throes of a panic attack.

"Maybe a solution is for me to do the research ASAP," she said. "That way, Rowan won't be involved for long. Besides, I'm not sure Rowan will actually find anything."

"He already has," Brody disagreed. The scowl returned, and he went to his desk, picked up several pieces of paper that'd been stapled together and he handed it to her. "Rowan went through old newspaper articles and internet searches and came up with that. He found it on a blog where people post their unresolved legal complaints."

That, she soon realized as she read through it, was definitely something.

"Your father, Jimmy, filed a lawsuit against Abe," Janessa summarized. "Why haven't I heard any gossip about this?" But she stopped when she saw the answer to her own question. "Because Jimmy filed the lawsuit in San Antonio where he was living at the time."

She went further down the page, and holy moly, Jimmy had made some pretty startling claims in that lawsuit.

"Yeah," Brody repeated, no doubt interpreting the look on her face. "My father claimed Abe used his power and money to destroy his business, ruin his marriage and force him to leave town."

Janessa did some facial interpretation of Brody, too, and she saw this had given him a hard punch. "It might not be true," she reminded him.

"Go to the next page," Brody instructed.

She did, and Janessa groaned when she looked at the accusations. "Abe paid off the suppliers to your father's hardware store to get them to stop doing business with him. Abe offered deep discounts of the same supplies until it forced your father into bankruptcy, and then Abe bought the store from the bank and had the building torn down and completely rebuilt.

Janessa stopped to take a much-needed breath, but she continued to read. After Abe had ruined Jimmy, he'd made it next to impossible for him to get a job in Last Ride. Broke and with his marriage on the rocks, Abe had then offered Jimmy money if he'd leave Last Ride and never come back. Jimmy had taken the cash, given it to Darcia and left.

"This happened when I was about ten," Brody filled in for her.

Oh, mercy. It was definitely an eyeful of the steps Abe had allegedly taken to get Jimmy out of town.

She looked up, her gaze meeting his. "I'm guessing your father wrote this blog post?"

"You'd think, but take a look at the last page."

Janessa's ESP/facial reading failed her this time, but she turned to the last page, and her gaze zoomed to the bottom.

Where she saw none other than her mother's name.

CHAPTER ELEVEN

BRODY CLIMBED ONTO the back of the Brahma bull named Foya. AKA Fall on Your Ass. And while Foya snorted beneath him, Brody began to question why the hell he'd agreed, once again, to do this particular ride. Yes, it'd add some money to the Abe Parkman Holiday Gala fund for various town charities, but there had to be an easier way to raise some cash.

Then the adrenaline kicked in.

So did Foya when the gate opened, and the bull charged out, bucking and tossing his muscled body around to fling off the rider he probably considered an idiot. Maybe Brody was indeed an idiot for letting himself just get slung around like this, but that adrenaline kick was something else. A good something else.

He heard the cheers of the onlookers, and everything inside him pinpointed to moving with the bull, hanging on, knowing that at any second his ass could land hard on the ground. Brody didn't consider himself an adrenaline junkie or thrill seeker, but he could appreciate this high. A high that went up many significant notches when the bell clanged to signal the end of the ride and that he hadn't busted his butt after all.

The rodeo clowns rushed forward to distract the bull so that Brody could slide off and head to the fence.

Where he immediately spotted Janessa.

Somehow, he was able to pick her out of the crowd of at least two hundred still-cheering people who'd plopped down ten bucks just to watch the three rides that'd taken place this evening. She was on the other side of the riding arena, her gaze glued to him, and she was eyeing him with interest and lust.

Obviously, Brody was doing the same to her.

Waving and responding to the cheers and whoops still going on, Brody walked toward her, telling himself that he needed to talk to her about Sophia and the blog Rowan had found. But the lust was definitely playing into the reason his boots were headed in her direction.

She was wearing snug black jeans with really sparkly shoes, a red sweater and coat, and she'd pulled her hair back in a ponytail. Her face was a little rosy from the chilly temps, and all of that combined made one hell of a picture.

"Great ride," she said, smiling before she took a small bite from a brown ball of something on a stick. Nothing about it looked appetizing or even edible. "You're the star attraction."

"The last ride of the night," he corrected. He put on his jacket, which one of the ground assistants handed him. "There really aren't any stars in an event this small."

She shrugged. "Looked like a star-quality ride to me."

Because Janessa's rodeo knowledge was probably somewhat limited, Brody didn't want to feel good about the praise. But he did. He rested his arms on the top of the fence between them, and he was well aware that they'd attracted a whole lot of attention.

"What's that you're eating?" he asked.

"Fried cotton candy."

Nothing about it sounded appetizing or edible, either, but he knew pretty much any gross-sounding food option was available at the festival. Some delicious ones, too. He planned to grab some nachos before the night was over.

"I got it from a booth between the fried Oreos and fried beer," she added, and her smile pumped up to a full-fledged grin when he scowled. "Better hurry if you want some because they're selling out fast."

"I'll pass. I want to hold on to as much of my stomach lining as possible."

She chuckled, had another nibble of the blob and pointed to the massive banner strung just above them. Abe Parkman Holiday Gala emblazoned in gold on a black background. Twin pictures of Abe graced both ends of the banner.

"This is another penis deal," she remarked. "Look at me, look at me. See how important I am."

He couldn't argue that. Abe had definitely had an ego. "I take it you haven't found anything in your research that proves Abe had redeeming qualities."

She looked straight into his eyes. "Well, he was good to you and was smart enough to give you free rein in running the ranch. So far, though, that's about it. FYI, he has some ranching files in his office that you might want to move to yours."

Before Brody could issue a *will do*, someone called out his name.

Alyssa Cooke.

The tall brunette was sort of a penis deal, too, but in a womanly kind of way. Alyssa dressed to draw maximum attention, and tonight was no exception. Her purple jeans looked as if they could seriously restrict blood flow in her thighs and crotch. Ditto for the sparkly silver sweater that squeezed and pushed up her D-cups and made every movement seem as if it could quickly turn into a planned wardrobe malfunction. She was gorgeous, and she knew it.

She also had made it plenty clear that she wanted him.

Brody wasn't biting, though. He preferred relationships that had a longer shelf life than deep-fried cotton candy. That wasn't the popular view when it came to most cowboys, but sex—any sex—in a small town meant coming face-to-face with that sexual partner when things went south.

Alyssa kept her attention locked on him while she licked her chocolate-covered banana. Yes, licked. And yes, it was also on a stick, completing the penis metaphor.

"I'm sure she's not doing that because it's sexually suggestive or anything," Janessa muttered.

Brody bit back a laugh. Going the minimal politeness route, he gave Alyssa a quick wave to acknowledge he'd noticed her and heard her call out his name. What he didn't do was give the woman any kind of signal that he wanted her to come closer with her mouth licking and sucking on that chocolate banana, and he turned back to Janessa.

"Did you ever get a chance to talk to your mother about the blog post that Rowan found?" Brody asked after he glanced around and made sure no one was close enough to hear.

There wasn't. Other than Alyssa, people had given them a wide-ish berth, but just in case anyone had bat hearing, he kept his voice low.

"Not really. My mom's a master at avoidance and has been holed up in her room at the inn. I haven't pestered her about it too much because I don't want to get mad and therefore give her a reason to leave town."

There was that. "I did some internet searches and didn't find anything else."

"Same here," Janessa admitted. "I also read the blog post multiple times, and if it's true, Abe really did screw over your father. Do you remember any of this happening? Any talk about it? Anything?"

Brody had already given this plenty of thought so he didn't have to figure out an answer. "My dad left when I was ten, and most of the memories I have are of him working long hours at the store. He and my mom rarely mentioned Abe around me."

In private, though, they'd likely had some big-assed discussions about the man who'd once been his father's best friend. And his mother's boyfriend. Hard to totally omit something like that from marital conversations. Or maybe they had because it'd been such a touchy subject.

"After my dad lost the store," Brody went on, "I recall him drinking a lot. Being bitter. A lot. So, I'm not surprised at the bitterness in the blog."

"Abe could have done all those things, right?" Janessa asked after a long pause.

Here he went, speaking ill of the dead, but he'd done some speaking ill of the living, too. "Abe could have, but it's possible my father wasn't a saint in all of this. What they were going through was an all-out feud, and I'm sure plenty of it splashed onto my mother. It's one of the reasons she's so bitter about Abe."

He'd cut his mother some slack. Because of the things she'd been through. But he wasn't in a slack-cutting mood when it came to Abe and his father. If all of the info in the blog had come to light when Abe was alive, Brody would have definitely confronted him about it, and it was highly likely that he wouldn't have taken over running Abe's ranch.

"Sorry," she murmured as if picking up on the bad vibes coming off him. There wasn't much left of that adrenaline from the ride.

"This might help." She held out the ball of fried cotton

candy for him to sample. "There's a lot to be said about a sugar high that comes with absolutely zero nutritional benefits."

What the hell. It was possible he took a bite only to get the cheap thrill of touching something her mouth had just touched. Still, the taste wasn't nearly as bad as it'd sounded. It was a little like strawberry shortcake.

"We came here sixteen years ago," Janessa remarked, glancing around. "Remember? It was for the Fourth of July festival."

Of course he remembered. He might forget a dental appointment or what he'd had for breakfast that very morning, but details about Janessa just seemed to stick in his mind.

"We stayed for the fireworks," she added a moment later. "Well, some of them anyway."

He remembered that, too. They'd left so they could go make out in his truck. Over the next weeks, the making out had continued, and continued, until they'd passed the threshold of holding onto their willpower and had sex.

She kept glancing around, then stopped. Smiled. Brody followed her gaze and spotted Margo and Teagan coming toward them. Both had sticks with blobs on them. Brody also saw Sherry McKinnon, one of the ranch hands trailing along behind them. Sherry was on bodyguard duty tonight and would stay with Teagan until the girl was safely back at the ranch.

"We saw your bull ride," Margo immediately said. "We were on the other side of the arena. Don't know how you kept that fine butt of yours on that Brahma, but you managed it. Great job."

He thanked her, and because Teagan was looking plenty uncomfortable, he made sure he kept an easygoing expression. "Fried cotton candy?" he asked, tipping his head to the blob.

"Fried ice cream. Miss Margo got the fried cotton candy." Teagan paused. "Thank you for having your ranch hand watch out for me." She glanced at Sherry who'd stayed back a few feet. "No one has seen Riggs around, right?"

"Right," Brody assured her.

"And he'll stay gone," Margo said as if it were gospel instead of wishful thinking. "That boy's probably figured out that trying to come back here would mean taking on the whole ranch. Me included."

Margo stopped, and making oh-how-cute sounds, she peered down at Janessa's shoes. "You wore them. They look perfect with your outfit."

Brody should have known the footwear was Margo's doing, and while he couldn't say they were perfect, they did suit the occasion.

Margo turned from her shoe admiring and pointed to a couple about ten yards away. "There's Millie Parkman and Joe McCann." Since Brody knew both of them, her info was obviously aimed at Janessa, and Margo pointed to the couple holding hands and looking seriously starry-eyed at each other. "Remember, I told you about them. They fell in love when they were doing research for the Last Ride Society."

Margo then turned a sly smile toward Brody and Janessa. "All sorts of good things can happen when you're not expecting it."

He lifted an eyebrow and nearly pointed out that all sorts of bad things could happen, too. Case in point, Abe's sudden death and his will. But Brody didn't want to stir up any more fear for Teagan.

Joe lifted his chin in greeting when he spotted Brody, and Millie, he and Joe's six-year-old nephew, Tanner Parkman, Jr., came over. Even though Joe was a year older than Brody, they'd become friends playing football in high school, and their friendship had continued.

"Janessa," Millie said. "It's good to see you again. I met her at the drawing," Millie added to Brody.

He'd heard all about that. Brody had also heard rumblings that Joe was smitten with Millie. Yes, smitten. It was a good thing to see since Brody knew Joe had been through a tough time after losing his wife in a car accident over two years ago.

Brody climbed over the fence, dropping down next to Janessa. He made introductions, even though he was certain that Janessa remembered Joe from the summer she'd spent here. However, when he got to the boy, Brody used the name that most people called him. Little T.

"You rode a bull with a big hump on its neck," Little T announced with the sugar high and enthusiasm of a six-year-old. "Can I ride it, too?"

"When you're thirty and eleven feet tall," Joe automatically answered.

Little T came up on his tiptoes and stretched his neck as if he might be able to grow those extra feet in the next couple of seconds.

Millie took a business card from her purse and handed it to Janessa. "In two and a half weeks, we're having a pre-holiday party at my antique shop, Once Upon a Time, and I'd love for you to come. It'll be a chance to see some of the new art we've put up in the local artists' gallery. You come, too, of course," she said to Brody, Margo and Teagan, and she gave all of them cards, as well. "Some of Darcia's pottery pieces will be on display."

Until she'd said that last part, Brody had been about to decline. He wasn't a fan of parties, but he'd go to support his mother. Especially since she loved making and teaching pottery as much as she did nursing.

Janessa looked at Teagan and Margo and got eager nods from both of them. "We'd love to come," Janessa told her.

"Great," Millie answered. "We'll see you then."

Joe, Millie and Little T had barely taken a step away when Brody saw someone else walking toward them. Someone he definitely hadn't expected to see here.

Sophia.

Brody had figured she'd avoid anything named after a man she loathed, perhaps keep avoiding her daughter, too, but Sophia made a beeline toward them. She greeted the four of them but then stopped a moment, though, to smirk at the banner that cracked and snapped in the evening breeze.

"Gala," Sophia mocked. "Because it sounds more important than festival. I guess there wasn't enough room on the sign for Display of Pompous Assery by a Pompous Ass."

"Probably not," Margo agreed, "but maybe we can do that next year if we use a smaller font." She gave Sophia a gentle nudge with her elbow. "I didn't think you were coming."

"Changed my mind. Curt asked me to meet him by the longhorn sculptures made entirely from root vegetables." Sophia said that with a straight face. Mostly.

Brody hadn't seen this year's displays, but they were usually impressive in a small-town gala sort of way. He also didn't miss the lift in Sophia's voice when she said Curt's name. He'd heard rumors about the two hooking up and not just for legal discussions about Abe's will, either, and he hoped that didn't come back to bite them in the butt. If things fizzled and then fizzled between Sophia and her fellow lawyer, then it might spur Sophia to head out of town.

"You've been dodging my calls," Janessa told her mom.

"Yes, I have," Sophia readily admitted.

That admission seemed to be enough to get Margo to make a comment about Teagan and her being *just as eager as can be* to get a look at the turnip-and-carrot longhorn sculpture that people were buzzing about. Margo and Teagan headed in that direction with Sherry right behind them.

"Alone at last," Sophia remarked. "Judging from the voice mails and texts you left me, you want to know about a blog post that Jimmy wrote years ago." She plucked off a tiny bit of the fried cotton candy and popped it into her mouth. "Well, my name was there because I was Jimmy's lawyer."

In a no-shit surprise contest, Brody wasn't sure who would have won. Him or Janessa.

"How'd that happen?" Janessa asked.

Sophia shrugged. "Jimmy came to me and asked me to file a lawsuit against Abe. I suppose he knew how I felt about Abe and he thought that I'd jump at the chance to get back at my ex." She paused. "And I jumped."

"You never mentioned any of this to me," Janessa pointed out.

"I often don't mention things about my clients. Besides, you were young, just a child, and you didn't even know Brody back then. It happened around the time Abe gave up his custody fight."

Brody did the math. That would have been when Janessa and he were twelve so his father would have gone to Sophia about two years after he'd already lost his business and left Last Ride.

"According to the blog, the lawsuit was filed in San Antonio, but you're in Dallas," Brody pointed out.

"That's where Jimmy was living at the time so I did all the paperwork as he requested and had a colleague in San

Antonio file it. We lost the suit," Sophia added, "and that's when Jimmy and I put together that blog post."

Janessa made a sound that had a let-me-see-if-I'm-getting-this vibe to it. "So, after I came home from Last Ride that summer and doodled Brody everywhere, you ran a background on him. You would have found out that he was Jimmy's son."

"Doodled?" Brody asked. He wasn't sure if that was literal or what.

"I'll explain later," Janessa muttered to him and then faced her mother again. "You knew he was Jimmy's son." And it wasn't a question.

"I did," Sophia admitted not with any embarrassment that she'd kept something like that from her daughter. "I knew, and it was why I was glad you were no longer involved with him. I'm sorry," she added to Brody, "but Jimmy is a very angry man, filled with hatred for Abe. I didn't want Janessa caught in the middle if Jimmy blew up over his son getting involved with Abe's daughter."

Brody could see a mother feeling that way, but there was still some puzzling parts about this conversation. The doodled part he'd put on hold since Janessa had said she'd explain that, but he didn't want the other bit to slide.

"You ran a background check on me?" Brody asked Sophia.

"I did," Sophia repeated, and again there wasn't even a smidge of remorse. "I wanted to know all about the boy who'd hurt her and caused her to cry herself to sleep at night."

"Mom," Janessa scolded, sounding very much like a teenager.

"Well, you did, and I can't see why Brody shouldn't know that. You got hurt. Heck, maybe he did, too. But if there's one thing I've learned from all of my bad relationships, it's don't make the same mistake twice." She checked her watch and started walking away. "I need to get to the longhorn booth because Curt is probably waiting for me."

They stood there, watched her go, and Brody gave it a couple of seconds before he asked, "Doodled?"

Janessa sighed. "I was a teenage girl, and I took out some of my angst by scribbling your name in places where my mom obviously saw it."

Okay, he could see her doing that. He'd certainly cursed Janessa's name often enough back then for her running out on him.

"And the crying yourself to sleep?" he pressed.

"Once or twice," she admitted. "Three times, tops. Sophia obviously had Mom ears because she heard me."

Well, hell. That made him feel like a dick. Of course, at the time he'd thought she was the dick after she'd left. He hadn't known that the real dick in all of this had been Abe.

Some static crunched through the air, and a couple of seconds later a voice came through the huge speakers positioned throughout the fairgrounds. "Might want to find a comfortable spot, folks. Fireworks will start in ten minutes."

Brody thought they might end up missing the bulk of those again, but for a different reason this time. Not so they could run off to make out but because the conversation with Sophia had put a serious damper on his mood.

"I should probably find out where Margo and Teagan are," Janessa muttered. She took out her phone and sent a text to Margo.

Within seconds, Brody saw Margo's response on Janessa's phone.

We're all sitting with the Last Ride Society ladies at the big picnic table by the fried-spaghetti booth. Join us. They've got heaters, and we have a great view for the fireworks.

"I wish they'd picked a table by a better booth," Janessa mumbled, and she tossed the rest of her fried cotton candy in the trash. "You'll sit with us?"

Brody was trying to find a polite way to turn her down when someone called out to him. Not Alyssa this time. It was Dewayne Milton. Along with owning a portrait studio, he also took pictures for the town's weekly newspaper.

"I was hoping I'd run into the two of you," Dewayne greeted as he pulled something from the enormous canvas bag he had hooked over his shoulder.

A photo.

"It's Brody and you way back when," Dewayne told Janessa.

It was indeed a picture of them that'd been snapped during the fireworks display. There were plenty of other people in the shot, most sitting on blankets or in lawn chairs they'd brought out for the occasion, but Janessa and he were standing. Or rather leaning against the old oak tree in the picnic area of the fairgrounds. They had the tree to themselves because the huge branches obstructed the view of the night sky and therefore the fireworks. But they clearly weren't focused on anything that was happening above them.

Nope.

They were facing each other, eyes locked, hands on each other's waists, with lust waves spinning around them. Brody couldn't recall the exact moment, but he was betting he'd been about to move in for a kiss.

"I thought you two would like that," Dewayne said,

handing Janessa the picture. He started glancing around. "I've got one of Margo, too."

"She's by the fried-spaghetti booth," Janessa answered with her attention still on the photograph, and she added a "Thanks," as Dewayne hurried off.

"Well," Janessa murmured when they were alone. "Well," she repeated, and she looked up at him.

Again, they were face-to-face, eyes locked, and the lust waves were hot and plentiful. "Well?" he questioned, not because he wanted her to answer it, but because he figured if he was using his mouth for talking, he wouldn't kiss her.

But he was wrong.

He'd barely spoken that *well* when there was a loud boom, and from the corner of his eye, Brody saw the first of the fireworks burst overhead. It was followed by lots of squeals, oohs and aahs.

And a kiss.

Janessa moved toward him just as Brody moved toward her, and it was pretty clear they had the same goal in mind. To do a very dumb thing in a very public place. Their mouths met and just kept on meeting until they sank into the kiss.

She tasted sweet, of course, but it wasn't all from the deep-fried cotton candy. This was Janessa, and that taste dipped right into all his hot spots, all his needs, all the stupid parts of him. Their tongues met, played around and just kept on playing until all those stupid parts of him made some decisions. That this was the best idea he'd ever had and that he should deepen the stupidity by taking hold of her hips and pulling her even closer to him.

The fireworks continued to boom and burst. The sounds of the festival-goers continued, and in the back of his mind,

Brody hoped everyone had their attention on the sky show and not on Janessa and him.

But he was wrong about that, too.

When he heard a throat clearing, Brody pulled back from Janessa and saw Rowan standing right next to them. Brody expected his brother to flash a grin and dole out some kind of smart-ass remark. He didn't. Nor was Rowan oohing or aahing over the fireworks.

"It's Mom," Rowan said.

Brody's stomach dropped. "What happened? What's wrong?"

"Somebody sent her a picture of Layla." Rowan stopped, dragged in a deep breath. "There was no note or anything. Just a picture of Layla from her high school yearbook."

Brody didn't relax, not even a little. While it wasn't the bad news that he'd been braced to hear—a car accident, a heart attack, etc.—he figured it must have upset his mother to get something like that.

"Who sent it?" Brody asked.

Rowan shook his head but gave Janessa a split-second glance. "Mom thought it might be Janessa's mother. I told her it was probably just some kid playing a bad joke, but it rattled her. She's at home now, and she said I shouldn't tell you, but I knew you'd want to know."

"I do. How'd you get here?"

"Rode my bike," Rowan answered. "It's chained up by the entrance."

"Get it," Brody instructed, "and meet me at my truck. I'm parked just over there. We'll load it in the back, and I'll drive you home." He motioned to the other side of the arena, and his brother hurried off.

"My mother wouldn't have sent something like that to Darcia," Janessa insisted.

He believed her, but that left him with a huge question. Who the hell had done it? Because this didn't feel like a kid's prank.

"I have to go," Brody told her.

Janessa nodded. "If there's anything I can do to help, let me know."

Brody wished to hell there were something she or anyone else could do. But the core of this wasn't fixable.

"What have you heard about Layla?" he asked.

She kept her eyes locked with his. "Only bits and pieces. That Abe had loaned her the car even though Darcia hadn't wanted him to do that."

Brody nodded. That was one piece all right. But there was a bigger one. One that would cause him and his family grief for the rest of their lives.

"I'm the one responsible for her death. Abe might have been the one who lent her the car, but I'm the reason Layla's dead."

While the fireworks lit up the sky over the Abe Parkman Holiday Gala banner, Brody turned and walked away.

CHAPTER TWELVE

JANESSA GLANCED AROUND Abe's office and sighed. Velma Sue had prompted her, again, to come in here and start sorting through Abe's things, but the room just felt creepy to her. At the top of the creep pile was the portrait of Abe, staring down at whoever deemed to walk into his space. He might as well have hung a huge Bow Before Me, Peons sign.

Someone, probably Velma Sue, had left empty boxes around the room. No doubt meant for packing up anything Janessa didn't want to keep. Which would probably be everything. She couldn't imagine hanging on to anything in here unless it was a photo of Abe and Sophia or if it had something to do with answering all the questions she had about the man who'd fathered her.

Teagan stepped into the doorway with her, and as Janessa had done, she made a sweeping glance around the room. "It kind of reminds me of the lobbies in fancy hotels."

That was better than the comparison Janessa had come up with. It was like walking into a really big mausoleum, similar to those she'd seen at the Parkman cemetery.

"I can help," Teagan said. "Just tell me what you need me to do."

It wasn't the girl's first offer. Teagan had done that at breakfast when she jumped in to volunteer after Velma Sue had mentioned sorting through Abe's stuff. Janessa did have some work to do for Bright Hope and she needed to take Teagan to her doctor's appointment in a couple of hours, but she could get started on this particular chore.

But where to start?

In addition to the desk with all its drawers, there were filing cabinets, bookshelves and not one but two computers. Janessa couldn't imagine this would be any fun for a teenage girl.

"You could open the gifts in the storage room if you want," Janessa suggested.

"No. That's something you should do. I'd like to watch, though, or help you when you do it."

Janessa wasn't exactly in a gift-opening mood, and when she glanced out the massive bay window, she saw one of the reasons for her mood.

Brody.

He was getting out of his truck and heading to the barn. Where he would no doubt continue to avoid her. Something he'd been doing for the past two weeks since the gala. Since he'd dropped that bombshell and walked away.

I'm the reason Layla's dead.

He certainly hadn't explained what he'd meant by that, and she hadn't wanted to ask Velma Sue or Margo. It felt too much like the gossip she was coming to loathe. But Janessa had a hard time believing that Brody was actually responsible.

"What will you do with this room, this house?" Teagan asked, going to the desk.

"To be determined." Janessa was still taking things day by day in case Sophia changed her mind and left. She joined Teagan at the desk. "For now, though, we could pack up the computers and any of the files that are connected to the ranch and take them to Brody's office. Don't lift anything heavy, though," Janessa reminded her.

Janessa started to unhook the desktop computer, leaving the laptop for Teagan. Instead of boxing the desktop, though, Janessa took the various pieces down the hall and set them outside the closed door of Brody's office. She wasn't sure if he was in there, but once she hauled down some of the files, she would knock and let him know what she was doing.

Hopefully, she could talk to him, too.

She wanted to know about Layla, but she also just wanted to see him. And yes, maybe kiss him again. She missed him and hated that the photo someone had sent his mother had stirred up such bad memories for both of them.

Sophia certainly hadn't dodged her when Janessa had asked her if she'd sent Darcia a photo of her daughter. "No, why would I?" had been her mother's response. One that Janessa had expected and believed. Even if Sophia was the sort to torment people, there was no reason for her to aim that torment at Brody's mom.

Janessa set the monitor and keyboard outside Brody's office and went back to Abe's to help Teagan with the files. But she wasn't alone. Rowan was there.

"Oh, hey," the boy greeted Janessa. "I didn't like just come in or anything. One of the housekeepers let me in."

"It's all right," Janessa assured him. "It's good to see you."

"Good to see you, too. My mom dropped me off so I could check on some of the horses." He looked at his phone. "In about twenty minutes, I'm hitching a ride to school with one of the hands who's dropping off his kid. I figured I'd come in and check on you."

Since Rowan was yet someone else she needed to talk to, she was glad he'd come. However, what she wouldn't bring up was Layla, though she really wanted to know who'd sent Darcia that picture. And why.

"I think it'd be a good idea for you to back off on doing the research," she told him. Even though Brody had asked her not to mention this, Janessa definitely didn't want to add any more pain for Darcia, and the research had high potential for stirring up bad memories.

Rowan nodded, and his sigh let her know that while he might not be happy about the backing off, he knew it was the right thing to do.

"I didn't want to leave it all for you," Rowan explained. "I mean, since he was your dad and all, and I figured it'd be hard for you to keep reading about him. But your mom said she'd help so that kind of makes up for me dropping out."

Janessa pulled back her shoulders. "My mom told you she'd help me with the Society research?"

Rowan nodded and then shrugged as if it weren't a big deal. "I saw her in town yesterday, and when I said I was going to have to tell you I wouldn't be able to do the research after all, she said not to worry, that she'd help you with it."

Janessa tried to think of some ulterior motive why Sophia would have done that, and she came up with zilch. There was no reason whatsoever for her to jump into finding facts about a man she despised. Well, unless Sophia was planning on gloating over the bad stuff they'd no doubt find about Abe.

"I can move that," Rowan volunteered when Janessa lifted one of the file boxes that Teagan had packed.

"Thanks. I appreciate it. Just put it outside your brother's office for now."

Rowan stepped out, just as Brody stepped in. The air in Janessa's lungs backed up a little. Man, oh, man, did he have her number. Of course, it was a number he likely didn't want, but neither of them seemed to be doing a halfway decent job of nipping this attraction in the bud.

"Uh, I'll see if Rowan needs any help," Teagan said, and she hurried as much as she could out of the room.

The girl had no doubt made a swift exit because she'd picked up on the sudden change in the air. Or maybe she'd heard about the scorcher kiss between Brody and her at the festival and figured to give them some time alone. Either way, Janessa welcomed it because like with Rowan, she had some things to say to Brody, as well.

Janessa started with a blanket apology. "I'm sorry."

He stared at her a moment. "About?"

She felt like squirming. Janessa had hoped that he would help her out here so that she didn't jump into something he didn't want to talk about. His sister. His mother. The kiss. Anything and everything else going on. But at least Janessa had a smidge of good news to add.

"My mother didn't send a picture or anything to Darcia," Janessa told him.

"I didn't figure she had. I'm guessing it was some kind of stupid prank."

That was a better theory than anything she'd come up with. Still, she'd considered one possible long shot.

"Maybe it was Riggs," she threw out there. "I know that sounds far-fetched, but you stepped in to get him off the ranch, and he could resent it. He might figure a way to get back at you is to take a jab at your mother."

Brody stayed quiet a moment, obviously processing that. "Has Riggs taken any kind of jabs at you? Because you also stepped in to get him to leave."

"True, but he'd see you as the bigger threat. Plus, I don't have any obvious things to jab. So what if he were to send me something bad about Abe? I don't have the to-the-bone kind of grief for him that you and your mother have for your sister."

There. She'd given him the opening if he wanted to talk about his sister, but Brody didn't exactly jump on that opening. He took several moments.

"Layla's birthday is coming up. That's always a tough time for my mom. For all of us," he amended. "Getting that picture obviously didn't help."

"No," she agreed. "But you can let Darcia know that Rowan won't be doing the research. That might make her feel better."

"Yeah, that's probably for the best, given what's happened," he muttered.

She paused, studied him. "Will Darcia go to Millie's party at Once Upon a Time?"

"Probably. Why?" he asked.

"Because I was thinking of going," Janessa admitted, "but I won't if you believe it'll spoil her evening. I know there's gossip about tension between Darcia and me," she added.

"There's gossip about everything. Always will be. Go to the party if you want. I'll give my mother a heads-up that you might be there."

She opened her mouth, intending to thank him, but that wasn't what came out. "Do you want to go?"

He leveled those amazing eyes on her. "Are you asking me out on a date?"

Janessa decided to woman-up. It was the quickest way to get the chance to try out that amazing mouth of his again. "Yes."

His expression didn't change much, but she got the feeling that he was fighting back a smile. Or maybe that was a grimace. "All right, but I'll likely have Rowan with me."

"Great. Because I'll have Margo and Teagan with me."

"And me," someone said from the doorway. "Millie asked me to come, too."

It was her mother.

Sophia was smiling when she came in. "Sounds like a fun evening," she said, "unless you don't want me tagging along."

"No, it's fine. The more the merrier," Brody muttered with absolutely no enthusiasm whatsoever.

"Oh, I'm having some of the stuff in here moved to your office," Janessa told him when he headed for the door. "But if there's anything else you want, you should just take it."

He stopped, made a sweeping glance around the room before his gaze paused on her. Instant heat. Instant hope of those kisses after all. Well, once they were away from her mother, that is.

"I'll let you know," Brody said in a drawl as slow and easy as good sex, and he walked out.

"Correct me if I'm wrong," Sophia remarked after Brody was gone, "but you're not doing a whole lot of resisting when it comes to Brody."

"No, I'm not," Janessa verified. "Are you resisting when it comes to Curt Dayton?"

"Of course not," her mother answered without pausing a beat. "But I'm not risking a broken heart with Curt. You are with Brody."

Yes, she was. A crushed, stomped-on broken heart. And yet she was still going for it. A holiday fling at Colts Creek was worth it.

She hoped.

Rowan and Teagan peered in through the doorway. "I've got to head to school now," the boy said, "but if you need anything else moved, I can do it later today."

"Thank you," Janessa told him as he headed off.

"I need to get changed for the doctor's appointment," Teagan reminded her, leaving, too. Janessa suspected the girl had done that to give Sophia and her some alone time.

"Someone sent me a picture," Sophia said, getting Janessa's attention off alone time, Brody, sex and broken hearts.

Frowning, Janessa asked, "What kind of picture?"

Sophia took a five-by-seven brown envelope from her purse. "It was addressed to me at the inn, and the postmark is from Dallas." She pulled out the photo and handed it to Janessa.

It was a black-and-white shot of a man and a woman. Their arms were wrapped around each other. Their bodies pressed together. It was obviously wintertime because they were wearing coats, and the woman had on a knit hat. She was turned so that the camera only caught part of her face, and the image was fuzzy. Well, it was fuzzy there anyway. The man's mouth was on the woman's neck, and his face was crystal clear.

Abe.

A young Abe at that. Janessa guessed he was in his late twenties. Since that would have been about the time he was married to her mother, she had a closer look at the woman. Not Sophia. At least Janessa didn't believe it was, but it was hard to tell.

"According to the date on the back, it was taken the month after Abe and I got married," Sophia supplied.

Janessa's head whipped up so she could study her mother's expression. Not hurt. Not even any anger. But, yes, the handwritten date on the back was indeed when she would have been married to Abe.

"The person who sent this could have written that to

upset you," Janessa pointed out. "The picture might have been taken before you even met Abe."

"No," Sophia said, and then she sighed. "This isn't the first time someone has sent me this particular photo. I got a copy of it years ago, right before I left Abe." She paused, cleared her throat. "He cheated on me."

Janessa just stared at her. Trying to process that. And suddenly things got a whole lot clearer. "This is why you divorced him."

"That's why I divorced him," Sophia verified. She glanced away, brushing at some nonexistent lint on her top. "Needless to say, I was crushed. I have firsthand knowledge of broken hearts, betrayal, etc."

Sophia had clearly gone for a nonchalant it-no-longer-matters tone with her explanation, but she failed. Janessa saw and heard the emotion. Yes, her mother did know all about broken hearts.

"Who's the woman?" Janessa asked.

Sophia shook her head. "I don't know. When I got the first one, I went to Abe, showed it to him and he denied having an affair. In fact, he accused *me* of having one." Now, there was some anger. The really-pissed-off kind of anger. "I was four months pregnant, and he said he'd insist on having a DNA test done to prove the baby wasn't my lover's." Her mouth tightened, her eyes went to slits. "I left that day."

Yes, that would have definitely sent Sophia packing, and Janessa couldn't blame her. It would have been beyond heart crushing to have her husband accuse her that way. Especially if he was the one who was having an affair.

Janessa looked at the picture again while she tried to figure out who would have sent this to her mother. And why? Why dredge up all of these old memories?

Since the woman's face and body weren't visible, Janessa studied her hat. Nothing descript about it. But she was wearing a bracelet that had some kind of stone set in metal.

"Did you try to find out who the woman is?" Janessa pressed.

"No. I figured, whoever she was, she was welcome to my lying, cheating son-of-a-bitch husband. And speaking of the SOB," Sophia said, taking another envelope out of her purse. "These are some details about how I met the SOB, how he proposed, yada yada. I figured you could use it for the research."

"Thanks." Janessa took it, but her attention was still on the photo. "Since this was taken before I was born, maybe Velma Sue would know who the woman is."

"You're right, but I don't know why it would matter after all this time." Sophia used her hand to mime a bridge and water flowing under it.

"It might tell us who sent you the photo," Janessa reminded her. "Because I don't think the sender has good intentions. This was meant to stir up old bad feelings. Maybe feelings that would cause you to leave town in a hurry so that we can't fulfill Abe's will."

Judging from her mother's shrug, Sophia had already considered that. "It'd take more than an old picture to do that. I told you I'd stay, and I will."

Yes, but the sender might not realize just how fast and hard Sophia could dig in her heels.

With the picture in hand, they headed to the kitchen where they found Velma Sue at the breakfast table with Margo. They were sipping coffee while Margo ogled—yes, ogled—two cowboys by the corral. After getting a quick glimpse of them, Janessa decided the ogling was justified since one of them was Brody.

After a quick good morning, Janessa handed Velma Sue

the photo. "Someone sent this to my mom. Do you have any idea who the woman is?"

Velma Sue slipped on the reading glasses that dangled from a string necklace and took the picture. Studying it, she shook her head. "I'm bettin' Abe didn't know somebody took that. If he had, he would have pitched a fit about it."

Since the shot was grainy, Janessa suspected it'd been taken from a distance and then enlarged. So, yes, it was possible that Abe hadn't had a clue that he was being photographed.

Margo stood and went around the table to stand behind Velma Sue. The woman smirked. "Yep, he would have pitched a fit all right. That was taken a while back," she added with her attention still on the picture.

"At least thirty-three years ago," Sophia supplied. "Someone sent me a copy of it right before I left the ranch."

Both Velma Sue and Margo looked at Sophia, and Margo muttered a curse that had Velma Sue scolding her. "Abe cheated." She cursed some more, got another scolding. "He accused me of cheating. I didn't," Margo quickly added, "but Abe was convinced I had."

"Same here," Sophia admitted. "We'll have to get together sometime and compare notes," she said with a dry smile.

Margo smiled, too, and had another look at the picture. Her forehead bunched up. "Hey, I recognize that." She tapped the bracelet. "I sure as heck do. She used to wear it all the time."

"Who?" Janessa asked.

Margo's smile vanished, and her gaze drifted out to the corral. To Brody. "I think the woman in the picture is Darcia."

CHAPTER THIRTEEN

BRODY FIGURED THE timing for this was lousy, but he'd put it off long enough. Not intentionally put it off. He'd just been busy with the ranch. And with other things. But he needed to talk to his mother before she heard gossip about it from someone else.

He rang his mother's doorbell and didn't have to wait long before she opened the door. She was hopping around on one foot while she was putting a shoe on the other. Dressy shoes, a reminder that she was no doubt getting ready for Millie's party.

"Is something wrong?" Darcia immediately asked. "Is Rowan okay?"

It occurred to him then that he almost certainly had a serious look on his face, and since Darcia usually jumped to a worst-case scenario when it came to her kids, Brody tried to relax. Hard to do, though, considering why he'd come.

"Rowan's fine," he assured her. "And nothing's wrong."

Brody stepped in and noticed that she'd already done her makeup and hair, signals that Janessa, Margo, Teagan and Sophia had likely done the same. He'd need to be meeting them at the ranch house so they could all drive over in one of the ranch's big SUVs.

"Are you here to tell me you'll be taking Janessa to the party?" Darcia asked.

He shook his head. "But I am taking her and three others." Brody paused. "Sophia will be one of them."

"I see." Darcia went a little stiff. "She called me and said she hadn't sent me the picture of Layla."

He waited to see if that was all Sophia had volunteered. Apparently, it was because his mother didn't add more.

"I believe her," Brody said. And that was about as good of a lead-in as he was going to get. "In fact, someone sent Sophia a picture, too."

Since there was a generous amount of surprise in her eyes, it confirmed that Sophia hadn't mentioned it. Brody took a copy of the photo from the envelope he was holding. A copy that Janessa had given him, and he handed it to his mother.

"Someone sent this to Sophia twice," he explained. "The first came right before she left Abe, and then a second one arrived a couple of days ago."

He couldn't help but notice her fingers tremble a little when she took the picture, and Brody kept his attention pinned to her face. Looking for any signal that she recognized herself in the shot.

"Any idea who that is?" he asked when she didn't say anything.

"No." Lifting her gaze to meet his, she gave the photo back to him. "I have no idea."

"You're sure? Because Margo thought that bracelet looked like one you used to wear."

"Well, it's not my bracelet, and it's not me." Now there was a little anger mixed with a smidge of outrage. "I don't appreciate Margo saying it was, either."

"Duly noted," he said and continued to watch her. "Whoever sent this to Sophia might have been the one who sent you the photo of Layla. Janessa thinks it could be someone stirring up trouble. Maybe because of Abe's will."

"That has nothing to do with me," she insisted. "Neither does his will. You said you thought the person who sent Layla's picture did it as a sick prank."

Brody nodded. "I still think that. I also believe it might be connected with Sophia. Maybe someone who wants to take a jab at Janessa and me by sending pictures like these to our mothers."

She touched her fingers to her mouth. "Are you talking about that young man who came to the ranch? The boyfriend of the girl who's staying with Janessa?"

"Ex-boyfriend," he corrected. "That's the one." And now he needed to do something to soothe the worry on her face. "I don't believe he'd do anything to harm you."

"But Rowan—"

"I don't think he'd try anything with Rowan, either. But I've already talked to him and told him to be on watch. You should be, too."

"I will," she assured him. "In fact, I'll ask Rowan to go to the party with me."

"Where is he?" Brody asked.

"In town with friends. They're eating at O'Riley's, but I can stop by there on the way to the party and pick him up."

Brody was about 100 percent sure that Rowan would rather hang with friends than attend a party with his mother, but his kid brother knew the score. Rowan would see that Darcia was worried, and he'd do whatever it took to make her feel safe. Even if he believed there was no reason whatsoever for her safety concerns.

He kissed his mother's cheek, said goodbye and went back to his truck. Unlike his mother, he had no plans to change into anything dressy or fancy. He'd put on clean jeans and a shirt and made sure there wasn't any horse shit on his boots. Oh, and he'd combed his hair with his hand after he'd showered. That was about as good as it was going to get.

When he got to the ranch house, he found his "escorts" waiting for him in the foyer. Margo had definitely gone the fancy route and was wearing a sapphire blue cocktail dress with matching neck-breaker heels. Sophia had opted for a little black dress. Teagan, a white maternity top and pants. But Janessa had apparently decided to see if his tongue could land on the floor because she had on a body-skimming red dress that made him take notice of her curves.

Her wicked little smile told him she knew exactly what she'd done.

And what he had done right back to her.

She took a breath through her mouth when her gaze skimmed down his body and back up again. That gaze-skimming certainly seemed like multiple carnal invitations. Ones that at best would have to wait. At worst, they might be invitations he should wisely pass up. Of course, nothing about him was feeling wise at the moment.

A ranch hand brought around one of the SUVs, and after they'd gotten on their coats, they started out of the house toward it. Janessa stayed back, though, keeping pace next to him.

"My mother said it wasn't her in the photo," Brody volunteered since he knew she'd want to know.

"She was positive?" But she waved that off. "Do you believe she was positive?" Janessa amended.

Brody jumped straight between a rock and a hard place. No, he wasn't at all sure he believed Darcia, but it seemed like backstabbing his mother to admit that to Janessa.

"I don't know," he settled for saying.

She didn't scowl or sneer over his holding back. Janessa simply nodded. "Sophia wants to have the photo analyzed by one of the computer geeks who works on some of her cases."

"Why would your mother care after all this time?" Brody asked.

Janessa sighed. "Because that's just the way she is. Someone has taken a jab at her. A jab that's brought back some bad memories, and she wants to get to the bottom of it. If her computer geeks get an ID, the truth will come out."

Yeah, and he'd deal with it if and when it turned out to be his mother. "I just don't know why she'd lie," he admitted. "I mean, no one knows exactly when the photo was taken so it could have been done when Abe and she were still together."

But the moment he spelled it all out, Brody thought of a reason for a possible lie. If that snuggle and neck kiss caught on camera happened when Abe was married to Sophia, then Darcia might believe a good fibbing was in order rather than confess something like that to her son.

So, they were back at square one.

As the women got into the SUV, they all agreed that he should drive and that Teagan should sit up front with him so that she wouldn't have to climb into the back seat. The girl was nervous, and Brody noticed her glancing at their surroundings as he drove away from the ranch. He silently cursed Riggs for putting her through this, and if Riggs was behind the mystery photos, then Brody would do more than curse. He'd hunt him down and have a little chat with him about being an asshole.

Since the party guests living in town had likely gone on

foot to the party, that left room in the parking lot for the SUV so Teagan didn't have to walk far to reach the shop.

Once Upon a Time was a good fit for its name since it was one of the first Victorian homes built in Last Ride, and it'd kept most of its original exterior. Along with taking up a third of the block, it had porches, lattices, towers and even a gargoyle.

The wide front window featured a Victorian Christmas display, complete with old editions of Charles Dickens's books. It definitely wasn't a place that Brody frequented, but he'd been here once or twice with Darcia.

Millie's shop assistant, Monte Klein, greeted them at the door, and he was dressed in party mode with his Santa's helper outfit. He took their coats, stacking them on a table behind him. "The new art display will be unveiled in about a half hour so feel free to follow the signs and mingle."

The signs were on easels just inside the entrance. The one to the left said G-rated, For All Ages. The sign with an arrow pointed straight ahead said PG-13. The one on the right said, Adults Only—Prepare to Blush.

Millie hadn't limited the holiday decorations to just the display window. Nope. There were lit-up trees tucked in every available space and tiny lights were scattered everywhere. It was a reminder that it was something Abe normally did at Colts Creek. For a man who didn't seem to care much for others, Abe had definitely enjoyed decking the halls.

"FYI," Monte added to Sophia, "Curt Dayton's already here, and he went that way." He tipped his head to the PG-13 area. "He might have been influenced by the promise of O'Riley's sliders and nachos, but he said I was to let you know where he was."

Sophia hooked her arm through Teagan's. "Well, why

don't we go that way, too? A blush won't look good with the shade of lipstick I'm wearing so we'll avoid the Adults Only." She led her in the direction of the PG-13 section, and Curt.

"A second FYI," Monte went on, talking to Brody now, "your mom and brother went that way." He motioned to the G-rated section. "Not sure it was much of a lure for Rowan, but there are Christmas cookies to die for and hot chocolate so it won't be a total bust for him."

The food would surely appeal to his brother, but since Rowan was fifteen, he probably would have preferred the PG-13 area. Or the Prepare to Blush if no one would have objected to him going in there. Brody made a mental note to have another chat with Darcia about treating Rowan like a teenager and not a toddler.

"Well, I'm going there," Margo insisted. She apparently wasn't worried about color-clashing issues because she went straight into the Prepare to Blush.

"My advice," Monte whispered to Janessa and him. "Go for the blush. Along with having some yummy party food, Millie's got a serious stash of sexy antique stuff that she had us put out for this shindig."

Brody tried to wrap his mind around that. Millie was as wholesome looking as wholesome got, and she hardly seemed the sexy antique type. Then again, he'd heard some stories about her wild grandmother so maybe this was something that'd been handed down to her.

Apparently, Janessa was all for the blush because she took hold of Brody's arm to get him moving in that direction. "I've never seen sexy antique stuff," she said to explain her choice.

Brody blamed it on his guy genes, but he didn't have to be convinced to go in any area where sex was involved.

Even if it was stupid to go into such areas with Janessa along. Then again, he thought about sex with her even when she wasn't in a room that would stir up such things.

They stepped in through the opening created by display shelves. There were more Christmas decorations and lights here, but Brody immediately saw a table with some sheets of paper. The sign sitting on top of the paper said, Take One, and When You Finish, Collect Your Prize. An arrow pointed to some small gold-foil-wrapped gift boxes on the table. Your Prize was on a label lying next to them.

When Brody complied and took one of the papers, he realized it was a scavenger hunt. They were to look through the fifteen hundred or so square feet of wall-to-wall "stuff" and find the items on the list.

Not alone, either.

There were at least a dozen other people, including Margo. Judging from the way she was walking around with her gaze volleying between the paper and the displays, she was already on her own scavenger hunt.

"The first thing we have to find is a dirty cocktail," Janessa said, leaning in to read the paper.

Since Brody had already noticed the small bar in the corner, that's where they headed. Millie's other shop assistant, Haylee Rickert, was obviously playing bartender. Or something similar anyway. She was dressed like Santa's elf but had added some jewelry and a headband that seemed more suited for the 1960s.

"What will it be?" Haylee asked. "Pink Panty Dropper, Slippery Nipple or a Super Stud of Many Inches beer?" She offered those without so much as a blush or a smirk.

Brody wasn't sure he wanted any of them. Or to say them aloud. So when Janessa ordered a beer, he held up two fingers to let Haylee know he wanted one, as well.

Haylee retrieved the longneck bottles from an ice-filled barrel, wrapped napkins around them and passed them to Janessa and him.

"Since this is sort of our first date, sort of," Janessa emphasized, "I didn't figure our relationship was at the Slippery Nipple or Panty Dropper stage." She opened her beer, dropped the cap into an antique bowl on the bar and smiled around the sip she took of the brew.

"But you're okay with the Super Stud of Many Inches?" Brody asked before he thought his question all the way through.

He really should have given it some thought.

"Walked right into that one, didn't you?" she said, giving him a playful jab with her elbow.

But there wasn't much playfulness in that look in her eyes. There was lust. Oh, yeah. He had no trouble recognizing it, and since looks could lead to kissing, Brody decided it was best to look at the next item of their scavenger hunt.

"Find and take a picture of a naughty cowboy," he read aloud. "Well, there's no way we can get lusty thoughts when searching for that," he added with more than eight inches of sarcasm.

Janessa laughed, and mercy, was it good to hear. She'd laughed plenty when they were teenagers, but there hadn't been much of a reason for it in these three and a half weeks since she'd been here.

Stepping away from the bar, they headed into the maze of displays, some on tables, others on shelves, easels and even the wall. Obviously, someone had spent a lot of time putting this all together. There were semi-nudes on old postcards, a hand-crank spanking machine, corsets with holes for the nipples to peek out and some weird devices labeled as Self-Pleasurers that looked like kitchen utensils.

Some of the items had tiny price tags on them, a reminder that this was Millie's business. A successful one from all he'd heard. But most of the items in this area were labeled as Private Display, Not for Sale. Brody could see why. Last Ride wasn't exactly a thriving market for Smutty R Us paraphernalia. Not in public anyway. But he was betting Millie would get plenty of takers if a buyer's identity was guaranteed to remain anonymous.

"I was in the market for one of these," Janessa joked when they stopped to study, well, whatever the hell it was.

It looked like a cross between a spinning wheel, a lady's black lace glove and a bicycle. The label on this one said "It's a Victorian Cure for Hysteria. As for how it manages to do that, your guess is as good as ours."

"Have you found a Peeing Peeping Tom?" Margo asked when she spotted them. She hurried in their direction. "Or a hand-crank air blower for personal areas?"

Brody frowned. "Are you making that up?"

"No," Margo assured him. "It's right here." She tapped her paper. "Have you found them?

He shook his head. "Haven't seen either of those things, and they're not on our list. We're looking for a naughty cowboy."

Margo snickered. "There's a mirror over there. Go and take a look, and I'm betting you'll see plenty of naughty." She fluttered her fingers to her right, and she was still snickering when she hurried off in another direction.

"Funny," he grumbled under his breath.

Brody didn't especially want to see his own reflection, which was what he thought Margo had meant. However, as Janessa and he got closer to the tall stand-alone mirror, he saw the engraved Texas flag at the top. He also saw the two dozen or so men and women who had been carved into the wood frame. They were naked except for the men's cowboy hats. While the couples weren't actually having sex, or even kissing for that matter, there was enough touching, fondling and clothing removal going on to land them in the naughty category.

"Well, they're certainly agile," Janessa remarked. Setting down her beer, she took a photo with her phone. She put the phone back in the purse that she had hooked over her shoulder and then ran her finger over one of the men's butt cheeks. "But he's not anywhere near worthy of Super Stud of Many Inches status."

Maybe it was the sexually charged vibe in the air, but it felt as if she'd touched his own butt cheek—and that unlike the carved guy, she might actually consider him Super Stud worthy.

"We only have one more thing on the list," he said, hoping to get his mind back on the game. Not that he especially wanted to play the game, but it was better than standing there and watching Janessa touch carved naked people. "Get a photo of a hot summer kiss," Brody read from the paper.

Of course, there was no mention if it was a statue, birdbath, mirror or a weird spinning wheel cure for hysteria. After Janessa picked up her beer, they started strolling again while they continued to look around. They passed by the table of party food, which did indeed look good, and just a few feet away he spotted what appeared to be a small birdbath.

"Ah, it's Margo's Peeing Peeping Tom," Janessa said.

It was the figurine of a peeing man, who was also peeping up the long billowing skirt of a woman on the perch above him. The little card next to it identified it as an Edwardian conversation garden piece. Obviously, someone had thought this was worthy of being made. And preserved.

They went past a display of feather whips, masks and other pieces that had likely belonged in some early version of a red room. Janessa stopped a moment to linger over a display of antique jewelry and memorabilia. There was an etched Cupid on a bracelet, lovebirds on a necklace and tiny dangling heart earrings with pearls inside. An antique brass compass with a turquoise-studded arrow had been positioned to point at the lovebirds.

It was all interesting enough, but there wasn't a kiss in sight. When they reached the end of the displays, Brody figured they would either just have to give up or start back through again.

Then he saw it.

A framed photograph no bigger than his hand. It was hanging on the wall, surrounded by much larger ones. Ones of provocatively clothed people in various poses. But the couple in the photo were fully clothed. They were standing in the dark beneath a tree and were locked in a heated kiss while fireworks lit up overhead.

"It's us," Janessa blurted out.

Brody had just brought his beer to his mouth for another sip, but he stopped. Leaned in. And he cursed. Because it sure as hell was them. Crap, what was it doing there on display?

"Dewayne took it," she added in a mumble. Janessa pointed to the label beneath the photo that ID'd the photo as Hot Summer Kiss and Dewayne as the photographer. The label also said more of his photos were on display at the new local artists' exhibit in the shop.

Great. Brody only hoped the "more" didn't include Janessa and him. He especially didn't appreciate Dewayne doing this without so much as mentioning it. Or asking their permission. If Dewayne had said something about it at the holiday gala when he'd given them the other photo, then Brody would have told him no way in hell did he want their picture on display.

"Might as well finish the game." Janessa handed him her beer so she could snap a picture of the photo with her phone. "Maybe no one else will see it." Looking up at him, she smiled a little. "I suppose we should be flattered that Dewayne considered us art quality subjects."

There was that. And Dewayne had gotten the title right, too. It was indeed a hot kiss. Hotter than any of the antiques and other pieces they'd seen in this part of the shop. Then again, maybe he felt that way because he remembered that kiss in perfect detail. Hell, he remembered lots of kisses with Janessa.

"We're going to have to do something about this," he heard himself say.

Janessa didn't lift an eyebrow, didn't question what he meant, but she did remind him of something very important. "I want to do something about it," she said. "But I'm here for only two more months and one week."

Yeah, there was that. For a man who didn't go looking for temporary, it was an in-his-face reminder that two months and one week qualified as a textbook definition of *temporary*.

She looked up at him. "Want to go on another date?" Janessa asked.

Brody answered that by pulling her to him and kissing that smiling mouth. If he was going to make a mistake, he might as well go all in. *Temporary* was going to get a whole lot hotter.

CHAPTER FOURTEEN

"UH, WHAT IS IT?" Teagan asked as she stood back and studied the present she'd just opened.

Janessa had been going through her emails on her phone while she hung out with Teagan, but she stopped and studied it, too. She had a moment of déjà vu from the scavenger hunt at Millie's party three days earlier. Not because there was anything about the gift that was blushing material but because she didn't have a clue what it was. It looked like a jumbled heap of various colored wood.

"This was for your first Christmas," Teagan said, reading the tag. "It says to pull the lever."

Janessa went closer, looking for a lever, and found a strap of sorts at the bottom. When she pulled it, the jumble started to expand. She kept pulling, it kept expanding, and when she was done, the jumble became like a pop-up version of the grounds of the ranch with the large barn in the center. There were even some wooden horses and cowboys, all grounded into their popped-up place so they couldn't even be moved.

This one was much larger than the dollhouse and spread out in a good five-foot square. Like the dollhouse, though, it was in no way an appropriate gift for a baby. It was simply something to look at if you were so inclined to look at a replica instead of going outside or to the window and seeing the real deal.

That reminded her of Millie's party, too.

Or more specifically, a reminder of Brody. The photo of them had been a nicely captured image, but it was nothing compared to the man himself. Which brought on yet another reminder. A man she hoped she'd be seeing soon so they could see where more kissing would take them.

It was a risk, of course, because her remaining two months and a couple of days were dwindling away, but Janessa was positive she didn't want to leave Last Ride until she'd had a chance to have more of those nicely captured images with Brody. Now, they just needed to figure out the time for it. Between her work schedule and his business trips, they'd only managed some texts and a few short conversations.

No kissing involved.

"Your dad sure liked to flex," Teagan remarked, and then she flushed a little, probably because she thought flex or showing off was an insult. In Abe's case, it was the truth.

"Yes," Janessa agreed. "Everything I've found in my research about him so far says he was indeed *flex*. But I have to believe he wasn't always that way or he never would have attracted Darcia, my mother or Margo."

"Rowan said something about his mom and Abe hooking up way back when," Teagan commented.

Janessa turned from the gift to her. "Rowan talked about that?"

Teagan shrugged. "He just mentioned it, that's all, when we were looking at his mom's pottery pieces at the party."

Janessa remembered that Teagan and Rowan had been standing together during the unveiling. Darcia had noticed as well, and she'd given Janessa a little of the stink eye, maybe because she thought her son shouldn't be talking to a pregnant teenager. She could understand Darcia's concern to a point, but Janessa doubted that being around Teagan would cause Rowan to go out and knock up some girl.

"His mom's pottery was pretty," Teagan went on, rubbing her back and stretching.

Janessa made a sound of agreement. Darcia clearly had talent and hers were definitely some of the best pieces in the new exhibit.

"His mom's also sort of protective of him," Teagan added a moment later, and her inflection made it sound as if it were an opening to something else she had to say. But whatever it was, she didn't spill it.

"Is something wrong?" Janessa came out and asked. "Did Rowan's mother say something to you?"

Teagan's eyes widened. "No, nothing like that." She shook her head and turned her attention back to the ranch that was now side by side with the dollhouse. "It's just it made me think about this baby, that's all." She moved her rubbing hands to her stomach.

Janessa walked closer, moving so she could see the girl's eyes. "Teagan, are you having second thoughts about going through with the adoption?"

"No." She said it fast and with no hesitation. "I'm not going to change my mind. I swear I'm not. I was just thinking about what kind of mom Char will be."

Her sister, Air Force Sergeant Charlotte Talley.

"From everything I researched and learned about Char, she'll make a great mother," Janessa said.

That wasn't lip service, either. Janessa had had several long conversations with her, and Char had convinced her that she and her husband wanted children that they so far hadn't been able to have. Char was twenty-eight and had been married for five years, and the marriage seemed rock-solid.

Teagan nodded. "You're right, and she's so excited about the baby. She wishes she could be here for the birth, but I told her you'd be there so it's okay."

Janessa certainly hadn't forgotten that Teagan wanted her in the delivery room. A first for her. And that first wouldn't be long now at all. At Teagan's last appointment, the doctor had told her that she was about thirty-six weeks. So, only one more month to go if the baby arrived on time.

"Remember, I don't want to see the baby," Teagan went on. "I don't feel as if she's mine, and I don't want to start feeling that way."

"I understand." Though it did tug at Janessa's heart. It was such a grown-up thing to do for someone who barely qualified as a grown-up. "But you'll probably see the baby at some point, when you visit your sister," Janessa reminded her.

Teagan gave another nod. "I won't visit for a while. Not until the child is older, like two or three. Then, I won't see him or her as the baby I gave birth to. He or she will be Char's and her husband's son or daughter."

Again, that was adult logic, and while Janessa didn't think Teagan would change her mind, those visits wouldn't be easy.

They turned at the sound behind them, and Janessa's heart did a different kind of tug when she saw Brody standing there.

"Sorry I'm interrupting," he said, and she thought from his expression that he was uncomfortable at overhearing their conversation.

Janessa had to stop herself from running to him and kissing him. She'd do that later, she decided.

"You're not," Teagan assured him. "I just opened another of the presents Janessa's father got for her."

"This one was for my first Christmas," Janessa supplied. "I would have been only a couple of months old."

Brody walked closer, stared at it and frowned. "Well, it's big." That was possibly the only compliment he could come up with.

Teagan checked the time on her phone. "I told Miss Velma Sue I'd help her pick out which china and silverware to use for tomorrow's Thanksgiving dinner, but I've got about an hour before that. I can do some more research on your father if you'd like."

"Sure. Thanks. You got the copy of the stories my mother gave me?"

Teagan nodded. "There's not a lot of detail in them. Just dates and places. But I can add it to the other newspaper articles I found."

"Articles?" Brody asked.

"Nothing personal, not really," Teagan explained. "Just events like the Cattleman's Ball he attended. There are some stories, too, about his wedding to Janessa's mom and Miss Margo. I like writing reports so I don't mind putting it all together."

And Janessa was thankful for that since it was somewhat depressing uncovering Abe's layers.

"I met Miss Alma Parkman at the party, and she gave me her number so I could call her," Teagan added as she walked to the door. "She said she had a few stories about Abe I could use."

Since Alma was in her eighties, she likely would have a tale or two. Maybe even info about Abe as a child. Alma was president of the Last Ride Society so obviously she was interested in preserving the town's history. That would include Abe's, hopefully. Janessa thought she might get in touch with the woman, as well.

"I haven't seen you much since the party," Janessa said, and she leaned in to brush her mouth over his. She got a nice hit of heat for such a quick touch.

"Always lots to do around here during the holidays. Happy Thanksgiving Eve," he tacked onto that.

"Happy Thanksgiving Eve to you." She gave him another quick kiss. "Velma Sue and the kitchen help are already in full prep mode. You're sure you won't join us?" But she knew the answer before he even spoke.

Brody shook his head. "My mom does a big dinner, and she'll expect me there."

Of course, she would. Sophia wasn't into cooking so Thanksgiving had never been a huge deal when she'd been growing up, but she suspected it had been for Darcia. Family was important to the woman.

"I brought some things from Abe's office to yours this morning, but you weren't in," she remarked.

"I've been driving out to look at other ranches and properties for sale around the area," he answered.

That stopped her from taking another kiss hit. "For sale?" She was ready to tack on a whole bunch of questions and comments about that, but he continued before she could say anything else.

"I want to run my own ranch." His tone was almost matter-of-fact. However, she could see the concern in his eyes. Not concern for himself, though. But for her reaction.

"You can run this ranch, just as you've done for years," Janessa quickly pointed out.

"I'll repeat what I overheard Teagan say about her baby. I don't want to feel as if this place is mine because it isn't."

Janessa was just as fast with a comeback to that. "But it will be. If it's anywhere in my power, I'll give you the ranch."

He calmly took her by the shoulders and looked into her eyes. "No, you won't. If Abe had wanted me to have it, then he would have left it to me. He didn't. The ranch is yours, and you can decide what to do with it. You just can't decide to give it to me."

No fast comeback this time. Stunned, she stood there and stared at him. "Your home is here."

"My *house* is here," he corrected. "I own it outright so I'll sell it and use the money as a down payment on a place with more acreage. Margo has said she'd be interested in buying just an acre of my land and having her house moved there. That way, it won't matter if someone else takes over the ranch."

"You talked to Margo about this," she muttered. Janessa heard her own voice and decided she sounded as shell-shocked as she felt.

"I did. I've talked to a lot of people," he continued. "The ranch next to Joe McCann's is a strong possibility. The owner's getting on in years, and he's put out the word that he might be interested in selling."

Obviously, he'd given this a lot of thought, along with a lot of talk, and here she hadn't had a clue. Obviously, the gossip mill was falling down on the job if word of any of this hadn't gotten back to her.

"One of the big reasons I stayed in Last Ride was so you and a lot of other people wouldn't get screwed over with Abe's will," Janessa said.

"I know." On a sigh, he gave her a quick kiss. "And thank you for that. But I'm giving you an out. Don't stay for me because no matter what happens, I'll be moving. If you decide to stay for other reasons, like Margo and the people who work here, then I can help you find another ranch manager, one who'd be amenable to keeping on the present crew. I might even be able to convince my top hand, Clayton Erle, to take over."

She took a moment to let that sink in. Then another. It turned out she needed a lot of extra moments. "What brought this on?" she asked.

"You," he said without hesitation. "And all this foreplay we've been playing around with."

Janessa shook her head. "I don't understand."

Brody looked her straight in the eyes. "Don't be insulted by this, but I don't want you to kill time with me just because you feel you have to be here to save my ass. You can go, and it'll all work out fine." He paused, muttered some profanity. "And if you stay, it might work out fine, too. I just want to take Abe and saving my ass out of this particular equation."

Janessa knew this wasn't a light moment, far from it, but she said the first thing that popped into her head. "It's impossible to leave your ass out of any equation, Brody. Some things are just too noticeable to ignore."

The corner of his mouth turned up just a little. "I could say the same for yours."

"Oh?" She smiled despite her mind whirling with the news of Brody not staying on at Colts Creek. Later, she'd sit down and give that some thought.

"Oh," he verified, and he moved in for what would no doubt be a very satisfying kiss. At least it no doubt would have been had her phone not rang.

"So help me, if Alisha's used her curling iron to cook something else, I'm having Kyle confiscate the damn thing," she muttered.

But it wasn't Kyle's name on the screen. It was a local number. Since she doubted this would be a routine call on Thanksgiving, she answered it right away.

"Janessa Parkman?" the caller asked. "I'm Dr. Marshall Dayton," he continued once she'd verified that. "I was your father's doctor."

"Oh," she muttered, and this time there was nothing remotely light or sexual about it. "I'd left a message with your nurse yesterday, asking if there was anything in my father's medical records you could go over with me."

"Yes, I got the message, and I'm sorry I'm just now getting back to you. And yes, there are some things I can tell you. During your father's visit to my clinic, which was about a week before he died, he added you as a designated personal representative to his medical records. That gives you access to anything in his files."

Abe hadn't said anything about that in his letter, and it made her wonder why he'd done it. Or why he hadn't added Brody.

"Another reason I'm calling is to let you know that I just got Abe's autopsy results," the doctor added. "The county coroner is a friend of mine, and he thought the news would be better coming from me."

That didn't help the knot that'd formed in her stomach. Janessa just stayed quiet and waited for him to continue. However, she tried to steel herself up in case the doctor was about to tell her that Abe had been poisoned or had passed away after a secret, painful illness.

"Abe died from an aneurysm that ruptured in his brain," Dr. Dayton explained, and he probably heard the loud breath of relief. "I can give you a more detailed explanation if you want."

Even though Abe had been dead for weeks, this brought on a sudden wave of grief. He might have been a horrible man, but he was still her father.

"No," Janessa said, "but can you tell me if he was in

pain?" Because something had caused him to send her that letter.

"He'd been having headaches," the doctor said after a long pause. "About a week before he died, he showed up at my office and asked for a script for pain meds. That's when he made you his designated representative. At that time, I gave him a small supply of meds with the agreement that he schedule an exam. He balked about that and finally came in the day before he died. I ran a lot of tests but didn't have the results yet when I got the call that he'd passed away."

Janessa had to squeeze her eyes shut a moment, and she felt Brody put his hand on her arm. She hadn't put the call on Speaker, but obviously he'd heard enough to know what she was feeling.

"Around the time he came in for that exam, he wrote me a letter, and he said he was dying," Janessa explained to the doctor. "Had you told him that he might have an aneurysm?"

"Yes, I did tell him that was a possibility, along with a stroke or an infection. That's why I wanted the tests. But even if I'd had the results back, it likely wouldn't have helped. Once this type of aneurysm ruptures, there's nothing we can do. He could have been in the hospital, and the result would have been the same."

Janessa had to swallow hard before she could ask her next question. "Do you think he suffered when he died?"

"It would have been fast," the doctor assured her.

Maybe a lie. The kind of lies medical professionals told to spare the family. Janessa realized she wanted to be spared. She didn't want to think of Abe suffering.

"I think Abe might have sensed he was dying," Dr. Dayton went on. "He said something about trying to make things right, and during the exam, he got a call. Which he took. Since I was standing right there, I heard bits and pieces of the conversation. From what I gathered, the caller was a private investigator, and he was looking into some things that'd happened in Abe's past. Did Abe mention anything like that in the letter he sent you?"

"No," Janessa said, looking up at Brody to see if he knew anything about it. But he only shook his head. "No," she repeated to Dr. Dayton. "Do you happen to remember the PI's name?"

"Sorry, but I don't. I just recall Abe saying, not in a pleasant kind of way either, that the person was supposed to be one of the best PIs in the business so he should do his damn job."

So, Abe hadn't been pleased with this PI. Or heck, maybe Abe talked like that to most people. Janessa thanked the doctor, asked him to call her if he thought of anything else, and when she ended the call, she turned to Brody.

"Abe never told me anything about hiring a PI," Brody said before she could ask. "It's possible, though, that he wanted a background check on an owner of a business or some land he was interested in buying." He paused. "But I don't recall him ever doing anything like that."

It was the timing of the PI that worried Janessa. "All of this happened around the same time he wrote me that letter, and I still don't know what he wanted to tell me or what he believed I could fix."

Brody made a sound of agreement. "Well, if he hired a PI, then he would have had to pay him. That should be in his personal financial records on his computer. He didn't pay for him through any of the ranch accounts. If he had, I would have seen it since I handle all of those."

Janessa followed him when Brody headed down the hall to his office. He snagged the laptop and charger cord from the floor and carried them to his desk. The moment he had the computer plugged in, he booted it up.

"Please tell me you know his password," Janessa commented.

"There won't be one to get into the computer itself, and the password for his bank will be saved on the site. At least that's what Abe told me in case I ever needed to get into his account."

That was a reminder of how much Abe had trusted Brody, which made all of this so puzzling. He hadn't told Brody about the will, the letter to her and now the PI.

Brody sat in his chair, navigated to the bank website and logged in. Just as Abe had said, the password was indeed there. "I'll start with his credit cards," Brody explained, "but it's possible he wrote the guy a check. If so, we can go through the bank statements."

Janessa stood over his shoulder and looked at the credit card info that Brody accessed. Of course, there were no charges since his death, and Asher had put a freeze on it to make sure no one tried to use it. But it was obvious that Abe preferred plastic over checks, and he spent a lot of money on restaurants, clothes and travel.

It didn't take Brody long though to zoom in on the payment to Barton Investigations. The five-thousand-dollar charge, which was possibly a retainer, had been made about two weeks before Abe's death. There didn't appear to be any other payments before that.

"Barton Investigations," Brody repeated, switching to a search engine so he could pull up info. "Solid reviews," he muttered, glancing at that first before he went to the actual web page.

"Victor Barton is the owner," Janessa read. There were

several other PIs listed, but she figured Abe would have gone for the boss, not one of his employees.

She used her phone to call the number on the site, and she was surprised when someone answered. She'd thought that maybe the office would be closed since it was the day before Thanksgiving.

"Barton Investigations," a woman greeted. "I'm Olivia Martinez, office manager. How may I help you?"

"I need to speak to Victor Barton."

"I'm sorry, but he's on vacation for a week," the woman responded. "I can take a message, and he'll get back to you as soon as he can, or you can speak to one of our other investigators."

Janessa had a quick debate as to how to handle this. "I'm Janessa Parkman, and my father, Abe Parkman, recently passed away. I was going through some of his things and found that he'd hired Mr. Barton. Could you please tell me what Mr. Barton was investigating for my father?"

There was a short silence on the other end of the line. "I'm sorry, I can't give you that information. You can bring in the death certificate, along with proof that you're Mr. Parkman's next of kin, and then we can make copies of our files."

According to what she'd last heard from Asher, she wouldn't get the death certificate for another month or so. Janessa didn't want to wait a month or for the PI to return from vacation. She had a gut feeling that the PI could answer a whole lot of their questions.

So Janessa pushed with a lie. "My father thought that someone might be trying to harm him. And me," she added to make this sound more urgent. "Please help me. I need to know if I'm in danger."

There was another short silence, followed by a sigh. "Let me access the file and see what's there."

Janessa didn't exactly hold her breath, but she was certain she wasn't taking in as much air as she should. She assured herself if this failed, then she could go the other route and find the info in a month or two. It was also possible that this had nothing to do with Abe's personal life and was merely, as Brody had suggested, part of a business deal.

"I've just pulled up the file," the office manager said several long moments later, "and it does say that your father felt there was some kind of threat."

Oh, mercy. Apparently, her gut feeling had been right.

"I can't go into the details of the investigation," the woman continued, "because Mr. Barton hasn't included the info, but I can see from the billable hours that he did at least some of the background work that your father had wanted."

"What kind of background work?" Janessa asked.

"Financials, interviews, that sort of thing. According to the initial contract, your father had received some disturbing photos. It doesn't say what those photos were, but he almost certainly gave Mr. Barton copies."

Photos. That seemed to be going around, what with the one of Layla that someone had sent to Darcia and the one that Sophia had gotten of Abe with the mystery woman.

"Mr. Parkman requested any and all information on two people. Father and son," the office manager clarified. "And because there might be a threat, I'll tell you that their names are Jimmy and Brody Harrell."

CHAPTER FIFTEEN

BRODY SAT ON his porch, sipping a Lone Star while he watched the setting sunlight glint off the pond. The view was just about as perfect as perfect could get, and he considered finishing his beer in the hammock that he'd strung up between two oaks by the pond. It wasn't exactly toasty warm with the temps in the high forties, but he had a firepit. Plus, it'd be worth the chill just to sit there and let himself level out.

He'd had plenty of evenings just like this, and he'd never taken a single one of them for granted. Having his own place had always meant something to him. He didn't take it for granted now, either, but he knew he wouldn't have many more nights like this one.

He refused to feel bitter about that. He'd known the risks of building his place on what had once been part of the ranch. With the ranch literally surrounding him, there was no way for him to expand, especially since Abe had made it clear he didn't want to sell any more of the adjoining land. But Brody had gone through with buying the five acres and building on it because he'd loved this particular spot. However, he'd always known that if Abe and he ever had a falling out, then he might have to leave.

Well, the falling out had apparently happened.

Of course, Brody had been completely unaware of it, not until four days ago—the day before Thanksgiving—when he'd learned that Abe had hired that PI to look for *any and all information* on him and his father. That certainly explained why Abe had basically cut him out of the will, but what Brody couldn't figure out was why Abe had started to distrust him in the first place.

Abe had gotten some *disturbing photos* the office manager had explained to Janessa. Abe hadn't mentioned that, either, but Brody had to wonder if it was connected to Layla's death. The same person who sent a photo to Darcia could have also sent one to Abe. But why would Abe have believed he'd have any part in that? Yeah, Abe had lent Layla the car, but the blame for her being behind the wheel that night was on Brody's shoulders.

Where it weighed him down like a mountain of boulders. Always would.

The memories came. They always did. Of that sweltering summer night. Of the storm that had come raging through.

Of his sister's death.

A couple of weeks after the funeral, Abe had apologized for lending her the car, but he hadn't dwelled on it. Or rather he hadn't seemed to do that, but maybe there'd been enough kernels of guilt for Abe to believe all these years later that Brody blamed him. Brody didn't.

But it was possible that Jimmy had.

Equally possible that Abe had believed Brody knew something about Jimmy's involvement and considered that whole falsehood of blood being thicker than water. It wasn't. Brody had no father–son feelings left for Jimmy, but he had had some of that for Abe. In hindsight, Abe hadn't felt any of that for him.

Yeah, it was time to move on.

That confirmation came at the exact same moment he spotted the headlights of the car coming toward the house.

It was dark now, but he could make out enough of the vehicle to know it was Janessa. That brought on a new wave of memories. Not bad ones. But complicated ones. They had definitely been doing the foreplay dance around each other, and it was probably time to dive in or nip it in the bud.

Janessa parked, stepped from the car, and after one glance, Brody knew there'd be no nipping. Nope, this was a dive-in sort of thing that was already in motion.

"Are you up for some company?" she asked in a silky siren's voice.

All right, maybe the voice was his imagination, but that smile was definitely an invitation for them to pick up where they'd left off four days ago. Those kisses hadn't been of the long steamy variety, but they'd had plenty of potential.

"I'm up for it," he assured her. Of course, he could have worded that so it didn't sound dirty, but he had the feeling she'd come here for dirty.

Janessa was wearing jeans with a sweater and coat, and she didn't limp when she made her way onto the porch. That was good because it meant that broken toe was finally healing.

"Margo and Velma Sue are at the house with Teagan," she said, taking his beer and having a sip. "Margo's new boyfriend is there, too."

Deputy Ollie Bellows. Brody had definitely heard the gossip about that. "Ollie's a good guy," he assured her.

"He seems it. Margo said he's moving a little slow with her, though."

Slow for Margo meant Ollie hadn't groped her and hauled her off to bed on their first date. Ollie would either end up frustrating Margo or else he'd get the woman to slow down and enjoy the ride.

"Nothing back from the PI yet," Janessa continued. The

breeze stirred her hair. "I called his office again, and the office manager said he was at his hunting cabin in Montana and that he didn't answer his phone while he was there."

Brody wasn't planning on sitting on pins and needles for the guy to call back. Especially since it likely wouldn't be good news. Brody certainly couldn't think of a good reason why Abe would have wanted him investigated.

"Have you been avoiding me again?" she came out and asked—after she gave him an instant hard-on by leaning down and brushing her mouth over his.

He shook his head. "No. Work. I was tied up."

She smiled again. "Now, that's an interesting image to have in my head."

He'd had enough of the playful teasing so Brody merely caught onto her waist and pulled her down to him. Her butt landed on his lap. Not a bad place for her to be at all. She touched her mouth to his again. Pulled back and smiled. He hadn't turned on the porch light, but the moon made it pretty easy for him to see her face.

"You seemed…settled or something," she said. So, obviously she had no trouble seeing him, either.

"That's one word for it." A good word, too, for the peace he'd found over selling this place and moving on.

Moving on from Abe, as well.

Brody refused to believe the last decade and a half of his life had been wasted. Just the opposite. He'd learned a lot running Abe's ranch, and he'd put that experience to good use on his next place.

"You seem…unconflicted," he settled for saying.

She laughed. "I have two months left here, and I want to spend some of that with you. I hate that you won't be running this ranch, hate what Abe did to you, but I decided I could keep dwelling on that or come over here and see if you're…unconflicted, too."

Brody didn't answer her. Not with words anyway. Setting his beer down on the porch, he kissed her. It wasn't a touch or a brush, either. He kissed her the way he'd been thinking about kissing her for the entire month she'd been back in Last Ride. Nothing unconflicted about this.

Well, not about the heat anyway.

It was there and felt ready to blaze right out of control. He decided to take Janessa's approach and not dwell on the possibility that they might end up regretting anything they did here tonight.

She was clearly on the same page with him because she went right with the kiss. Moving into him, making a moan of hungry pleasure when he turned it French. He recalled her teasing him with that whole "French kiss him and see where it'd go." Well, it was going just fine. Then again, her mouth had turned his brain to mush so it was entirely possible that he wasn't even having a sane, logical thought right now.

Brody didn't break the kiss, but he took hold of her, moving her. That, of course, meant there was some very groin-tightening contact going on. Plenty of touching. Sliding. Hitting all the right spots. He savored every one of the moments that it took him to position her so that she was straddling him.

And, man, did that make the "right spots" contact even better.

With the heat firing, he had to touch her. Had to keep kissing her. So, he slid his hand between them and cupped her breast. She did a little hand sliding of her own, and her clever fingers found their way to his chest. Then she shoved up his shirt and put her hands on his bare stomach.

All in all, it was a good way to keep revving up things. And speaking of up and revving, in all the maneuvering on his lap, her sweater had slid up, making it very easy for him to do some more maneuvering. Brody trailed his hand first to her breasts. And then lower, lower, lower into her jeans. So he could touch the front of her white lace panties.

She gasped, moaned, and her eyes practically rolled back in pleasure. "Just how private is your front porch?" she muttered.

"Private," he assured her. But he had no intention of having sex with her in a rocking chair. This was just the foreplay. A very heated round of foreplay, but he intended to take her to his bed to finish what they'd started here.

Hooking both his arms around her, Brody stood so he could begin that trek to his bedroom. Just as her phone rang.

"Crap, crap, crappity, crap," she grumbled. Janessa hooked her legs around his waist, kissed him and then yanked her phone from the pocket of her jeans. She repeated her crap profanity when she saw the name on the screen.

"It's Teagan," she muttered. "I have to take it."

Of course, she did, and Brody's first thought—a bad one—was that Riggs had shown up and was trying to get in the house. That wouldn't be a smart move on his part, what with a deputy inside, but Riggs might not know that.

"Teagan," Janessa said when she answered, "is everything okay?"

"No. You need to come fast," Teagan answered, and Brody set Janessa back on her feet when they heard the fear in her voice. "Fast," she repeated. "I need to get to the hospital. My water broke."

JANESSA NEVER CONSIDERED herself a pacer, but that's what she was doing now. So were Margo and Sophia. Margo and

Deputy Bellows had made the frantic drive to the hospital behind Brody and her after they'd picked up Teagan.

Literally.

The moment they'd gotten to the ranch house, Brody had scooped up the girl, put her in his truck, and they'd taken Teagan to Labor and Delivery. Velma Sue had called Sophia, and since the inn was just up the street, Sophia had beaten them all to the hospital.

Brody wasn't pacing, though. He was leaning against the wall in the small waiting area, his arms folded over his chest and his boots crossed at the ankles. To a casual observer, he might appear to be lounging, but Janessa could see the tight set of his jaw.

"The baby's coming too early," Janessa muttered, not for the first time this evening, either. She'd been saying similar statements since a nurse had wheeled Teagan away to an exam room.

Sophia must have heard her mutterings because she gave a variation of something she'd been saying during that hour. "Both Teagan and the baby will be fine. You'll see." But like Brody's tight jaw, there was tension in her mother's voice.

Janessa prayed Sophia was right, that both would be fine, but the baby was coming a month early, and there could be complications. She silently cursed her decision to let Teagan stay here. Even though the girl had seemed to settle in and even relax some at the ranch, it probably would have been better had she stayed in Dallas so she'd have access to a medical center rather than a small-town hospital.

She paced her way toward Brody, knowing that just being near him would soothe her. It did. Funny how that worked. Right before Teagan's call, he definitely hadn't been soothing. He'd been firing up every part of her body, and they'd been within minutes of having sex. Maybe seconds since she wasn't at all sure they would have actually made it to his bedroom.

There'd be other chances for them to haul each other off to bed. Janessa was sure of that. But for now, she took a different kind of release from him. She went straight into his arms when he reached out for her.

"Teagan hasn't even finished her childbirth classes," Janessa said. "The last one is supposed to be tomorrow night, and they were going to take a tour of Labor and Delivery."

She was well aware she was babbling, and Brody let her while he brushed a kiss on the top of her head.

"I should have gone back there with her," Janessa went on. "I mean, I know Teagan's doctor said for me to wait here until they'd done the tests and gotten her settled, but…"

"Waiting's hard?" Brody filled in for her.

Yes, this was what she needed, and she squeezed her eyes shut and just leaned against him.

"Tell me about the other babies you've fostered." His voice was calm, and some of the tension was gone from his jaw, too. So maybe she was helping him, as well.

"There've been two, both boys." Janessa figured this conversation was meant to help her get her thoughts off what was happening with Teagan, but she didn't mind. "The first one's mother was only fifteen, and while she didn't want to keep the baby, both sets of grandparents were fighting for custody. I kept him only a week before they reached a compromise."

"And the second?" he asked when she paused.

"His mother was at Bright Hope for about a month before she went into labor. She gave birth, and a couple of hours later, she sneaked out of the hospital. She left a note, saying she wanted me to foster the child until he could be adopted. I considered adopting him myself, but Kyle wasn't in a good place back then."

He lifted his eyebrow just a fraction, and while he didn't ask for more info, Janessa just kept on babbling.

"He was clinically depressed and sort of a mess," she explained. Except it wasn't just *sort of*, he had indeed fallen into the *mess* category. "He'd recently lost his cushy high-paying job at his father's real-estate investment firm, which had only deepened his depression. We'd been dating a couple of months when that happened so I asked him to do some volunteer work at Bright Hope."

"That must have been not long after you started the place," he commented.

"It was. Less than a year, and I needed the help." Along with needing to fix Kyle, but there was no sense babbling about that. "Anyway, after Kyle got on the right meds, he decided he loved working at Bright Hope so he donated a huge chunk of his inheritance to make some upgrades. Then he eventually took over running the office and pretty much anything else that cropped up."

"Upgrades," Brody repeated. His forehead bunched up. "I forgot to mention this earlier, but when I was going through Abe's financials to look for why he was having me and my father investigated, I found an expense Abe had labeled as anonymous donation for upgrades. He'd gotten a cashier's check for fifty grand and paid for a courier to take it to Dallas. He did this about fifteen months ago, and I just wondered if, well, the money had gone to Bright Hope."

Janessa didn't have to think long or hard about this. Bright Hope rarely got anonymous donations, especially for that large of an amount. Most donors wanted the tax write-off. But she remembered one for fifty grand, and the timing was right.

"I recall the courier just showing up at the office with the check. The money probably came from Abe." She had to shake her head. "Just when I think I might have him figured out, something like this pops up."

And that money had popped up at a much-needed time. Bright Hope House was a hundred-year-old building, and they'd needed some dire plumbing repairs. Again. There wasn't nearly enough money in the budget so Janessa had made dozens of calls, hoping they could pull together the funds. Then the check had just shown up.

She wanted to take a moment just to let that sink in, but she heard footsteps coming toward the waiting room. Janessa stepped away from Brody. But it wasn't Teagan's OB, Dr. Sanchez, who walked in. It was Darcia, and she was wearing pale yellow scrubs. She gave Brody one of those reassuring smiles that medical staff sometimes gave before she turned to Janessa.

"Dr. Sanchez asked me to bring you back to delivery. Teagan's labor is progressing extremely fast, and she wants you there when the baby's born." No reassuring smile this time, but Darcia didn't give her the fish-eye as she usually did. She was in full medical mode right now. "Teagan said I was to remind you that she doesn't want to see or hold the baby, that she wants you to take the newborn from the delivery room as soon as possible."

Janessa managed a nod, but it must have looked pretty shaky because Brody came to stand by her side. "Is the baby okay?" he asked his mother.

"The baby's heart rate is good. Strong," Darcia qualified. "Dr. Sanchez has already called in the pediatrician, Dr. Ellen Mendelson, but I'll be standing by in delivery, too. Come with me," she added to Janessa. "We need to get you washed up and ready. Have you attended a delivery before?"

Janessa shook her head, muttered, "No," and gave a glance back at Brody while his mother led her away.

"Well, I hope you're not the squeamish type," Darcia commented.

Janessa assured her she wasn't and she washed up and put on a paper gown when Darcia took her into a prep area. However, after one step into the delivery room, Janessa decided she might indeed be squeamish after all. Not because of anything she saw in the birthing area but because of Teagan. The girl was beaded with sweat, and her face was a mask of straining muscles.

"This is going to be even faster than I thought it'd be," Dr. Sanchez explained, sparing Janessa and Darcia a glance. The doctor was also positioned for the delivery so Janessa hurried to Teagan.

Who immediately cursed and yelled at her.

"Get it out now!" Teagan shouted, and she clamped onto Janessa's hand with a vise grip.

Janessa couldn't complain about the bone-crushing pain she was feeling because it was obvious Teagan's pain was a hell of a lot worse.

"Breathe," Janessa instructed as she remembered the things they'd learned in the birthing classes.

Teagan yelled at her and cursed her again. It wasn't pleasant, but at least Teagan was indeed breathing the way the instructor had taught her. Janessa tried another technique from the class—distraction. Unfortunately, she was having a hard time coming up with any good topics so she went with the one that popped into her head.

"What do you bet one of those gifts Abe left for me is a replica of the horses? Or the stables?" Janessa asked.

Teagan yelled and cursed at her.

"Here comes the baby," Dr. Sanchez said, but Janessa focused on wiping the sweat from Teagan's face.

Moments later, Janessa heard the cry. Not a kitten-like mewl, either. This cry was nearly as loud as Teagan's yelling and profanity had been.

"It's a girl," the doctor announced, and he handed the crying, squirming baby to Darcia.

Teagan quit straining. Quit moving. She went perfectly still while her eyes locked with Janessa. "Please take her out of here. Please," she repeated with her bottom lip trembling.

"Come with me," Darcia told Janessa.

Janessa gave Teagan's hand a gentle squeeze, and the girl's eyes filled with tears. Tears that slid through the sweat down her cheeks.

"Please just take her now," Teagan begged.

And with tears in her own eyes, Janessa followed Darcia and the baby out of the room.

CHAPTER SIXTEEN

BRODY WALKED THROUGH the hospital toward the nursery and, glancing around, he saw exactly what he wanted to see. One of the ranch hands, Jeff Chavez, was in a chair in the hall. Keeping watch for Riggs. Jeff was a former linebacker and would have no trouble handling the idiot if he decided to show up and try to cause some trouble.

"Sherry will relieve you in a couple of hours," Brody told Jeff as he walked by him.

And after that, he had someone ready to relieve Sherry so that Teagan and the baby would be covered 24/7. Something he'd had in place for the last three days since the little girl had been born. As far as Brody was concerned, the guards would stay as long as necessary.

The hospital wasn't big by anyone's standards, so it didn't take Brody long to make his way down the hall to the nursery. He peered through the glass so he could get a look at the baby. Hard to do, though, what with Velma Sue, Sophia and Margo blocking the view.

He shifted, craned his neck and finally saw Janessa in a rocking chair, and she was holding the blanket-wrapped baby while the other women peered down at them. Not right over them, though. They were wearing medical masks and paper exam gowns over their clothes. Since the door next to the observation glass was open, Brody could also hear them all cooing and making baby sounds, but they were doing that from a distance.

Judging from the updates he'd gotten from Janessa, Margo, Velma Sue and Sophia had been constant visitors. The little girl might not have a name yet, but she wasn't lacking attention, and the women were all eager to get their turn to hold her.

"Brody," he heard his mother say, and he looked up the hall to see Darcia making her way toward him.

Since it was her job to take care of the babies, it wasn't unusual for her to be in this part of the hospital, but he could tell she was surprised to see him there. Or maybe not surprised but rather worried.

"Everything okay?" she asked, moving to stand beside him. Like Brody, she peered through the glass at the newborn and the women.

"I was going to ask you the same thing. All is fine with me. How's the baby doing?"

Darcia gave a little sigh, causing him to have a sharp spike of concern. "She's doing very well," she quickly explained, no doubt because she noted that concern.

"Janessa told me the baby had lost some weight, that it was to be expected, but she's already so little." Four and a half pounds. That's all she'd weighed when she was born. Brody figured she was tiny enough to fit in his cowboy hat.

"She lost a couple of ounces, and yes, that usually happens. The loss is basically from water weight and can vary from newborn to newborn. I haven't spoken with the doctor today, but I suspect he'll want to keep her a while longer. Her vitals have all remained good, and she's eating well," she added, "and that's why the doctor didn't transfer her to a NICU in San Antonio."

Brody hadn't exactly become a baby expert, but he'd

learned that NICU was a Newborn Intensive Care Unit. Obviously, a baby would have to be in serious condition to land there so it was good that she was still here.

"Her good vitals are also the reason the doctor allowed her to be held," Darcia added and then paused. "They're bickering over names."

"Excuse me?" Brody asked, but Darcia didn't have to explain because at that exact moment he heard Margo.

"She really looks like a Chloe to me," Margo said. "I mean, that face has Chloe written all over it."

"I still see Evelyn on that face," Velma Sue argued.

It didn't take long for Sophia to say, "Chloe and Evelyn will be too hard for her to pronounce. She needs something simpler."

"You mean like Janessa," Janessa said with plenty of sarcasm that told him she was well aware of the name bickering and was tired of it. "Her parents will name her." Which was no doubt something she'd repeated a lot to the trio.

With the baby still snuggled in her arms, Janessa stood, her gaze meeting his through the glass. She smiled, but the smile faded a bit when her attention shifted to Darcia. He hated that there was this tension between Janessa and his mother. Hated even more that his mother had reason for concern because she didn't want to see him get hurt.

Apparently, it was Sophia's turn to hold the baby because she hurried to take her seat in the rocking chair, and Janessa carefully made the transfer to Sophia's waiting arms. Janessa kissed the baby on the top of the head and then came out in the hall to join them.

"Did you need to examine her?" Janessa asked his mother.

"Not yet." Darcia patted Brody's arm. "I'll see you Thursday night," she muttered and strolled away.

"For dinner," Brody explained. He stopped, gave it a few seconds of thought. "Why don't you come with me?"

Janessa got a classic deer-in-the-headlights look. "That's not a good idea. Your mother doesn't like me."

"My mother just remembers all the moping I did the last time you left. But it won't be that way this time because I know you're leaving."

That was something that'd finally sunk in. There'd be no shock over her quick departure because he already had that departure circled on his calendar. Janessa still had weeks to go on Abe's three-month condition.

"Your mother might not have gotten the no-moping memo," Janessa muttered. She motioned toward the end of the hall. "Teagan is being released this morning, and Kyle's here to drive her back to Dallas. She wants to go," she added. "Actually, she insisted on going."

"She didn't change her mind about seeing the baby?" Brody asked as they started walking.

Janessa shook her head. "Teagan doesn't even want us to talk about her." She paused, shook her head again. "I don't think she's processed that she'll eventually see her child because her sister, Char, is adopting her. She and her sister had a horrible home life, which is why Teagan ended up at Bright Hope, but Char and she are fairly close. Anytime Char visits Teagan, she'll likely have her daughter with her."

That was a huge downside, considering that Teagan obviously wanted to keep some emotional distance from the baby. However, it had to be comforting, too, because Teagan wouldn't have wanted this adoption if she hadn't believed her sister would be a good mother to the child.

They stopped outside of Teagan's room, which was still in sight of both the guard and the nursery. "Teagan will want to say goodbye to you, too," Janessa assured him when she reached for the door. "Rowan's already been by."

Yeah, Brody had known about that because Rowan had told him right before he started his shift. Brody had to admire his brother for continuing his friendship with Teagan. Darcia wouldn't have demanded he not see Teagan, but she would have given Rowan plenty of her quiet disapproval. That was Darcia's specialty, and Brody knew firsthand that it wasn't always easy to stand up to that.

Janessa knocked on the door, said, "It's Brody and me," and Teagan called out, "Come in."

They did, and Brody saw that Teagan was already dressed and sitting on the foot of the bed. Her suitcase was on the floor, and the three vases of flowers she'd gotten, including the one from Brody, were next to the suitcase. Teagan was obviously ready to go.

He shifted his attention to the man standing across from her. Kyle, no doubt. The guy was tall, buff and blond. In fact, Janessa and Kyle sort of looked like the old-fashioned Ken and Barbie dolls.

Brody didn't like the hard knock of jealousy he got from how perfect they looked together. It was totally unwarranted since Janessa and Kyle were no longer together. Still, there'd been something about the man that had not only attracted her but made her fall in love with him. That, Brody realized, was at the core of the jealousy. Janessa certainly hadn't fallen in love with him.

Kyle stuck out his hand for Brody to shake, and even though the guy smiled, Brody detected some kind of mental assessment going on when Kyle's gaze skimmed over him. Maybe he thought Brody was vying to be his replacement. But nope. Brody was just trying to figure out how to deal with this aching need he felt for Janessa. A round of good sex would soothe the ache, but he doubted that one round would be the cure.

"Kyle's already picked up my things from the ranch. We're just waiting for my release forms," Teagan said.

She got up from the bed, and even though she was moving cautiously, she gave Janessa a hard hug. Teagan surprised Brody by hugging him, too.

"Thank you both for everything," Teagan murmured. She eased away and picked up a file folder from the bed and handed it to Janessa. "That's the research I've been doing on your father for the past three days. I had Margo print it out for me."

Janessa opened the folder that was practically bulging with papers and started to thumb through it. "Thank you, Teagan. This is a lot of work."

The girl shrugged. "Not much else to do in a hospital, and it kept my mind off other things."

Since it seemed as if Teagan wanted an alone moment with Janessa, Brody gave Kyle a quick look. "Ken" picked up on it, too.

"Teagan, you want Brody and me to go ahead and start taking that stuff out to the car?" Kyle asked her.

Teagan smiled. "Yes, thank you. I really want to be able to leave when they give me the release."

Kyle put on his coat, fished out his keys from the pocket of his khakis and gathered up the flowers while Brody grabbed the suitcase. In silence, they walked out, and the silence stayed in place until they passed by the ranch hand who was still standing guard.

"I'm sure Teagan and Janessa have already thanked you for the security," Kyle said as they made their way down the hall and toward the exit. "But I'd like to add my thanks, as well. Teagan was pretty shaken up about Riggs."

Brody figured she was still shaken up. "What'll stop him from coming to Bright Hope to try to see her?"

"Well, there's a temporary restraining order, which is practically worthless if Riggs is dead set on seeing her. We'll do as Janessa and you have done here and at the ranch. Lock the doors and keep the security system on. But Teagan will be moving out soon. She wants to go to college next semester in Houston."

Rowan had mentioned that, and Brody thought it was a good thing that Teagan was making these kinds of changes in her life. Still, that didn't mean Riggs wouldn't eventually find her. He'd mention that to Janessa so she could have a talk with Teagan.

They went out through the ER doors and into the chilly November air. The temps had really dropped and were barely above freezing. "The flowers won't last long in the car," Brody pointed out.

"True, but I think Teagan will feel better just knowing that we're speeding things along. She's really anxious to leave. At first, I thought that was because she didn't want to be tempted to see the baby, but I think it has more to do with wanting to start the next stage of her life." Kyle headed toward an older model red SUV. "She never got over you, you know?"

Because Kyle hadn't paused before that question, it took Brody a moment to shift gears. Kyle definitely wasn't talking about Teagan anymore but rather Janessa. And he was dead wrong.

"Are you thinking the reason your marriage failed was because she still has feelings for me?" Brody came out and asked.

"No, the marriage failed because we weren't in love.

Now, that maybe had something to do with you. Hard to fall in love when you've got unresolved issues with your ex."

Brody frowned at the *ex* label. Hell, they'd been teenagers. *Ex* seemed more of an adult deal. "It was years between the time Janessa left Last Ride and when she married you. If she really hadn't gotten over me, she could have come back."

The moment the words left his mouth, Brody got a flash of clarity. Definitely something he wouldn't have had as a teenager. Janessa couldn't have come back because of Abe's threat. Because Abe had hurt her to the core. Her leaving had far more to do with Abe than it ever had to do with him. For some reason that soothed him. A teenage broken heart had a long-assed memory, but it wasn't any match for hard-earned common sense.

Kyle popped open the back of the SUV so that Brody could add the suitcase he was carrying to the two others that were already back there. Then the man poured out the water from the vases and began to anchor the flowers in between the suitcases.

"Is she doing okay?" Kyle asked, and Brody knew they were still talking about Janessa. "I mean, is it getting to her to be here with all the memories of her father?"

"Janessa's handling it," Brody said, but then he thought of the things they'd learned so far about Abe. Some good things, but there were also plenty of bad. Added to that, she now had to deal with the baby and the fact she'd put her life on hold for three months. So he mentally amended his answer to, "I hope she's handling it."

Kyle had just closed the back of the SUV when Brody spotted Janessa and Teagan making their way toward them. Janessa still had the file folder Teagan had given her, and Teagan was clutching some papers. No doubt those release forms. Obviously, freedom pleased her because she gave Brody and Janessa another hug.

"I'll text you when we make it to Dallas," Kyle assured Janessa. "Stay out of trouble," he added and then flashed a grin at Brody.

Janessa waved as they drove away, and they stood there until the SUV was out of sight. "Are you okay?" he asked.

She nodded, and it seemed steady enough. Janessa lifted the file. "Want to sit in my car with the heat on while we look at this?"

Since there were possibly things in that folder to shake her steadiness, Brody matched her nod, but instead of going to her car, he motioned for her to follow him to his truck because it was closer. He cranked the heat to the max as soon as they got in, and Janessa didn't waste any time opening the file.

Brody leaned in to look at the first page. It was a bio of sorts, and Teagan had even cited her resources of internet searches, online newspaper articles and interviews with Alma Parkman and Fannie June Dayton, who had the distinction of being the oldest resident of Last Ride. The woman was 101 years old. Brody had no idea just how good Fannie June's memory was, but Teagan had spoken with her for over three hours.

"Abe was born sixty-one years ago at the old Last Ride Hospital," Janessa summarized as she skimmed through the lines. "His mother, my grandmother, Norma Dayton, ran off with another man when Abe was six." She paused. "That's probably the start of Abe's abandonment issues."

"Abandonment issues?" Brody questioned.

"Oh, he had them in spades. He turned against your mother when she dumped him. He turned against both of his ex-wives. And he turned against me when I was twelve and told the judge I wanted to live with my mother."

When put like that, Brody supposed *abandonment issues* was as good a name for it as any.

"His mother never came back to see him," Janessa went on. "She left Abe with his father who was…as tough as a stewed skunk. That's a quote from Fannie June," she added, looking up at Brody. "I'm guessing that's pretty tough?"

Brody had to shrug on that one, but the snips and snaps he'd heard about Abraham Lincoln Parkman III all centered on him being a hard man.

"Fannie June calls Abe a poor little rich boy whose stewed skunk father wouldn't scratch his own mama's fleas. That's another quote," Janessa provided. "I think the translation for that is Abe, the third, was not very generous with his time when it came to his son."

Brody made a sound of agreement and did some skimming, too, when Janessa flipped to the next page. Fannie June recalled Abe running away from home many times. The woman also stated he was often seen around town with bruises and once had a black eye.

He stopped reading and cursed. Even though this had all happened a lifetime ago, it sickened Brody to think of Abe as a kid going through something like that. Worse, most people wouldn't have stepped up to help because Abe's father had been one of the richest men in town. Added to that, there might not have even been a system in place sixty years ago to report something like this.

"His father died when Abe was only sixteen," Janessa continued to summarize, "leaving him a huge estate to run. According to Fannie June, Abe did a good job building the businesses and the ranch, and he got along with most people until Darcia left him and took up with his best friend."

Janessa stopped and looked at him. "This wasn't your mother's fault. She's not responsible in any way for how Abe handled their breakup."

No, not her fault, but Brody wasn't doubting any of what Fannie June had recalled. Maybe it'd felt like another abandonment for Abe to lose Darcia to his best friend. Abandonment layered with betrayal. That might cause a man to snap and start acting like his stewed skunk of a father.

Janessa groaned, shook her head. "How do I make sense of all of this? Abe was abused and turned bitter. Part of me wants to forgive him for every wrong he's ever done solely because of that, but I was on the receiving end of some of those wrongs. You were, too."

"Some," he admitted, and he thought about the cut-to-the-bone feeling when he'd heard Abe was having him investigated. "Maybe there's no way to make sense of it. You and I have both dealt with upheavals in our lives, and it didn't cause us to become mean and bitter."

He wrapped his mind around that for a moment. No bitterness, but like their parents, they hadn't exactly been lucky in love. Janessa looked up at him again, her eyes skimming over him as if she was trying to figure out what he was thinking. His thoughts shifted from love, luck and old wounds to her face, her mouth. To her. And just like that, his mood shifted.

Brody leaned in and dropped a kiss on her mouth. "Come to dinner with me tomorrow night."

The quick kiss had caused her to smile, but the smile vanished when she pulled back and met his gaze. "Do you usually take your dates to family dinners?" she asked.

"No." Never, in fact. And maybe that's why he wanted to do it now.

Same ol', same ol' just wasn't working for him anymore.

He would have to try to explain that to Janessa while trying to understand it better himself. But he didn't want this temporary thing with Janessa to be just about sex. Yes, he definitely wanted the sex, but he wanted to make these next eight weeks count. However, before Brody could even attempt an explanation, Janessa's phone rang.

"It's the PI agency," she said when she glanced at the screen. She hit the answer button right away and put the call on Speaker.

"This is Victor Barton," the man said, "returning Janessa Parkman's call."

"I'm Janessa. Thank you for getting back to me."

"Sorry that it took so long, but I make a habit of not taking my phone on vacation." His tone was all business. "I understand you have some questions about your father and the investigation he hired me to do."

"Exactly what did he hire you to do?" she asked.

"Plenty. Abe came to me with old photos and emails that seemed to prove his two ex-wives were cheating on him. He wanted me to find out who'd sent them."

Janessa paused a moment. "All of that happened years ago. When did my father ask you to look into it?"

"About four months ago. He said it was just something that had been bugging him, and he wanted to know the truth," Barton added.

That would have been three months before Abe's death. Brody thought back to that time, but he couldn't recall any kind of trigger that would have caused Abe to do this.

"I checked, and I found the emails came from an account that closed right after they were sent," the PI continued. "The postmarks on the envelopes for the pictures didn't pan out, either. But then I had someone take a harder look. The pictures were all Photoshopped. A good job of it, too."

"Photoshopped," Janessa repeated. "So, neither Margo nor my mother cheated on Abe."

"Can't say that for sure, but I didn't find any evidence of it. Just the opposite, in fact. Other than those bogus pictures and emails, I couldn't find a single person who could verify that either woman had ever engaged in any extramarital affairs."

Janessa groaned softly. "Yet that's why he ended his marriages."

"He did indeed," Barton verified. "Needless to say, Abe didn't take the news well that his ex-wives were innocent of cheating."

No, he wouldn't have. Because it would mean he'd been wrong.

"Abe told me to keep digging," the PI continued, "that it didn't matter how much it cost or how many people I had to hire, he wanted the whole truth. So, I got some computer experts to study the photos themselves, and they tracked them back to a guy named Delbert Bodell. After having a long chat with him and offering him payment, he admitted someone had hired him to alter the photos."

"Who?" Janessa pressed when Barton paused.

"Jimmy Harrell," the PI said.

Well, hell. Brody did a whole lot of mental cursing. His father had done this. He'd set this shit in motion, and it'd led to two divorces and a whole bunch of pain.

Suddenly, things got clearer, too, on why Abe had asked for the PI to investigate Jimmy. And him. Abe would have wanted to make sure Brody had had no part in any of this.

Brody took a pen from the glove compartment and used the file folder to write out a question he wanted her to ask the PI. He didn't want to do it himself because Barton might clam up if he realized someone other than Abe's daughter was listening in on the conversation.

"Only Jimmy was behind the photos and emails?" Janessa pressed the PI after looking at what Brody had written.

"The evidence points to it being only Jimmy," he verified. "Abe had me look into Jimmy's ex-wife and son, but there was nothing I could find. I did track down Jimmy, but he refused to talk to me. Abe tried to contact him and got the same result. That's when Abe told me to keep digging, to find out if Jimmy had done anything else to screw him over."

Brody suspected there had indeed been other things. Maybe not something that could be traced directly back to Jimmy, but it wasn't hard to start gossip that could stir up trouble.

How long had this been going on? At least back to when Sophia and Abe were married, but it was possible his father had done things even before that.

"There's another matter that Abe hired me to look into," the PI said, drawing Brody's attention back to the phone.

"What do you mean *another matter*?" Janessa asked.

Again, the PI hesitated. "I'm still working on it, and I'm not comfortable getting into that with you because there are other people involved. I need to speak to…someone first and make sure it's okay to tell you. If it is, I'll get back to you."

"Does this have something to do with my father's will?" she asked.

But she was talking to the air because the PI had already ended the call.

CHAPTER SEVENTEEN

JANESSA SAT AT the dining room table and thought of all the things on her to-do list. The baby would be released from the hospital tomorrow, and she should be checking the nursery she'd set up to make sure everything was as it should be. She also had some paperwork to do for Bright Hope along with wanting to talk to Sophia some more about the things Brody and she had learned from the PI.

But Janessa wasn't doing any of those things tonight.

Instead, she was having dinner with Darcia, Brody, Rowan and his date, Aspen Granger. An awkward dinner at that. In fact, it likely broke many records for its level of awkwardness. Darcia was being polite enough, maybe too polite, but Janessa could feel the tension smeared over her with the same thickness that Rowan was slathering butter on a roll.

Janessa took another bite of the lasagna and met Brody's gaze from across the table. And suddenly she forgot all about the things she should be doing and remembered why she was here. It was because Brody had wanted her to come, and she'd wanted to be with him. That was worth the meet-the-family kind of pressure. In fact, she was pretty sure she'd be willing to put up with just about anything to be with him.

Not good.

Because when she was looking at him like this, she tended to forget that what was going on between them was just a holiday fling. And flings should be about sex and hungry kisses in the moonlight. It shouldn't include family dinners or an ache inside her that went well beyond the fling stage.

The sex would happen. She was certain of that. Sooner or later, there'd be no interruptions, and the making out would carry them straight to the bed, floor or whatever nearby surface there happened to be. Every inch of her body was burning for that, but her heart had gotten in on this, too. When she went back to Dallas, she'd end up doodling his name.

And wondering if she wanted to be without him.

Of course, any mention of that would likely send him running. Brody had made no comment about anything permanent between them. Still—

"A lot of people are still talking about it," Janessa heard Aspen say. The girl's voice cut through the monologue Janessa had going on in her head. "Mr. Parkman's will and what'll happen 'cause of it. But it's a good sign that you and your mother have stayed here this long."

Janessa made a sound of agreement. It wasn't just a good sign. It was a miracle, one that Janessa could partially thank Curt for since, according to the gossip, he'd been keeping Sophia occupied.

"I'm optimistic," Janessa said, though she put a mental asterisk next to her comment. The optimism would stay as long as Abe didn't throw them any more curveballs.

"Lots of stuff's going to change around Last Ride," Aspen went on, looking at Brody. "I heard about you maybe buying my great-uncle's ranch."

All eyes went to Brody. Well, they did after Janessa gave Darcia a quick glance. Apparently, talk about this particular *lots of changes* hadn't made it back to Darcia.

"Your great-uncle?" Darcia repeated.

Aspen nodded and didn't seem to have a clue that she'd

just let the cat out of the bag. Well, a potential cat and bag anyway.

"Elmer Tasker," Brody provided. "He has the ranch next to Joe's. He raises Charolais, but it'd be good pasture for horses."

"And you're buying it?" Darcia's gaze shifted from Brody to Janessa. Great. Darcia clearly thought she was the reason for this.

"Maybe," Brody answered. "Elmer and I are trying to work out a fair price."

"I see." Darcia moved around some bits of salad with her fork. Her *I see* had a definite tinge of disapproval.

"Janessa offered to give me Colts Creek if her inheritance goes through," Brody added. "I turned her down."

That got Darcia's attention off poking at the cherry tomatoes in her salad and back on to her son. She opened her mouth, probably to ask if he'd lost his mind or why the heck he would turn down owning the ranch he already ran. But she must have decided that was a mother-to-son chat best left for later because the cherry tomatoes got more pokes.

"Are you ready for the baby to come home tomorrow?" Rowan asked, turning to Janessa. The boy might only be fifteen, but he knew when to fill in dinner conversation.

"Hopefully. It's been a couple of years since I've fostered, but I have help. Plenty of help," she added in a mumble. "My mother's set up a schedule." And she left it at that. Sophia was a force to be reckoned with when it came to her temporary grandchild, and spreadsheets.

"And Teagan's sister?" Rowan added. "When does she get here?"

"In about six weeks. She's coming in from Germany to pick up the baby and take her to a new assignment in Florida." Janessa sincerely hoped that during those six weeks Sophia and Margo didn't become too attached to the little girl.

Darcia cleared her throat, obviously ready to jump back into dinner chatter. "Teagan's doing well?" she asked.

"She's back at Bright Hope and will move to Houston next month to start college," Rowan said before Janessa could answer. "We keep in touch through texts," he explained when Darcia, Brody and Janessa looked at him.

Since Aspen didn't seem the least bit bothered, or surprised, about that, it meant Rowan had already told her all about Teagan. Darcia probably objected to Rowan's continued contact with a teenager who'd just had a baby. A teenager who was technically an adult. But judging from the glances Darcia was giving Brody, she was more concerned with him.

It seemed to take several months, but they finally finished the meal. "I'll take care of the dishes," Darcia insisted, already gathering some plates. "There's apple pie in the family room. I'll be in there in a few minutes."

Rowan and Aspen didn't need further invitation to head that way, but Janessa and Brody stayed put.

"Janessa, could you just grab the water glasses for me?" Darcia added. "Brody, maybe you can give Janessa and me a minute?"

"Why?" Brody asked his mother while Janessa went ahead and gathered up the glasses.

Darcia sighed. "I won't keep her long. Please go ahead and have some pie. It's your favorite."

Janessa could see the debate Brody was having with himself, and she gave him a wink and a nod to try to assure him all would be just fine. That was probably true. Probably.

Brody finally tapped his watch as if counting down that

minute his mother had requested, and he went toward the family room. Janessa followed Darcia to the kitchen.

"Why'd Brody turn down Colts Creek?" Darcia immediately asked.

Janessa didn't mind the woman jumping right to the point since those seconds were ticking away. "I think a lot of reasons. Reasons that should come from him."

Darcia paused and then gave a stiff nod. "Well, it was a decent thing for you to do, to offer him the ranch. It was something Abe should have done."

"I agree," Janessa said without hesitation. "Abe screwed over a lot of people with that will, but Brody got the worst of it."

Darcia eased the plates into the sink, and her next nod wasn't so stiff. "Brody told me about the PI Abe hired," she said with her attention fastened to the faucet she turned on. "I swear I didn't know Jimmy had sent Abe those photos and emails."

Janessa heard the tone. Not defensive exactly but close. "I didn't think you had," she assured Darcia. "My mother didn't know he'd done it, either. I haven't had a chance to have a long conversation with her about it, but I suspect Jimmy arranged for the Photoshopping of the picture she got. The one of Abe with the mystery woman."

Darcia groaned. "So much damage." She finally turned and looked at Janessa. "Abe and Jimmy started this war between them because of me, and it spilled over into so many lives. Sophia's, Margo's, yours."

Yes, and countless others. Brody was caught up in that, too, because if Abe hadn't been "at war" with Jimmy, he might not have objected to her being with Brody that summer they were teenagers. Abe might not have torn them apart and sent Janessa running back to Dallas.

Janessa figured that Brody would be coming into the kitchen any second now, but she went ahead with what she wanted to bring up to Darcia. "The PI said Abe had given him another assignment, but he wouldn't go into detail about it. I've called him, pressed him, but he won't budge. Do you have any idea what that assignment would have been?"

Darcia shook her head, but Janessa thought she might be considering all the things that Abe would have wanted the PI to dig into. Especially once Abe had learned that Jimmy was responsible.

"Did Brody tell you that Abe was having both you and him investigated, too?" Janessa pressed.

"Yes, he told me." Darcia huffed. "I hate that Abe believed Brody and I had any part in what Jimmy had done. It's probably why Abe wrote his will the way he did. He wrote it and then didn't have time to change it before he died."

Maybe. And Janessa wanted to believe that Abe had had those intentions. Still, there was something missing in this odd puzzle. Some reason why Abe had dragged her into the middle of this and not given Colts Creek to its rightful owner—Brody.

"Thank you," Darcia muttered.

Janessa looked at her. "For what?"

"For not being like Abe. And for not telling me to go to hell in a handbasket when I glared at you for being with Brody."

Janessa smiled. "You're pretty good at glaring," she said, trying to keep things light. "But I also know you love your son and want to protect him."

"I couldn't protect him from Abe," Darcia said under her breath just as Brody came into the kitchen.

Brody volleyed glances at both Darcia and her. No doubt checking to see if they were upset. Janessa kept the smile on her face, and she thought Darcia did a decent enough job looking as if all were well with their world. It wasn't. There was still plenty to be worked out, but Janessa thought Darcia and she had just reached some kind of truce. Good. Because Janessa didn't want Brody to have to endure his mother's wrath just for being with her.

"Aspen says she has to be home soon," Brody explained. "Janessa and I can get our pie to go and drop her off."

Darcia wiped her hands on a dish towel. "No, I can take her. You and Janessa just stay here and have your dessert."

"Actually, I should be going, too," Janessa said, thinking of her to-do list and Brody. Mainly Brody.

"Of course." Darcia nodded. "You have things to do, what with the baby being released tomorrow."

Darcia took two small plastic containers from a cabinet and carried them into the family room. Where Rowan and Aspen immediately jumped away from each other as if they'd been scalded. The jumping, however, wasn't quite fast enough because they all got a glimpse of the kiss they'd tried to hide.

Darcia didn't say a word about the lip-lock she'd just witnessed. She simply went to the coffee table, put two slices of the pie in the containers and handed them to Brody and Janessa. She surprised Janessa then by hugging her. So, yes, there was indeed a truce.

"Thank you for dinner," Janessa told her when they all headed out. Rowan and Aspen with Darcia to her car. Janessa and Brody to his truck.

"So?" Brody asked the moment they were inside.

"So," she repeated, stretching it out a few syllables. "I

think you're going to need to have the safe-sex talk with your brother."

He gave her a flat look. "I've already done that. What'd you and my mother chat about?"

"The expected," Janessa settled for saying. "She didn't know anything about what Jimmy was doing, she's still pissed about Abe's will and she likes that I offered you Colts Creek. She doesn't like that you didn't accept."

"*I* wouldn't have liked it had I accepted," he grumbled as he drove away. "If all of this plays out, then I'll sell my place, buy Elmer's and either help you find a buyer for Colts Creek or a ranch manager if you decide to keep it."

So, he was trying to tie up everything in a neat little package. Trying to fix it. Something that was normally her role.

Janessa didn't mind him stepping up like this. She needed his help. But part of her wished that in all his plans, Brody would have included the possibility of *them*. As in him and her somehow being a couple after they'd had their way with each other for the next two months. Janessa wasn't 100 percent positive she wanted that, but she hated that it wasn't even on his radar. In Brody's mind, she was leaving, period.

Janessa wasn't sure if it was hurt, annoyance or lust that caused her to lean across the seat and tongue kiss his ear. Something that she recalled he enjoyed very much.

And still did, apparently.

The sound Brody made certainly wasn't a protest, and Janessa was pretty sure the heat in the truck went up some serious notches. Some of that heat was in the quick glance he gave her before he pulled over.

"I'm guessing you did that for a reason?" he drawled.

"Yes," she confirmed. But she thought it best not to get

into that reason now. Brody probably wouldn't want to hear that she was considering that whole couple thing. Besides, that was on the back burner now because her tongue kiss had clearly moved sex to the front of the stove.

Good.

It was about time.

Thankfully, they were already out of town and on a stretch of road where there was little traffic because Brody unsnapped their seat belts and hauled her to him.

BRODY HAD A split second to consider that this probably wasn't the best idea he'd ever had since they were in his truck and on the side of the road. But only a split second. Once he had his mouth on Janessa's, the notion of good or bad items became toast. One taste of her and that toast label applied to him, too.

Janessa managed to laugh despite the sudden burst of wild heat. Even when she'd been with him that first time, she'd had some playful moments. Obviously, that hadn't changed, and Brody was very appreciative about it. More appreciative, though, of the well-placed kisses she dropped on his neck and, yes, his ear. The woman had a good memory for his hot spots.

Brody had to shift his position and move to the right edge of his seat so there'd be room to pull Janessa onto his lap. It certainly wasn't a comfortable position what with the gearshift gouging into his thigh and his arm pressed against the steering wheel. Still, he wasn't giving up this first round of kisses for the sake of comfort. Nope. He intended to keep stoking this fire, and then he could somehow drive to his house and get her in bed.

That was a lofty goal, he soon realized.

Janessa didn't stop at the kisses on his ear and neck.

She slid her hands under his shirt, creating some mind-blowing skin-to-skin contact. Creating more contact when she did her own shifting and managed to straddle him. Now it was her butt against the steering wheel and her left knee jammed down into the gear console. No complaints from her, though, and soon, very soon, Brody couldn't have voiced a complaint even if he'd been in excruciating pain.

"Ever noticed sex talk is only sexy if you're aroused?" she asked, tugging his shirt over his head and lowering, somehow, to put her mouth on his chest.

Brody was reasonably sure he'd never noticed that.

"Sex talk like tongue kiss me there," she went on, demonstrating that on his stomach. "Make me scream your name." She undid his belt, unzipped him. "Use me. Deeper. Harder. *Faster, faster, faster.* Make me come. See? That's not sexy at all unless I'm doing something like this."

She shoved down the top of his boxers, somehow managed to put her mouth on him and blew. Then she laughed. The breath from her laughter nearly took off the top of his head. It also had him rethinking that whole notion—which had obviously been stupid—of driving back to his house.

Cursing her and the cramped space of the truck, Brody took matters into his own hands. And mouth. He kissed her *deeper* and *harder* while moving onto the passenger's side. With her still on his lap, he hit the recline button on the seat to give them more room.

And he got to work.

"Tongue kiss," he growled, and he went after her neck. Just a sample or two because he remembered that wasn't nearly as much of a hot button for her. That's when he peeled off her sweater, shoved down the cups of her white lace bra and did some tongue kissing on her nipples.

That got the response he wanted. She moaned, long and

silky. The sound of pure pleasure, and Brody gave her that pleasure while he slid his hand under her skirt and into her panties.

"It's not necessary to scream my name," he said with his mouth against her now-wet nipple. His fingers had found another wet spot to toy with, and he went in slow and deep.

"Brody," she screamed.

Partly deaf now but pleased with himself and her reaction, he kept touching while he sucked her nipple into his mouth.

More name screaming, followed by her yanking him from his boxers. "You'd better have a condom," she snapped. "If not, you're going to make me come before we go get one."

No problem. He fished out a condom from his wallet, but he decided to give her both. Brody continued the mouth play on her nipples. Continued the finger strokes inside her. And he felt her tight wet muscles contract.

"Brody," she breathed out. Not a scream but the sound of that desperate relief from the desperate heat.

She was still in the throes of that relief and heat when he got the condom on, and he thrust inside her. Now he was the one breathing out her name, and there was no relief in his own voice. Just the need, and the overwhelming sensations of feeling her squeeze around him.

"Deeper, harder, faster," he told her. And he gave her that, too. Of course, he was giving it to himself, as well.

He held back, giving her time to rebuild. Gripping onto her hips and angling her so that his dick could slide against her number one hot spot. He had no trouble finding it. No trouble taking her right back up to that needy peak where she took hold of fistfuls of his hair and muttered his name as a repeating oath.

"Make me come," he told her.

Janessa did just that. And then she did the same for him.

CHAPTER EIGHTEEN

JANESSA FIGURED IT was wrong to have such raunchy thoughts about Brody when she was driving the baby from the hospital to the ranch.

Still, the thoughts were there. So was the buzzing slack feeling in her body that had come from good raunchy sex with Brody the night before. He'd definitely sated her, twice, but he'd also left her wanting a whole lot more of him.

She glanced in the rearview mirror at Margo and Sophia who were on either side of the baby's car seat. Janessa couldn't actually see the baby because the seat was rear-facing, but she had no doubt the little girl was fine.

Along with having plenty of attention.

Plenty of concern, too. Margo and her mother had grilled the doctor to make sure a preemie could come home from the hospital so soon, and the doctor had assured them there was no reason for the baby not to be released. The baby wasn't having any medical problems and was in fact, thriving. Janessa expected that thriving to continue, but if something did go wrong, she wouldn't hesitate to call the pediatrician.

Both Margo and Sophia were taking turns talking to the baby, describing every little thing along the route to Colts Creek. Janessa heard words like *moo cow*, *horsey*, *doggy*, but it grabbed her full attention when she heard Margo say, "Brody."

Janessa glanced around and spotted him in the front pasture. Oh, my. He was straddled atop an impressive black stallion, one that was sleek and muscled. Just like Brody himself.

She wasn't going fast, but she slowed the car to a crawl to take in the view. He was in full cowboy mode today and appeared to be using the stallion to herd some calves toward the back of the pasture. A pair of blue heeler dogs were helping.

"Well," Margo muttered, "there are sights and there are sights. He's a sight all right."

Janessa didn't need to follow the woman's gaze to know she was talking about Brody. She could hear the "admiration" in Margo's voice.

Brody spotted them, tipped his hat in greeting, smiled in a way that only he and a cocky Greek god could have pulled off. Then he went back to doing the work that made Janessa want to tongue kiss him from head to toe. She might experiment with that the next time they were together. Whenever that would be. With the baby out of the hospital, there would be fewer opportunities for truck sex.

Janessa got the car moving again toward the house, and she passed by a crew that was setting up Christmas decorations. Lots of them. Apparently, it was a tradition at Colts Creek to have lights and garland on the long stretches of fence that flanked the road to the house. Another tradition was to decorate the trees that stood about fifteen yards apart along the fence line. It was something Abe had already contracted and paid to happen for the next ten years.

She parked directly in front of the porch. It was still morning, and the temps were chilly enough that she didn't want the baby out in it any longer than necessary. However, before Janessa could even get out, Sophia and Margo were working together to lift the infant seat from the holder, and Sophia carried the baby onto the porch where Velma Sue already had the door open for them.

Velma Sue did her own cooing and baby talk as they made their way up the stairs to the guest room that they'd converted to a nursery. It was right across the hall from Janessa's and next door to the suite that Margo had already said she'd be using so she could cover some of the nightshifts.

Janessa stopped in the doorway and was pretty sure her mouth dropped open. When she'd done a final check of the room the previous night, before she'd gone to dinner at Darcia's, there hadn't been nearly as much stuff as there was now. There'd been a crib, changing table, a mobile and two rocking chairs. All things suitable for a temporary nursery.

Emphasis on the *temporary*.

But the room was now filled with not one but *four* huge stuffed teddy bears, horses and dolls larger than a preschooler. There were four of those, too. The landscape oil paintings that once graced the walls had all been replaced by colorful artwork of ponies, calves, kittens and puppies.

Emphasis on colorful.

There was plenty of pink in the color scheme, including the fuzzy rug by the crib. It matched the equally fuzzy pillows in the rocking chairs.

Someone had brought up the large dollhouse and pasture from the storage room next to Abe's office. They weren't suitable for a newborn, but Janessa had to admit they looked good in the room. Ditto for the floor-to-ceiling fully decorated Christmas tree in the corner—complete with wrapped gifts.

"Uh, Sophia and I added a few things last night," Margo murmured as she took the sleeping baby from her infant seat. "We just wanted to spruce things up a bit."

Janessa sighed, but she wasn't sure either her mother or Margo heard her because they already had their attention back on the baby. Velma Sue was easing back the blanket to count fingers and toes.

"We also thought you should go through the rest of the presents Abe got you," Sophia added. "There could be other buildings from the ranch. She can't play with them, of course, but anything ranch-related would go with the theme."

Janessa sighed again. "You shouldn't get attached to her," she reminded them all. For the umpteenth time. "She'll be leaving with her parents soon."

She got a couple of murmured "Of course" comments, which made it seem as if they did understand. But their actions said differently. Velma Sue and Sophia went across the room with Margo, and all three stayed put, looking down at the baby even after Margo eased her into the crib.

"The three of us agreed to call her Sweet Pea for now," Margo whispered, sparing Janessa a glance. "I mean, it's better than just saying *her* or *baby*."

Maybe, but Sweet Pea was a nickname, which was perilously close to an actual name. Something they shouldn't be doing. That should come from the baby's parents.

Janessa checked the time. "I'll call Teagan's sister, Char, and see if she's picked a name yet. The hospital gave us a deadline of fourteen days to fill out the paperwork with the baby's name, but the sooner we get that done, the better."

"I agree," Sophia answered, and she didn't even spare a glance. It was all about the baby.

Janessa was truly thankful for all the help, but it

wouldn't hurt to find out if Char would be able to get the baby sooner than she'd planned. Obviously, Velma Sue, Sophia and Margo were going to get attached, along with being very much involved. The chart next to the changing table was proof of that.

Someone, probably Sophia, had come up with a spread-sheet to show the eight-hour shifts and to spell out who would be watching the baby and when. Janessa wouldn't be "on duty" for another twenty-four hours. However, that didn't mean she wouldn't be spending some of that twenty-four hours with the baby. She was after all the foster mother. Even if she hadn't been, though, she would have wanted that time with the newborn.

While Janessa went downstairs, she took out her phone and sent a text to Char, asking her to call her the first chance she got. She'd already sent Char and her husband, Mark, many pictures of the baby, but Janessa fired off an-other. This one was of the baby being discharged from the hospital. They were no doubt chomping at the proverbial bit to be with their little girl.

She walked into Abe's office and got a pang of guilt when she saw the file folder on the desk. It contained the research for the Last Ride Society. Research that mainly Teagan and Rowan had done. Janessa still had weeks to complete it, but she'd basically put both Abe and the re-search aside. She'd just have to schedule it in along with taking care of the baby, her work for Bright Hope and the winter fling she intended to continue with Brody. She was more eager to focus on all three than find out why her fa-ther had become the man he'd turned out to be. Maybe that meant she'd found some kind of peace with him after all.

She went to the storage room, hoping that Teagan or someone else had actually opened the presents. But no.

The remaining ones were still wrapped. Eleven for her birthday, eleven more for Christmas. Gathering her breath, she went to the birthday corner, sat down on the floor and started opening.

One thing was for certain—Abe hadn't known how to go small. Or pick out gifts that would be fun for a girl aged one to twelve. Case in point, when she ripped open the present for her second birthday, she found a horse. Not a cute stuffed pony like the one in the nursery. Nope. This was a wooden painted deal like from a carousel at an amusement park. The only thing you could do with it was look at it, but since the baby might enjoy the bright colors, she set it aside to haul up to the nursery.

The present for her third birthday continued to confirm Abe's clueless gift choices for his toddler daughter. It was a sign with the Colts Creek Ranch name and logo, a black colt chomping grass in a pasture. Oh, well. Since it might go with the nursery decor, she set it aside, too.

Janessa tackled birthdays four and five at the same time, ripping off the paper with both hands. They were more building replicas. One of the stables, which should please Sophia and Margo, and another one of the barns.

She tore through more paper, not really taking the time to even study the gifts until she had them all unwrapped. When she was done, Janessa stepped back and realized that with the house and pasture already in the nursery, Abe had given her replicas of the entire ranch, right down to the bunkhouse, gazebo and even the gardens. It made her more than a little sad. She wasn't sure if Abe had been trying to show off with these things or give her a clear visual of what she could have if she lived at the ranch.

Janessa kicked, shoved and pushed the mountain of paper aside and was steeling herself up to tackle the Christmas presents when she spotted the small package on the floor. It wasn't wrapped in the glitz and sparkle of the others. It was a simple white box with a tiny pink ribbon.

Puzzled, she picked it up and read the label. To Janessa, for Your 13th Birthday. From, Your Father.

She had to mentally shake her head. She'd turned thirteen only months after she'd told the judge she wanted to live with her mother. Abe had stormed out and not spoken to Sophia or her again until Janessa came to Last Ride. Janessa had been sure he'd washed his hands of her that very day.

So, why had he bought the gift?

She was still considering that when Brody walked in. Even a puzzler of a gift couldn't hold her attention when this particular hot cowboy came into the room.

"Having fun?" Brody asked, tipping his head to the mountain of wrapping paper.

"I am now," she told him.

Brody didn't disappoint. He walked straight to her and kissed her. That really got her attention and held it until he'd had his way with her. Well, as much of a way as he could have with just a kiss.

He pulled back, smiled. "When I saw you in your car earlier, I wanted to do that."

"I had something similar in mind. Maybe involving more tongue and more…inches." Janessa bumped her body against his just in case he'd missed the dirty reference.

"I happen to have some inches." He kissed her again, letting her know that he hadn't missed diddly-squat with her cute wording.

This kiss went on for several incredible moments, but when she went to pull him into her arms, Brody held back. "It's cold out there, but I still worked up a sweat."

"Yes, I know." She laughed. Kissed him. And licked his lips. "You're a walking, talking sweaty fantasy. Did you come in here to fulfill that fantasy?"

"After a shower and the rest of my morning meetings, I could arrange that."

She didn't even bother to hold back her disappointment. Sex right now would have been a bad idea anyway since Margo, Velma Sue or Sophia could come looking for her.

"Seriously, what are you doing in here?" Brody asked.

"Enduring blasts from the past." She showed him the small gift box. "Did you know Abe got me a gift after he lost the custody battle?"

Brody shook his head. "But then I didn't know he'd gotten you all of this. What will you do with this stuff?"

"To be determined, but some of it will go into the nursery. You know, the nursery that isn't supposed to have a lot of things in it because it's just temporary. Right now, it looks like a storefront for Infants R Us at Christmastime."

Brody smiled again. "How's the baby?"

"Well looked after. They're calling her Sweet Pea."

He made a sound to indicate he'd picked up on her mild disapproval about that. "Cute. I'm going to grab a shower in my office bathroom and then I'll go up and look in on her before my meetings start. Anything you want me to emphasize to the three GeeGees?"

"GeeGees?" she asked.

"Yeah, that's how I heard Margo refer to herself when she was holding the baby in the hospital."

"Great," Janessa muttered. "I'll talk to them." She hooked her fingers over his belt buckle, pulled him closer and kissed him.

"When can I see you about those inches?" he asked when she eased back.

"Tonight. I'm apparently not on the spreadsheet for baby duty."

"Good. I'll see you later, then." He kissed her one more time before he headed out.

Janessa just stood there, enjoying the view when he walked away. The man had a superior backside. That image occupied her thoughts for a couple of seconds before she looked at the gift box in her hand again. She would have opened it, but her phone rang, and she saw that it was from Char. Good. Maybe they could get this name business worked out.

"What'd you think of the pictures I texted?" Janessa asked the moment she answered.

"Beautiful. She's such a beautiful baby."

Janessa went still. She'd only spoken to Char two other times, but she thought she heard something off in the woman's voice.

"Is everything okay?" Janessa asked, and she got a flutter in her stomach, not a good one either when Char hesitated.

"I'm in the hospital," the woman finally said. "I had a little bit of a scare." She paused again. "I just found out I'm pregnant, and I started spotting."

Janessa did some hesitating of her own. "Are you all right?" she finally settled for saying.

"I'm better. The spotting has stopped, but the doctor wants to keep me overnight. Obviously, I'd given up on having my own baby so the pregnancy was, well, a shock. A really good shock," she added with a laugh that didn't have any humor in it.

"I can only imagine," Janessa muttered, and her mind began to spin with the possibilities of how this might play out. She didn't speak, though. She just waited for Char to continue.

"It's twins," Char finally went on. "Guess all those months of fertility treatments finally worked." She chuckled again, and while it was filled with nerves, there was happiness there, too. "Anyway, I wanted you to know that my husband and I are still reeling from the news I'm pregnant so we'll take some time to think all of this over once I'm out of the hospital."

"*Think all of this over*?" Janessa repeated. She pulled in her breath, held it.

"Yes," Char confirmed. No attempted chuckle this time. The sound the woman made was a hoarse sob. "I haven't talked to my sister about this yet so just keep it to yourself for now. But it's possible we're not going to be able to adopt Teagan's baby after all."

BRODY WASN'T SURE how working couples with a baby actually managed to have sex. Janessa and he certainly hadn't worked it into their schedules after their hookup in his truck. The "inches" date they'd planned hadn't panned out because the baby had thrown up her entire bottle. Reflux, Janessa had called it, and it was a big enough deal that Janessa had canceled the date so she could personally feed the newborn and keep her elevated or in "up time" to ensure she held down the preemie formula.

He certainly wasn't upset that Janessa had put the baby first. It was exactly what she needed to do, but her baby duties weren't the only thing that had prevented them from rescheduling their date.

Both of them had many, many irons in the fire.

Her, taking care of the baby and dealing with the constant flow of work for Bright Hope House. Him, running the ranch, trying to buy a new place and looking for a new ranch manager for Colts Creek. The assistant manager, Clayton, was still debating if he wanted to move out of his current job.

Brody wasn't sure Janessa was going to keep the place, but if she did, he wanted her to have options. Especially since she likely wouldn't be around much to see to the daily operations of the ranch. He tried not to think too hard about that. For now, he wanted to focus on the things he could fix, and he had someone in mind for the manager position. Calling him was something else on his to-do list.

Janessa was also dealing with the possibility that Teagan's sister wouldn't be adopting the baby after all. Brody had learned about that from one of his and Janessa's quick conversations in his office. That had to be weighing on her, but Janessa hadn't told Teagan or the "GeeGees" yet. She'd reasoned there was no need to worry them until she was certain there was indeed something to worry about. Brody figured, though, Janessa was probably already trying to work out a contingency plan.

If Teagan didn't know of someone else to adopt the baby, then there'd need to be a search for suitable parents. No way would Janessa just leave that to the foster system. Hell, neither would he. That had nothing to do with the don't-get-attached-to-her warnings that Janessa had repeatedly told them. It simply had to do, well, with wanting what was right for her.

Brody fired off the emails with the holiday work schedule to the ranch hands and got started on the contracts and invoices. Definitely not his favorite part of the job, but paperwork was part of ranching.

He looked up when there was movement in the doorway of his office, and for a moment he thought it might be

Janessa. Over the past week, she'd gotten into the habit of bringing by the baby just so they could say hello. Often, there was a kiss or two to go along with that hello, and Brody realized he'd started looking forward to it. But this time it wasn't Janessa.

It was Rowan.

With his hands bracketed on both sides of the doorjamb, Rowan stood there and stared at him. One look told Brody something was wrong.

"What happened?" Brody demanded.

On a heavy sigh, Rowan stepped in and shut the door. Hell, this was not going to be good.

"Are you in some kind of trouble?" Brody asked.

"No." He leveled his gaze on Brody. "But is Mom in trouble?"

That question certainly hadn't been on Brody's radar. "Not that I know of. Why do you ask?"

"Because this private investigator came to the house last night. Mom stepped out on the porch with him because I'm guessing she didn't want me to listen, but I overheard him say she hadn't returned his calls and that he was there because he had to talk to her."

That answer hadn't been on his radar, either, and Brody eased out of the chair. "What was the PI's name?"

"Victor Barton. You know him?"

Brody had a quick debate with how much to tell his brother and decided to spill all. Well, spill as much as he knew anyway. Barton still hadn't fessed up about the *other matter* that Abe had wanted him to investigate.

"Abe hired Barton to look into some pictures and emails he'd gotten over the years," Brody explained. "Pictures and emails that caused him a lot of personal trouble. Abe thought Mom, my dad or I could be behind them. Did you hear Barton say anything about that?"

Apparently, this was the day for bad radars because he could tell Rowan was genuinely surprised by that. "You or Mom wouldn't have done that."

"No, my dad would have. At least that's what Barton believes. I haven't actually seen proof."

But Brody had tried to contact Jimmy. Just yesterday, Brody had gotten Jimmy's phone number from one of his old friends and had called him. Jimmy hadn't answered, but he'd left a message saying it was important they speak. Apparently, Jimmy had blown that off just as Darcia had the calls from the PI.

In his mother's case, though, she probably hadn't dodged the PI because she'd done something wrong. More likely she just hadn't wanted to deal with anything Abe had set in motion. Being accused of harassment wasn't fun, and it didn't matter that the accuser was no longer alive.

"Mom got that picture of Layla," Rowan pointed out. "Was the PI investigating that, too?"

"No. But they might be connected. Jimmy could have sent it."

And that was the main reason Brody wanted to talk to his sperm-donor/deadbeat dad. Not because of how he'd harassed Abe all these years but because Brody wanted to make it clear that he wouldn't let the asshole torment Darcia.

But that didn't explain why the PI had gone to see his mother.

Maybe that was something Abe had instructed him to do? If so, Brody wanted to have a chat with Barton about that, too.

"What else did you hear the PI say to Mom?" Brody pressed.

Rowan shook his head. "Mom kept her voice very low, and she didn't stay out on the porch with the PI for long. Less than five minutes." He paused. "She was upset, though, when she came back in."

Brody cursed. Yeah, he'd definitely be having a chat with Barton about that. "I'm guessing she didn't tell you what the visit was about?"

Another headshake. "I asked her if she was okay, and she blew me off. You know, with one of those fake smiles when she wants us to believe there's nothing wrong?"

He did indeed know that smile, and along with calling Barton, Brody would drop by to see his mother tonight.

Brody heard the now-familiar sound of a fussing baby in the hallway, and he figured that Janessa had dropped by for her morning visit. She didn't knock, though, probably because she thought he was in a meeting so Brody went to the door and opened it. Yep, it was Janessa all right, and she'd already started to walk away.

"It's okay," Brody assured her. "Rowan and I were just finishing up. Tell me if you remember anything else about Barton's visit," he added to Rowan.

"Will do." Rowan grinned when he turned his attention to the baby. Who was indeed doing some fussing. Her little face was screwed up as if she was ready to let out one of those loud cries she was thoroughly capable of.

"Hey, Sweet Pea," Rowan greeted, and he gave the baby's toes a gentle jiggle.

The baby's expression instantly changed, and while she didn't smile, her mood seemed to shift when she studied Rowan. His brother gave her another toe jiggle, added a "Catch you later" before he headed out.

Janessa waited until Rowan was gone before she asked the question Brody knew was coming. "Barton visited Rowan and your mom?"

"Last night. I don't have any details," Brody explained, "but I soon will." Then he would find out why he'd had to hear the news from Rowan rather than his mother.

There was uneasiness in Janessa's eyes. Until she met his gaze, that is. Then she smiled, and with the baby snuggled in her arm, she bent forward to kiss him. It was better than a coffee hit.

"Margo's covering the night shift with the baby," she said when she pulled back from the kiss. "She'll spend the night in the nursery and told my mother and me not to worry about showing up until nine tomorrow morning. Well, that's provided the baby doesn't throw up an entire bottle again."

Brody ran his fingers over the baby's hand while he kept his eyes locked with Janessa's. "This probably isn't the most romantic way to go about this, but if the baby doesn't puke, would you like to go out with me?" he asked.

She smiled. "Yes, especially if the date involves...other things."

He smiled, too, and kissed her again. "Other things can definitely be arranged. Just come over when you're done for the day, and we'll go from there. If the baby has trouble with the reflux, just let me know, and we'll keep rescheduling until the forces of the universe align in our favor."

Brody wanted to kiss her again, but his phone rang, and when he saw the name on the screen, he knew he had to answer it. "Lucian Granger," he relayed to Janessa. "He's buying some horses."

She nodded, said a quick goodbye. And while gently rocking the baby, Janessa left him thinking about tonight and about this aching need he had for her. An ache he pushed aside so he could take the call. As usual, Lucian was all business, which suited Brody just fine. They worked out the deal for buying six of the ranch's cutting horses, and while Lucian was still on the phone, Brody emailed him the standard contract for the sale.

When he finished with Lucian, Brody didn't put his phone away. He went ahead and called Barton. Brody expected to have to leave him a message, but his assistant put the call right through.

Brody dispensed with a greeting and went right to the heart of the matter. "Why did you go to my mother's house last night?"

Barton certainly didn't jump into an explanation, though. He took several long moments before he finally said, "What did your mother tell you?"

That counter question definitely didn't sit well with Brody. "Why were you at her house?" he repeated, and this time he made sure it sounded like the demand that it was.

Barton's huff was plenty loud enough for Brody to hear. "I'm sorry, but I can't get into this with you."

"*This*?" Brody snarled.

"I'm sorry," Barton repeated. "If you want to know what your mother and I discussed, then you should ask her." The PI muttered a goodbye before he ended the call.

Brody sat there staring at his phone and cursing. Not because the PI had hung up on him but because he knew what he had to do next. He was pretty sure his mom was at work today, but Brody still tried her number. When it rang and then went to voice mail, he didn't leave a message. What would he have said anyway?

I demand to know why Abe's hired PI went to see you.

That wouldn't play well with his mother. If that visit was

something she wanted him to know about, she'd tell him when she was ready. If she didn't want Brody to know, then she'd dodge him. Without a message, she'd be curious, or worried, enough to call him back the first chance she got. It was possible that she still wouldn't explain the PI's visit, but at least this was a start.

Brody was about to put his phone away again so he could go out and have a chat with one of the supervisors who handled training the ranch hands, when it rang. He figured it was Darcia. But it wasn't.

It was Jimmy.

Brody hit the answer button, and like with the PI, he didn't greet his father. Nor did he wait for the scumbag to say anything. "I know about the photos and emails you've sent Abe over the years so don't even think about trying to bullshit your way out of it."

"Well, hello to you, too, *son*." Jimmy said that last word as if it were a gnat to be swatted. If the man had ever loved him, and Brody wondered sometimes if he ever had, there was certainly no love now. The feeling was mutual.

Brody answered with his own gnat-swatting tone. "You're a petty asshole, and I want you to stop dicking around with people's lives."

"I don't know what you mean. It has stopped. Abe's dead, remember?"

"I'm not talking about the photos and emails that ruined Abe's marriages and plenty of business deals. This is about Mom," Brody snapped. "You will stop trying to get back at her for whatever wrong or slight you feel she's done."

"Well, now that's an interesting accusation," Jimmy said, his voice still calm and cool. "What exactly is it you think I've done to her?"

"You sent her a photo of Layla." Brody wasn't doing so

well with the calm and cool because the photo was just for starters. It was possible Jimmy had done something that had spurred the PI to make that visit.

"Oh, that. Yeah, I sent it. I wanted her to remember the anniversary of our daughter's death."

Brody wished he could reach through the phone and punch this jerk. Damn it. That photo had caused his mother to cry and twisted her into knots. He wouldn't give Jimmy the satisfaction of hearing that, though.

"My mother has no trouble remembering Layla's death," Brody spat out. "You, on the other hand, weren't even here and haven't been since she died. You should have sent the photo to yourself, you worthless son of a bitch."

"Me? I'm the son of a bitch?" Jimmy growled. Apparently, he was also ditching the calm and cool. "Abe ruined me, and I'm pretty damn sure he did that with your mother's help. They worked together so I'd lose my business, so I'd have to leave town. As far as I'm concerned, they deserved a hell of a lot more than pictures and emails."

Brody wanted to shake his head. "You believe Darcia helped Abe ruin you?"

"I know she did." The anger in his voice was fresh and raw. "Darcia isn't as squeaky clean as she likes people to believe. She's a liar, Brody, and if you want to know the truth about why your sister died, you should ask her."

CHAPTER NINETEEN

JANESSA GLANCED AROUND and decided it didn't get much better than Christmas twilight at Colts Creek. The winter breeze stirred the tiny lights and garlands on the fences, making it look like ribbons of fireflies. The trees, also lit, dotted the grounds so that everywhere you looked, you got a taste of Christmas.

The decorations continued along the road to Brody's, and they dazzled even brighter as she drove away from the lights of the main house. She might never know why a grouch like Abe would want something like this, but maybe it came down to the simple beauty of it. A beauty that even grouches could appreciate.

Janessa parked her car in front of Brody's and stepped out into the crisp night air. She immediately caught a whiff of fragrant wood burning. Heard the horses whickering in the corral off the barn. The winter breeze brushed slow, soft and damp against her skin.

Snuggling her coat tighter around her, she walked toward Brody's porch where he'd left a light on for their *date*. Part of her wanted to laugh at that label when this was clearly a scheduled evening of sex, but it felt like a date, too, what with the romance of this place.

She'd risked the cold and worn a dress. A winter wool red one that she'd bought at a shop in town. It hit her mid-calf so she'd paired it with black cowboy boots that she'd found at the same shop. Putting the outfit together and slathering on some makeup had definitely taken some time. Probably too much time, considering the clothes wouldn't be on her for long. That thought warmed her despite the chilly temps. But what warmed her more was when she looked in the direction of the pond.

And she saw Brody.

Well, she could see the silhouette of him anyway. He was by the pond, standing next to a firepit, the source of that burning wood she'd smelled. There was another Christmas tree there and it was all lit up, making a perfect mirror reflection on the surface of the indigo water.

His back was to her, his hands propped on his hips. What a picture he made standing there. Tall and lean in his great-fitting jeans, buckskin jacket and cowboy hat.

No, Christmas at Colts Creek didn't get much better than this.

He looked at her from over his shoulder, and even though it was hard to see his eyes, she knew they were on her as she made her way toward him. With the tiny lights and fire dancing off the water and flickering over his face, Janessa stepped into his arms when he reached for her, and she slid right into the kiss. A kiss with plenty of heat and need.

But there was something else.

Something simmering just below the surface of that kiss. She thought it might be a different kind of need.

His face was cold, letting her know that he'd been standing out here for a while. She couldn't blame him, though. This place was magic, and with the heat from the firepit, they wouldn't freeze.

"Is everything okay?" she asked when she eased back. Janessa kept her mouth right against his, drawing in his breath, savoring the taste of him.

She expected a quick, short answer along the lines of *fine* and for him to then ask her how her day had gone. But she didn't need to see his eyes to know that *fine* wasn't going to cut it.

"Jimmy called this morning," Brody told her. "He admitted to sending the photos and emails to Abe and the picture of Layla to my mother."

Well, at least he'd owned up to it, but she didn't think Jimmy's confession was what had put Brody in this mood. Janessa didn't push for more. She just slid her arms around his waist, stealing some of the warmth of his body, and waited.

"Jimmy implied that my mother had something to do with Layla's death," Brody finally went on. "He didn't get into specifics, but he claimed she was a liar. I don't want to ask her about it because God knows how many bad memories this will stir up for her."

It was obviously stirring up plenty for Brody, too. "It's possible Jimmy said that to hurt you. He probably knows that the fastest way to hurt Darcia is through you, so he could be trying to drive a wedge between the two of you."

She wanted to ask the obvious—had Darcia had anything to do with his daughter's death? Anything even in an accidental sort of way. But Janessa recalled what Brody had said.

I'm the reason Layla's dead.

Not Darcia. Not Abe. Brody felt he was the cause.

Brody nodded. "Yeah, I can see Jimmy trying to create a wedge especially since he's at the core of Abe's divorces. But I just don't know why Jimmy would go after my mother. He's the one who left. She's the one who stayed to raise Layla and me."

"Unhappy people often try to make others unhappy."

That was the best reason Janessa could come up with. However, that wasn't going to answer these questions Jimmy's call had put in Brody's head. Those answers would have to come from Darcia. Maybe Brody wouldn't risk upsetting Darcia to get to the truth, and if so, he might have to get the truth elsewhere.

"Can the PI verify or disprove what Jimmy told you?" she asked.

Brody shook his head. "I called him after I talked with Jimmy, and he said he didn't have any idea what Jimmy meant. And FYI, Barton is still refusing to say what other matter Abe hired him to do."

Janessa couldn't see how all of this was connected. The emails and photos Jimmy had sent. His sister's fatal car accident. This *other matter*. And the PI's visit to Darcia. But maybe it was.

"If you think it would help, I could ask my mother to talk to Jimmy," Janessa offered.

He looked at her. Really looked at her. Not the eye contact of a man with something else on his mind. For whatever reason, she had now moved front and center of his thoughts.

"Thanks, but don't bother Sophia about this." Using a single finger, he moved a strand of hair off her forehead, and in the same motion, he touched his mouth to hers. It was extremely effective. A whole lot of heat for such minimal contact.

"We're supposed to be on a date," he reminded her. "I've got steaks in the fridge."

Janessa was hungry, but steaks could wait. So could going back to his house. First, she wanted to make sure he was truly all right.

She tipped her head to the hammock. "Why don't we

just lie there for a while, snuggle up to stay warm, look at the Christmas tree and count the stars?"

Now that her eyes had adjusted to the darkness, she had no trouble seeing his eyebrow lift. "If you're thinking about having sex in that thing, you should know we'd likely end up on our asses."

He smiled, and mercy, that was good to see. Still, it wouldn't hurt to linger down here for a while. And possibly fall on their asses.

"That sounds like a challenge," she said, and Janessa went in for a kiss. One of those long slow ones that made her feel as if the rest of the world had just floated away.

"The bed could be a challenge, too," he reminded her. "You know, the bed in a heated room in the heated house. You never know when you can get a paper cut from one of those mattress tags you're not supposed to take off."

She laughed, kissed him again, and taking hold of the waist of his jeans, she backed them toward the hammock. Janessa was pleased to see a plaid blanket, which told her that Brody used this even in wintertime.

"Rowan camps out here sometimes so it's a waterproof camping blanket," he explained when he followed her gaze.

Even better, though, there was no rain in the forecast until morning. Still, if they fell asleep out here, they wouldn't risk getting soaked.

"We'll just count the stars, fool around a little and then take the fooling around back to the bed. Oh, look—" Janessa pointed to the sky "—there's one star. See if you can find another."

He didn't look up. Brody took her mouth as if it'd been years instead of seconds since they'd last kissed. The man could certainly make mouth-to-mouth contact into something sizzling hot.

When she felt the back of her legs hit against the hammock, she took hold of Brody and dropped back. And they promptly tumbled right onto the ground. Janessa's butt did indeed hit, but she thought Brody's shoulder took the brunt of the fall. She was laughing, trying to apologize and making sure he was okay all at the same time when he kissed her again.

She forgot all about possible bruised butt cheeks, the December cold, the inevitable grass stains on her new dress and everything else. The fire that his kiss created had her focus pinpointing just on Brody.

He pulled her into his lap, giving her body something else to think about. Specifically, think about feeling the already hard length of him in just the right spot. Mercy, she already wanted him. Too much want to try to fulfill that fooling-around promise and then make it all the way back to the house.

Brody must have felt the same way about the fifty or so yards of distance between them and the house because with her arms wrapped around his neck and legs around his waist, he managed to move to his knees. Then get to his feet. With slow gentle movements, he eased onto his back on the hammock, which put her on top of him again. But at least they weren't on the ground. And they weren't toppling out.

"The trick is not to make any sudden movements to the side," he instructed, and he managed to toss the blanket over them.

"You seem to know the ins and outs of hammock sex."

Janessa wasn't jealous or disappointed about that, though. Right now, she'd take all the expertise she could get. And the speed. A quickie would work to burn off some of this ache, and then they could do a bedroom follow-up.

With that plan set in her mind, she went after his belt, but he stopped her. "Indulge me," Brody told her.

That was the only warning she got before he worked his way inside her coat and pushed up her dress. Not a fast movement with his clever hands. Nope. This was a slow slide up her body with his palms sliding over each inch of her skin that he bared. Many scalding moments later, he finally had the dress pooled up above her breasts.

Janessa didn't consider herself an overly modest person, but she made one quick glance around. She didn't see lights from any nearby house or barn. That didn't mean there weren't any, though. "I asked something similar when we were in your truck, but how private is it out here?"

"Private," he assured her, "but not as private as my bedroom would be."

She smiled. "We can save the bedroom for later. Sort of like the main course. This can be an appetizer."

"Am I going to be able to walk after this appetizer?" he asked, but there was absolutely no wariness or concern in his tone or expression. All the blues over his mother were now on the back burner. Exactly where she wanted them to be.

And speaking of where things should be, Brody somehow shifted them again. Using that same slow pace he had with her dress, he eased her to her side so that she was snuggled against him. It was, well, nice, but Janessa had preferred the full-body contact.

She got it.

When Brody moved on top of her. The hammock swayed, rocking them, and Janessa got an even better angle on that full-body contact deal.

Brody used the new position to shove down the cups of her bra and kiss her breasts. While the heat inside her continued to climb and climb, he went lower and lower, kissing her along the way. Kissing her, too, as he shimmied down her panties and gave her a kiss that caused her to gasp, arch and send the hammock jiggling.

The jiggling created some interesting sensations. So did Brody's chuckle. The kind of sensations that were going to end way too soon. Yes, she wanted a quickie, but she didn't intend for it to be a solo act.

Janessa caught onto him, dragging him back up her body, and she decided to do some torturing of her own by kissing those vulnerable places on his neck and ear. She did that while she managed to get his shirt unbuttoned, and her reward was his bare chest against hers. Definitely a good way to move this quickie along.

While she kissed and Brody touched—the man used his fingers where his mouth had just been—Janessa tackled his belt and zipper. She was about to free him from his boxers when she realized something.

"Please tell me you put another condom in your wallet," she managed to say.

"Two of them." Wiggling and pressing against her, he worked his wallet out of his back pocket.

She grinned because she might get both the quickie and the follow-up right here. Then again, she wouldn't mind having Brody in bed, especially since she could stay the whole night.

He did some amazing multitasking by French kissing her while he worked on the condom. Since they were smushed right against each other, that involved lots and lots of touching. So much so that Janessa nearly climaxed before he could even get inside her. But once he made that thrust into her, she was so glad she'd managed to wait. Because this was the kind of orgasm that racked through her whole body.

One long stroke and she was a willing, ready and able goner.

She took hold of Brody, matching his strokes until he was a goner right along with her.

JANESSA STRETCHED LIKE a lazy, sated cat. One with a hot naked cowboy next to her in his bed and a clock on the nightstand that told her it was a little past seven in the morning. That meant she still had another hour with him before she'd need to make her way back to the ranch house.

She blew off the idea of getting up so she could do some work stuff before it was time for her to take over baby duty. Some of the work stuff might be important, but right now, waking up next to Brody was something she wanted to savor a little longer.

He was still asleep on his stomach, and while the sheet covered his butt, the rest of him was right there for her viewing pleasure. So, she viewed. And recalled exactly what he'd managed to do to her with that amazing body of his.

Outside, the rain pattered and pinged on the tin roof. The vents from the heater stirred the gauzy white curtains, and the air brushed over her skin like a lover's touch. Well, some lovers anyway. Brody's touch was more masterful at stirring her up rather that brushing her like air.

He didn't move, but since she was watching him, she saw his eyes open. Unlike her waking up, there was no indication that he was puzzled as to why she was there. Of course, he was waking up in his own bed, and it was entirely possible that he often woke up to see a lover looking at him.

Smiling a lazy smile, he took hold of her arm, pulling her down to him for a kiss. "Morning," he drawled, and then he cursed when his gaze shifted to the clock. "I don't usually sleep in."

Apparently, they had entirely different notions as to what constituted sleeping in. "It's Saturday," she reminded him. "You have work?"

"Unfortunately, yes." He cursed again, and sitting up, he scrubbed his hand over his face. Then kissed her long and hard enough to scramble her mind. "I got a text last night right before you got here. I have a meeting in my office at eight."

Crud. That meant there'd be no time for a quickie, especially since he'd need to get dressed.

"Any chance you can come back tonight?" he asked, getting out of bed and giving her a prime peep show. It was a reminder that she still had plans to tongue kiss him from head to toe.

"Possibly. I need to check the baby schedule and see what's going on at Bright Hope."

"You want to grab a shower with me?" he asked. "It'd have to be a fast one."

She was about to take him up on that offer, but there was a knock at the door. "Janessa, it's me," she heard her mother call out. "I really need to talk to you."

Well, heck. This couldn't be good, and Janessa prayed nothing had happened with the baby.

"Go ahead and take your shower," she told Brody as she threw back the covers and got out of bed. "I'll deal with Sophia."

"No, I want to see why she's here." He began pulling on his jeans.

Janessa spotted her dress on the floor, but she didn't see her panties and bra. They had to be somewhere in Brody's house, though. After their incredible hammock sex, she had slipped back on her dress, gathered her underwear and boots, and they'd kissed and groped their way across the pasture to his house. The kissing and groping had been a serious and delicious distraction so she wasn't sure where the bra and panties had ended up.

Because Sophia knocked and called out to her again, Janessa skipped the underwear search, threw on the dress and hurried out of the bedroom and through the house. Brody was right behind her, and he managed to get his jeans zipped up just as Janessa opened the door. She immediately got hit with some of the icy rain that was slanting onto the porch.

"Is the baby okay?" Janessa blurted out.

"She's fine," Sophia insisted. "There's nothing wrong with her."

Janessa's breath swooshed out, and that's when she realized Sophia wasn't alone. Curt was with her, and Janessa didn't miss that both he and her mother looked as if they'd also hastily thrown on their clothes.

"It's about Riggs. It's all taken care of," Sophia quickly added. "Since I was almost positive you'd be here with Brody, I decided to come over and tell you myself. I just didn't want you to hear about it from Dallas PD or Kyle."

Oh, mercy. The cops were involved in this. "What happened?"

"Kyle called to tell me that Riggs showed up at Bright Hope about an hour ago, and he set off the security alarms when he tried to get in. Riggs never got in," Sophia emphasized. "The cops got there fast. So did Kyle. And Riggs was arrested for violating the restraining order."

Janessa shook her head. She was beyond relieved that Riggs hadn't gotten into the house, but there was something here that didn't make sense. "Why did Kyle call you and not me?"

"Because that's what I told him to do. He and I were talking yesterday since it's time to get another extension on the restraining order. The judge had issued the last extension for only fourteen more days, and it was set to expire today. But with this stunt Riggs just pulled, we can go for something much longer. I'm pressing for a year. I told Kyle to hold off calling you so I could come and tell you in person."

Blowing out a long breath, Janessa leaned against the doorframe and let it all sink in. Sophia would have known she would be upset, and she was, but being upset was a drop in the bucket to how Teagan must be feeling.

"I'll call Teagan and Kyle in a couple of minutes," Janessa muttered. Then she looked up at Brody. "Go ahead and get ready for your meeting. I don't want you to be late."

She saw the quick debate in his eyes. "I'll reschedule it," he said. "Let me grab that quick shower and get dressed. Then I'll beef up the security detail around the ranch." He shifted his attention to Sophia. "Because I'm guessing Riggs will soon be out on bail if he isn't already."

Sophia sighed, nodded. "He'll probably be out by this afternoon."

Brody sighed as well, stepped back and motioned for them to come. "Make yourselves some coffee. I won't be long."

Janessa figured with the news about Riggs delivered, her mother and Curt would leave. They didn't. They both stepped inside, and Curt headed to the kitchen, no doubt to get that coffee. Sophia, however, glanced around.

"This is a nice place," Sophia said. After she'd finished the sweeping glance, her gaze settled back on Janessa. Her mother didn't say anything else, but she was clearly waiting for some kind of details.

"Don't ask me about my night with Brody," Janessa advised her, "and I won't ask about yours with Curt."

"I don't mind telling you about Curt." Sophia flashed a

Cheshire cat smile while she went to the fireplace to run her fingers along the smooth stones.

Janessa ignored both the smile, the offer to tell and her mother's *inspection* of Brody's house. Instead, Janessa fired off a text to Kyle, asking him to call her so they could discuss what'd happened with Riggs. After they talked, she'd get in touch with Teagan.

She then headed into the kitchen with Curt. Janessa wasn't sure if Curt had ever been here, but the man certainly had no trouble finding his way around the kitchen. He grabbed four mugs from a cupboard and popped the first pod into the single-serving coffee maker.

"I'm guessing you need the first cup more than the rest of us," Sophia said, joining them. "It appears you didn't get much sleep last night. Oh, by the way, I saw something on the grass between here and the pond. Definitely a bra with perhaps matching panties. If you and Brody tried to have sex in a hammock, you've probably got some bruises."

Janessa had no intention of confirming the hammock sex, but they did indeed have bruises. A few scrapes, too. Any and all injuries were totally worth it, though.

Curt thrust the first cup of coffee at Sophia and kissed her. Not a sweet little peck, either. It was a lover's kiss that Janessa in no way wanted to see. That's why she took the coffee from her mother and stepped away.

"There," Curt said when he pulled back from Sophia to get another cup brewing.

His *there* seemed to be the start of some kind of lecture, maybe even a scolding for her to back off teasing her daughter, but Curt didn't add more. A lawyer who was also a man of few words. Even more surprising was that his there/kiss combo had worked. Sophia looked chastised, smug and satisfied all at once.

"I've asked the judge to extend the TRO so that Riggs can't get near Sweet Pea," Sophia said once Curt had given her the coffee. "It's just a precaution. I don't think Riggs will come back here, but—"

"Thank you," Janessa interrupted. She held gazes with her mother for a moment to let her know the thank-you was not only genuine but very much appreciated. Sophia had certainly stepped up when it came to the baby.

And that's the reason Janessa needed to tell her about Char.

No time like the present. But before Janessa could even get started, Sophia's phone rang. "I have to take this," she said, glancing at the screen. "It's another client who's got some issues going on." As she hit Answer, Sophia headed into the living room, no doubt so she'd have some privacy.

"Thank you, too, for the interference," Janessa told Curt.

He smiled, added some sugar to the coffee that he'd just brewed, and he started another cup. "Sophia's worried about you. Apparently, she has strong memories of you falling apart after your last encounter with Brody." Janessa opened her mouth to argue that she hadn't fallen apart and to defend Brody, but Curt continued before she could speak. "Sophia's wrong. People reconnect, and it all turns out just fine. Take Sophia and me, for instance."

Janessa stared at him from over the rim of her cup. "You and my mother…connected?" Because there must have been a connection for the *re* to occur. "When?"

"When she was madly in love with Abe. She was about twenty-four, and I was ten." He smiled again. "I had a crazy crush on her and thought she was the prettiest girl I'd ever seen."

"Uh, you were a child," she pointed out.

"A child with eyes and apparently wisdom beyond my

years. I was both thrilled and heartbroken when she left Abe. I was glad she was no longer married to my cousin, but I missed seeing her. I took many riding lessons at the ranch just so I could see her."

"Did my mother know?" Janessa asked. Relaxing a little, she leaned back against the edge of the counter.

"She did. Surprised the heck out of me. I thought when I confessed all to her about a month ago that she'd be shocked, but she apparently knew about my crush and riding ploy." He paused, sipped his coffee. "And now the most beautiful woman I've ever seen and I are lovers. I hope we'll keep seeing each other after Abe's will is settled."

Janessa had no intention of dashing his hopes, but Sophia went through relationships darn fast. That probably stemmed from being hurt by Abe, but her mother's love-'em-and-leave-'em-before-they-leave-you pattern didn't bode well for Curt. Too bad because he seemed like a nice guy.

Sophia finished her call, and when she joined them in the kitchen, Curt handed her the coffee he'd made for her. "Everything okay with your client?" he asked.

Her mother made a sound of agreement and looked at Janessa. "That was Jimmy on the phone."

Janessa groaned. She'd hoped they'd heard the last of him.

"Jimmy?" Brody said as he came out of his bedroom. He was all showered and dressed and clearly wanted to know why his father had called.

"Your father has agreed to back off and not cause any more trouble for anyone, including your mother," Sophia explained.

"And you believe him?" Brody fired back.

Sophia lifted her shoulder. "I believe he understands that I'll help Darcia sue his sorry ass for harassment and stalking if he pulls another stunt like sending her a photo of your late sister. You'd have to help with that," she added to Curt. "It'd be a conflict of interest for me to actually go after him, but you could do it for me."

"No worries," Curt assured her. "It's been a while since I've arranged to sue a sorry ass. Hope that doesn't offend you," he told Brody.

"Believe me, it doesn't. I don't want him ever doing anything like that to her again." Brody shook his head, checked the time. "I have to go. I rescheduled my meeting, but I want to draw up a new security-watch schedule."

Janessa nodded, and pushing aside any remarks it might cause Sophia to make, she kissed him. It wasn't hammock-sex foreplay kissing, but it was solid enough.

"Stay as long as you want," Brody told them. "There's bacon and eggs in the fridge if you're hungry."

They all murmured their thanks as he left, and Janessa motioned toward the pond. "I'd better collect my underwear, get dressed and go to the house to check on the baby."

"You should turn the house into Bright Hope Two," Sophia said, stopping Janessa in her tracks. She'd already headed toward the door, but she stopped and stared. Or rather, she goggled.

"Bright Hope Two?" Janessa questioned. "Are you suggesting I stay in Last Ride?"

"No." Sophia was plenty fast with that response. "But you could set it all up, and someone else could run it."

"Uh, like who?" Janessa considered everything Curt had just told her. "You?"

Sophia laughed as if that were the most absurd thing she'd ever heard. "No. I was thinking more along the lines of Darcia and Margo. Darcia's already certified as a foster parent, and she obviously loves kids."

"And she has a job along with being the mother of a teenager," Janessa pointed out.

"A home for troubled teens could appeal to her, and Margo obviously has plenty of time on her hands. Or she will have after Sweet Pea's adoption. I could do the legal work for it, of course, but I could do that from Dallas." She paused, smiled and lifted her coffee cup as if making a toast. "You could call it All Abe's Exes Making Up for His Bad Karma. Or AAEMUFHBK," she added slowly as she obviously went through the first letter of each of those words.

Janessa wanted to mimic Sophia's laugh to note the absurdity, but that seed of thought had been planted in her head. And other than the name, it wasn't a totally stupid idea. She could add it to the list of possibilities of what would happen to the house and the ranch in six weeks.

First, though, she needed to deal with what was happening now.

"I don't want to say anything about this to Teagan yet," Janessa started, "but her sister, Char, recently found out she's pregnant with twins."

Janessa watched her mother process that, but Sophia didn't say anything.

"Char's had some complications," Janessa went on, "and I've stayed in contact with her through texts." She paused. "It's possible that Char will decide not to adopt Teagan's daughter."

"Well," Sophia finally said. She set her cup on the counter and then stared at it for several seconds before she lifted her gaze to meet Janessa's. "Well," she repeated, "you can tell Teagan that no way Sweet Pea's going into foster care. If Char doesn't adopt the baby, then you'll have to do it."

CHAPTER TWENTY

BRODY KNEW HE had put off this visit long enough. Along with it being Christmas Eve, it'd been a little over two weeks since Rowan had told him about the private investigator's visit to see Darcia. Two weeks of Brody hoping that his mother would come to him and volunteer what the visit had been all about.

But she hadn't.

That's why he pulled to a stop in front of her house and, steeling himself up, Brody walked toward her porch. The air was cold and heavy, the clouds thick and gray, which meant there was talk about the rare possibility of a white Christmas. It was more likely to be an icy one, but he supposed that still qualified as white.

Brody knew his mother was home because he'd already checked. Earlier, he'd texted her to see if he could drop by, and she'd said that was fine, that she didn't have any plans for the day. Well, he had plenty of plans. Plenty to do. But this was the first thing he had to deal with. Then he'd have to handle a whole pile of fallout if this visit didn't go well.

Because it was entirely possible he was going to hear something he didn't want to hear.

He caught the scent of cinnamon and sugar before he even knocked. The scent got stronger when his mother opened the door.

"I just took a fresh batch of Christmas cookies out of the

oven," she greeted with a huge smile. Motioning for him to follow her to the kitchen, they walked past the sprawling tree by the fireplace. "I've already dropped Rowan off at Colts Creek so I figured you and I could have a late breakfast. I made cinnamon rolls."

Brody knew Rowan wasn't there. It was something he'd already checked on, and his brother was indeed at Colts Creek. The ranch hands were having their annual Christmas breakfast gathering that would last for at least a couple of hours. Brody wasn't sure how this conversation with his mother would go, and he hadn't wanted to risk Rowan being around for it.

Darcia's smile faded when she studied his face. "What's wrong? Did something happen to Sweet Pea?"

Sweet Pea. Janessa really needed to come up with an actual name before that stuck. It was cute now, but Brody doubted the girl would want people calling her that when she was a teenager.

"Nothing's wrong with the baby," was all he said when he stepped inside. He took a moment to settle himself. "Mom, we need to talk about the visit you got from the PI Abe hired."

She turned away from him but not before he saw the surprise in her eyes. Surprise because she hadn't expected him to know about that.

"It was nothing," she said, walking toward the kitchen. "He just wanted to ask me about the photo of Layla that Jimmy had sent me."

He had no trouble recalling word for word what Jimmy had said about Darcia, that she was a liar and that she'd had some part in Layla's death. Of course, with all the crap that Jimmy had done, there was no reason to believe him. But still it was eating away at him.

Brody followed his mother into the kitchen and watched as she used a spatula to place some of the cinnamon rolls on plates. "Are you planning on marrying Janessa so she can keep the baby?" she asked.

His brain did a sort of mental stutter. "What?"

Darcia just kept on plating up the rolls, but she also lifted her shoulder in a shrug. "Sophia said something. She was vague about it, but I got the impression that the adoptive mother might be trying to back out."

Yeah, and that was more than an impression. Janessa hadn't pressured Char to give her an answer, nor had she told Teagan what was going on, but as the days and weeks dragged on, it seemed clear to him that Janessa needed to be looking at other options for the little girl.

As for his own options, he obviously needed to make something crystal clear. "No, I won't be marrying Janessa so she can keep the baby."

Darcia put the plates on the table, but she gave him a quick glance before she turned away again and started pouring some coffee. "But you might want to marry her for other reasons?"

No need for Darcia to fill in the blanks on that. It was a really bad attempt to ask if he was in love with Janessa. He wasn't. Nor were there any proposal or marriage plans in his future.

"Janessa doesn't need to be married to me or anyone else to adopt a baby," he reminded her. "You should know because you weren't married when you adopted Rowan."

With her back still to him, he saw her stiffen a little. "Yes. But Sophia thought that, well… It doesn't matter what she thought."

Again, no need for blank-filling. Sophia and his mother had obviously had a conversation about their kids possibly being in love. Something that neither mom would likely approve of because of the way things had ended with Janessa and him a lifetime ago.

"Janessa and I aren't kids," he reminded her. "And she's going back to Dallas at the end of next month." The next weeks would no doubt fly by.

That was all he intended to say about his temporary sex life. Plus, he recognized dodging and stalling when he saw it, and his mother was definitely doing both of those things.

Brody sat at the table, cupping his coffee in his hands, and he waited for Darcia to take the chair next to him. He'd considered how to start this chat but wasn't sure if he had the right angle of throwing out a hot button to see if it spurred his mother into telling him the truth about Abe's investigation and that visit from the PI.

"My mind keeps circling around what happened to Layla," he started. "I know I'm the reason she was in that car—"

"No," Darcia interrupted. "Your sister was in that car because Abe lent it to her."

Brody had wished a million or more times that what his mother had just said was true. It wasn't.

"I was the reason," he insisted. "If I hadn't argued with her, if I'd handled things better, she wouldn't have been in that car in the first place."

She reached out and slid her hand over his. "You shouldn't have had to *handle* things with her. You were only seventeen. I'm the parent, and I should have dealt with it, with her, before things went from bad to the worst possible thing that could happen."

Brody was well aware that his mother felt plenty of her own guilt about what'd happened that night, and yes, she was the parent. But Darcia hadn't known all the stuff going on because Brody had kept it from her.

"I knew that Layla had been sneaking around and drinking," Brody explained. Not for the first time, either. It was something he'd repeated the few times that his mother had actually been willing to talk about the daughter she'd lost. "I didn't tell you because I thought I could get her to straighten up."

Darcia shook her head and closed her eyes as if trying to shut out the memories. Brody knew for a fact that doing those things didn't work. The memories were always right there behind you, ready to bite you in the ass.

"Layla was acting out," his mother muttered. "Some of it was normal teen stuff, but part of it was because she felt abandoned by her father. You felt that, too, but you handled it in a different kind of way."

Yes, by drinking and sneaking out at night. The car Abe had loaned her gave Layla an easier way of doing those things, but Brody figured she would have found another way had she not had that vehicle.

"If I hadn't been at work that night," Darcia added, "the outcome of this could have been different."

He doubted that. Like finding another vehicle, Layla would have come up with a way to get around their mother.

"I took away her keys that night," Brody went on, "but I didn't think to look for a spare." That had been a big-assed mistake. So had arguing with Layla. "I told her she was acting like an idiot." He'd also called her stupid and a couple of other choice words.

It'd been like pouring gasoline on a blazing fire.

Layla hadn't run out then and there because she knew he would have gone after her. Nope. She'd shouted some predictable profanity at him, stormed into her room, slammed the door and locked it. Then, while Brody had been stewing over the argument and doing his own cursing, Layla sneaked out through her bedroom window, got in the car and sped away.

And that's where Brody's string of big-assed mistakes exploded with a huge bang.

He'd gone after her in his truck and caught up with her on the stretch of road that led to the interstate. Brody hadn't been sure where she was going, but it'd been obvious she was trying to put some distance between him and her.

She'd managed it, too.

Brody had sped up. So had she. Until both of them were driving too damn fast. Because he had a little experience driving that particular road, he'd known to slow down on the deep curve just before the Longhorn bridge.

Layla hadn't done the same.

She'd slammed into a tree, and by the time Brody had gotten to her, she was already dead. Sometimes, like now, the image of seeing her in that mangled wreck was as fresh and raw as it had been in the moment it'd happened.

Brody pushed that grief aside as he'd done countless times. It wouldn't stay gone, but he needed a reprieve so he could finish this conversation with his mother.

"So, did Abe want the PI to investigate Layla's death?" Brody came out and asked. "Is that why you don't want to talk to me about it?"

Darcia's eyes widened, and her hand shook when she set her coffee cup on the table. "No. Why would you think that?"

Because there was indeed something about her death to be investigated. Something to be revealed anyway. Maybe Abe had gotten wind of it and wanted it confirmed.

"There's a reason the PI didn't come to me with this,"

Brody went on. "I'm thinking that reason was because Abe didn't want to throw the hell of that night back in my face. So, Abe could have told the PI to talk to you instead."

Though that still would have been some hell-throwing since his mother was just as torn up about Layla's death as he was. But Abe might not have minded Darcia being upset, and it was possible he'd wanted to spare Brody until he'd gotten to the truth, the whole truth and nothing but the truth.

"Was that visit about Layla?" Brody pressed. "Was Layla the *other matter* that Abe wanted him to investigate?"

"No," Darcia repeated.

Brody cursed under his breath when tears filled her eyes, and on a sigh, he started to get up so he could pull her into his arms. But Darcia stopped him by catching onto his hand.

"Please sit down," she said, her voice no louder than a whisper. "There's something you need to know."

"Something about Layla," he concluded.

She shook her head, and it felt like a kick in the teeth when he saw twin tears spill down her cheeks. "Not about Layla. It's about Rowan."

Everything inside Brody went still. He sure as hell hadn't expected his brother's name to come up, but his mind began to whirl with some really bad possibilities.

"Are Rowan's birth parents trying to get him back?" Brody snapped, and that was another kick in the teeth mixed with a hefty dose of anger. Because no one was going to take Rowan. He'd already lost a sister, and he wasn't going to lose a brother, too.

"No," Darcia said once again. This time she took both of his hands, and her gaze locked with his. "Because I'm Rowan's birth mother."

Well, hell. Brody tried to let the shock of hearing that sink in, but it didn't.

"Rowan is your son?" he managed to ask.

"Yes, I gave birth to him when I was in California." More tears came. Not hoarse sobs. They fell as quietly as her voice. "I had fake adoption papers done, and then I lied to everyone. Including Rowan and you."

Brody shoved his way past that shock and tried to follow this through. "Abe found out about Rowan, and he hired the PI to find the truth?"

Darcia nodded, squeezed his hand even harder. "So did Jimmy. When he found out that Abe was having him investigated, he followed the PI, and Jimmy put enough pieces together to come up with the big picture." His mother paused, sighed. "And the big picture is that Abe was Rowan's father."

"Sweet Pea's smiling," Margo announced, bringing the baby into Abe's office where Janessa was working.

Janessa immediately set aside the email she was answering to look at the baby who may or may not have been smiling. The corner of her tiny mouth was indeed lifted, and her eyes seemed to be fixed on Margo.

"It's a reflex smile," Janessa said. "I read about them. Most experts believe babies don't actually smile until they're about six weeks old." Which wouldn't be for another two weeks. "It could be longer for her since she's a preemie." Janessa had read all about that, as well. It was a nice change of pace from all the teen books and articles she'd studied since creating Bright Hope.

"Well, she's a fast learner," Margo concluded with an exaggerated pout and a firm nod. However, there was nothing firm about her expression when she turned back to the baby. "Aren't you a cutsie-wootsie fast learner, jelly bean? You're GeeGee Margo's Sweet Pea Patootie, and tomorrow you'll have your very first Christmas-Missmass."

Janessa winced a little at the baby talk, but she didn't insist Margo knock it off. She'd done some reading on this, too, and the experts were divided on whether it was good or bad. What was good was to have a lot of interaction with the baby, and Margo was clearly doing that. The woman had also clearly gone overboard with the Christmas-Missmass presents, too. There were at least a dozen presents under the massive tree in the great room.

"Thank you for stepping up to take care of the baby," Janessa said, and it had Margo looking up at her in surprise. "You're amazing with her."

Margo brushed a kiss on the top of the baby's head. "It's not hard to be amazing with someone this precious." Her eyes teared up a little. "Not having children is my biggest regret. Yes, an even bigger regret than letting Abe treat me the way he did by tossing me out."

Wow, then her no-children regret was huge since Janessa knew the depths of Margo's hatred for Abe. After all, they'd both kicked Abe's tombstone.

"You could foster," Janessa suggested. Then she thought of something else. Something she was still mulling around, but it was a good time to get Margo's take on it. Especially since the conditions of Abe's will would soon be fulfilled.

"Did Sophia say anything to you about her suggestion of turning this house into a teen shelter?" Janessa asked.

Margo beamed. "Yes, and I had some ideas about that. What if you used it for a transition house? You know, for those teens who are too old for Bright Hope but still haven't gotten their lives together yet. Some could work here or finish school."

Obviously, Margo had given this more thought than Janessa had. There was a need for such a place, and it was the reason she'd often ignored a teenager's eighteenth birthday just so he or she would have a little more time.

"I'm not sure how the folks of Last Ride would like having a place like that here," Janessa remarked.

"Maybe a few sourpusses wouldn't approve, but they're just poopy-doopy sourpusses, aren't they?" she added to Sweet Pea.

That was possibly true, but it was something Janessa needed to look into. She could talk to Alma from the Last Ride Society. Or get Sophia to start asking around. Since it was her mother's idea in the first place, Sophia would likely jump right on doing that. If Janessa went to Alma, then the woman would likely have questions about the research she hadn't finished yet.

"Why are you working in here?" Margo asked, her gaze skirting over the now-empty walls and shelves. With the exception of the desk, chair and his sneering portrait, all of Abe's things had now been boxed up and moved into one of the storage rooms.

Janessa shrugged. "The chair's more comfortable than the one I was using in my bedroom, and there are electrical plugs everywhere." She tapped her foot to the ones on the floor beneath the desk. "Plus, the view is great."

It was. She could see some of the pastures and one of the barns, which meant she often caught glimpses of Brody.

"What's this?" Margo moved closer to the desk and the small wrapped gift box that was tucked on the side of some files Kyle had sent her from Bright Hope.

"My thirteenth birthday gift from Abe." Janessa picked up the box, and as she'd done since she'd first discovered it, she put it back down.

"You're not going to open it?" Margo asked.

"Eventually. I just keep thinking that I should do it when I'm not busy and when the mood is right."

Margo snorted. "Which might be never. You should open it tomorrow, on Christmas." She looked back down at the baby. "Oh, look. Sweet Pea's smiling at you now." Margo finished that off with some cooing and babbling.

The baby was doing another of those reflex smiles, but it looked like the real deal to Janessa. It didn't spur her to baby talk, but she went closer so she could kiss the tiny fingers that were clutching onto the leg of her pink onesie.

"Here, she wants you to hold her," Margo insisted.

Janessa decided to go with that theory, too, and she took the baby, snuggling her in her arms. Margo stayed right there, smiling down at the precious little face. The woman also appeared ready and willing to take the baby back at any moment.

There was a knock on the jamb of the open door, and when Janessa looked up, she spotted Velma Sue. Not alone. A lanky man with black hair was with her.

"Oh, Matt," Margo said, hurrying to him for a hug. "Well, you're a sight for sore eyes. Actually, you're a real sight for any and all eyes."

"Matt," Janessa mentally repeated, and she recalled Brody mentioning a foster brother, Matt, who was a cop. This guy looked more cowboy than cop in his jeans, boots and pale gray shirt. He was even carrying a Stetson, and if he had a weapon, she didn't see it.

Margo eased back from the hug and turned the man to face Janessa. "This is Matt Corbin. Matt, this is Abe's daughter, Janessa."

Oh, yeah, he had that cowboy smile down pat, too. Sort of a slightly lopsided grin that showed plenty of charm and verified Margo's comment about his being a real sight. Janessa wasn't tempted by this tasty-looking guy when she had Brody, but Matt was solidly in the hot-guy category.

"Good to meet you," Matt said, crossing the room toward her.

Matt shifted that cool lopsided grin from the baby to Janessa. "And this must be the baby you're fostering. Brody mentioned her last time we talked," he added. "What's her name?"

"To be determined," Janessa answered before Margo could spout out Sweet Pea. No need to add another person calling the baby by the nickname. "It's good to meet you, too, Matt. Are you here to see Brody?"

"I am. I drove down from Amarillo yesterday with my son and ex-wife so they could spend Christmas with her folks," he added. "Figured I'd catch up with Brody while I was in Last Ride, but he's not in his office. Not at his house or Darcia's, either. Since he's not answering his phone, I thought he might be here."

That got Janessa's attention. "He's not answering his phone?"

Matt's grin faded, and now she saw the first trace of cop in his eyes. There was concern, and she knew why. It wasn't like Brody not to take a call.

"It's Darcia's day off," Matt explained, "and if she's driving, she'll let a call go to voice mail. I was going to try Rowan, but I didn't want to worry him if there's nothing to worry about."

"Rowan's here today for the ranch-hand breakfast," Janessa said, motioning out the window. "I saw him earlier in the corral."

Matt nodded. "Then maybe I'll just go out and speak to him. Brody's phone battery probably died or something.

Or he could be out looking at some horses where there's no cell reception. I'm sure there's nothing wrong."

There was some cop subtext in that assurance. Matt wanted to believe there was nothing wrong, but until he ruled it out, there was indeed something to worry about.

"How long ago were you at Brody's?" she asked Matt.

He checked the time. "About a half hour ago, maybe a little more." He paused. "Again, it was good to meet you," Matt said. He smiled at the baby, slid on his hat and went to the door where he gave Margo another hug before heading out. No doubt to find Rowan who would in turn help him find Brody.

"Margo, could you take the baby?" she asked, and once Margo had done that, Janessa texted Brody. Where are you?

A few seconds crawled by. Is everything okay? he texted back.

Janessa learned two things from that. Brody hadn't answered her question, and he wanted to make sure there wasn't something wrong with the baby.

We're all okay she messaged back. Are you? Matt was just here looking for you.

More seconds ticked by. Then more. And finally he responded. I've got a lot on my plate today.

Interesting because the plate didn't include anything at the ranch. Or responding to phone calls from a foster brother.

Gotta go, Brody added to his text. I'll talk to you later.

It was the sort of thing people said all the time, but Janessa got a bad feeling about it. Bad enough for her to grab her purse and her keys.

"Is it all right if I drive over to Brody's and see if he's there?" she asked Margo.

"Of course," Margo readily agreed. "You'll let us know if you find him?"

Janessa assured the woman she would, then gave the baby a quick kiss and hurried out after bundling her coat. She got in her car and headed to Brody's. Even though Matt had said he wasn't there, it was a starting point. She could leave Brody an actual note, one that might let him know how concerned she was once he read it.

When she reached his house, she saw that his truck wasn't in the driveway so Janessa dug out a pen from her purse, then a piece of paper. Or rather a receipt.

"I need to see you," she wrote and then looked around for something to stick it to his door. The only thing she could find was some cinnamon gum.

Chewing two pieces, she went to his porch, chewed some more, and when she thought she finally had the gum at the right consistency, she used the red blob to glue the note in place. She was about to go back to her car to start a drive around town, but she heard the sound of an engine. A couple of moments later, Brody pulled to a stop in his driveway.

One look at his face and she knew he wasn't happy to see her. She also knew that something was wrong.

"I'm okay," he said in such a way that in no way assured her that he was.

With her gaze locked on his face, she waited on the porch as he walked toward her. "Matt came by the ranch house," she told him. "He was worried about you."

Brody made a sound that could have meant anything, took out his phone and fired off a quick text. "I told him I'm fine," Brody relayed to her. Then he repeated it to Janessa.

She nearly mimicked that sound of his, the one that could have meant anything, but no way did she want to blow this up into an argument. Something was wrong, and Janessa wanted to know what.

He plucked the note from the door, read it and then looked at the gum. She shrugged. "I wanted to make sure it didn't blow away."

And to make sure Brody didn't send her away, Janessa slid her hand around the back of his neck, pulled him down to her and kissed him. In what was a first in this kissing history, he didn't slip right into it. No tongue, no heat. But Janessa didn't give up. She kept kissing him while she eased her arms around him. She didn't stop until they both had reached the level of serious oxygen deprivation.

"Want to tell me what you don't want to talk about?" she asked.

On a heavy sigh and some muttered profanity, he unlocked the door so they could go inside. He went to the fridge and came back with two beers. Since it wasn't even lunchtime yet, it was early for a drink, but Janessa took it, and when he dropped down onto the sofa, she sat on the stone-top coffee table across from him so they'd be face-to-face. Janessa didn't say anything else, didn't kiss him again. She just waited him out.

"I talked to my mom about the visit from the PI that Abe hired," Brody finally said. "I thought it had something to do with my sister's death."

As serious of a subject as that was, and it was indeed as serious as it got, Janessa was relieved that she wasn't the reason for his obviously dark mood.

"There were some things about her death that my mother didn't know, but I thought maybe Abe had found out about it and paid to have it investigated." He paused, had a long pull of his beer. "My sister killed herself because she was pissed off at me."

Janessa tried to combine sympathy with a flat, level look. "There had to have been more to it than an argument with you."

"Many arguments," he corrected. "But that night, her mood was the worst I'd ever seen. She'd been drinking, and after I yelled at her, she sneaked out and ended up driving her car right into a tree." He paused again. "She didn't even hit the brakes."

Janessa took a moment to let that sink in, and she had to bite off the *holy hell* she nearly muttered. He believed his sister had committed suicide. Janessa wanted to ask if it was possible that the girl had simply lost control of the vehicle, but she doubted that would make Brody's guilt go away. Guilt that he didn't deserve, but a lot of crappy things happened that people didn't deserve.

She set her beer aside and took hold of his hand. "I'm sorry." It was a puny response, but it was heartfelt, and much to her surprise, it seemed to help.

Brody cursed, groaned and dropped the back of his head against the sofa. His mood didn't brighten, but at least now she could see more than just the guilt and grief. There was frustration and maybe something else.

"So, did the PI visit Darcia to talk to her about Layla?" Janessa asked.

Brody laughed, but there wasn't a drop of humor in it. "No." He lifted his head, drank more beer and met her gaze. "The visit was about Rowan."

At the mention of his brother's name, Janessa instantly got a bad thought. "Was there something wrong with his adoption? Did Darcia cut any corners?"

"Oh, there was something wrong with it all right," Brody verified. "There wasn't one because my mother gave birth to Rowan."

Janessa hadn't instantly got that thought at all. And now she did say that "Holy hell."

"Yeah," Brody verified, "and that's not even the big surprise in all of this. Abe is Rowan's father."

Janessa froze. Any other *holy hell* that was still trapped in her throat just stalled there. It took her a moment and chugging some beer before she could finally ask, "How the heck did that happen?"

"Apparently, there was some residual lust left over from their younger years." There was more than a tinge of sarcasm in his voice.

Since Brody and she had that same residual lust, Janessa totally got it. But she couldn't get Abe and Darcia being together after they'd fought and feuded for years. Still, she could see how this might play out. One bad night, perhaps some alcohol, but instead of driving a car into a tree, Abe and Darcia had landed in bed. Darcia had gotten pregnant, and… Janessa had to stop.

"Did Abe know?" she asked.

"He found out. I don't know how," Brody quickly added. "It was probably when he was having the background checks done on Jimmy, Darcia and me. Rowan was the other matter that Abe hired the PI to investigate."

Her brain was too frazzled right now to consider how Abe would have handled news like that, but he would have absolutely wanted proof that Rowan was his son. Abe had done a DNA test on her after all. So, maybe the PI was supposed to get that proof.

She thought of Abe's letter that he'd sent to her right before he'd died. *I need you to come to the ranch ASAP. There are some things I have to tell you, some things I have to fix.* Had Abe been talking about Rowan?

Possibly.

Probably, she amended.

Once Abe had found out that Rowan was his son, Abe would have wanted him. The child with him and his first love. Heck yes, Abe would have wanted him, but a custody battle wouldn't have worked because Rowan was already old enough to nix such a fight. No way would Rowan choose Abe over Darcia. So, Abe had needed a strategy, a fix, for drawing his son into his life. Abe had needed her maybe to help him mend fences with Darcia so he could in turn build a relationship with his son.

"Why didn't Darcia tell Rowan? Or you?" Janessa asked Brody.

"I didn't get into that with her, but I suspect she was ashamed of sleeping with her sworn enemy."

Janessa could understand his mother feeling that way, but something else occurred to her, too. Something that was going to take her a while to process. "Rowan's my half brother. Yours, too."

"Yeah." That was all Brody said for several long moments. "And now I have to tell our kid brother that his life has been pretty much a big-assed lie."

CHAPTER TWENTY-ONE

BRODY WAS QUICKLY learning that fixing big-assed lies wasn't easy. Life got in the way. Specifically, life in the form of Rowan having a hot Christmas Eve date. One that Brody had decided not to shoot to hell and back by telling his brother the truth about his parents. Instead, Brody had delayed lie-fixing for the night.

Now that it was morning, he wished he could keep delaying it.

Darcia no doubt felt the same. After all, it was Christmas, but this wasn't news they should sit on any longer. The odds were slim that Rowan would hear this from someone else, but it could be devastating if the boy had to hear it from anyone other than family. Heaven knew what the truth would do to him, but Brody was betting this wasn't a case of the truth setting him or anyone else free. Still, it had to be done.

They'd already opened presents and had their traditional family breakfast before Rowan went to his room for a shower and to no doubt test out the new video game Brody had gotten him. That left Darcia and Brody waiting in the living room.

And waiting.

Brody thought he was doing a decent job of holding back his frayed nerves, but his mother was failing big time. She was clutching and unclutching her cross necklace while running the fingers of her other hand over the silk scarf Rowan had given her for Christmas. Brody had gone big scale and given her the plans for the new pottery studio he was having built for her, and Darcia had her gaze fixed on those plans that she'd spread out on the coffee table.

"I told Janessa," Brody said, his voice cutting through the silence.

He saw the muscle do a quick jump in her throat, saw the equally quick objection in her eyes. Then the resignation came. Janessa needed to know because Rowan was her brother. *Their* brother, Brody mentally corrected, which would make for a weird family reunion if they ever had one. His lover's father and his mother had created a child together.

"Janessa must think I'm the worst kind of parent," Darcia muttered.

"No, she doesn't. She's just trying to come to terms with this like I am. It's not easy to come to terms when we have to deal with the image of her father having sex with my mother." He shrugged. "But actually the whole idea of parental sex isn't something we want to imagine."

Darcia managed a brief smile. One that came to a fast end, and her forehead bunched up. "I was a mess after Layla died. You remember," she muttered in a whisper.

He certainly did. He'd been a mess, too. Brody considered the timing of that and merged it with the timing of Rowan's conception, his mother becoming a traveling nurse and Rowan's birth.

Brody cursed and, even though it was warranted, the language earned him a scolding glance from Darcia. Once a mother, always a mother. "Abe took advantage of you," Brody concluded. "You were grieving, and he—"

"Abe has plenty of sins, but that isn't one of them," Darcia interrupted. "As much as you don't want to think about parental sex, I'm the one who went to Abe. At first, it was just to confront him again about that blasted car he'd lent Layla, but then I started crying. Abe pulled me into his arms, and one thing led to another."

It sure sounded like Abe taking advantage, but Brody remembered something else. Abe had grieved, too. Even as a teenager, Brody had seen that.

"That was the first and only time I had sex with Abe," Darcia went on. "When I realized I was pregnant, I left so I could have the baby in secret. I'm sorry about that," she added to Brody. "Because I know I left you when you were only eighteen and in a very bad place about your sister."

He had indeed been in a bad place, what with Janessa leaving and Layla's death. But he had to give his mother an out here. "Truth is, you weren't really helping with the grief," he confessed. "Don't get me wrong, I love you and I missed you when you weren't here, but we weren't doing much to fix each other. What helped was when you came back with Rowan."

The muscles in her face relaxed, and some relief practically washed over her. She tensed, though, when his phone dinged with a text. Brody glanced at it and, even though it was something he'd want to share with her eventually, for now he sent a quick reply and put his phone away.

Just as they heard Rowan come out of his room.

They stayed put, waiting, and a few seconds later, Rowan came in. "Hope there are more of those cinnamon rolls," his brother immediately said.

Then he stopped, looked at their faces. Rowan didn't curse, not out loud anyway, but Brody was positive there were some choice words and some WTFs going through the boy's head.

"Are you sick?" Rowan asked, the question directed at his mother before he shifted to Brody. "Did you get Janessa pregnant?"

"Wrong on both counts," Brody assured him, and he added a scowl for the second question.

Darcia stood and faced Rowan. "I have something to tell you, but before I do, I want you to know that I love you so very much."

"Crap," Rowan blurted out. "This is bad. Real bad. What happened?"

His mother swallowed hard. "Rowan, you're my son. *My son*," she emphasized, pressing her hand to her stomach. "And Abe Parkman was your father."

Brody had to hand it to his mother. She'd gotten it all out there without so much as a stutter or a crack in her voice, and she'd kept her eyes on Rowan the whole time.

Rowan stood there, volleying confused glances between Brody and Darcia. Since it seemed Rowan was looking for some confirmation, Brody gave him a nod. He stood as well in case Rowan fell apart or tried to do a deny-and-bolt. Brody didn't want to give another sibling the chance to run off in a rage.

But Rowan didn't rage, bolt or deny. Groaning softly, he went to the sofa and plopped down. "Well, this explains a lot," the boy grumbled.

Now, it was Darcia and Brody who exchanged surprised glances. "What do you mean?" Brody asked.

"Well, when I applied for an after-school job at the ranch, Mr. Parkman called me into his office to talk to me. This was just a couple of weeks before he died. He kept looking at me funny. You know, the way you'd study a painting or something."

Or something. In this case, Abe was looking for any

resemblance. There wasn't one. Well, in hindsight, Brody could see that Rowan and Abe had the same shaped eyes, but the Parkman DNA wasn't as obvious in Rowan as it was in Janessa and plenty of others.

"Mr. Parkman didn't really say anything about the job," Rowan added. "He just asked me questions about how I was doing in school, what I wanted to be, that sort of thing."

Since Abe rarely had anything to do with the hiring and firing of ranch hands, calling Rowan into his office would have definitely clanged some bells for Brody if he'd known about it. Still, he wouldn't have made the stretch to Rowan being Abe's son. Brody would have just figured that Abe was trying to wheedle info as to how Darcia felt about Rowan working at the ranch. Of course, Abe could have also been trying to figure out if Rowan knew the truth.

"Then I was at O'Riley's later that day and was having my usual nachos and a Coke," Rowan went on. "When I finished, I tossed my cup and plate in the trash and left, but one of my friends said after I was gone, this guy went through the trash and took out the cup. He was trying to be all stealthy like, but my friend saw him. I just figured the guy wanted the cup because it was one of those that O'Riley's had printed up for the holiday gala. Some people collect junk like that."

Brody was about 100 percent sure this wasn't about adding to a junk collection. "The man who took it must have been the PI Abe hired," he explained to Rowan. "And he likely used the cup to get your DNA so Abe could prove his paternity."

"Crap," Rowan muttered again. He repeated it a couple more times and scrubbed his hands over his face before he fastened his gaze to Darcia. "It's true? You really gave birth to me?"

Darcia nodded. "I didn't tell you because then I would have had to also explain that Abe was your father. I didn't want him to know because he would have tried to get custody of you. I figured I'd tell you when you were old enough." She paused. "But then when you got *old enough*, I convinced myself that you were better off with a lie than the truth. I'm truly sorry about that," she insisted.

Rowan certainly didn't jump to accept her apology. No surprise there. If Brody was having trouble dealing with this, then it had to be much, much worse for Rowan.

"And you didn't know?" Rowan asked him.

Brody shook his head. "Mom told me yesterday, and no, I didn't suspect anything." Going with another round of hindsight, Brody hadn't *wanted* to suspect anything. He'd just been so damn glad that having a baby around might help Darcia's grief over Layla.

Darcia went closer to Rowan as if she might try to hug him, but Rowan backed away from her. There was still no rage. Still no fired off insults as to what a huge mistake this had been for her not to tell him.

Rowan held out his hand in a don't-come-closer gesture. All things considered, it was a fairly mild reaction, but Brody saw that it cut Darcia to the core.

"I, uh, think I want go for a ride around the ranch," Rowan said to Brody. "Mind if I use Thorn or one of your other horses?"

"No, I don't mind. But choose any horse other than Thorn unless you want to deal with his pissy mood. You want me to go with you?"

Rowan shook his head. "I just need some time to myself," he said, aiming that at their mother. "I won't do anything stupid."

His brother had probably said that because he knew this

would cause a flashback or two back to the night Layla had died. Later, when things had settled down, Brody would thank Rowan for saying it to her.

"It's cold out there," Darcia told him. "It might snow."

"I'll bundle up, and I won't do anything stupid," Rowan repeated. He grabbed his coat and headed out the back door toward the barn.

Brody expected Darcia to stay put, to wait until Rowan came back. Whenever that would be.

Darcia's gaze drifted to the window that faced the barn. "He'll be all right by himself?"

Brody nodded. "Rowan's a good rider, and I believe him when he said the doing-nothing-stupid part."

That didn't mean Brody wouldn't check on him. He'd give Rowan a couple of hours, then text him. If he got any bad vibes from the text response, or no response at all, then Brody would ride out to whatever part of the ranch Rowan had gone. All of his horses had trackers on them so it wouldn't take long to find him.

Darcia brushed a kiss on his cheek. "Thank you for everything, and let me know if Rowan wants to see me."

He would, but that might take a while. "Rowan might want to stay here until he's worked out some things in his head."

Her sad, weary sigh coupled with a sad, weary nod told Brody she had already resigned herself to that. She was probably also terrified that she'd lost her son forever. Not in a car wreck like Layla. But it was possible that Rowan might never be able to forgive her.

With that dismal thought hanging in the air like lead, Brody gave his mother a hug and left. It was indeed cold, right at freezing, and it certainly felt damp enough for something to start falling from the sky. Maybe if it started sleeting, that would be enough to get Rowan to come home.

Once he was in his truck, Brody used the tracker app on his phone to see that Rowan had indeed taken Thorn out for his ride. Apparently, his brother wanted a pissy horse to go with his mood. No way did he want to wait around for hours while he stewed and worried about Rowan, so he set the app to alert him when Rowan brought Thorn back.

Hoping to help with his own mood, Brody drove to Colts Creek, and he immediately spotted Janessa in the front doorway that she'd obviously just opened. She was wearing her red coat, a white knit hat, and she was tugging on some gloves.

Janessa smiled at him, waved, and that smile fixed some of the lead-weight air, which seemed to lift a little. She continued to smile when she opened the front door for him, but apparently *worry* was the word of the day because he could see plenty of that for him in her eyes.

"Should I ask how it went with Rowan?" she said. The moment he was on the porch, she caught onto his hand, pulling him into the foyer. Once the door was shut, she leaned in and kissed him.

That kiss did some weight lifting, too, and Brody leaned into it for a moment, taking all that she was offering and then some. When he finally eased back from her, he showed her the app with the moving, pulsing dot.

"Rowan's out riding," Brody explained, giving her the condensed version. "He's confused, probably pissed off some, probably hurt. But he's not a hothead. I think he'll be okay. Well, okay-ish anyway."

"Okay-ish is a good start," Janessa assured him.

Yeah, it was, and Brody needed to hang on to the good that was going on in his life. Which brought him to one of the reasons he was here. He'd wanted that smile and kiss from Janessa, but there was something else.

"You're going somewhere?" he asked, motioning to her coat.

"To the inn to see Mom. She was here earlier when we opened presents, but she asked me to come for coffee. Then I was going to stop by your place and give you your Christmas present." She took out a small box from her coat pocket to show him.

It was wrapped in gold foil, very similar in color and size to the gift he had for her in his truck.

Janessa motioned to the stairs. "Margo and Velma Sue are with the baby while she's taking her morning nap. Deputy Ollie's with them."

Good. Because despite everything else going on, the baby's safety was still at the top of everyone's list.

"I can text my mother and tell her I need a raincheck," Janessa suggested.

"Do that," he said, not feeling the least bit guilty for screwing up whatever plans Sophia had. "I want to show you something. And I want to give you your Christmas present. It's hard to explain, but I need to take a step forward today."

"You don't have to explain, and I want to give you your present, too," she assured him while she followed him to his truck. "It's flattering that you'd want to make that step forward with me around." She froze. "Uh, you're not going to ask me to marry you, are you?"

Her tone stung just a little because she made it sound as if that was a really out-there idea. And it was. They weren't in love and were in the middle of a holiday fling. Flings by definition weren't permanent and didn't usually lead to marriage. Still, Brody would have preferred she didn't look so dumbfounded.

"Rowan asked if I'd knocked you up," he grumbled as he drove away. "So, I guess it's the day for wild conclusions. No, this isn't a drive so I can propose."

Though the possibility of it didn't dumbfound him, and it could perhaps even happen if a whole boatload of things changed. Not just the falling-in-love and the fling parts, either. There was that whole wacky notion of Janessa's life not being here, and Brody knew he was a long, long way from being her *life*.

He took a back road, driving past the string of small ranches that were east of Colts Creek. No black stone houses and fences here. This was the heart and soul of the county.

"That's Joe's place," Brody pointed out when they went by the sign for Saddle Run.

In the distance from the main house, Brody spotted the ground that was being cleared for Joe's new place. One that he would no doubt end up sharing with Millie. They weren't engaged yet, but Brody thought that was on the near horizon for his good friend.

Brody only had to drive another quarter of a mile before he got to the next ranch, and he pulled into the gravel driveway. He stopped the truck, sat there, taking in the view. The white limestone and pine house, the freshly painted barn and corral fence.

"This is the place you want to buy?" she asked, moving to the edge of the seat so she could look around.

"It's the place I bought," he corrected. "Right before we talked to Rowan, I got a text from the Realtor saying that the owner had accepted my offer. I should be able to close on it the end of next month."

And because life was just filled with a crapload of irony,

that would be when Abe's will would be done and Janessa would be heading back to Dallas.

"It's eighty acres," Brody continued. "And there's a good stretch of the creek running through the property so I'll be able to get a lot more horses than I have now. I want to focus on the breed stock, building a name and reputation."

"Like you did at Colts Creek," she muttered. She made a sweeping glance around the place before her gaze came back to his. "You're sure this is what you want?"

He nearly told her he wanted a lot of things. Her included. Instead, he ran his thumb over her bottom lip, gathering up her taste and brought it to his own mouth. It gave him exactly the heat kick that he'd expected.

"I'm sure," Brody said. "The Realtor's putting my place on the market as we speak." Heaven knew how long it'd take to sell, but he could financially swing both places for a while.

"Let me check on Rowan and then we can have a look around." Brody took out his phone, opened the app. "Rowan's still riding," he explained as he followed the little dot on the screen. "The abrupt stops are probably because Thorn's acting like an ass."

"He'll be okay?" Janessa asked.

"Rowan, yes. Thorn, no. But Rowan can handle Thorn."

In fact, the horse's orneriness might help Rowan focus on something other than his own anger. Still, the boy was going to have to deal with that shock and anger and come to terms with forgiving Darcia for holding back like this.

"Here," Janessa said, taking the gift from her coat pocket. "You look as if you could use this. Maybe it'll cheer you up."

He eyed the box, then her. "Is this an engagement ring?" he joked.

"No." She stretched that out a few syllables. "It's something to keep you on the right path."

Well, he needed help in that area so Brody opened the box, and he smiled when he saw the antique compass inside. A brass one with turquoise studs on the arrow. "This was at Once Upon a Time during the scavenger hunt."

"Yes, it was." She flipped it over so he could see the back. An etched rearing horse pawing at the air.

Since he hadn't picked it up the night of the party, he definitely hadn't noticed that, but it suited him. Suited him more because it was a gift from Janessa.

"Thanks." He kissed her, lingered some doing that, and then Brody took out her gift from the glove compartment. "Not an engagement ring," he told her right off.

Unlike him, Janessa didn't hesitate opening the tiny box, and he watched the smile bloom on her mouth when she saw the antique heart-and-pearl earrings. Yep, the very ones she'd eyed at the party.

"I went back to Once Upon a Time to buy them," Janessa said, her voice a little misty with emotion, "but Millie told me they'd already been sold." She plucked them from the box and threaded the delicate gold backs through her pierced ears. She took a moment to look at them in the vanity mirror before she kissed him. "Thank you. I love them. And they'll remind me of you."

That had a bittersweet tinge to it. Because she wouldn't need to be reminded of him if she were here.

"Now, let's see the ranch," Janessa insisted, getting out of the truck. Brody turned off the engine and got out with her. Janessa motioned around her. "So, this is your house, your barn, your fences?"

"It soon will be. The owner, Elmer Tasker, moved out a couple of days ago. He went to Florida to live with his daughter." Brody pointed to the Charolais cattle in the pasture. "He sold the livestock to a broker over in Wrangler's Creek, and someone will be coming to get them in a couple of days."

She turned to him, and for a moment he thought she was about to caution him about moving too fast. Or try to talk him into staying at Colts Creek. But she merely smiled. Not an I-want-to-distract-you-from-your-troubles smile. This one had some heat to it.

"I think you should kiss me by the fence and in that barn," she said, leading him in that direction. It was cold enough for her breath to create a wispy fog between them. "Sort of a christening like whacking a champagne bottle against a ship when it's dedicated. Then, when you move into the house, you can christen me there, too."

She might not be there for his move-in, but Brody wasn't an idiot so he kept that depressing thought to himself. And he stopped and kissed her before they got to the fence.

"We should christen the driveway," he muttered against her mouth.

Circling their arms around each other and while kissing, they began to inch their way to the nearest fence. It wasn't easy since neither one of them could actually see where they were going. This could turn into another hammock deal where they ended up with scrapes and bruises.

Then again, that had turned out to be a sky-high rating on the pleasure meter.

They stumbled and kissed all the way to the fence, and Brody was mindful of not stepping on her toes. Literally. He didn't want to risk reinjuring the toe she'd broken so he lifted her, sitting her on the top rung. The fence was a standard four and a quarter feet high and with him at six-two, that put Janessa's mouth higher than his. But she remedied that by leaning down and kissing him as if this was to be the hottest, best christening in history.

Brody certainly didn't object to her enthusiasm and thoroughness. Nope. He just let her have her way with him until she laughed and then jumped off the railing and into his arms. Kissing her, he carried her in the direction of the barn. He doubted they'd get any visitors, but if Joe had seen them drive by, he might come to check if the sale had gone through. Brody didn't have plans for sex. Then again, he hadn't planned all this kissing, either. It was a nice bonus to buying his place.

"Does the ranch have a name?" she asked. She hooked her legs around his waist as Brody walked.

"No. Maybe you can give it one."

That'd be a nice perk, remembering Janessa every time someone said the name of his ranch. Though it might not be a reminder he wanted if things didn't end well between them. Sort of like getting a tat of the person you thought you'd love forever and ever, only to have to go through tat removal when it turned out forever had a much shorter shelf life than expected.

"I'll give it some thought," she assured him.

She kept the leg lock around him while he carried her to the barn. Then he stopped when he felt something cold and wet land on his face.

"It's snowing," Janessa gushed with loads of enthusiasm. Probably more than warranted since it was only a couple of flakes. Still, it seemed as if everything, including Mother Nature, was cooperating to make this very special.

He walked into the barn where Janessa's warm scent immediately blended with that of the hay and saddle leather. Brody didn't waste any time backing her against a wood stall door. There was a high risk of splinters, but he was pretty sure this was going to be worth it.

With her anchored against the stall, he could free up one of his hands to slide between their bodies and swipe his thumb over her nipple. He also untangled their tongues so he could go after her neck.

The sound Janessa made was part lust, part laughter. "This dedication is heating up."

Yeah, it was, but the heat did a nosedive when his phone dinged with a text. "It might be Rowan," he managed to say.

With his breathing ragged and his body hard and aching, he eased Janessa to her feet so he could dig out his phone from his pocket. Not Rowan.

"It's Betty Parkman, the real-estate agent," he grumbled.

Brody nearly declined the call, especially since it was Christmas and there was no way the woman should be working. However, there might be a problem with the sale of this place so he held up his finger in a wait-a-second gesture to Janessa, and he answered.

"Good news," Betty greeted him.

"Yeah, I got your text about Elmer accepting my offer. Thanks." He was about to end the call when Betty continued.

"Double good news, then," Betty amended. "Merry Christmas, Brody. I already have a buyer for your place."

That didn't cool him down, but it did get his attention. "Is it even officially on the market yet?"

"Nope, but word gets around, and you have a buyer for the full listing price we discussed."

Brody tried to wrap his mind around that, and he frowned at Janessa. "Did you do this?" he asked.

Obviously, she'd heard the conversation. Hard not to since they were still plastered against each other, and she had her hand on his belt buckle. Janessa shook her head. "It wasn't me."

"Who wants to buy my place?" Brody came out and asked Betty.

"Well, it's a surprise, that's for sure," the woman said in her overly cheery voice. "It's Sophia Parkman."

CHAPTER TWENTY-TWO

JANESSA CONTINUED TO open the old Christmas presents from Abe while she listened to Kyle's update.

"I broke down and bought Alisha a grilled-cheese maker for Christmas," Kyle continued. "And I plan to have a second fire alarm installed in her room."

Janessa didn't ask if it would have been easier just to get the girl kitchen privileges because it wouldn't be. Bright Hope's cook, Thelma Garcia, fixed amazing meals on a budget, but she ruled the kitchen roost and never allowed kids in there. Never. It was the reason Janessa had bought another fridge and had had another pantry built in the rec room. That way, the residents could still have snacks without bothering Thelma.

"Good call," Janessa agreed—especially since Kyle's update from the day before had included another bad grilled-cheese attempt from Alisha. This time with aluminum foil and candles.

"You okay?" Kyle asked. "I hear rustling."

"Christmas wrapping paper," she supplied, tearing off another swatch to reveal, well, a doll. One that was about three feet high, and it looked a lot like her when she'd been six—which was how old she'd been when Abe had gotten this particular gift.

"It's December twenty-eighth," Kyle pointed out.

"Yes, but I'm still going through the old gifts I found

from Abe. I need to get them all opened so I can either give them away or burn them."

Though Janessa wasn't sure she could do either. That would seem ungrateful. And she wasn't. So far, everything she'd unwrapped had taken plenty of thought and money, and it didn't seem right just to get rid of them. Which meant they'd likely end up in yet another storage room.

"Three days after Christmas," Kyle repeated. "As it's only five more weeks until the end of January."

She knew that was a prompt for her to spill her feelings about there being only one month left on Abe's wonky will conditions. She'd been here two months, and while time hadn't exactly flown, it had gone by pretty fast. She suddenly wished she could dig her fingernails into time and slow it down a bit. Because then she could spend those slowed moments with Brody and the baby. After all, Sweet Pea wouldn't be here much longer, either.

Well, probably wouldn't.

Char was still on bed rest, still on the fence about the adoption, and Janessa had decided not to try to fix that particular situation. She'd leave it to Char and Teagan to work out, or rather to continue to work it out since they'd already spoken about it several times on the phone. But each day Sweet Pea was around, Sophia and Margo were growing more and more attached.

"Are you coming home at the end of next month?" Kyle came out and asked when she didn't say anything.

"That's the plan," she settled for saying. "Sophia says she'll tie up any legal loose ends for me with Abe's estate."

"Because she's not coming home," Kyle concluded.

"To be determined. She's buying Brody's house and land and says it's just a vacation home, but she's pretty cozy with the lawyer." Janessa suspected the vacation home would be a nookie nest where Sophia hooked up with Curt anytime she was in Last Ride, which could be often if the youth house actually became a reality.

When she heard the movement in the doorway, she looked up and saw exactly whom she wanted to see.

Brody.

"Gotta go," she told Kyle, and she ended the call.

Brody had been way too busy the last couple of days with Rowan and the new ranch, and she hadn't seen nearly enough of him. Since she wasn't on baby duty, she'd planned on letting him see plenty of her by showing up at his house, stripping off her clothes and greeting him butt naked.

And had then planned on getting him equally butt naked.

"You're having dirty thoughts about me," he said. "I can tell." He went to her, hauled her up off the floor and kissed her. All in all, it was the best form of hello, and she wished she could bottle it.

He was smiling when he pulled back from the kiss. "You're in a good mood," she remarked.

"I am. Just checked on the baby, and she was sleeping, well, like a baby. All's going well with the new place. And last but certainly not least, Rowan's still a little shaky, but he's back with Mom."

That was indeed a reason for a good mood since Rowan had been staying in the ranch bunkhouse. Brody had offered Rowan his guest room, but the boy had apparently wanted some space from family. That apparently included Janessa, though Brody doubted Rowan had completely come to terms with the fact that she was his half-sister. He would though. Eventually, it would all sink in.

Brody glanced around the room, his attention settling on the doll she'd just unwrapped. "I guess that's supposed to be a replica of you."

"Yep. Me, minus the plastic skin, glassy eyes and vacant stare."

"Damn, I don't know if that's creepy or creative."

"It's both. It'll go someplace where it won't scare small children." She pointed to another recently unwrapped gift, this one for her tenth Christmas. "That, on the other hand, isn't creepy."

It was an oil painting of the ranch, not the way it looked now, but the earlier days. Abe had included a clipping on a newspaper article and photo that the artist had used to recreate it.

"I want to hang it somewhere in the house," she explained as he went closer to examine it. "Maybe in Abe's office to replace that horrible portrait of him."

"I think that's supposed to be Abe." Brody pointed to one of the barns in the painting.

Janessa went closer, too. She hadn't seen it earlier, but she certainly saw it now. The little blond-haired boy in the doorway of the open barn. She reexamined the newspaper photo, and Abe was indeed ID'd as the child.

She did the math and realized the photo would have been taken when he was about ten, right around the time his mother had deserted him. In the painting, he was all smiles, but in the photo, he looked lost and sad. It broke her heart a little to know that he likely had been and that he'd tried to erase some of the loss and sadness by making the boy happy in the painting.

"I just can't reconcile the mean-spirited man with the father who'd have something like that painted for me," she said. "In some ways, it feels as if Abe was bragging, but in other ways, I think he was trying to make me a part of what he'd built."

Brody turned from the painting and back to her. "You are a part of it. That's why Abe left the ranch to you."

"Maybe. But since he knew about Rowan, he should have left something to him and to you. I suspect, though, that he knew I'd make it right. I'm trying very hard to make it right," she added in a mumble.

She cursed the tears she had to blink back. This wasn't a boo-hooing moment. She had nothing to boo-hoo about, and she sure as heck wasn't going to become another poor little rich kid like Abe.

"You'll make it right," he insisted, and there was absolute confidence in that. "You've probably already started."

She shrugged, but she was pleased with the plan she was coming up with. A plan with holes, yes, but she had started one, and she wanted to bounce some of her ideas off Brody so he could start helping her plug those holes.

"Along with Velma Sue, there are two full-time housekeepers, one part-time and a part-time cook," Janessa explained. "Abe hasn't given them raises in years, and they don't have retirement packages. I'll fix that."

He gave a nod of approval. "I'm sure they'll appreciate it."

"Abe's businesses make a lot of money," she went on, "and if this house is turned into a youth home, some of that money from those businesses can be funneled into the daily operation instead of stockpiling it the way Abe did. I'll also set up salary packages for Margo and anyone else who ends up running the house."

Another nod of approval. "You'll put the money to good use."

She'd certainly try. "That leaves you." Janessa looked him straight in the eyes, and in that moment, she got clarity that had been floating away before she could latch on to it. Well, she latched on now. "I can't replace you, Brody."

He nodded as if it were only part of the plan and changes she'd just been doling out to him. "I told you I'd help you find another ranch manager—"

"It's not just about the ranch, though I will need a manager. It's about other things." Things that she had been mulling around, but clarity had fixed that little red wagon. "I'll give you a whole bunch of horses from Colts Creek in exchange for sex."

"Really?" He didn't sound at all serious.

"Well, I want the sex whether or not you take the horses. I was looking over the paperwork for the ranch, and it looks as if we're due to clear out some stock soon. I want you to take those horses."

His *really* remark amusement faded, and she knew he was taking it seriously now.

"Think about it," she added when he just kept staring at her.

He finally nodded after some snail-crawling moments. "I'll think about it."

Which was Brody-speak for "no way in hell will I take that from you. It'd be like charity," yada yada. Maybe she could put bows or gift-wrap on them so it felt less charity-like and more like a gift. Which it was.

"When you look out the window of your new house and see the horses in the pasture, I want you to think of me," she added. "Yes, that's selfish, but I think the horses would be a better keepsake than a doll or a painting."

He continued to stare at her, and she could tell she'd totally cooled down the heat from their earlier kisses. She'd have to work on building it back up.

"One more thing," she went on. Best to get all the business finished first. "I was also thinking about offering the ranch itself to Rowan when he turns eighteen. He could still hire a ranch manager until he's ready to take over. If he wants to take over, that is," she amended. "I don't want it to be a burden, but it should be his birthright."

"You've given this a lot of thought," Brody said after several moments.

Well, he hadn't objected or said it was a totally stupid idea, so that was something at least. "I'm a fixer," she settled for saying. And now it was time to start fixing this moment and making it more about them than the situation Abe had left behind.

"Let's play a sex game." Janessa hurried across the room to lock the door.

The corner of his mouth lifted. "Let me guess. A game that will lead to, well, sex?"

Janessa matched his naughty smile, went back to him and touched her tongue to his lips. "You got it. But maybe we can make it more interesting by spelling things out in a smutty kind of way." While his hot gaze stayed on her, she trailed her fingers down the front of his shirt. "Something like feel my mouth here." She circled his left nipple. "And here." She slid her hand lower to his stomach. "Then here." She pressed her palm to the front of his jeans.

His gaze heated up even more, and Janessa expected him to start touching her. And he did. Sort of. "Feel my mouth here," he mimicked. But it wasn't only his hand he put on her.

In one quick motion, she was in his arms, and his mouth was on hers. He stole her breath along with pretty much the rest of her. He pressed hard, shaping her lips with his, making their bodies fit in a way that was already well past the foreplay stage. Brody simply kissed and took. It was as simple and as complex as that.

And Janessa welcomed it.

She was lost. Willingly lost and wasn't sure she ever wanted to find her way back again.

Apparently, Brody was ready to be lost, too, because with the kiss still raging, he pulled her to the floor onto the heap of Christmas wrapping paper that crackled, crumpled and shifted beneath them. Not exactly the most comfortable of beds, but they were past the point of comfort. They were already in that desperate I-have-to-have-you-now zone.

It wasn't words that undressed her. It was Brody's hands. Janessa didn't mind one bit because he continued to use his mouth for kissing. Her mouth and then, as he peeled off her jeans and top, he went after the very spots on her that she'd touched on him when she'd been trying to do the sexy talk. Her nipple, her stomach and the front of her panties. She wasn't sure how he managed to get that much of his breath through the fabric, but he did. It was like getting an incredible preview to what would no doubt be kisses to remember.

Janessa liked kisses in that particular area, but there was times, and this was one of them, when she wanted their bodies pressed together. With his weight on her. She wanted him inside her and let him know that by latching on to him and pulling him back up so she could take his mouth.

And his belt and zipper.

She shoved his jeans and boxers down his hips while Brody got out the condom from his wallet. Later, she'd thank him for replenishing his supply, but for now she just lifted her hips and took him inside her the moment he had the condom in place.

The slam of pleasure came. That desperate ache to take more, more, more. Thankfully, Brody didn't have any trouble with her taking, and he let her set the pace. The rhythm.

The blood rushed to her head. And other parts of her.

She could feel her pulse, thick and throbbing, which was also what those other parts of her were doing while he pushed into her.

She could feel the edge of the climax and tried to hang on. Tried to harness this delicious, desperate need so she could savor it a little longer. She managed it for a few incredible seconds before her body said to heck with this, and the orgasm avalanched through her. Brody wasn't far behind.

Janessa buried her face against his neck and just held on to him. Her body was floating, and she was getting those cheap thrill aftershocks of the climax. But the best part was having his weight on her while they were still puzzled around each other. Evidently, Christmas wrapping paper made a good bed after all.

After he'd returned to planet earth, Brody did a quick stop in the hall bathroom, but he came right back to her. He located her mouth and kissed her. Then he looked down at her. Not with post-orgasmic hazy eyes but as if he were studying her.

"I know this isn't something you want to hear," he said, "but I'm falling in love with you."

Well, that finished off her hazy eyes and mind. Janessa mentally snapped to attention. "Uh, what?"

"I'm falling in love with you," he repeated. He didn't choke on the words. Didn't wince. Didn't fumble around and say it was mindless sex talk. "I know it doesn't fix anything, but it's how I feel."

No, it definitely didn't fix stuff. It complicated an already complicated situation. All the plans and fixes she was making were so that the ranch, the house and Abe's other businesses could operate with her being in Dallas.

All the plans Brody was making with his new ranch would require him to be here.

Janessa was trying to figure out how to remind him of that when she heard Velma Sue's shout.

"Brody, Janessa," the woman called out. "Come quick. That boy, Riggs, is here, and he's trying to get the baby."

BRODY LEAPED UP, thankful that he'd already zipped up his jeans, and he didn't wait for Janessa. He had a gun in his office up the hall, but he didn't use up what might be precious seconds going to get it. Instead, he ran toward the sound of Velma Sue's shout.

A dozen things went through his head, none good, but he pushed possibilities aside and hurried to stop Riggs. No way was he going to let that hothead SOB get anywhere near the baby.

There was another shout. Not from Velma Sue this time. It was Riggs. "Bring our baby out here now!"

A dozen hells would freeze over before that happened. Brody ran to the foyer where he found Velma Sue peering out the side window of the closed front door.

"He's out there," Velma Sue said, pointing to the yard.

He eased the woman aside to have a look, and he spotted Riggs all right. He was at the bottom of the porch, and he wasn't alone. Shit.

Teagan was with him.

One glance at the girl's face and he knew she hadn't come willingly. She was terrified. Added to that, Riggs was behind her, his arm around her neck in a choke hold.

Teagan's hands were tied in front of her with a bright yellow bungee cord. She wasn't struggling, probably because Riggs would tighten his grip on her throat if she did, and there were tears spilling down her cheeks. Brody intended to make this asswipe pay for every single one of those tears.

"Where is he?" Janessa called out, and Brody heard her running footsteps. "Oh, God," she said when she had her own look out the window.

Brody glanced at her, then at the top of the stairs where he saw Margo clutching the baby against her. Good. That ruled out one of his worst-case scenarios, that Riggs had already managed to get the baby.

"I've already called the cops," Margo said, her voice as shaky as the rest of her. In contrast, though, the baby was quiet, maybe even still sleeping which qualified as another good.

"Margo, take Sweet Pea to the nursery," Brody instructed. He hadn't seen a weapon on Riggs, but in case the idiot had one, he didn't want the baby to be anywhere near this. "Stay back," he added to Janessa and Velma Sue.

And he opened the door.

The cold blast of air hit him, and he stepped out onto the porch that had some patches of ice. There was some leftover Christmas snow still on the ground, too. Only thin patches of it since it hadn't snowed a lot, but it was enough to make his footing unsteady.

Of course, Janessa didn't stay back. Neither did Velma Sue. With an umbrella aimed like a sword, Janessa came out, and Velma Sue was "armed" with her sturdy thick-soled shoe. Not her own since she was wearing hers, but neither Janessa nor Velma Sue were wearing coats.

"You can't do this," Janessa insisted.

Riggs kept his attention on Brody, no doubt because the idiot wisely considered him the bigger threat. He was, and Brody gave him a stare straight from those twelve hells that he'd just imagined.

Brody had felt this kind of fear before. When he'd seen his sister crash into that tree. But he'd been just a kid then. Now, he used that anger to pinpoint everything inside him so he could deal with this piece of shit.

"You've got one chance," Brody warned Riggs. Several of the ranch hands ran toward the house, but Brody motioned them back as he stepped closer to Riggs. "Let go of Teagan, or you'll be yelling in pain."

Riggs tried to sneer. Hard to do that, though, with all his jaw muscles locked up in anger. Anger that was in his fiery eyes. "Me and Teagan are a family. Give us our baby now so we can get out of here."

Brody didn't bother repeating his threat or clarifying. He didn't intend to wait for the cops, either. Or for Janessa and Velma Sue to do whatever it was they were planning on doing. Without taking his eyes off Riggs, Brody snatched the shoe from Velma Sue and bashed it against Riggs's head.

Cursing and yelling, Riggs didn't go down, but he did let go of Teagan, and that's when Brody moved in. He tossed the shoe onto the steps, gently moved Teagan aside and rammed his fist into Riggs's face. He heard the satisfying crunch of broken cartilage, and Riggs's nose spewed with blood. Still, the idiot didn't go down. He tried to grab Teagan again, no doubt so he could use her as a shield.

Janessa fixed that.

Swinging the umbrella like a baseball bat, she slammed it against the side of his head, and she kept slamming until Riggs dropped down to his knees. And yeah, he yelled in pain.

Brody caught a blur of motion from the corner of his eye and saw Velma Sue's shoe fly past him. Obviously, she'd picked it up, and it bashed into Riggs's already broken nose. This time, the yell of pain was more like a sobbing howl.

"Are you all right?" Janessa asked Teagan. Teagan gave a shaky nod as Janessa got off the bungee cord.

"I'll take that," Brody told her, and when she tossed him the cord, he used it as makeshift handcuffs to restrain Riggs. He also had to stop Velma Sue from hurling her other shoe at Riggs.

"He's not getting Sweet Pea," Velma Sue declared, and it was by far the most emotion Brody had ever heard in her voice. That tone could have gotten death row inmates to back off.

In the distance, Brody heard the police sirens. So did Riggs, and proving that he was indeed a moron, he tried to scramble away. That was such a bad idea. Brody merely stepped to the side and let Velma Sue hurl that shoe. It bashed right into Riggs's balls. Well, that was assuming he had any. There must have been something in that general region because it put him on the ground where he howled, groaned and yelled.

Since there were now nearly a dozen hands in the yard, Riggs wouldn't be going anywhere so Brody turned his attention to Teagan. She was still sobbing, and seeing those tears made Brody want to punch Riggs again. Instead, he sank down on the other side of Janessa so he was facing Teagan.

"I'm so sorry," Brody told her.

Teagan shook her head. "I'm the one who's sorry. I'm so sorry. I was going to work, and I didn't see Riggs before he jumped out and grabbed me. He put me in his car and forced me to come here with him."

That meant Riggs could be charged with kidnapping and forced imprisonment for starters, and hopefully that would keep him behind bars for a long, long time especially since he already had a record.

All three Last Ride cruisers came to a stop in the driveway, and the sheriff and deputies poured out. "The little shit was trying to take Sweet Pea," Velma Sue told them, and she walked toward them, no doubt to fill them in.

The sheriff would want to question all of them, but for now Brody continued to sit next to Teagan. "Why don't you come inside?" he asked. "It's cold out here, and you could probably use something warm to drink."

Teagan shook her head, and she gave a wary look over her shoulder toward the still-open front door. "The baby's here?"

"Yes," Janessa assured her. "And she's safe. She's upstairs with Margo."

"Then no. I don't want to go in. I don't want to see her." Teagan's tears came pouring again. "I can't see her."

"I understand." Janessa's voice was a soft, soothing purr. A contrast to the "chaos" that was now going on in the yard with the deputies hauling a still-howling Riggs away.

Teagan lifted her teary eyes to meet Janessa's. "I was going to call you today to tell you that Char can't take her. She says it'll be too much for her to handle, what with the twins."

Hell. Brody had known this could happen, but he'd held out hope that Char would still be able to take Sweet Pea.

"I don't want the baby to go into the foster system," Teagan went on, her attention still glued to Janessa. "Please don't let that happen. Janessa, I'm begging you to adopt her."

CHAPTER TWENTY-THREE

BUNDLED UP IN a blanket and with her thermos of hot chocolate, Janessa sat beneath a sprawling live oak, her tablet on her lap, and she stared at her father's tombstone. Maybe if she stared at it long enough, she'd be able to figure out how to finish the research paper for the Last Ride Society.

This definitely wasn't a comfortable or joyous way to spend a chilly Texas winter night, but once she'd left Colts Creek and started driving, she'd somehow ended up here.

Here, where it'd all started.

Abe's funeral seemed like a lifetime ago, but the fresh lettering and date on the tombstone let her know that a lifetime could happen in a single season. This particular lifetime of hers certainly had. That was rather deep musings, considering she should be writing this report and fixing stuff by making sure that all was well at the ranch. And with Brody. And with Teagan.

And with everyone else.

Including herself.

The only person she was certain wasn't still shaken up by what Riggs had tried to do was Sweet Pea. That's because the baby was thankfully too young to realize that her sperm-donor dad was basically—to borrow one of Margo's expressions—a flamin' bunghole. The baby had slept through the ordeal and afterward had shown absolutely no signs of stress. Janessa had personally made sure of that once the aftermath of the flamin' bunghole's antics had been brought to a stop.

The aftermath had started with Riggs being carted away in a police cruiser. His destination was the hospital followed by the jail. Where he would remain until the cops worked out who would charge him, try him and then lock him away for a good portion of his life.

During Teagan's aftermath, she'd been examined, too, not at the hospital but rather by the EMTs. Once they'd given her the all clear to leave and she'd given her statement to the cops, Brody had put her in his truck to drive her back to Dallas.

Janessa was thankful he'd volunteered to do that, and she could tell that Teagan had been, too. The girl had wanted to leave fast, and she probably wouldn't have been as comfortable with a ranch hand or deputy that she didn't know.

Continuing with her own aftermath, Janessa had said a teary goodbye to Teagan and waved Brody and her off, and then she'd gone to the nursery. There, she'd just rocked the baby while the minutes and the hours ticked by. Janessa had fed her, changed her and rocked her some more, all the while wondering what the heck she was going to do. That's when she'd finally handed off the baby to Sophia and let everyone know she was going out, that she needed some thinking time.

The thinking time was a necessity, but she knew it had caused so many people to worry about her. The proof of that was the sheer volume of texts and calls she'd gotten after a couple of hours had passed. Apparently, they thought *thinking time* was code for her doing something stupid because Janessa could read the worry between the lines of the messages. Still, she hadn't been able to make herself move from this spot and go back to give everyone a face-to-face assurance that she wasn't falling into a million little pieces.

Sighing, Janessa took out her phone when it dinged with another text. It was Sophia wanting to know if she was all right. Her mother had used her own version of code, though, by saying Alma had just dropped off some fresh snicker-doodles and didn't she want one?

Save some for me, Janessa messaged back. Will be there in a while.

Of course, *in a while* might be a couple more hours. So far, her thinking time had resulted in zero decisions, and she wasn't going to give up on it just yet.

When she slipped her phone back in her purse, her fingers brushed against the small box. Her thirteenth birthday gift from Abe. She'd put it in her purse, intending to open it once she'd decided what to do with, well, everything and everyone, but Janessa took it out now and with a "What the heck," she tore off the paper and looked inside the box.

It was a necklace.

Not anything over the top or meant to show off his wealth, either. It was a delicate gold heart locket with her initials inscribed on it. When she opened it, there was a thumbnail-sized picture of her, one taken when she'd been about six or seven. On the other side of the heart was a wedding photo of Abe and Sophia. Janessa hadn't even known such photos of them existed, but as she looked closer, she had no doubt it was them. Either they were putting on an Oscar-worthy performance or they looked very much in love.

Janessa put the necklace on, fumbling around with the tiny latch until she got it on. She looked at Abe's tombstone to see if he was going to give her any kind of approval from beyond the grave.

A bat swooped and dipped through the night sky.

Well, that probably wasn't a sign from the hereafter, but she'd take it. She had too many unresolved issues in her life to mentally quibble about hereafter signs and how her father would feel about her now.

She didn't quibble either when the night breeze took a swipe at her hair and caused her earrings to jangle. Her Christmas gift from Brody. She hadn't taken them off except to shower and sleep, and she'd kept them right next to her bed. It made her feel a little like a lovesick teenager.

Her phone rang, again, and she knew it was a call she'd have to take when she saw Kyle's name on the screen. He had as much on his plate of worry as she did and was probably blaming himself for what Teagan had been through. Especially since there'd been enough time for it all to have sunk in. According to the text Janessa had gotten from Brody, he'd dropped Teagan off at Bright Hope nearly four hours ago. Four hours for Teagan to give Kyle her personal account. Four hours for Kyle to mentally kick himself.

"I'm okay," Janessa greeted as a preemptive strike. "And none of what happened was your fault. You couldn't have used your ESP or crystal ball to stop this."

Kyle's silence let her know that her preemptive strike was a direct hit. "I just hate that Teagan had to go through it."

"I know. I know," she repeated with another heavy sigh. "How is she?"

"As well as can be expected. Is everyone there okay?"

"Everyone but Riggs. He has a broken nose and sore balls. Brody punched him. I bashed him with an umbrella, and Velma Sue hit him in the balls with shoes. Really heavy shoes."

She nearly laughed after spelling that all out. Nearly.

But the image of a terrified Teagan was still too fresh in her mind.

"Riggs is in jail?" he asked.

"He is, and the sheriff here assured me that he was going to fight any quick bail because Riggs is a flight risk with a violent streak and a record. He intends to charge him with the forced imprisonment, assault and attempted kidnapping of the baby, and he'll transfer him to the county jail to await trial. Once he's convicted and sentenced to what should be several decades, then he'll face the kidnapping charges for Teagan in Dallas. That will add even more years to his time behind bars."

"Good. I'll make sure Teagan understands that. She's in her room right now having some downtime to process everything, but a group of us are having dinner with her tonight." He paused. "I didn't ask her about it, but I take it she didn't want to stay there in Last Ride?"

"Nope, and she didn't want to see the baby." Janessa paused, took that deep breath she needed so she could continue. "Teagan wants me to adopt Sweet Pea."

Kyle paused again. "So she said. And will you?"

"To be determined. My life feels like one of those thousand-piece jigsaw puzzles that have just been tossed into the air, and the pieces are all over the place."

Just as she said that, Janessa saw one of those pieces walking in the darkness toward her. Brody.

"Gotta go," she told Kyle. "I'll call you tomorrow."

Her heart did the little leap it always did when she saw Brody. The man certainly made a picture in his jeans and Stetson. A cowboy in winter moonlight. A cowboy she loved down to the soles of those boots.

She was betting Brody had wrestled with his confes-

CHRISTMAS AT COLTS CREEK

sion about that love on the drive back from Dallas. Janessa had, too.

"Being in love doesn't fix squat," she greeted him just as he'd leaned down to kiss her.

His mouth stopped and hovered above hers. "Oh?"

"Squat," she repeated. "I still have decisions to make. Big decisions. And this research for the Last Ride Society." Janessa set the tablet on top of her purse so she could pull Brody down to her for that kiss.

One touch of his lips and she felt some of those puzzle pieces slide right into place. Okay, so maybe being in love did fix some things after all.

"Big decisions," he repeated, sinking down on the ground. Not by her side but with them facing each other. A wise choice since it gave her a chance to look at him. At his eyes, that mouth.

"You look darn good in moonlight," she informed him, and she pulled him into the blanket with her.

"Same goes for you." With the corner of his hot kissable mouth slightly lifted, he used the tip of his index finger to push a strand of hair off her cheek.

Their gazes locked, held, and she could have sworn they had an entire conversation. One where Brody assured her that everything would turn out all right. A few more of those puzzle piece wiggled right where they were supposed to be.

"How much more research?" he asked, picking up the tablet.

"To be determined. I've written and tweaked all the stories and bio details. It's the ending I'm having trouble with. I read some of the other reports, and they all had a flourish of sorts at the end. Some of them quite dramatic. So-and-so forged unforged paths, was the brightest of stars, leaped tall buildings, etc." She put those last ones in air quotes.

Brody's smile kicked up even more. "How about just saying Abraham Lincoln Parkman IV was a rancher, businessman and my father. It's simple," Brody added, then paused. "That is if you think of him as your father."

Janessa took a moment to wrap her mind around that particular puzzle piece. "I do. He wasn't the best parental unit, but he wasn't the worst, either." She opened the heart locket for Brody to see. "His thirteenth birthday gift to me."

So maybe that piece had fallen into place, as well. An imperfect father, an imperfect man, yes, but life rarely dealt out perfection. It was all about handling the imperfections and making them work. Sliding them until they fit.

Like now.

As that single bat made a return and flitted through the air, she pulled Brody to her for one of those long slow, soul-soothing kisses. Of course, it had heat. This was Brody after all, so heat was a given, but a kiss from him was like one of those package deals. Lots of stuff and free shipping.

She felt a little drunk when she eased back from him. Drunk and incredibly clearheaded.

"I'm going to adopt Sweet Pea," she told him. "And I'm naming her Ava Elizabeth. Ava is Sophia's middle name. Elizabeth is Margo's middle name. That should make both GeeGees happy."

It seemed to make Brody happy, too, because his smile widened. "I think that's a wise choice, both on the adoption and the name." He paused. "Though you know they'll probably keep calling her Sweet Pea."

Yep, she'd figured that and was okay with it. Janessa was more than okay with a lot of things. For instance, Colts Creek House. She was going to let Sophia do some full steaming ahead with her plans for putting that together and running it with Margo.

That left Brody.

"Now, I'm going to tell you all the things I'm not going to do," she said. Janessa held up her finger to start counting them off. "I'm not leaving Last Ride. I'm not giving up managing Bright Hope."

She'd just have to take a trip there once or twice a month and continue to deal with the paperwork from here. That might take some adjustments for Kyle, but if it became a problem, they could hire some extra help. Especially since she was technically stinking rich now.

Janessa held up a second finger. "I'm also not going to raise Ava on Colts Creek Ranch. I'll find another place."

Again, being stinking rich would help with that, but she didn't want a house. She wanted a home.

She held up a third finger. "And I'm not going to let you take back the *I love you*. You're stuck with that, but I'll give you an out and say you don't have to do anything you don't want to do about that whole loving me deal. We can just keep going with this fling until one of us decides we don't want to fling anymore."

He didn't say anything. Not so much as a grunt or a sigh. Brody just stared at her for what seemed to be the entire life cycle of a bat.

"Well?" she prompted, pairing it with a huff. "I've just shown you all the pieces of my life, and—"

He pulled her to him and kissed her, but even then she could feel him smiling against her mouth. Well, smiling until he deepened the kiss, and he turned her mind to mush. Good mush. With lots and lots of heat and potential.

"You showed me yours," he drawled when they broke for air. And, mercy, he made that sound down and dirty.

"Now, I'll show you mine. Here's what I'm not going to do." He held up one finger but then used it to trace the outline of her right nipple. "I'm not going to back away from Colts Creek. I'll help you with it for as long as you need my help and until we find the right ranch manager."

Good. Because that was one of the puzzle pieces that looked as if it might have the possibility of some frayed edges. Janessa still intended to give Rowan the ranch, but it'd be years before he was ready to take it over.

Brody held up a second finger and used it to trace her mouth. "I'm not going to have a fling with you anymore."

Everything stopped. The air, her breathing, maybe even her heart. God, her heart.

"I'm not going to have a winter fling with you," he continued, "because I want a whole lot more. I want autumn, spring and summer." He paused. "I want you. And FYI, I'm not taking your out. I want that *I love you*, and in turn I'll give it right back to you."

God, her heart, she thought again. It was fluttering and dipping like that bat. "Then say it," she insisted. Because she so wanted to hear it.

He didn't stop with the nipple toying. Brody was doing his Brody thing. And he nipped her bottom lip. "I'm in love with you, Janessa."

Every puzzle piece in the universe fell into place, and just like that, everything started again. The air, her breathing and her heart.

"Good. I'm in love with you, too," she repeated since she was pretty sure he wanted to hear it.

Also, because turnabout was fair play, she danced her fingers over the front of his zipper. "Want to celebrate in your truck?" Because it didn't seem right to have sex in front of her father's grave. You know, just in case that bat was indeed a hereafter sign kind of deal.

Brody got right to his feet, stuffed the tablet in her purse so she could latch on to it. Just as he latched on to her and scooped her up.

There were so many things that were still to-be-determined, but this sure as heck wasn't one of them.

Snuggled in the blanket, and in his arms, Janessa kissed Brody all the way to his truck.

* * * * *

*Don't miss the next Last Ride, Texas book
from USA TODAY bestselling author Delores Fossen
when Summer at Stallion Ridge goes on sale
in April 2022, only from HQN Books!*

Get 4 FREE REWARDS!

We'll send you 2 FREE Books plus 2 FREE Mystery Gifts.

FREE
Value Over
$20

Both the **Romance** and **Suspense** collections feature compelling novels written by many of today's bestselling authors.

YES! Please send me 2 FREE novels from the Essential Romance or Essential Suspense Collection and my 2 FREE gifts (gifts are worth about $10 retail). After receiving them, if I don't wish to receive any more books, I can return the shipping statement marked "cancel." If I don't cancel, I will receive 4 brand-new novels every month and be billed just $7.24 each in the U.S. or $7.49 each in Canada. That's a savings of up to 28% off the cover price. It's quite a bargain! Shipping and handling is just 50¢ per book in the U.S. and $1.25 per book in Canada.* I understand that accepting the 2 free books and gifts places me under no obligation to buy anything. I can always return a shipment and cancel at any time. The free books and gifts are mine to keep no matter what I decide.

Choose one: □ **Essential Romance**
(194/394 MDN GQ6M)

□ **Essential Suspense**
(191/391 MDN GQ6M)

Name (please print)

Address   Apt. #

City   State/Province   Zip/Postal Code

Email: Please check this box □ if you would like to receive newsletters and promotional emails from Harlequin Enterprises ULC and its affiliates. You can unsubscribe anytime.

Mail to the Harlequin Reader Service:
IN U.S.A.: P.O. Box 1341, Buffalo, NY 14240-8531
IN CANADA: P.O. Box 603, Fort Erie, Ontario L2A 5X3

Want to try 2 free books from another series? Call 1-800-873-8635 or visit www.ReaderService.com.

*Terms and prices subject to change without notice. Prices do not include sales taxes, which will be charged (if applicable) based on your state or country of residence. Canadian residents will be charged applicable taxes. Offer not valid in Quebec. This offer is limited to one order per household. Books received may not be as shown. Not valid for current subscribers to the Essential Romance or Essential Suspense Collection. All orders subject to approval. Credit or debit balances in a customer's account(s) may be offset by any other outstanding balance owed by or to the customer. Please allow 4 to 6 weeks for delivery. Offer available while quantities last.

Your Privacy—Your information is being collected by Harlequin Enterprises ULC, operating as Harlequin Reader Service. For a complete summary of the information we collect, how we use this information and to whom it is disclosed, please visit our privacy notice located at corporate.harlequin.com/privacy-notice. From time to time we may also exchange your personal information with reputable third parties. If you wish to opt out of this sharing of your personal information, please visit readerservice.com/consumerchoice or call 1-800-873-8635. **Notice to California Residents**—Under California law, you have specific rights to control and access your data. For more information on these rights and how to exercise them, visit corporate.harlequin.com/california-privacy.

STRS21MAXR2